FROSTGRAVE
SECOND CHANCES

OSPREY
GAMES

Osprey Games, an imprint of Osprey Publishing Ltd
c/o Bloomsbury Publishing Plc
PO Box 883, Oxford, OX1 9PL, UK
www.ospreygames.co.uk
OSPREY and OSPREY GAMES are trademarks of Osprey Publishing Ltd,
a division of Bloomsbury Publishing Plc.
First published in Great Britain in 2017

A CIP catalogue record for this book is available from the British Library.
Matthew Ward has asserted his right under the Copyright, Designs and
Patents Act, 1988, to be identified as the author of this book.

ISBN:

PB: 9781472824646
ePub: 9781472824653
ePDF: 9781472824660
XML 9781472824677

17 18 19 20 21   10 9 8 7 6 5 4 3 2 1
Typeset in Adobe Garamond Pro
Originated by PDQ Digital Media Solutions, Bungay, UK
Printed and bound in Great Britain by
CPI (Group) UK Ltd, Croydon CR0 4YY

Cover and interior artwork by Dmitry and Kate Burmak

Osprey Publishing supports the Woodland Trust, the UK's leading
woodland conservation charity. Between 2014 and 2018 our donations are
being spent on their Centenary Woods project in the UK.

FROSTGRAVE

SECOND CHANCES

MATTHEW WARD

CHAPTER ONE

A lantern's glow suffused the tunnel mouth, casting distorted reflections across the ice-sheathed stone. They danced and skittered across the cavern floor, across the surface of the still, dark pool – rare sparks of light and life in a chamber long-bereft of both. A heartbeat after, the tunnel mouth fell into darkness once again. The reflections vanished. Not much of a warning, unless you were watching for one.

Mirika gripped her stone perch tight, and pinched her eyes shut. The lantern's brief flare had destroyed her night vision, but even in the pitch-black depths, there was memory of light. Casting herself adrift from the present, she plunged a portion of herself into the past, seeking a time before the darkness reigned supreme. She found it centuries back, when the bronze finials had yet to corrode, and the now-silent stanchions blazed with flame. Mirika embraced that moment and opened her eyes.

For the first time, the cavern lay revealed in all its faded glory. Its foundations had been laid down as a tomb, the largest chamber in the Temple of Draconostra's crypt. Colossal statues, each easily four or five times Mirika's height, peered out across the darkness with empty eyes, their faces worn and cracked by the passage of time and the ingress of water. Swollen facades bulged from the walls, their facing stones distorted by the inexorable onset of ice.

The first intruder – curiously toy-like at that distance – stood in the tunnel mouth, darkened lantern still clasped in one hand. Other shapes fanned hesitantly out across the broken, mossy flagstones. Drawn weapons confirmed suspicions provoked by the doused lantern.

They knew she was there.

With a last glance downwards, Mirika ghosted back along the spine of the toppled statue that served as her perch. How the mighty had fallen. She doubted the long-dead Szarnos had been quite so noble of form or figure as that of the colossal graven likeness, but then tomb complexes were seldom commissioned by men and women of modest bents.

How long until the pursuers caught up? Depended on how cautious they were. A minute to skirt the pool. Another two to ascend the zigzag stairway and series of half-landings? Perhaps longer, now they were operating in the dark. Frostgrave had a knack for punishing the unwary. If the newcomers were who she suspected, they knew, and would advance accordingly.

Mirika reached the end of her makeshift path and dropped to the uneven dais. One entrance. One stairway to the burial vault of Szarnos the Great, the steps doubling back three times across the chamber. A choke point half a mile long, end to end. Mirika smiled. She'd have fun with this.

'Hurry up,' she whispered.

The fur-swathed figure kneeling beside the vault door didn't even look up.

'I *am* hurrying,' Yelen breathed.

Her fingertips traced spirals across the flagstones, leaving charcoal sigils in their wake. Gutter magic, but effective enough against curses for all that. There was more to opening some doors than simply picking a lock.

Mirika peered at the door – a patchwork of granite and corroded bronze, a jagged serpent rune carved at its heart. Like the rest of the tomb, it'd come remarkably unscathed through the quake that had buried this section of the city. That was good news and bad. Good, because that surely meant the contents hadn't been spirited away by another delver. Bad, because it also promised that the locks and protections were still intact.

'How much longer?'

At last, Yelen met her gaze, lips twisting. Familiar impatience danced behind her cold blue eyes. Her hand dipped to her belt. Lock picks glinted. 'About twice as long if you keep interrupting. Only the best for tyrants like Szarnos. *And* some of us are working in the dark, remember?'

Mirika winced at the reminder of what separated them. Outwardly they could perhaps have passed for twins, even with the handful of years separating them. Same dark braids. Same watchful eyes, though Mirika's own were more grey than blue.

Same defiant scowl, when the need was there.

A sharp *crunch* of stone on stone sounded from below. A choked-off curse followed, the harsh waylander syllables echoing strangely about the stalactite-encrusted ceiling.

A little of the defiance faded from Yelen's thin face. 'How many?'

'At least half a dozen. How much longer?'

Yelen scowled. 'Too long. I haven't even started on the lock. Unless…?'

'No!' Mirika shook her head, all too aware of what had gone unsaid. 'I'll handle this.'

'Let me help!'

'You can help me by getting that door open.' Mirika took a deep breath, knowing she'd spoken more harshly than she'd intended. It was too easy to fall back into old habits. She squeezed Yelen's shoulder. 'Don't worry, little sister. It's only the Gilded Rose. I'll be fine.'

* * *

Yelen set to work on the lock, her thoughts more on Mirika's retreating footsteps than the mechanism. It was always the same. Fewer than three years separated them, but Mirika always insisted on playing the big sister, always watching out for her. It had been comforting when they'd been younger. Now…?

The irony was, Mirika could have opened the vault in moments. But no, she had to show off.

With an effort, Yelen returned her attention to the lock – to the sounds of metal scraping on metal. Twelve tumblers, and what she knew from bitter experience to be a deadfall trip. One false move, and she'd trigger whatever precautions the designers had chosen to install. She'd heard of whole complexes sinking into the snows, ancient scuttling mechanisms tripped by a delver's single mistake.

Drunken old Azra claimed to have survived such a disaster where the rest of his band hadn't. Perhaps it was true, perhaps it wasn't. Azra loved to tell stories almost as much as he loved his liquor. But Yelen had nearly lost an arm to one such trap just weeks before. The false tumbler in the door at Koroz Sanctum had collapsed the doorway, sealing the chamber beyond. Master Torik had been furious when they'd returned empty-handed. Yelen had just been glad to return with both hands, and endured the old man's scorn and the fall of his fist in silence. Not that Mirika had seen the latter. Torik was always careful not to upset his prize pupil.

Yelen's hands trembled as the old, familiar anger surfaced. At Torik for his hateful manner. At Mirika for excusing it. And at herself, for allowing the situation to continue. Deep down, the old man was afraid of her. Damn right. She could snap him in half, if she wanted. Just like she could open this vault without this rigmarole of lock picks and skeleton-craft. Maybe she would.

At least this commission was the last. Then they'd be free. Of Torik, and of…

Bleak laughter echoed around Yelen's thoughts. The sour taste of sulphur crept across her tongue. Her fingers slipped. The tumbler shifted the wrong way. Heart leaping into her throat, Yelen steadied the hook pick and forced the anger back down. She had to concentrate. She glanced down at her wrist. A waste of time – her skin was covered. The tattoo was concealed.

Hand still trembling, she eased the pick back to resting position. Something heavy *clunked* into place behind the door. Yelen held her breath, waiting for the rumble of stone on stone that would betray the collapse to come. Nothing happened. The only sounds were her own frantic heartbeat, and the intruders' footsteps on the stairs.

At her feet, the charcoal sigils glowed dull red, flecks of orange flaring at the edges as the vault's curse ate away at the warding. Taking a deep breath, Yelen set the hook pick moving again – this time, in the correct direction. But the laughter? The laughter remained.

* * *

The rope hissed through Mirika's gloved hands. The stale air of the tomb rushed across her face like a stiff sea-breeze. Above her, the robed statue peered out into the dark, its noble features haunted by some unspeakable malice, the end of the rope tied tight around its outstretched hand. Below, the vanguard of the Gilded Rose crept up the stairs. Two shadows clad in leathers and furs, their cloaks cinched at the neck by golden rose-shaped brooches. Each carried a naked blade. Each moved with the caution of a man whose night vision was not all it could be.

Mirika grinned with exhilaration and anticipation. Done right, delving was deathly dull. Keep to the correct paths. Don't stray into the wrong districts. Know when to run. Get your prize. Get out. Those were the delver's rules – the rules for turning a profit while keeping your parts and pieces intact. But this? Tweaking the noses of your rivals? There was joy in that. More to the point, she and Yelen had a reputation to build if they wanted to prosper in the frozen city. Reputations didn't forge themselves.

Her feet struck stone half a dozen steps below the two shadows. Too loud.

'What was that?' The larger shadow turned. The time-shifted light revealed a craggy face that had seen the losing end of one too many brawls. Yet if his face suggested too many bouts lost, it surely wasn't for lack of fortitude – the man was built like a mountain.

'The frozen hells with this,' growled the other. He was shorter, swarthier than his companion, and his beard prickled with frost. 'I can't see a damn thing.'

The lantern in his hand flared, bathing the upper stairway in greasy light. The interplay of ancient and present-day luminance cast strange shapes across the ice that sheathed flagstones, statues and rubble alike. But this was Frostgrave. Ice was never in short supply hereabouts. Only the pool at the base of the stairs was free of it. Whatever liquid rippled gently beneath the icicle-strewn chandeliers, it wasn't water, that was for sure.

Mirika shielded her eyes and severed the connection with the past. The shapes faded along with the long-vanished light.

The brawler's laughter echoed around the chamber. 'Mirika Semova. I thought it had to be you.' The voice was a poor match for the mangled face, each elucidated syllable dropped into position with a scholar's precision.

She swept her hand down, shifting her feet and making a quarter-turn to transform the motion into a florid bow. Her sword, she left in its scabbard. 'You were expecting someone else, Darrick?'

He shook his head. 'The boss isn't happy at you for stealing the Markriese crown out from under us.'

Mirika snorted. 'I didn't steal it. We got there first. Finders keep, remember?'

The other man snorted and started down the stairs towards her, blade levelled and his expression hard. He was a stranger to Mirika. Fresh muscle bought in after the Markriese job, perhaps?

'Enough talk,' he rumbled. 'I don't get paid if we don't get the bauble. And I like getting paid.'

11

Darrick set a restraining hand on the swarthy man's shoulder. 'No. We wait for the boss, as agreed.'

Mirika frowned, her pulse quickening. That changed things. 'Magnis is here?'

He shrugged. 'Like I said, he's not happy. Wanted this one to go without a hitch.'

Mirika was struck by the sudden urge to peer over her shoulder. Just how close were the others, anyway? She should have checked. 'Walk away, Darrick. No one needs to get hurt.'

He sighed. 'Sadly, I also like getting paid.'

The swarthy man tore free of Darrick's grip. 'Then let's to it!' Leaping forward, he hacked down at Mirika like a woodsman splitting timber.

Darrick shook his head. 'Oh dear.'

The steel arced down. A dull, watery rumble filled Mirika's ears as she reached into the timeflow, increasing her personal tempo a hundredfold. The sword slowed inches from her brow, the whip-quick motion suddenly turgid.

Mirika darted aside, lantern light taking on a ruddy hue as her personal timeline snapped clear. Ducking clear under his weapon arm, she rammed the heel of her palm into the swarthy man's back, releasing her grip on the timeflow as she did so. Red light snapped back to greasy yellow.

Her blow, accelerated by the inrush of time, struck like a battering ram. The swarthy man shot across the stairway with a *whumph* of suddenly-expelled air. He struck a granite column with a *crack*, rebounded and collapsed.

Mirika spun on her heel, vision blurring with fatigue. It'd pass, given the chance, but if he rushed her now... Fortunately, Darrick hadn't moved.

'He's new, I take it?' she asked.

He shrugged. 'I tried to warn him. Killed a yeti with his bare hands, so I understand. Easy to underestimate a slip of a girl with something like that under your belt.' He stepped closer. 'Speaking of which, I don't suppose you'll go easy on me, for old times' sake?'

Mirika laughed and shook her head. Slip of a girl, indeed. She'd nineteen winters behind her. 'I don't have any old times, Darrick. Just this moment. As often as needs be.' At last, the tiredness was passing. Not enough to pull the same trick again so soon, but that didn't matter. She drew her sword with a flourish, and pulled on the timeflow just enough to slow Darrick's reactions relative to hers. 'Shall we?'

* * *

A man's bellow echoed up the stairway, the musical ring of steel on steel chasing it along. Mirika's laughter followed both, carefree… or possibly careless.

Yelen wiped a bead of sweat from her forehead. Her back ached from the half-hunched pose demanded by the lock's placement, and her arms felt heavy as lead. But seven tumblers down, and she still wasn't dead.

Hooray.

At her feet, the charcoal sigils blazed like fire. The serpent rune on the door glowed. Minutes left, if she was lucky. Not that she and luck had more than a nodding acquaintance.

'Not that I'd notice another curse, anyway,' she muttered, raking the lock's innards with the diamond-toothed pick. A tumbler clicked. Eight down. Four to go.

The laughter faded from the back of Yelen's mind.

'And I thought we were becoming friends...' The feminine tones flowed like spiced honey through her thoughts, at once mocking, soothing and hinting at a threat to come.

Yelen swallowed. The taste of sulphur remained. 'Shut up. I'm concentrating.'

'Why bother? It'll all become dust soon enough. Or it can. *Let me assist you.'*

'I don't want your help.'

'Really? That's not what you said at Koroz.'

Yelen took a deep breath and steadied herself against the door. She couldn't argue with the truth. 'That was different. Mirika would have died.'

'And she might yet today. She's so reckless.*'*

Yelen glanced down at her wrist, and at the hidden tattoo. 'She's not the only one.' She fought the sudden urge to scratch at her wrist. 'Korov was a mistake. I want nothing from you.'

The laughter returned, sweet as mead and cold as ice. *'That's what you always say. I can wait.'*

And with that, Yelen felt the presence slither back into the depths of her mind. Trying to likewise banish the sounds of swordplay from her thoughts, she returned her attention to the lock.

* * *

Mirika shook her head and hefted the lantern she'd taken from Darrick. Her sword was still unblooded. She was a delver, not a killer – she stripped Frostgrave of its treasures, not her competitors of their lives. Bruises and embarrassed memories were another matter. Those she gladly gave out to all-comers.

The arrow's telltale whistle came too late. The broadhead sliced a hot, sharp trail across Mirika's upper arm and sped away into the darkness. Yelping with pain, she flung the lantern aside and dived face-first onto the stairway's flagstones. She winced as her knees cracked against stone. Another arrow whistled away over her shoulder.

Mirika pressed a hand to her wound. Only a scratch, although Yelen would be unlikely to see it as such. Another lecture waited. Still, she'd been lucky. Blinded by the loss of her lantern, she called forth the light of times past and peered down the stairs.

'Where are you?'

The archer stood on the half-landing overlooking the tunnel mouth, staring vainly into the darkness.

Scrambling to her feet, Mirika took the steps three at a time. The archer nocked and fired, the wild shot accurate beyond his wildest dreams, his arrow flying true for Mirika's heart. She reached into the timeflow just long enough to slow the arrow's tempo, and struck it aside with the flat of her blade. As time snapped back to normal, she launched herself into space.

Boots slammed into the archer's chest. He staggered backwards, missed his footing and abandoned his bow in a mad scramble for a handhold. When Mirika hauled herself upright, she found him dangling from the fingers of one hand.

'Please, help me!'

Mirika stepped closer, her right knee stiff from the awkwardness of her landing. It was only a dozen or so feet from the half-landing to the pool. Of course, the archer couldn't see that. 'You just tried to kill me.'

His eyes widened. 'A mistake… Magnis wants you alive.'

Mirika glanced down the last run of steps. Two figures approached the foot of the stairway, one a man in fur-lined silk robes, trimmed with golden cloth, a lantern held at arm's length, as if he expected the flame within to bite him. The other was a woman, clad shoulder to foot in chain and plate, the blue and gold heraldry on her breastplate scuffed beyond recognition.

Darrick hadn't lied. Cavril Magnis had indeed shown up in person. Mirika had no idea as to the woman's identity. A bodyguard perhaps, hired to replenish the ranks after the Markriese debacle. It didn't matter. Mirika already felt the dull claws of temporal fatigue tearing at her. She'd done too much, too swiftly. There was no cheating the Clock of Ages. You could borrow, but not steal. If she was to end this, she'd have to do so now.

The archer scrabbled at the stairway's edge with his free hand, but his fingers found no purchase on the ice-locked stone. 'Please…'

Mirika stamped on his fingers. The man's wailing cry ended in a splash as his body struck the rippling black waters of the pool far below. Then she reached into the timeflow one last time, and went to confront the master of the Gilded Rose.

* * *

The tenth tumbler yielded in the same moment Mirika's pained cry echoed up from below.

'*Told you.*'

'Shut up!'

Wedging the picks in place to prevent her work coming undone, Yelen hurried away from the vault and peered down into the darkness. Twin spots of lantern-light glowed on the stairs. One partway up, one at the very foot. As she watched, the closest lantern went out.

Choking back the instinct to call out for her sister, Yelen glanced back at the vault door. The charcoal sigils glowed white-hot. Moments left. Maybe not enough. But what about Mirika?

A bowstring sang out. A scream split the air. A man's scream. Yelen's shoulders slumped in relief. Mirika was still alive. Still doing her part. Relying on Yelen to do hers.

Yelen turned towards the vault, and found a dagger-point at her throat.

'I don't want to kill you, love.' The woman didn't sound much like she cared either way. Even in the poor lichen-light, she looked weary, well-worn. The patch over her right eye was mildewed, its corners turning up at the edges, the hems of her greatcoat moth-eaten and as ragged as her straw-blonde hair. But the dagger gleamed as only a beloved possession could. 'Up. Up. Up. Hands where I can see them.'

Yelen complied, the gesture spurred on by the dagger pressing at the soft tissue under her chin. 'How did you get up here?'

The woman shrugged like a carrion-crow resettling on its perch. The point of the dagger didn't move. 'Hid in the shadows while your sister clobbered Darrick and Marcan. She ran straight past me.'

'*You sure you don't want my help?*' The languid syllables dripped across Yelen's thoughts.

'Be quiet.'

The blonde woman shrugged again. 'You asked.' Her free hand danced across Yelen's tunic and trews, tugged the short dagger from her belt, and tossed it to the floor. 'Maybe you feel like talking a bit yourself? Door's got a deadfall, I take it?' Yelen glared at her, but offered no reply. 'How many tumblers? Does it have a false threshold? A jangler's tilt?' Receiving no more of a reply than before, the woman sighed. 'Look, you cooperate, I'll tie you up. Otherwise, I'll have to give you a little tap on the head to keep you *docile*. 'Less you struggle, that is. Then you get the blade. You know how it is.'

'*Hardly matters.*' Had the voice possessed physical form, it would have been examining its fingernails, or engaged in some equally trivial activity. '*Dead or bound, you'll not be able to stop them. Nor help your sister. And that's if she's telling the truth. But of course…*'

The blonde woman leaned closer and grabbed Yelen's shoulder. The point of the dagger drifted downwards, running across Yelen's ribs to rest against her midriff. A single hazel eye gazed unblinking into hers. 'What's it to be, love?'

'*Yes. What's it to be?*'

'I told you to shut up!'

Yelen slammed her forehead forward. Dark spots burst behind her eyes, a dull pain rushing in close behind. The woman shrieked, and collapsed like a sack of tubers, her dagger skittering away across the flagstones. On the second attempt, she propped herself up on one elbow, a second dagger appearing like magic from beneath her greatcoat. 'That's it, love. You're getting the…'

The woman fell silent as Yelen's boot connected with her temple. She collapsed once again, this time going still. Shaking her head to clear it, Yelen kicked once, twice, three times more, and then flung herself at the lock.

At her feet, the first of the sigils burst into dust.

* * *

Mirika doubted that Magnis even saw her coming. Riding the timeflow to a spot immediately behind him pushed her dangerously close to her limits. But it was worth it to hear his breathing quicken as the blade of her sword settled against his throat – to see the supercilious expression falter as her arm slipped under his, pinning him tight.

'Hello, Cavril.'

'Ah, Miss Semova.' The close-cropped blond moustache creaked into a knowing smile. The words were measured, spoken seemingly in ignorance of a life hanging by a thread. Cavril Magnis wasn't the type to remain flustered for long.

Ahead, the armoured woman stiffened and spun around. The chain links of her armour rustled like metallic leaves as she slid the bastard sword from its shoulder-mounted scabbard. It made Mirika's short sword look like a toothpick. Her eyes drowned in darkness, her close-cropped hair black as night, save for a streak of silver running about her temples.

'Step away, delver.'

Mirika drew the blade closer to her captive's throat. 'Actually, I'm comfortable here. Aren't you, Cavril?'

Magnis extended a hand, palm outward, in the woman's direction. 'Let her be, Kain. It's fine.'

Kain's posture shifted. Not enough to suggest ease, but her grip on the widowmaking sword relaxed just enough for Mirika to believe she wasn't about to embark on a headlong charge. But her expression didn't alter. The coal-black stare didn't even flicker. 'Of course.' She upended the sword and set the point against the flagstones.

Magnis cleared his throat. 'Miss Semova. *Mirika*. I assume there's something you want of me? Otherwise you'd be gone by now.'

Mirika leaned closer, her lips brushing his ear. 'Order your lackeys out of here.' Kain's scowl darkened a few shades at the word 'lackey'. Mirika offered her a sweet smile. 'We were here first. It's ours.'

Magnis snorted. 'And when you say "ours", you of course mean you'll deliver it to that haggard old fool.'

'Does it matter?'

'I suppose not. And if I refuse?'

Mirika drew the sword closer so that the steel kissed Magnis' skin. 'You're a scholar. You'll work it out.'

Kain edged forward, but halted at another gesture from Magnis.

'I thought you didn't kill.'

She paused before replying. The better to show a confidence she didn't entirely feel. 'At least two of your lackeys just tried to kill me. I'm reconsidering.'

The corner of Magnis' mouth twisted into a lopsided smile. 'You'd miss me if I weren't here.'

His tone invited agreement, craved it, even. But then, Cavril Magnis had always been a silver-tongued devil. At least, compared to most of the outcasts and robber-kings seeking their fortunes in Frostgrave. He was even handsome, if in a soft, decadent way that suggested he'd snap if caught in a strong breeze. Even now, days into an expedition, he'd barely a hair out of place. To look at him, he could be standing upon the veranda of his agreeable mansion, some five hundred leagues to the south, in the softest and most indolent stretch of the heartlands.

With an effort, Mirika kept the threat in her voice. 'Keep this up, and I guess we'll find out.'

Magnis sighed. 'So sad. You're wasted in this blighted city, working for that cantankerous old fool. Which reminds me. I have a counter offer. Instead of slitting my worthless throat and thus breaking hearts in every tavern for miles around, why don't you sign on with the Gilded Rose? And your sister, naturally.'

'I already have an employer.'

'Hah. "Employer" suggests that you're paid, but Torik doesn't have two crowns to rub together, so that can't be the way of things. What is it he has on you, I wonder?' The smile turned sly. 'What secret are you hiding? Or… maybe it's not you. Your sister, perhaps?'

Mirika bit her lip, not daring to speak for fear of giving anything away. Magnis' guesses were already too close to the mark.

Fortunately, he didn't seem to notice. 'I'll pay you, and pay you well. Look at Kain over there. A Knight of Dawn doesn't come cheap, even when you can find one who'll take the coin.' At last, Kain's gaze flickered, transferring briefly from Mirika to regard Magnis no less coldly. Again, Magnis didn't seem to notice, a man at ease with his station in the world, even with a sword at his throat. 'Think of a number, then double it. I can afford it.'

Mirika shook her head. 'You're mad.'

Magnis laughed. 'Not at all. You'll earn every crown.'

Despite herself, Mirika was tempted. Certainly, the Gilded Rose always had coin for new hirelings. They weren't even a bad bunch, by the standards of delvers. The frozen city attracted all sorts, but most of those who survived were desperate, wild or worse. And Cavril Magnis certainly wasn't desperate. Unlike most of the magi, mystics and luminaries that composed the self-appointed elite of Frostgrave's scattered encampments, he hadn't come to the frozen wasteland in search of a fortune. He already had one waiting back home, or so rumour said. That meant he was in this for the chase, for the excitement. Just like she was. Would it really be so bad to say 'yes'?

But then there was Yelen, as always. She had no future with the Gilded Rose, not as things stood.

'The answer's no,' Mirika said. 'Now, you going to call off your dogs, or do I slit your throat?'

Magnis sighed. 'I'd hoped to avoid this. Kain, please don't kill her. She really is something quite special.'

Mirika frowned, suddenly aware that something was off-key. 'Have you forgotten the sword at your throat?'

He laughed. 'Ah yes. About that.'

He faded into nothing, leaving Mirika clutching at empty air. She swore softly under her breath. An illusion! And she'd fallen for it! He had to be here somewhere, but where? She glanced around, but caught no sign. A clink of armour dragged her back to more immediate concerns.

'Well then.' Kain's lips twisted into a malevolent smile. 'Do you want to do this the easy way, or the hard?'

Banishing her self-recrimination, Mirika pivoted on her heel and reached into the timeflow. A mistake. The world lurched and spun. She'd pushed herself too hard, too fast. The Clock of Ages sought its due. She gritted her teeth, forcing back nausea. It'd have to wait. The job wasn't done. Moment by meticulous moment, she hastened her tempo until every second crawled by in the span intended for two. It'd be enough.

Mirika sprang at Kain, her sword-point aimed for the join between breastplate and pauldron. A shoulder wound. Painful, certainly. Incapacitating? Maybe. Fatal? Probably not. But it'd slow her.

Steel chimed against steel. Mirika's blade clattered away, slowing as it tore free of her altered tempo. Kain's sword, point down against the flagstones a heartbeat before, was now held crosswise in front of her body, the broad steel angled to deflect a strike the Knight of Dawn couldn't possibly have seen coming.

Mirika didn't realise she'd lost her grip on the timeflow until Kain's mailed fist closed around one of her braids. Her head snapped back, nausea flooding in as her tempo abruptly realigned. The light of ages slipped away, plunging the chamber into darkness.

'Run out of tricks?'

Kain yanked on Mirika's braids. Her head jerked back. The rest of her body followed, reeled in like a gaffed fish. She barely saw the mailed fist that slammed into the side of her head, shattering already precarious balance. She hit the flagstones, her wrist folding beneath her. Bones snapped like rotten boughs, the agonised scream ripping free before she realised it was her own.

* * *

'Mirika!' Yelen twisted away from the vault, heart in her throat.

The scream had been her sister's. Hadn't it? She strained her ears, listening for a clue to what had transpired below. The scream wasn't repeated. Its absence only made things

23

worse.

'*It certainly sounded like her. By the way, have you forgotten something?*'

'No!' Yelen dived for the lock, already knowing she was too late.

The hook pick, no longer held in place, pinged free of the lock housing. A series of grinding clicks sounded from within the door – the hard-won victories over the tumblers undone as they rumbled back into place. To Yelen, they sounded like they were sealing her in, not out. Trapping her in a lifetime of servitude. Without what lay inside, she'd never be free. And without Mirika…

She choked back a sob. No, she had to be stronger than that.

Two paces away, the woman with the eyepatch groaned and shifted against her bonds. The last of the charcoal sigils flared white, its remaining moments burning away. Yelen glanced from one to the other, and back to the outer darkness of the cavern. She could repick the lock now she knew the tumblers' patterns – she could even restore the sigils – but it would all take time. Time she didn't have.

Time Mirika didn't have, if it wasn't already too late.

'*Are you sure you don't want my help?*'

Yelen clenched her fists. To the frozen hells with it, anyway. 'Open the vault.'

At once, she felt the voice slither free from its nest in the base of her mind. She gagged as the sour taste of sulphur crowded her tongue.

'*At last.*' A honeyed chuckle rippled across her thoughts. '*Place your hands on the stone.*'

Yelen did as she was bidden, her breathing quickening as the waves of the timeflow washed over her. The sounds of the cavern grew muffled, distant – subsumed by the booming, sonorous pulse of the Clock of Ages. She lost herself in the rush of it, of nerves set afire. It was the sensation – the power – she'd envied ever since Mirika's talent had first blossomed. The talent she'd always lacked, except in that one, small way.

Red light crept across the door as the magic took hold, the timeflow doubling and redoubling through the conduit of Yelen's flesh and bone. The bronze yielded first, peeling away and falling into dust as a thousand seasons of corrosion overtook it. The granite lasted longer, but beneath the assault of the writhing timeflow such distinctions barely mattered. Ten thousand, thousand relative years later, it succumbed. Cracks zigzagged across smooth stone, spreading and deepening into fissures. Dust ran between Yelen's fingers, the vapour swirling about her feet.

With a yawning, tortured groan, the door collapsed inwards. Yelen twisted aside. The lintel hurtled past her, smashing into fragments and hurling clouds of dust into the air.

'*As commanded*,' laughed the voice, coiling back into the depths of Yelen's mind.

The timeflow slipped from Yelen's grasp, all at once distant, unreachable. The familiar sense of loss billowed in to replace it, as if a piece of her had been stolen with its departure – the piece that made her truly whole. The tang of sulphur receded. Then came the pain, her left wrist burning like fire.

Gasping, Yelen propped herself against the ruined architrave. The pain would pass, just as the sense of loss would not. She trembled with withdrawal, and with guilt. She'd sworn never to do that again. She'd promised Mirika.

But what was done, was done.

The dust cleared. Beyond the wreckage of the vault door, a skeleton lay in silent repose. The scarlets of its silk robes had dulled with the passing centuries. Its flesh was long since eaten away. But gold still glinted at its throat and wrists. Gemstones on the tarnished crown glimmered in the lichen-light. And in its hands, folded across its emaciated chest like a priest in prayer, sat an onyx cube the size of a man's fist, marked with the familiar serpent rune, just as Torik had predicted.

Yelen sighed with relief and reached inside. 'I'll take that, Lord Szarnos.'

Even in death, Szarnos the Great was reluctant to relinquish his prize, but Yelen was in no mood to be thwarted by a corpse – no matter the legends that had surrounded it in life. Bones snapped and scattered as she dragged the cube clear. Even through the glove, her skin crawled.

All the while feeling the empty eye sockets of the skull upon her, she ran headlong for the stairs, haversack bouncing against her shoulder.

* * *

Mirika staggered to her feet, cradling her shattered wrist, urging her eyes to adapt to the lichen-light. Hot spikes lanced through her forearm with every breath. She trembled in a way that had nothing to do with Frostgrave's habitual chill. Three years as a delver, and not a scratch. Now this.

'How? How did you do that?' Her voice sounded distant, unfamiliar. It belonged to a woman fearful for her life, not to her.

Kain shook her head and stomped closer, the blade of

her sword resting lazily against her shoulder. 'You think you're the first time witch to cross my path?'

Now she was closer, Mirika made out the scars high on the knight's left cheek and brow. Judging by the pattern, she'd been lucky not to lose an eye. As to Kain's age, it was anyone's guess. She moved with the confidence of an older woman, but the grace of her steps – in full armour, no less – spoke of a body not yet in its prime.

'You need to learn that this isn't a game,' said Kain, 'or you're going to get yourself killed.'

Mirika retreated towards the pool, hissing as the motion sent fresh agonies sparking up and down her wrist. 'By you?'

Kain advanced, side-stepping ever so slightly to cut off her retreat to the tunnel mouth. 'Doesn't have to be. Sit your skinny rump down, stay quiet, and let us collect what we came for. You'll keep breathing, and learn a lesson. It's a fair bargain. Take it.'

'Is that what this is about? Teaching me a lesson for Korov, and Markriese and the others? I need that reliquary…'

'Need counts for nothing around here. You keep what you can hold. You know that…' Kain's lip twisted in contempt. 'Or you should.'

Anger at the knight's disdain burnt away a little of Mirika's pain. Enough to focus on forming a plan. 'Why does Cavril even want the reliquary?' She edged further around the pool, choosing her next words with care. 'You don't know, do you? You're just a good little mercenary, following your paymaster's commands. I thought the Order of Dawn was good for more than that.'

Kain strode closer, eyes flaring. 'Keep running your

mouth and you'll see what I'm good for.'

In truth, Mirika had never heard of the Order of Dawn before Magnis had mentioned it minutes earlier, but she knew a sore topic when she heard one. 'What *would* your brothers and sisters say to see you now, grubbing around in the darkness like a delver, jumping at the snap of a southerner's fingers?'

Kain lunged, her gauntleted hand reaching for Mirika's shoulder. 'I'm warning you…'

Mirika never discovered the nature of the warning. As Kain came forward, she moved. Not towards the knight, but took a pair of long, loping steps towards the pool. Seizing what little of the timeflow remained in her grasp, she extended her tempo to breaking point, and vaulted the inky waters.

The timeflow ripped free mid-leap, but by then Mirika had all the momentum she needed. She crunched down on the far side of the pool, boots skidding on the impacted ice. A brief, one-handed flail for balance brought that under control, and then she was running. Not for the tunnel mouth – Kain was too close to the exit to take the chance – but for the foot of the stairs.

As she approached, a waif-like figure appeared on the half-landing, a black cube clutched tight in her hands. 'Mirika?'

* * *

Yelen's joy at seeing her sister alive quickly yielded to concern. Mirika's face was pale, save for the fierce bruise already forming above her brow. And the way she held her left hand…

'What's happened? Are you alright?'

Mirika took the stairs two at a time. 'Go! Go!'

Behind her, an armoured figure advanced around the edge of the pool, her expression thunderous and a sword as tall as Yelen ready in her hands.

Yelen turned and made for the upward flight. A fleshy thump sounded behind her, closely followed by Mirika's muttered curse. Turning, she saw her sister lying sidelong across the stairway, expression taut.

Careful of her own footing, Yelen ran to her sister's side and hauled her upright.

Mirika hissed in pain. 'Careful. Wrist's broken.'

'What? How?'

She nodded down at the knight, drawing inexorably closer to the foot of the stairs. 'We had a disagreement. I fell over.'

Yelen took in her livid bruise, seeing it in a new light. 'How'd she even touch you?'

Mirika winced. 'I don't know.'

The knight reached the foot of the stairs. As she did so, she refracted into six identical figures. Yelen recognized the style at once. It was one of Magnis' favourite tricks – you couldn't avoid pursuit if you didn't know which pursuers were real and which were not.

'We can't stay here,' said Mirika. 'Back up the stairs.'

Yelen glanced up in the direction of the shattered vault. The last thing she wanted was Mirika asking questions about how it had gotten that way. Not that she'd need to ask. A glance would tell her everything. 'There's at least one still up there.'

Mirika staggered onto the half-landing, pained expression giving way to a mischievous glint. 'Then we'll have to be clever, won't we?'

Yelen's heart sank. 'You know I hate that.'

'It'll work. Do you have a better idea?'

'*I've one or two,*' breathed the voice. '*you've only to ask.*'

For a moment, Yelen was tempted. She longed to touch the timeflow again, if only for a moment, to feel the seconds dancing at her command. Her thoughts drifted to the tattoo on her wrist. What time did it show? Was she down to minutes? Or did only seconds remain? There was no way to tell. No. She couldn't take the risk. Mirika would only blame herself.

Drawing down a deep breath, Yelen clasped Mirika's uninjured hand and closed her eyes. Nausea blossomed as their tempos, never entirely synchronous, blurred together. They'd first tried this when children, playing hide and seek for the highest stakes in the gutters of Karamasz. The one sliver of birthright she and Mirika shared, and it made her sick to the stomach every time. But in Karamasz, it'd saved them from a branding for pocket-dipping. It'd save them here, or so she hoped.

Yelen opened her eyes. The nausea faded, just a little.

Mirika's grey stare met hers, more confident than before. 'Ready?'

She nodded. 'Ready.' With a last glance behind, Yelen followed her sister back up the stairs.

* * *

Mirika forced her weary limbs on. Distance was important. They had to draw Kain further in, or it'd all be for nothing. Yelen kept pace alongside, reliquary tucked inside the crook of her elbow.

They passed Darrick at the third half-landing. The big man was still unconscious. A glass jaw to belie his physique.

Mirika glanced down the stairway. Kain had crossed the

first landing. Nearly there. Everything after this was a bonus.

A patch of darkness detached itself from a nearby column. Mirika barely saw it in time, caught the barest glint of steel as it lunged towards Yelen's back.

'Yelen!'

Mirika moved without conscious thought. Her shoulder struck Yelen's, jarring her injured wrist into fresh agony. Yelen yelped and sprawled across the stairs. Mirika had the barest glimpse of a thickly bearded face – the yeti-slayer – then something struck her in the gut. The world turned red.

The next Mirika knew, she lay on the stairs, good hand clasped to her belly. Her fingers were warm, but she shivered all the same. A shadow loomed. Yelen shouted something, a wordless cry – all emotion, no meaning. The shadow bellowed, and tumbled away down the stairs.

Fingers found hers. Squeezed them. A little of the red faded from the world.

Yelen dropped to her knees, blue eyes awash with concern. 'What did you do?' She blinked, and glanced briefly away. 'Let me see.'

Mirika shook her head. 'It'll be alright. Help me up.'

'You're not alright!' Anger flared through the tears. 'He cut you open!' Yelen's lips narrowed. When she spoke again, it was in a tone of command. 'Give me your hand.'

Mirika shook her head, and gasped as the motion awoke the fire in her gut. 'Help me up.'

With Yelen's help, Mirika staggered on up. She'd never have made it alone. Her feet dragged like lumps of firewood, her knees buckled every time they were forced to take any weight. Each step took an eternity, lit by the ache from her wrist and raw, sodden pain at her waist. Yelen didn't say a word. Each time Mirika looked at her face, it was almost that of a stranger, pinched with cold fury, with a glint of… was that red amongst the blue of her irises?

As they reached the next landing, Yelen lowered her to the ground. 'This is as far as we go.'

Mirika sank to the ground, and stared out across the flagstones. Was it her imagination, or was it growing darker? She couldn't even see the start of the next run. 'What! Why?'

Robes swirled. Cavril Magnis strode out of the darkness. The real one, or another doppelgänger?

'Stay back!' snapped Yelen. A dagger gleamed in one hand, the onyx reliquary in the other.

Magnis raised a calming hand and squatted down, setting a lantern at his side. He peered at Mirika, face tight. Unreadable. 'Who did this?'

'The…' Mirika swallowed. It helped. 'The bearded one.'

Magnis nodded. Raising a hand, he beckoned behind him. 'Serene?'

A woman emerged from the encroaching gloom. Her right eye lay hidden beneath a patch, and her shock of blonde hair was matted with blood. 'Cavril?'

'Find Marcan. Explain our rules to him. Again. Give him reason not to forget.'

The woman gave a sharp, aquiline nod, and strode away, careful to keep her distance as she continued down the stairs.

Magnis inched closer. 'I'm truly sorry. I'd no intention for it to end this way.' He sighed. 'You should have taken my offer. If your sister surrenders the reliquary, I'll see she's taken care of. You have my word.'

'Go to hell!' Yelen brandished the dagger, murder in

her voice and her eyes.

'Sshh, little sister. It doesn't matter.'

Mirika beckoned Magnis closer. He looked genuinely upset, but then Cavril Magnis always looked genuine. That was the problem. Was this even him? There was no way to know for sure. She reached out and cradled his jaw. She caught a flicker of revulsion as her warm, sticky hand touched his cheek. Perhaps it really was him, after all. Maybe he even cared. Just a little.

She coughed, grimacing at the metallic taste. Time, usually her closest ally, was slipping away. The pain had become distant, like it belonged to someone else. That wasn't a good sign. No choices left. None at all.

'Guess you won't be learning anything after all.' Kain's voice held no inflection. Not regret. Not triumph. 'Should've listened.'

Mirika gave a small, gurgling laugh. 'I don't know. There's always a lesson.' She patted Magnis' cheek. 'And Cavril? Yelen had it right... Go to hell.'

She raised her hand above her head. Thin fingers clutched hers tight.

The world lurched.

* * *

Yelen swam on a sea of blurring reds and blues. Direction had no meaning. Nor did sound, sight or any other of her senses save one. Even the colours were lies, her mind trying to explain the inexplicable. She clamped her eyes closed, and focused on the Clock of Ages, its sonorous pulse screaming outrage at violation. Only Mirika's hand was real, and Yelen clutched it tight. All the devils in all the frozen hells couldn't have broken her grip.

The pulse of the clock slowed. Yelen's vision cleared. Up and down regained meaning. She felt solid ground beneath her boots, cold air on her face.

Yelen opened her eyes. Mirika grinned back. 'Told you it'd work.'

Her sister stood facing her on the lowest half-landing, in the very spot where they'd synced their tempos. Her clothes were unbloodied, and she stood tall, eyes that had so lately crowded with pain once more alive with mischief. She still held her wrist awkwardly – the time walk could do nothing for injury sustained before its invocation – but the ragged wound at her waist was gone as if it had never been. Which as far as the world was concerned, was precisely the case.

Yelen squeezed Szarnos' reliquary tight, and glanced at the uppermost landing. Cavril Magnis stood silhouetted against lantern light. For him and the rest of the Gilded Rose – for the rest of the world – nothing had changed. 'We'd better go before Magnis works it out.'

A frustrated cry echoed out across the cavern.

Mirika grinned, then winced and cradled her injured arm. 'I think he just did.'

The sisters ran for the unguarded tunnel, wild laughter ringing in their wake.

CHAPTER TWO

The thin fire pattered and spat, fuelled by a meagre portion of kindling and a handful of alchemist's powder. Yelen hated the stink of the latter. Thick and brackish, it reminded her only too well of something else. Nonetheless, she drew her thin blankets tight and huddled closer as the wind howled around the shattered stones. Warmth was fleeting in the Broken Strand, and not to be lightly shunned – whatever memories it brought to the surface.

Restless, Yelen crossed to the broken arch of the window, jagged pebbles scattering from her boots. A full moon blazed down, lighting the snow-covered cobbles almost as bright as day. The towering buildings were packed into the tight streets like teeth in a jawbone – broken teeth, for most were missing roofs or walls. A few were little more than teetering piles of shattered stone, manmade structures only in the imagination of the beholder. The quakes had seen to that. The quakes, and whatever wild magic had drowned the city in ice. Only the Temple of Draconostra, capstone on the tomb so lately escaped, had survived fully intact.

Yet nowhere was there a surviving building fewer than five storeys tall. Here and there, they hit seven or eight –

twice that of the tallest building in the Karamasz guttermarch. Yelen and Mirika had scraped a squalid living beneath such dwellings after their mother had died, sifting through midden and muck for anything that might have value. Coin. Bones. Teeth. Anything.

Yelen had few fond memories of Karamasz, and most of those had grown suspect with age – a child's recollection of better times. But the city had been beautiful when the sun shone, she remembered that, the terracotta tiles and whitewashed walls of the wealthier districts glowing as if lit from within. Not like Frostgrave. The frozen city was always sullen, miserable – even on those rare occasions where Solastra's light broke through the clouds.

She hummed a few bars of a half-remembered lullaby, recalling the tale her mother had woven as the shadows lengthened in their cramped garret. Of the Queen of the Sun, and how she'd cast her unfaithful husband Belsanos from the heavens and banished him to the shadows. Solastra held a grudge still, or so the song told, and refused to bestow her magnificence on Belsanos' favourite haunts. Perhaps Frostgrave was such a place. Certainly, there was always bitterness on the air – a bitterness that had nothing to do with the cold. Meanness. Spite. As if the old stones longed for nothing more than to rise up and crush the delvers, brigands and adventurers who picked over their icy bones.

The notes died on Yelen's lips. The chorus. She could never remember how the chorus went, only that it was beautiful and sad at the same time, as if Solastra's love still tempered her hatred. Nice to know that family was complicated, even for the gods.

The wind howled past the window, the building swaying in its cold embrace. Yelen held her breath as she always did, waiting for the telltale creak of tortured stone that warned of imminent collapse. Mirika had chosen their campsite carefully, passing up four other buildings before settling on the one they now occupied. But you never knew. A bivouac in the Broken Strand was always a gamble. Too high, and you ran the risk of waking broken and bloody amidst the rubble of a fresh ruin. Too low, and you begged to end your days in a troll's belly. Even five storeys above the ground – even over the howl of the wind – Yelen heard the brutes howling at one another as they fought for territory. She'd take her chances in the ricketiest, most crack-ridden building before she put herself within a troll's reach. If tales were true, being eaten alive was the very best you could hope for.

The wail's pitch dropped. The building steadied. Yelen breathed a sigh of relief, knowing it'd be one of many as the night wore on. She glanced over at Mirika, wrapped tight in blankets and pressed up against a wall, the haversack holding the reliquary resting at her feet. Sleeping the sleep of the just, as she always did. Another knack Yelen envied.

Still jittery from her brief contact with the timeflow, Yelen had volunteered to take the first watch. Collapsing buildings and trollish curiosity notwithstanding, there was always the possibility the Gilded Rose had seen through their disguised tracks and would attempt to steal the reliquary. That, or something worse. There was no guarantee of safety once you strayed beyond the lights of the mismatched trading settlements and delver-gang strongholds. There were only probabilities. The Broken Strand had been... not safe, but safe *enough*... for as long as Yelen had been in the frozen city. But all it took was some fool to crack open the wrong tomb or break the wrong seal, and all bets would be off. Dead wasn't always dead hereabouts.

Ambling away from the window, Yelen planted herself on a fallen column and basked in the welcome heat of the fire until her skin prickled. She wasn't anyone to be pointing fingers at fools. Not after what she'd done.

The voice had stayed quiet ever since they left Szarnos' tomb, but Yelen felt it nevertheless, coiling around her thoughts with renewed confidence. Her fault. She'd given it power by asking for help – first in opening the vault, and again when she crumbled the stairway out from under the brute who'd stabbed Mirika. She hadn't even meant to call on it the second time, but her sister's scream… the spray of blood…

Yelen peeled back her left sleeve and peered down at her wrist. The tattoo stared back, its whorled, fibrous strands weaving together into a stylized clock face. There were no hands. Just a series of spurs around the circumference, the numbers writhing like worms, or tendrils of weed. When the tattoo had first appeared, the face of the clock had been clear. Now it was almost entirely black. Only a sliver of pale skin remained, marking the span between half-past twelve, and the impossible thirteen o'clock.

She pinched her eyes shut, heartbeat racing as she rocked backwards and forwards. So close! No wonder the voice had grown so confident. No. Not the voice. It had a name. There was no point pretending otherwise. It wasn't a figment of her imagination. Azzanar. Yelen wished she'd never heard it, had never listened to that huckster sage. At the time, she'd have given anything to be like her older sister.

Now, she'd give whatever was left just to be herself again.

'Yelen?' Footsteps approached. 'You alright?'

Hurriedly, Yelen covered her wrist. Things were bad enough without another lecture. Besides, the more Mirika worried, the more they argued. 'I'm fine. Just cold.'

Fingers squeezed her shoulder. She jumped, cursing the guilty reaction.

'Tell me,' Mirika said. 'I can't help if I don't know what's wrong.'

Yelen heard concern in her sister's voice, but something else as well. Not suspicion exactly, but the tone their mother had used whenever she'd thought her daughters weren't telling the whole truth. Not an accusation, not even a question, just a tacit promise that the matter wouldn't be dropped until she was satisfied. Yelen hated that tone. But she also knew how to outwit it: feed truth into the lie. Just enough to muddy things.

'You nearly died tonight,' she said. 'All because you were showing off.'

The grip slackened. Fingers danced across Yelen's shoulders. Mirika eased herself onto the fallen column, careful not to upset her splinted and bandaged wrist. 'Pffff. I had everything under control.'

Yelen bit her lip as old frustrations boiled to the surface. 'You know I don't like it when you lie to me. I'm not a child!'

She broke off, embarrassed as always at letting her emotions get the better of her. Not trusting herself to speak, she settled for staring at her sister – a stare she knew looked too sullen by half, but was at a loss as how to alter it. Part of her didn't want to.

Mirika regarded her in silence for a long moment. 'Alright. It didn't go exactly as I planned…'

'That's the understatement of a lifetime.'

'… but we came through it, that's what matters.' The stare softened. 'We're a team, you and me.' She shook her head. 'Saved by my little sister.'

'Do you have to say it like that?' snapped Yelen.

'Like what?'

'Like it's a surprise. A joke. *And you'll never guess what happened next…*'

Mirika sighed. 'For someone who doesn't want to be treated like a child, you're sure behaving like one.'

'And flirting with Cavril Magnis is better, is it?'

She stiffened. 'That's not what I was doing.'

Yelen snorted. 'You could have fooled me. I saw him making eyes at you at Markriese. I thought it was just him… But tonight…'

Mirika's eyes narrowed. 'What about tonight?'

'That longing deathbed stare you gave him. Don't think I didn't see it.'

'It wasn't like that.'

'Looked that way from where I was standing.' Yelen grinned inwardly, glad to have her sister on the defensive for a change. 'I was waiting for one of his goons to break into a mournful fiddle recital.'

Mirika's warning glare dissolved in a sigh of amused exasperation. 'You know what it's like around here. You want to make a good living – a clean living, without getting tangled up with Flintine or the rest of that mire-feeding dross – you need a reputation. The Gilded Rose has that reputation. The easiest way for us to make ours is to keep tweaking their noses, or…' She tailed off, her lips twisting wryly.

'Or what?'

'Or… maybe join them.'

'You're kidding.'

'And why not? Cavril's clearly impressed with what we can do…'

Yelen scowled. 'With what you can do, you mean.'

Mirika ignored her. 'And he's not bad people. How many delver bosses can you say that of? Remember that mess in the Rimewold? After we got swept away by that avalanche, he cleaned the place out, but left us a week's rations on the altar. He knew we'd lost everything…'

'Or he didn't want to make space for food when he could carry gold.'

'And you heard what Cavril said after I got stabbed…'

'By one of his people.' Had she forgotten that detail?

'By one of his people, yes. But I'll give you good odds that this Marcan of his is the worse for it right now. The Gilded Rose take their reputation seriously. Honour amongst delvers, and all that.' She shrugged. 'What's the alternative? Stick with Master Torik after we deliver the reliquary?'

Yelen rubbed at her cheek, and snatched her hand away. 'No! Gods, no.'

Mirika nodded. 'There you are. We can't strike out on our own. We don't have the contacts. There's no better recipe for becoming gnawed bones than wandering blindly around the ruins. And neither one of us wants to end up running with Flintine or Paras. You remember Crossmeet.'

She'd never forget. Not the sight of the bodies hanging from gallows posts, nor the smell of rotting meat that even the cold couldn't disguise. Crossmeet had been the largest trading settlement in the city's south-west reaches – until Ton Paras had taken offence at the tariffs levelled on his supply shipments and sent in his gang to… negotiate.

Yelen and Mirika had arrived two days after the massacre. Long enough for the fires to have died. Long enough for the crows to have started feasting on the dead.

'I remember. But Paras isn't a delver,' said Yelen. 'He was a thug back in Karamasz. He's a thug here.' Even as she spoke, she knew it wasn't true. In Karamasz, with its street wardens and courthouses, Paras was a thug. In the lawless snows of Frostgrave, he was a hedonistic monster.

Mirika leaned closer, eyes gleaming in the firelight. 'All the more reason for us to choose our associations carefully. Cavril's a rogue, but he has scruples. And he's interested. He's made an offer.'

'You already spoke to him?' Yelen sighed and rocked back on her haunches. 'Don't I get a say in this?'

'Of course you do. I didn't even bring it up, Cavril did. Like I said, he's interested.'

'Interested in you.' The words came out more defensive than Yelen intended, but there was no taking them back.

'In both of us. He knows we're a package.'

Yelen snorted. 'Like a merchant's barge and its ballast.'

Irritation crept into Mirika's tone. 'That's ridiculous, and you know it. You've skills. You got the vault open, didn't you? I couldn't have picked that lock.'

Yelen pressed a hand to her mouth, hoping that it looked like she was stifling a yawn, rather than the guilty grimace she felt creeping across her face. True, she could have picked the lock, given time and fewer interruptions. But she hadn't. 'I suppose.'

The corner of Mirika's mouth twitched. She took Yelen's gloved hand in her own. 'We're a team. Nothing changes that. Nothing will stop me looking out for my little sister. You wait and see. Frostgrave's going to make us both rich and famous.'

Her eyes gleamed with excitement. That was Mirika. Always planning for the future. Always blind to *now* – to what was right in front of her. Yelen suspected her connection to the timeflow made it worse. Why worry about the details of the present, when you could relive them again and again if need be? Mirika envisioned her ideal outcome, and trusted to instinct to see her clear of the obstacles in her path. But life wasn't like that, not for most people. Not for Yelen. Actions had consequences – if the tattoo was nothing else, it was reminder of that. She pulled her hand free and stared down into the fire.

'What if I don't want to stay here? Afterwards, I mean.'

'Where else would we go?' Yelen didn't need to see Mirika's face to picture the confusion upon it, not with that tone.

'I don't know. Back to Karamasz, maybe. Or further south, to the coast. I don't know. I don't care. I just want to be somewhere where I can feel the warmth of the sun when it shines. Where I can go for a walk without trudging through snowdrifts, or slipping on ice.' Yelen swallowed. She knew her next words would sting, but she had to say them. She should have said them months ago. 'Somewhere people know me as something more than Mirika Semova's little sister.'

Neither of them spoke for what seemed an eternity. Yelen's last words hung like the brimstone stink from the fire. Her cheeks warmed with guilt. Maybe she shouldn't have said anything. No. She had to. The feeling had been growing for months. Better she aired it now, rather than during a quarrel. Hurtful as the words might have been, in the heat of an argument they'd have been a weapon. And gods, but she felt better. Like a weight had lifted from her shoulders. It was like coming up for air after swimming underwater.

Yelen glanced up from the flames. Mirika was staring into the fire, her expression unusually thoughtful. Or maybe it wasn't thoughtful at all, but hurt. As if sensing Yelen's scrutiny, she raised her head. 'So it's not Frostgrave you want to leave. It's me.' She couldn't hide the tremor in her tone.

Yelen screwed her eyes shut. 'Yes. No. I don't know…' She took a deep breath. She'd always known this would be hard. Why did it feel like a betrayal? 'I just feel trapped. Like I can't move. Between…' She wrapped a hand around her wrist by way of explanation, unwilling to speak Azzanar's name aloud. 'And… We left Karamasz because you wanted to. Because you'd this grand idea of finding our fortune. We came here for the same reason. But I can't keep blindly following you around, Rika. I'll go mad. I have to do what's right for me. Even if that means we're not together.'

Mirika offered a small, sad smile. 'You haven't called me Rika for years.'

She shrugged, wondering what had provoked the slip of the tongue. 'It's a girl's nickname. But we're not girls anymore. Either of us.'

'No, I suppose not. Why didn't you tell me before?' Mirika shook her head. 'No, don't answer that. It doesn't matter.' She twisted away, but not before Yelen spotted the tears welling up in her eyes.

The guilt did nothing to extinguish Yelen's sense of relief. In its own way, that only made her feel worse. 'So what do we do next?'

Mirika cleared her throat and cuffed at her eyes. 'The plan's still the plan. We give Master Torik his prize, he comes through with what he promised, and we'll take it from there.' She gazed at Yelen, and forced a wry smile. 'I'm not angry, honestly I'm not. I just thought it'd take a little longer, that's all.'

'Mirika…' Yelen began.

Her sister cut her off. 'Get some sleep. It'll be a hard day tomorrow, even if the weather holds. I'll keep watch. I've lots to think about.' She spread her hands, winced, and drew her injured wrist back onto her knees.

Yelen shook her head. 'I still don't understand why you had me splint that. Can't you just step into the timeflow to heal it?'

'I could, if I wanted to lop two months off my life.' Mirika cocked her head. 'You really do want rid of me, don't you?'

'What? No!' It took Yelen a moment to notice Mirika's broad grin. She clapped a hand over her mouth to choke back an outburst of giggles.

'It's that, or have an arm older than the rest of me,' Mirika sniffed. 'Break enough bones, and I'll look like some patchwork crone before I'm thirty. Forget joining the Gilded Rose, I could earn good money in Rassel's freakshow. *If* I didn't aim to stay young and beautiful for as long as possible, that is.'

Unable to hold them back any longer, Yelen let the giggles have free rein. Mirika held her imperious pose a moment longer before joining in. As the laughter flowed, Yelen felt a little of her guilt bleed away. Everything would be alright, it truly would. So long as Torik came through on his promise.

* * *

Mirika stared out into the night. The wind had dropped, and the pressure with it. She welcomed the former, but the latter warned of snow to come. Another problem, and she'd collected too many on this expedition already. Hiking through a blizzard with only one good hand was sure to bring more.

Coming to a decision, Mirika plunged her injured wrist into the timeflow. Nerves jangled up and down the length of her forearm, the sensation like nothing so much as jarring an elbow. She gasped with the suddenness of it, and then it was gone, the pain with it.

'Mirika?' Yelen's drowsy voice drifted across from the dying fire.

'It's fine,' she replied without turning, 'go back to sleep.'

''k.' The response sounded distant, her sister already adrift on slumber's tides. Moments later, the soft, fluttering sounds of snoring filled the room.

Shaking her head, Mirika stripped away the bandage and splint, and flexed her wrist experimentally. It didn't *feel* older, but she supposed it never did. Master Torik had warned her about using the timeflow that way. He'd said it was akin to wishing away your ills and illnesses, and wishes always had a price, even when it wasn't obvious. On the other hand – Hah! The other hand! – a month or two, more or less, wouldn't do her any good if she fell into a crevasse the following morning.

'You were right, little sister,' she whispered. 'Always the practical one.'

She dropped the filthy bandage out of the window. It spiralled lazily through the air, tossed this way and that by the gusting wind. If only all her problems were so easily disposed of, hidden costs or no. Perhaps Yelen would feel different once Master Torik had worked his miracle, separated her from the… thing… tethered to her soul. She hoped so.

Being apart, when for so long they'd been all each other had? The idea was like a punch to Mirika's gut, every bit as bad as the memory of Marcan's knife. Or she thought so, anyway. The moments between that first clasping of hands and the triggering of the time walk were fading. They always did. After all, they'd no longer truly happened, and the mortal mind hated trying to make sense of the contradiction. Some parts would remain – Mirika knew she'd never forget the hot-cold sensation of torn flesh – but others would dissipate like waking dreams. Possibly they already had. The very nature of forgetting made accounting for it impossible.

Mirika's foot brushed the haversack. Stooping, she plucked the reliquary free, tracing her fingers across the whorls upon its surface. There was no crack, no obvious join in the stone. What did it contain? Master Torik hadn't said, but then he never did. She supposed it didn't matter, as long as he did what he'd promised.

With a sigh, Mirika leaned against the cracked windowsill. She stared out across the snow-drifted cobbles and listened to the rhythmic tremor of Yelen's snores – the same snores she never admitted to making. What if Yelen didn't feel different after Master Torik set her free? What then?

Mirika didn't want to leave. She'd fallen in love with the ruined city from the very first, with the opportunities it offered and the wildness of those who'd made it their home. Back home in Karamasz, she'd never have learnt to use her talents as she had here. She'd have been a street hustler, or perhaps a thief – until they'd caught her in the act of dabbling in the timeflow, then she'd have ended in a crow's cage. Here in Frostgrave, the possibilities were endless.

No. Not Frostgrave. What was the name Master Torik called it?

'Felstad.' Mirika whispered the word reverently, tasting the unfamiliar syllables as they rolled off her tongue. That was it. So much grander.

On a whim, she gazed out across a cityscape and reached out into ages past, this time not merely harnessing the memory of light, but the reflection of everything that light had touched. Ghostly images danced across the Broken Strand – in her mind's eye broken no longer, but a glorious promenade. The spires, no longer twisted and decaying, reached skyward like arms in prayer, flickering lights and swirls of brilliant colour dancing skyward. The collapsed roadway was collapsed no more, but led a winding path up to the Temple of Draconostra, itself now crowned by a magnificent bronze dome, rather than jagged and mangled metal.

The spiralling chimneys at the temple's rear gouted thick black smoke, stirring memories of old legends. Szarnos the Butcher. Szarnos the Mad. Szarnos the Damned. The list went on. Mirika had heard so many tales since coming to Frostgrave. Of how Szarnos had cast living servants into the fires, feasting on their life essence at the moment of death. Of the profane ceremonies, where his priests bathed in blood and slit one another's throats at the master's leaden command. The Charnel Feasts. The

Banquet of Souls. The Hidden Court of Draconostra, of which Szarnos was but a forerunner in some stories, and the unholy master in others. Had he been a priest, or a wayward sorcerer? No two tales agreed on the details. Like all of Frostgrave's secrets, they were whispered around campfires, multiplying like maggots as the ale flowed. The only thing on which the tales agreed, was that Szarnos' hour had ended long ago.

Far below, dark shapes crowded the streets. A processional? Citizenry going about their daily business? Sacrifices to Szarnos' mad dreams? It was impossible to tell. Time-light preserved the dead and the lifeless as if they were locked in ice, but the living? Their timelines were always in motion, even in the past, and cast only hazy shadows into the future. Or ordinarily so. One figure stood tall at the entrance to the temple, scarlet robes swirling about his feet. Even at that distance, the gold about his wrists and throat glimmered in the long ago sunlight and a black cube glinted in his hands. Was that…?

The skin of the reliquary blazed like fire.

'Ahhh!'

Mirika dropped the reliquary without thinking, her grip on the light of ages past slipping away. One corner struck the stone floor with a soft *chink*, and then it rolled to rest like a giant die. Over by the fire, Yelen snored on.

Mirika cursed softly under her breath, alternately shaking and sucking at her fingers to relieve a pain already fading. In all their years together, Master Torik had never raised his voice to her, but then again she'd never broken one of his precious artefacts. She squatted and stared at the cube. It didn't *look* damaged. Indeed, the impact had driven a splinter from the flagstone it had struck. She sighed with relief. A close call. Yelen was right. She did need to be more…

A dull roar sounded from outside. A troll. Not too close, but too close for comfort all the same.

Leaving the reliquary where it had fallen, Mirika twisted back to the window. Dawn's glow lit the horizon, the dark of night in full retreat before a new day. Almost directly below, at the foot of the building, a troll stood knee-deep in a snow drift, furred shoulders hunched as it lashed out. Not at another troll, but at a squat, bearded man in filthy leathers.

Marcan.

The blow connected with a dull *thud*. The swarthy man spun away into a snowdrift, sword falling from his hand. Mirika snorted. Serve him right.

A chill crept along her spine, spoiling the delicious schadenfreude of the moment. If Marcan was here, then the rest of the Gilded Rose wouldn't be far behind – assuming Cavril hadn't banished him for the almost-murder. They might even be in the building.

'Yelen!' she hissed. 'Yelen! Wake up!'

The bundle of blankets stirred. A gloved hand cuffed at sleep-crusted eyes. ''m awake.'

'Be *more* awake. It's time to leave.'

Mirika returned her attention to the growing contest below, now lit by the first grey light of the coming morning. Dawn had arrived more quickly than she'd thought. Had she gotten lost in the images of the past? It wasn't the first time that had happened. Marcan was on his feet again, swaying unsteadily. Then again, he was lucky to still have a head on his shoulders. He'd be lucky to keep it there. A second troll lurched into sight, a long-dead bough clutched in its hand as a makeshift club.

Marcan flickered and refracted, the dancing light coalescing into four identical images.

That settled it. Cavril was here. Whether or not Mirika's future lay with the Gilded Rose, the Szarnos reliquary belonged with Master Torik.

One troll lurched to a halt, dull-witted gaze sweeping back and forth across the unexpected puzzle. The other was of a more practical mind, and swung its primitive club at the nearest 'Marcan'.

The image shattered like breaking glass, shards dancing across the snows before vanishing entirely. The troll roared its victory, then stumbled away as an arrow thwacked into its shoulder. Mirika spotted the archer at the corner of the street, another arrow already nocked. Darrick charged past him, his battle cry unintelligible from that distance.

'Yelen! Come on! We have to go.'

Mirika's thoughts raced as she considered their next move. They couldn't leave at ground level without running into the growing skirmish – it didn't matter who won, she wanted no part of that. The roof. Get up to the roof and travel to the edge of the Broken Strand that way – assuming the wind remained in abeyance. They still had a rope. They could get down into Wailing Reach without setting foot on cobbles. Yes. That would do it.

'Yelen!'

'I'm here.' And she was, blankets already stuffed into their supply haversack. 'What's the calamity?' Another roar sounded from below. Yelen peered out of the window. 'Oh. You're sure you don't want to go down there? Take both groups on?'

'Very funny.'

One troll was reeling, an arrow in each shoulder, arms windmilling as it sought to land a blow. It fought not just

Marcan and Darrick now, but Serene as well. Not that numbers availed them greatly. As Mirika watched, Darrick ducked under the flailing fist and hacked at the beast's flank. The troll didn't stagger. There wasn't even any blood, the blow having wasted its force on the shaggy, matted pelt.

The second troll had but a single opponent. Kain stood before it, feet planted in the snows with the certainty of an aged oak, bastard sword held in a duellist's overhand stance. Where her fellows were edgy, hesitant in their blows – and with damn good reason, as far as Mirika was concerned – Kain exuded calm.

The troll's club came down. Kain twisted away. Not much. Just enough to avoid the blow grazing her armour. The bastard sword flashed. Blood sprayed from the troll's forearm, the droplets freezing in the clear air.

'Who is she?' Yelen breathed, wide-eyed.

'She's too good for the Gilded Rose, that's for sure,' Mirika replied. 'I wonder what she's running from.'

Yelen crouched. 'And why's this on the floor?'

Mirika started guiltily. She dropped to her knees, scooping the reliquary back into the haversack. It was no longer warm to the touch. Perhaps it never had been. 'I dropped it. Don't worry, it's fine.'

'Easy for you to say,' muttered Yelen. 'Torik won't blame you if it's broken.'

Mirika grimaced, but knew better than to take the bait. 'We'll go up to the roof. We can…'

'… cut across from there,' Yelen interrupted. 'I know. I unlocked the door while you were sleeping.'

Mirika shook her head. Two steps ahead, once again. Not bad for someone without access to the timeflow. 'You really do think of everything, don't you?'

Yelen's expression flickered with... something. 'Not even close.'

'Go on, get going.'

'Me? I was waiting for you.'

Mirika took a step towards the lopsided staircase, but some instinct held her back. Glancing out the window, she saw that a third troll had joined the fray, bearing down on Kain with single-minded determination. The first troll still held the bulk of the Gilded Rose at bay. The archer still lurked at the street corner, firing whenever a clear shot presented itself, which was seldom enough. Magnis – never really one for physical confrontation – stood close by.

Good as she was, Mirika couldn't see how Kain could fend off two trolls at once. Hells, even one was a challenge beyond the pale for most delvers, as the rest of the Gilded Rose were inadvertently proving. Mirika didn't know the woman. She wasn't sure she even liked her – the insults from Szarnos' tomb still rung too loudly in her ears for that. But still...

Coming to a decision, Mirika plucked a pebble from the floor. Leaning out over the window ledge, she held it at arm's length below her, taking the measure of the new-come troll's advance. Timing was everything, even for a time witch.

Steady. *Steady*.

At last, instinct declared the moment right. Mirika gave the pebble's tempo a hard shove, and released it. Time flowing over it at many times the speed of everything nearby, the pebble plunged, picking up more speed as gravity's acceleration took hold.

It struck the top of the troll's skull with a *crack* as sharp as it was brief. Frigid blood spattered the snow as the impact bored a ragged hole from the top of the beast's lumpen scalp to the base of its spine. With a last gargled roar, it toppled face first onto the cobbles.

Across the way, Magnis stared sharply up at Mirika's window, a thoughtful expression on his face.

'What are you doing?' Yelen asked. 'You've given us away.'

'They already knew,' said Mirika. 'And it felt right.'

Fingers closed around her arm. '*It felt right?* Will it feel right if Torik doesn't get his wretched box? Come on!'

Yelen ran for the stairs. With a last look out of the window, Mirika followed.

CHAPTER THREE

Yelen no longer remembered what it was to be warm. The wind howled across the maze of shattered monoliths and sunken sepulchres, slicing effortlessly through her robes. With each gust, a thousand icy needles pricked at her exposed skin. She walked hunched over, each plodding, leaden footstep following those Mirika had left behind. She seldom raised her eyes. What was the point? The path ahead lay hidden beneath the impenetrable blizzard, its fury funnelled and redoubled by the confines of the Broken Strand. Not for nothing was the sprawling grave-field known to delvers as the Wailing Reach.

The rope around Yelen's waist jerked once, twice. She tugged back, sending the 'all clear' signal into the swirling white, letting Mirika know she was still alive. Mirika could see, of course, drawing on long ago skies unchoked with clouds to pick a safe path through the graves. But the rope was necessary all the same.

They'd learnt that the hard way six months earlier, when Mirika had taken a tumble into a sunken crypt. The memory of the long, lonely hours of searching still burned bright in Yelen's thoughts. The rising sense of panic as time wore on, each passing minute bringing her closer to the looming reality of her sister's death. All in her mind, of course – she'd eventually found Mirika nursing a swollen ankle in the lee of an eagle-crested memorial – but it'd been too close a call, all the same. Mirika had been less than a hundred yards away the whole time, and the worry had nearly broken Yelen.

So how would she feel if Mirika was still delving in Frostgrave while she was leagues away in Karamasz?

Yelen jerked to halt, paralyzed by doubt and the shadow of future guilt. The rope went taut, occasioning a querulous double-tug from deeper in the blizzard. Stifling her embarrassment, she gave the all clear, and pressed on.

'You have to go,' she muttered. 'You have to.'

'Don't worry, poppet. You'll always have me.' Azzanar's voice rang out clear above the howling wind. More proof that fate hated her.

'I hope not.'

Yelen swayed slightly as another gust caught her off-balance. Experience had taught her that she didn't need to speak aloud for her tormentor to hear. That said, holding a one-sided conversation was less disconcerting than having the entire exchange play out inside her head.

'That's hardly kind.' Even in the biting cold of the blizzard, Azzanar's words maintained their syrupy warmth. *'And after all I've done for you.'*

'If you care that much, leave me the hell alone, and slink back to wherever that idiot plucked you from.'

'Sorry poppet. Promises were made. Blood exchanged. We're together 'till the end, like it or not. Anyway, I'm looking forward to stretching my legs.'

Yelen flinched as the skin at her left wrist started prickling. She scratched at it through her layered robes, already knowing the itch wouldn't fade. Likely it was all in her head, for whatever comfort that was. 'Your legs? Mine, you mean.'

Azzanar laughed like a parent amused by their child's unwitting witticism. *'Why quibble? It'll all be the same before long. I've already seen it.'*

Yelen gritted her teeth and trudged on. Azzanar often said such things as prophecy, asserting that the chime of thirteen was inevitable. Yelen didn't believe her. The demon never had anything else to say about the future. It was just another way to wear her down. Unfortunately, ignoring the taunts didn't discourage Azzanar in the slightest. In fact, Yelen had the horrible feeling she enjoyed the challenge – a cat enjoying the struggles of its prey.

Distracted by anger, Yelen misplaced her footing. Permafrosted mud crumbled away from her heel, spilling away down the sheer slope to her right. She lurched to her left, flailing for balance.

'We're going to have such fun, you and I.'

Yelen knew all too well what that meant. At the chime of thirteen, their positions would reverse – she'd be trapped in the depths of her own mind, and her body would become Azzanar's. Torik had been clear on that – gleefully so, when Mirika wasn't around. A favoured tactic of demon lords in ages past, he'd said. The prospect made Yelen sick to the stomach. Bad enough to die. But to stand as helpless witness to whatever Azzanar did with her body and in her name…?

But until then, she was still in control. For whatever that was worth.

'If you don't shut up, I'll untie this rope and throw myself into the next crevasse.'

Azzanar laughed. '*You're not going to do that. Think of what it would do to your sister.*'

Yelen halted and placed a hand on the knot. 'Try me.'

She felt the demon coiling in her thoughts, spiralling this way and that, weighing her conviction. Not for the first time, she was glad that Azzanar couldn't actually read her thoughts, only skim the meaning of silent conversation. Otherwise, she'd have seen that Yelen had no intention of following through with her threat.

'*Oh, have it your way,*' said Azzanar sulkily. Then, gloriously, she slid back into the depths.

Yelen allowed herself a moment of exultance before pressing on. A small victory, but no less satisfying for all that. Not that it changed anything. She'd called on the demon's help too many times. Never for trivial reasons, but that was the thing about last resorts – they cropped up more than you ever expected.

Bowing her head against the blizzard, Yelen trudged on.

* * *

At last, it loomed out of the snow – Blackstena crematorium, one of the few structures still standing in the Wailing Reach. The gate was ajar, but that meant nothing. The slab of stone was broader than Mirika was tall, and twice that in height. Only a colossal might could have budged it so much as an inch.

With a last surge of effort, Mirika waded through the deep-drifted snow, and into the gloomy interior. Wisps of snow blew in from small windows set high on the walls, but otherwise the floors were clear. Or almost so. A quick search uncovered a pile of blood-stained traveller's furs behind one of the chipped obsidian biers. Of the traveller, there was no sign. Not even bones. But nor was there any sign of what might have done the deed.

She made another sweep of the chamber, paying careful attention to the claw marks in the ice by the frost-locked kiln. Too large for wolves. A bear? Could be. She'd heard tell that they occasionally strayed this far south. Still, there was no sign of one now. And it was only a waystation. They wouldn't be there long.

Tugging three times on the rope, Mirika relinquished her time-sight. She already felt giddy from her brain trying to reconcile the light of past and present. A rest would help. So would a meal. That being the case, she busied herself setting a fire in the records room. At least, what she always called the records room. She found it easy to imagine a fussy clerk sitting behind the battered old desk, tutting at the grief of kith and kin as he scratched names off the ledger. In her mind, he was tall and thin – the very spit of the tyrant who ran the guttermarch orphanage. She hoped that he too was long dead.

Yelen arrived just as the fire caught hold. Mirika held her tongue at her sister's bow-legged and staggered gait, comical though it was – not out of politeness, but out of certainty that she looked every bit as ridiculous.

'Any sign of the Gilded Rose?'

Yelen planted herself beside the fire, gloved hands rubbing life back into her cheeks. 'You're joking. I couldn't even see you. Darrick could have been stomping away a pace behind me all across that last ridge, and I wouldn't have known. But I think they've more sense to be out in this.'

Mirika shot her a wry smile. 'Not like us?'

'Not like us.'

By the time the billy can had been fetched from the depths of Yelen's haversack, and fresh snow from the frozen wastes outside, Mirika was feeling almost warm. Almost. It took half a mug of sour chanin tea to chase the rest of the cold away. Propping herself up against the desk, she wolfed down a mouthful of bread and drew in a lungful of the smoky, bitter chanin steam. The smell alone held back the howl of the wind, evoking memories of comfortable evenings in more pleasurable climes. A little too much so, in fact.

'You're sure you didn't use too many of the leaves,' she asked. 'I don't want to start seeing things.'

There were plenty of hedge wizards in the frozen city who overindulged in chanin precisely *because* they wanted to start seeing things. But doing so while trapped in a blizzard on the Wailing Reach was hardly the place to try that. Not unless you wanted to separate mind from body permanently.

Yelen rubbed her hands together and held them, palm outward, towards the fire. 'Relax, we're well under the limits. At least, providing you don't drink all of it.'

Wincing, Mirika reluctantly handed the mug across the fire. 'Be like that. I'll have it all to myself when you're gone.'

Yelen froze mid-reach, her fingers inches away from the cup. A chasm yawned open at the base of Mirika's gut. She'd meant the words as a joke, to soften the prospect of a parting that might only be days away. But in addressing the idea aloud, all she'd done was to reinforce the reality to come. Judging by the stricken look on Yelen's face, they'd awoken a similar revelation in her.

'I… I'm sorry. I didn't mean…'

Yelen shook her head, and drew back her hand. 'It doesn't matter. Finish the tea. I'll make some more.'

Mirika twitched the mug. 'Don't be ridiculous. Drink it.'

Yelen hesitated. Then she took the mug and cradled it in both hands. 'Wouldn't kill you to think before speaking from time to time, you know?' A smile softened the harshness of the truth.

'That's what I've got you for, remember? I handle the bold action, and miraculous escapes. You do the worrying, and the thinking.' She shrugged, grinning at her own pomposity. 'It's worked out nicely so far.'

'I guess so.' Yelen raised the battered tin mug, tilting it slightly towards Mirika. 'To the Semova sisters – a selfish pair, but there's not a delver to match them.'

So saying, she knocked back a mouthful of tea.

'I can't return the toast without the mug,' Mirika observed.

'Or without tea,' Yelen observed, upending the vessel. Empty. 'I'll let you make some more.'

Shaking her head, Mirika trudged back to the doorway and stuffed the billy can with snow. The world beyond was awhirl with snow, so much so that she could barely see the two sentinel statues guarding the entrance. Yelen had walked all this way, seeing so little? Sometimes Mirika forgot what it was like not to have time-sight at your beck and call.

She stood there a while longer, imagining dark shapes amongst the white. Where were the Gilded Rose? There were only two or three safe paths through the Wailing Reach, so the odds were good that Cavril and his minions were even now closing the distance. Possibly, he'd even split up his expedition to follow all three routes. In which case, pursuit was certain. Something had to change.

Not that Yelen would like what she had in mind…

* * *

Yelen awoke, blinking to clear her thoughts and her eyes. She lurched to a sitting position, the bed creaking as her weight shifted. The smooth, ice-clad stones of the Blackstena crematorium had vanished, replaced by the buckled timbers of her attic room in the *Guttered Candle*.

She rubbed at her eyes with her palms. 'Mirika, what have you done now?'

Was it a trick? Payment for the thing with the tea? That would be childish even by Mirika's standards. Yelen didn't even know if such a thing could be done – erasing the long, cold walk from her mind by meddling with tempo and timeflow. Oh, she'd suffered similar pranks when they were younger – relived brief moments, as vibrant the second time as the first, only to be snapped out of it by her sister's mischievous grin. But to vanish a whole day? At least, Yelen hoped it was only a day. What she remembered of the hike across Wailing Reach promised a long, fraught journey.

Fire kindled in the pit of Yelen's stomach. Whatever Mirika had done, she was damn sure her sister didn't know what the consequences might be. 'Mirika!'

There was no answer. In fact, the whole tavern – seldom a place of riotous activity – seemed unusually quiet.

Pushing off from the bed frame, stooping low as ever to avoid bashing her head on the bowed beams, Yelen pulled on moth-eaten furs that served as her night robe, and made her way towards the door.

Halfway across the room, something caught her eye – a glint of light in the cracked mirror-pane. Frowning, Yelen changed course, running her fingers across the squat chimneybreast, her nails skipping and tugging across the uneven stones. Something wasn't right about the room, though she couldn't decide exactly what. Everything was in its proper place. The shelves holding her few meagre books. The statuette of Solastra she'd pilfered from that belligerent drunk down by the river wharf. The battered trunk housing her spare clothes. And, of course, the mirror itself; jagged and cracked, its edges chipped and discoloured.

Wrapping her arms tight about her thin frame, Yelen stared into the glass. No matter how hard she tried, she could dredge up no memory of anything after Mirika had left, billy can in hand.

With a growl of frustration, she planted a fist against the rotting plasterwork. Her mirror-image stared back, the two of them joined in silent fury at liberties taken. Taken aback at the reflected expression, Yelen took a deep breath and forced herself to something approaching calm. Better not to rise to it. Better not to… 'What has she done this time?'

'*Shhh…*' The reflection's lips twisted into a smile. '*You're leaping to conclusions.*'

Yelen's heart leapt into her mouth. For the first time, she noticed that her doppelgänger's eyes were not blue, but a deep, gold-flecked crimson.

She lurched on shaking legs, peering desperately around the attic. At last, she realised what was wrong. Everything was backwards. Reflected. Even the titles of her books. Through the mirror, everything was as it should have been. She was trapped in her own reflection.

'*I told you this was coming, poppet,*' crowed Azzanar. Her mouth parted to reveal a forked, black tongue. '*Now it's your turn to watch.*'

Yelen ground the heels of her hands into her temples. 'No! I didn't let you out! I didn't let you out!'

She ripped back the sleeve of the furs and stared at her left wrist. The clock face tattoo was completely black. The thirteen glowed red to match her reflection's eyes.

Yelen scrunched her eyes shut, the panicked sob choking off beneath a hot surge of anger. 'Let me out!'

The mirror shattered further beneath her fist, splintering Azzanar's image a dozen times over. Blood spattered across the glass. Yelen felt nothing. Again and again she hammered at the mirror, the demon's laughter billowing louder with every strike.

'I won't let you!' Another blow. Another sharp, brittle crunch. 'Let me go!'

Yelen drew back with a deep, shuddering breath. She stared at her trembling hands, the knuckles ripped and bloody. Mirika appeared in the fragmented mirror-image and set her hand on Azzanar's shoulder.

'It's time to go. I've booked passage as far as Karamasz. We can work out the rest as we go.'

'Mirika, no!' Yelen screamed for all she was worth. 'That's not me! That's her! Don't go!'

Mirika turned from the mirror and walked away. Azzanar offered Yelen a half shrug and a wink, then turned to follow.

'No! Mirika! That's not me! Mirika!'

Desperate, Yelen flung herself at the mirror. It exploded into bloody shards.

* * *

Alerted by the cry, Mirika caught Yelen's jack-knifing body before she plunged into the fire. Grabbing her sister by the shoulders, she hauled her bodily away from the flames and propped her against the wall. Yelen clutched at her arms, her breathing low and thready.

'Don't go with her! It's not me. It's not me!'

Grip still firm on Yelen's shoulders, Mirika gazed down into her sister's eyes. They stared back, glassy and unfocused.

Uncertainty pricked at Mirika's thoughts, its claws pricking along her spine. 'Yelen? Yelen, it's alright. Do you hear me?'

Yelen's breathing quickened. Her fingers tightened painfully around Mirika's upper arms. 'Don't go!'

With no other course of action obvious, Mirika flung her arms around Yelen and held her tight. Her sister's muscles were taut as ships' rigging. 'I'm not going anywhere. You hear me? I'm not.'

She held Yelen's thin, shivering form tight, repeating the mantra again and again. Little by little, Yelen's breathing slowed – the sharp, furtive gasps giving way to ragged lungfuls. Her body lost its stiffness. She sank into Mirika's arms, returning the embrace.

'I'm sorry. I'm sorry.' She whispered in a small voice, equal parts contrition and embarrassment. 'I must have dozed off. The nightmare was so real.'

'No kidding. I heard the snores all the way from the gate. As for the rest…' Mirika frowned. 'Show me your wrist?'

Yelen pulled away, a haunted look in her eyes. 'Why? What does it matter?'

Mirika's suspicions coalesced, dense as iron. 'It didn't. Not until you refused.' She sighed, and forced a sharper edge into her tone. 'Just show me.'

She didn't need to meet Yelen's defiant gaze to know that speaking so was a mistake, another incidence of the 'big sister knows best' attitude that was slowly driving them apart. But she couldn't back down. Not about this. Part of her was honest enough to admit that there'd probably never be a right topic to back down from, but sometimes big sister really *did* know best. If only Yelen had listened back in Karamasz, maybe none of this would have happened.

With a grimace, Yelen twisted away. Still not looking at Mirika, she stripped off her left glove and rolled back her sleeve. The clock face tattoo was darker than the last time Mirika had seen it, the black stain spread well past twelve o'clock. That could only mean one thing: Yelen had called on the demon for help. Exactly as she'd promised not to.

Mirika sank back beside the fire. 'When?'

Yelen kept her gaze fixed steadfastly on the wall. 'In the tomb. I heard you cry out, and I lost my grip on the lock picks.' Her voice quickened, the tone sharp, defensive. 'We were out of time. I thought you were hurt. We couldn't afford to start over, so I crumbled the vault to dust.' She drew herself up, at last shifting to regard Mirika with a cool, defiant stare. 'It had to be done.'

Mirika shook her head. The problem was, Yelen was right. The confrontation with the Gilded Rose – a confrontation Mirika herself had provoked – had been going badly. If Yelen hadn't breached the vault when she had, they might not have made it out at all, let alone with the reliquary. But still, the risk made Mirika sick to her stomach. It was one thing for her to have come as close to death, but if Yelen lost her battle with the demon in her soul…

'Yelen, listen…'

'It was only a dream,' said Yelen. 'Maybe I was wrong about the chanin.'

'Maybe. But it won't be next time. Not if you keep on like this.'

Yelen snorted. 'It doesn't matter, does it? You're still convinced Torik's going to cure me.'

The sudden bitterness in her tone caught Mirika off-guard. She chose her next words as carefully as she would her steps across a frozen lake. 'Of course he is. He promised, didn't he?'

'And how many times has he promised before?'

'So there were setbacks. Your situation's complicated. So is magic. He's doing everything he can.'

Yelen shook her head. 'You really believe that, don't you?'

'Of course. He's been nothing but good to us.'

'To you. To his beloved apprentice. I'm just the freak he keeps locked in the attic.'

The ice beneath Mirika's feet began creaking. 'What do you mean?'

'Why do you think I'm never there when he's holding his little gatherings, fanning his ego in front of the crowds? I'm just the price he pays to keep you around. An experiment gone out of hand. An embarrassment. Sometimes I wake up in a cold sweat, convinced he's in the room, watching me. But he never is. Or at least, I never see him.'

Mirika drew back. It was certainly true that Master Torik liked to play court when the fancy took him. He'd taken great care to introduce her to his peers, or perhaps rivals – in Frostgrave, the two were often one and the same. He'd even gifted her a time walker's scarlet robe – purchased at great expense, she didn't doubt, from one of the trade caravans that plied the eastern routes – so that she might properly look the part. Mirika had borne that gift, and the others that had followed, with suspicion at first, fearful that the friendliness would give way to more personal, more private, demands. Months had passed before she'd finally realised the truth. Despite his great age, or perhaps because of it, Master Torik was a deeply lonely man. He'd spoken many times about his fear of passing into the beyond without leaving another to fill his shoes. Though Mirika wasn't wholly convinced that she wanted to inherit his lonely, insular life, it did no harm to humour the old man – especially with Yelen's soul at stake.

'You stay away from Master Torik's parties because you hate people,' she pointed out. 'They bore you. Your words, not mine.'

Yelen's eyes flashed. 'I stay away from his parties because he made it quite clear what would happen if I didn't do as I was told.'

'And you always do what you're told? Right?'

She turned sharply away, fists clenching and unclenching.

Mirika choked back her own rising anger. 'Listen, I know you're scared. I know you're angry, but Master Torik…'

Yelen cut her off with a wave of her hand. 'You remember about three months back, when he invited Markos Tremojz and his band of thugs into the *Guttered Candle*?'

Mirika narrowed her eyes. Where was she going with

this? 'A peace offering, wasn't it? Some old squabble over an amulet, and a djinn. I remember Markos stank of beer even before he crossed the threshold. And that I didn't see you for a week afterwards.'

'I disobeyed Torik,' Yelen said. 'I came downstairs late in the evening. Saw them talking. I don't know where you were.'

Mirika shifted uneasily. 'I went down to the river. Markos *is* boring.'

In point of fact, she'd abandoned proceedings early on. Most of Markos' gang had been dour veterans, riddled with scars and ill-manners learnt during bitter years surviving Frostgrave. Elni was different. A few years older than Mirika, she'd smiled while the others had scowled, and alone had regarded her as an equal, rather than as another of Master Torik's exotic treasures. They'd got well and drunk that night, away from the crowd, sharing stories and laughter like old friends. A herd of mammoths could have trampled through the tavern that night, and Mirika wouldn't have noticed. Nor when she awoke on the wharfside the next morning, head thundering with the aftermath of excess.

Elni had died three days later, along with the rest of Markos' gang – the victim of some ill-advised expedition into the Grey District.

Yelen shrugged. 'Well, Torik caught me. He must've stepped into the timeflow, because I didn't even see him coming. Before I knew it, I was back in the attic. He stood over me...' Her fingers danced along one cheek. 'I can still smell the tobacco on his breath. He called me every name you can think of. I tried to pull away, but he's strong for a withered old fossil...'

Hairs prickled on the back of Mirika's neck. 'What happened?'

Yelen's lips contorted at the memory. 'He brought… He brought Azzan… *her* to the surface. Pushed me against the mirror, so I'd see her in my reflection. Said he'd bring her up all the way if I ever disobeyed him again. So I didn't.'

Mirika stared at her sister. Speechless, innards writhing like snakes. 'Why didn't you say anything?'

'Because you wouldn't have believed me,' snapped Yelen. She rolled back her sleeve, and slid her hand into the glove. 'And you don't, do you?'

Blue eyes, defiant as ever, met Mirika's. It'd be so easy to say what Yelen wanted to hear. Maybe even wise. 'I don't know.'

Yelen shook her head sadly. 'And that's why I didn't tell you. We may be sisters, but we don't live in the same world. Did you never wonder why the clock gained three hours in the space of days? Come on! I went wild back in Karamasz, yanked Bruel's gang through the timeflow so hard they were vomiting for days. Crumbled that old vulture's workhouse to dust, and that was just for starters.'

'I remember,' said Mirika. The memory even occasioned a small smile. She'd been proud of Yelen at the time. Had thought her gift had finally awoken. It was only afterwards that she learned the full horror of the bargain her sister had made.

'I bet they're still talking about it to this day.'

'Oh, you'll be a legend, sure enough.'

'An hour. That's all it cost me. An hour on the clock. One out of thirteen. Don't you think you'd have noticed if I'd let loose with three hours' worth in the space of one night?'

CHAPTER THREE

There was that, Mirika allowed. There was that. Yelen was telling the truth. She had to be. 'You should've told me.'

'You weren't there.' The words were mild, but there was no mistaking the accusation behind them. 'And then, when you were, it was easier not to say anything. You idolize that old vulture. What could I have said?'

'You could have started with what you've just told me,' snapped Mirika. Rising to her feet, she took a deep breath – angry at herself as much as at her sister. She wasn't surprised Yelen had remained silent. After all, she hadn't believed her, had she? No wonder she wanted to leave. 'He's going to help you. He promised.'

'I know you believe that.'

Mirika took a deep breath, collapsing all the anger and heartbreak into a single, implacable purpose. If there was a choice at hand, it was really no choice at all. 'You don't understand. *He's going to help you.* It doesn't matter what he's said or done to this point, or what he thinks he's going to do afterwards. You're my sister – we're a team, you and I. And he promised.'

To her relief, Yelen cracked a smile; small, wary and fragile, but a smile nonetheless. 'You're impressive at times, you know that?'

Hands on hips, Mirika tilted her head back, striking as heroic a pose as any tombstone warden in the Wailing Reach. 'And don't you forget it.' She held the pose a heartbeat longer, and let her shoulders slump. 'You still should have said something. How could you keep this from me?'

'It became normal. Everything does, if you do it for long enough.' For a moment, Yelen looked like she were about to expand on her theme, then she snorted and

71

clambered to her feet. 'How is it outside?'

Mirika watched her closely, distrusting the sudden shift of mood. 'Bad. Worse. Three days back to Rekamark, if the weather holds like this.'

'So it takes three days,' said Yelen, all business again. 'We've plenty of supplies, and it's not like the Gilded Rose can be making better time than us.'

'What if we took a shortcut?'

'What kind of shortcut?'

Mirika took a deep breath, but she was committed now. 'We leave the ridge behind, and cut across the east valley. That'll put the wind behind us. And the snow, with a bit of luck.'

Yelen scratched at her scalp. 'There's a reason we stick to the ridge.'

'I know, but…'

'You've heard the stories.'

Mirika waved her hand, sweeping the argument aside. 'This place is nothing but stories.'

'And some of them have corpses for punctuation.' She shot Mirika a sideways glance. 'This is about me, isn't it? You're worried I'll call on… her again, aren't you?'

'No!' Aware that the denial had been too forceful, Mirika paused before pressing on. 'I was already thinking about it. But now you mention it… The longer we're out here, the more likely something'll happen to force your hand.' She took Yelen's hands in hers. 'We've played things safe ever since we arrived here. We're due a risk. Let's take it. Given what you've just told me, the sooner we cut ties with Master Torik, the better.'

Yelen hesitated a moment, and then nodded. 'Alright. What did you have in mind?'

CHAPTER FOUR

Shattered monoliths marked the old funeral path – even in a blizzard, they left a trail Mirika could follow. Yelen trudged along the sheer pathway, the rope lifeline restored. The conversation in the crematorium haunted her steps. Did Mirika really believe her? Yelen wanted to think so. Should she have spoken up before? Would it have mattered? She shook her head and clutched the supply haversack all the tighter. No good came of second-guessing, not if she wanted to stay sane. Not when she was already teetering on the edge.

Even now, Yelen's pulse quickened whenever she recalled the dream – if indeed it had been a dream at all. It *could* have been the chanin, or… What if Azzanar had come so close to the surface that she was influencing her thoughts, her perceptions? Yelen clenched her teeth. No. She'd have noticed, surely? Unless part of that influence was to make her numb to what was really going on. If that were the case…

'No,' she whispered, the word snatched away into the storm. 'Getting paranoid doesn't help anyone.'

Azzanar's honeyed laugh trickled across her thoughts. *'Who's been telling you that you're paranoid? I wouldn't trust someone who said that to me.*

'Very funny,' muttered Yelen. 'So you *were* responsible for my dream.'

'*I don't deal in dreams. Nasty, flighty things that they are. We're a team, you and I, poppet. You'll understand that one day.*'

'I know,' she replied sourly. 'Your mind, my body. It won't happen.'

'*We'll see.*'

Yelen had the sense of someone walking beside her, a dark shape keeping pace through the blizzard. She turned, eyes tracking hopelessly through the blinding flurry. Nothing. 'Are you doing this?'

She stifled a yelp as fingers squeezed her shoulder. She spun around, dagger slipping free of its sheath as she did so.

And found herself staring into Mirika's grey eyes.

'Woah! It's me!' Mirika flung up her hands. 'I can't lead you through this if you cut my throat.' She stepped closer. 'You stopped walking. You didn't respond to my signals. What's wrong?'

Yelen sheathed her dagger, and tried to ignore Azzanar's distant laughter. 'Nothing. I'm going mad, that's all.'

Mirika slipped an arm around her, and gave her shoulders a reassuring squeeze. 'Just keep walking. We're nearly off the ridge. From there, it's a simple enough walk.'

Yelen nodded mutely and watched her sister vanish into the blizzard. How much time had passed since she'd stopped walking? She could have sworn it had only been seconds. 'That was you, wasn't it?'

'*So I get the blame for everything?*' Azzanar sounded more amused than hurt. '*Believe me when I tell you that if I start interfering, you'll not even notice until it's too late. But I won't. I don't need to. You'll embrace me with open arms. You'll beg me.'* The demon paused, its thoughts coiling around Yelen's. *'What did she mean "nearly off the ridge"?'*

Yelen snorted in triumph. Not only could Azzanar not read her thoughts, apparently she also didn't listen all the time, either. 'We're cutting through the valley.'

'That's a poor idea.'

'And I should care what you think?' She recalled her own cautioning words to Mirika, and pushed them to the back of her mind.

'Yes.'

Temptation prickled at Yelen's thoughts. What did the demon know? Did she know anything at all, or was she trying to trade for yet another sliver of the clock face?

The rope tugged twice. Gritting her teeth, Yelen gave the all clear. Then, shoulders hunched against the storm, she began the cold, thankless slog once again.

* * *

The skies cleared as they left the last of the marker monoliths behind, giving the impression that the foul weather had retreated behind the ridgeline. And perhaps it had. Yelen had been in Frostgrave long enough to know that even its unnatural climate seemed to possess a brooding and capricious personality. Maybe the defiance of the renowned Semova sisters had driven it to sulk out its storms on a distant field?

That ridiculous thought occasioned a slim smile as Yelen drew closer to her sister. Mirika waited in the lee of a weather-worn sepulchre. Yelen unknotted the safety rope, and Mirika reeled it in, the frayed length hissing through her hands as she wound it into a single coil. 'Told you it'd be better down here.'

Yelen stared out across the snow-covered mounds and jagged monuments, her unease returning. Emerald lights danced about the broken stones like swarms of mating firebugs in the midday light. They never strayed far, the groups never crossing the rings of stones surrounding each hummock, and certainly never mingling. All told, their behaviour gave Yelen the odd impression they were guarding their territory against others of their kind. 'You're sure this is a good idea?'

'We're here now,' Mirika replied, her evasive answer doing little to disguise the uncertainty in her voice. She kicked a spray of snow downhill. 'The snow's thinner. We'll make better time. If we pick up the pace, we can be home before midnight.'

Yelen blinked away a premonition of how the valley would appear beneath the night sky, the snows sickly and wan in the reflected wisp-light. 'Then let's get going. I'm not camping here overnight. Not for all the plunder in those barrows.'

Mirika scratched the back of her head. 'I suppose we could take a quick peek inside, as we're here.'

Yelen shot her sister a warning look. 'Mirika!'

She laughed. 'Oh, stop worrying. I'm joking. I've heard the stories, too. Here, your turn to carry the rope.'

'What am I, your pack mule?' Nonetheless, Yelen looped the rope over her shoulder.

'I'm carrying the prize.' Mirika hefted the reliquary's haversack. 'It's heavy enough. Swap you?'

Yelen shook her head. 'No. It's all yours.'

'Suit yourself.' So saying, Mirika strode lightly away through the snow.

Yelen shook her head, baffled as usual at her sister's levity, and trudged on behind. Mirika had been right about one thing, at least – the going was much easier. Up on the ridge, the snow had in places threatened to spill over the tops of her knee-high boots. Here, it barely crested her ankles. It was warmer too without the harsh embrace of the wind, and Yelen's extremities prickled as life returned to her fingers and toes. Still, the feeling of unease never entirely dissipated, not even when the sun broke through the thin clouds. It didn't help that Mirika set a brisk pace through the snowy hummocks, powered by a boundless vigour that Yelen could only envy from a distance.

'*This is unwise.*'

Yelen wasn't sure what worried her most: that Azzanar was unusually chatty today, or the worried tone the demon affected. Azzanar by turns delighted in smugness, self-gratification and mockery. The note of apprehension was new. Were they back in Rekamark, surrounded by the bright lights of what passed for civilization hereabouts, Yelen would have welcomed it. Here? If the demon was scared…?

'If you want to tell me something, then tell me. But I'm not asking.' Inspiration struck. 'What happens to you if something happens to me, I wonder?'

She felt the demon's hesitation. Her discomfort. Neither was so strong as the spark of delight at turning the tables for a change. '*This is a cursed place.*'

'That's rich, coming from you.'

'*There's hunger here. Older than the city. And you've skipped gaily into the larder, poppet.*'

'We haven't "skipped" anywhere,' said Yelen. 'As long as we don't cross the ghost-rings around a barrow, they'll leave us be. They can't break their bonds.'

'*And who says that?*'

'Delvers come here all the time.' *That* was an exaggeration. *Desperate* delvers came to the Wailing Reach occasionally. The tombs of Frostgrave's long-dead nobility might be stacked with the wealth of ages, but cracking a barrow was a high-stakes gamble. A wight's touch was not to be taken lightly. 'There are plenty of stories.'

'*I'm sure there are.*' Azzanar's voice lost its reluctance, taking on the aspect of a tutor disappointed in a promising student. '*And who tells those stories?*'

Yelen frowned. 'Azra, for one. And Markos. Real people. Not dusty myths or jumpy demons.' She tried not to think of the tales that ended with the teller's companions turned mottled blue by the chill grasp of a vengeful wight.

'*You're missing the point.*'

'And what's that? I'm getting bored of your games.'

'*The stories you've heard? They're all told by folk who came here and lived to speak of it. What tales would the dead recount, if you could but hear them?*'

'That's just scare-mongering, and you know it!'

'*Really, poppet?*' Azzanar's voice grew angry and... desperate? '*And what do I have to gain?*'

Yelen considered. 'Maybe you want me to run off in a blind panic, abandon Mirika so you have me all to yourself.' The words rang hollow even as she spoke them.

'*Fine. You caught me.*' Derision dribbled from every silent word. '*How's it going?*' Azzanar pressed on before Yelen could reply. '*Let's try something different. What marks the bounds of a ghost-fence?*'

'The stones.' Yelen frowned. 'They're sanctified. Pure. That's why the wisps don't cross them.'

'*Mortals.*' The sneer bled into laughter. '*These barrows aren't prisons, they're fortresses, buried by the passing aeons, and enchanted to prevent intrusion by rival spirits. The ghost-fences keep things out, not in.*'

'I've never heard of such a thing.'

'*Which of course means it's not true. Look behind you.*'

After a brief hesitation, Yelen did as instructed. Snow-covered hillocks stretched away towards the grey skies of the ridgeline, the dancing wisp-clouds swirling not around the statues on the crests, but along the trail of footsteps and freshly churned snow. They were following. At a distance – the ebb and billow of the swarms almost furtive – but they were definitely following.

'Mirika?' Her sister was gone, out of sight around the next bend. Eyes still on the wisp-clouds, Yelen picked up her pace.

'*Don't worry about them. Fragments of soul stuff, the remnants of cremated servants.*' Derision bloomed through Azzanar's tone. '*They're drawn to the time-spoor. To your sister.*'

'What?'

'*You think the undead have any hunger for flesh and blood? What use are they? No. Eternity is the coin in which they trade. Your beloved sister is steeped in it.*'

Yelen licked dry lips, head jerking back and forth as she tried to watch the path ahead and behind at the same time. 'Mirika? Where the hells are you?' Her shout bounced along the barrow-slopes, unanswered. 'How can I stop them?'

'*They're not even aware that they're aware. They certainly can't harm you.'* Azzanar paused. *'Their masters and mistresses? They're another matter. The hierarchy of the undead is as rigid as it is simple. The servants keep watch, and the masters prepare. I'd imagine they'll be waking up any time now.'*

The ground shook beneath Yelen's feet. A dull rumble echoed from around the shoulder of the next barrow. 'Mirika!'

Receiving no answer, she broke into a run.

* * *

The snowscape groaned, the force of the quake rattling Mirika's teeth in their sockets. Then she was falling, end over end, into the darkness.

The reliquary's haversack slipped from her grasp. Colour blazed behind her eyes as her head hit stone. Pain rushed in behind. A river of pebbles and fragmented ice spattered around her, heralds to a yawning, creaking groan. Mirika didn't see the boulder fall. She heard only the rumbling *crack* as it struck the floor somewhere beyond her outstretched legs.

Shaking her head to clear it, Mirika peered out into the gloom. Bright light revealed a jagged hole a dozen feet above, a thick layer of permafrosted soil visible above a cracked archway. The gap was easily twice as wide as the funeral path they'd followed down from the ridgeline. Just her luck to have been standing atop it all when it had finally chosen to give way.

Her pulse, racing from the shock of the fall, began to slow. The path had collapsed into the barrow below. Not ideal, but it could be worse. At least, if she got out before the occupant realised she was there. Fortunately, from what she could see of the chamber, it was a passageway, rather than one of the crypts. At least, she hoped so. There was too much darkness to her front.

Planting her hands against the chill stone, Mirika tried to rise. Her right foot wouldn't move. There was no pain, merely pressure. She recalled the spill of rubble that had accompanied her fall, and pursed her lips, pulse picking up. She'd feel it if something was broken, wouldn't she? What if she were numb with shock?

Instinctively, Mirika reached out for the light of times past. It fought her, dredged up from an era so distant, she couldn't guess at how far it had travelled to reach the present. Obsidian walls glinted all around her, the inlaid runework picked out in gold and scarlet. Alcoves lined the passageway, each home to a serpent statue with golden scales and multifaceted gemstone eyes.

As for her foot, it was trapped beneath a mass of stone and ice. The reliquary, thrown loose of its haversack by the fall, lay nearby. A deep crack split its once-marred flank, a gentle golden light spilling out from within.

Mirika swore under her breath. Master Torik had sworn the Szarnos reliquary was vital to curing Yelen's condition. If it had been damaged…

Turning her attention to her trapped leg, Mirika grasped the underside of the largest slab, and heaved. It didn't move an inch. Nor even a fraction of one.

'Fine,' she muttered. 'If that's how you want to play it. Dust it is.'

Gathering her concentration, she reached out into the timeflow, and turned her attention to the stone's dolorous tempo.

As she did so, something touched her mind. At least, that's the only way Mirika could describe it. All at once, she felt a presence, ancient and withered, pressing in on her thoughts. Numbness crept across her mind. Not cold exactly, for cold was simply the flipside of the same coin as heat. This was a creeping, insidious senselessness, trickling through her soul like a cursed amalgam of every thought of loss and sorrow. And it was hungry. Mirika didn't know how she knew that, but the certainty was as sudden as it was unshakeable.

Down the passageway, lost to sight beyond an arched junction, something moved. A clatter of bone upon stone. A breathy hiss that carried no language Mirika recognized.

'It's your imagination, that's all.'

Then the hiss came again, and she knew it wasn't.

Trying to ignore her pounding heartbeat, she returned her attention to the slab. The pressure grew stronger as she reached into the timeflow, thin fingers raking across her thoughts. Shivering, Mirika released her grip on the slab's tempo. At once, the pressure abated. Her magic, she realised. The wight was responding to her magic.

Hurriedly, she let go of the light of times past. Darkness rushed in. The presence retreated from her mind, leaving only a memory that chilled her to the marrow.

'Yelen?' Mirika called softly. 'Are you out there?'

She realised her mistake at once. Whether Yelen heard or not, the wight might. Or the wights.

'It didn't hear you,' she muttered. 'It didn't. Azra said they don't sense the mortal world like we do.'

Unfortunately, Azra said a lot of things, and not all of them were true.

As if in confirmation, the clattering, clacking sound

came again from the now pitch-black passage ahead.

Too late now. Abandoning all subtlety, Mirika called again, this time at the top of her lungs. 'Yelen!'

No reply came.

The darkness at the end of the passageway took on a greenish hue. The breathy hiss came again, more insistent. It arrived in Mirika's mind before reaching her ears, the soft, feathery caress of the sound like spiders on her skin.

Where the hells was Yelen?

Mirika grabbed the slab again. In the instant she touched the timeflow, the presence returned, hungrier than before. It took every scrap of self-control she had remaining to break contact, to choke the magic back down. Part of her wanted to stay, transfixed like a fly in a web. Heart in her throat, Mirika ripped her hands away.

'Yelen!'

The darkness in the cross-tunnel was no longer complete, but lit with a hazy green glow, like torchlight, save for the colour.

'Yelen!'

Mirika hammered at the slab with her free heel. On the third strike, it shifted in a spill of rubble. But not enough to free her ankle.

Flickering, mist-like tendrils crept across the junction floor. The hiss came again, fibrous and insistent. Mirika slammed her heel into the slab again and again. She begged. She swore. She pleaded.

She might as well have saved her breath for all the good it did.

'Yelen!'

A dark shape appeared, silhouetted against the sky. 'I'm here. What happened?'

What did she *think* had happened? 'My leg's trapped! I can't move!'

'Don't go anywhere.'

Mirika bit back her response at the ill-timed humour. 'Hurry up! Something's coming!'

Yelen jerked back from the edge. 'What? What's coming?'

'Just hurry!'

The mist at the cross-tunnel thickened, billowing like smoke from a damp timber fire.

The tail of a rope struck the rubble nearby. A thin hiss of gloves rushing against cord followed, and Yelen's boots crunched down. 'The other end's tied to a statue,' she gasped. 'It should hold.' Her eyes widened as she took in the mist-filled cross-tunnel. 'Hells…'

'Help me!' Mirika seized the edge of the slab. Yelen's gloved hands joined hers. 'On three. One. Two… Three!'

The sisters heaved as one. The slab shifted. Not enough to free Mirika's trapped leg, but enough to give her hope. 'Again! One. Two… Three!'

At last, the slab slid clear, crunching down the rubble spill. Mirika scrambled to her feet and flexed her ankle. Sore, but not sprained – and not broken, thank gods. 'Go on! Get out of here!'

Yelen hesitated.

Mirika shoved her towards the rope. 'I'll be right behind you.'

With a sharp, worried nod, Yelen locked her hands around the frayed cord and began to climb.

Turning her back, Mirika glanced desperately around. In the confusion, she'd somehow lost track of the reliquary. Had she buried it in her desperation to get free? A creaking hiss drew her gaze back to the cross-tunnel, now awash in green mist, a dark shape visible at its core. Master Torik had insisted there was something about Frostgrave's undead spirits more terrible than the largest troll or the most ferocious snow leopard. She'd not believed him. She wished she had.

'Right behind me, you said!' Yelen's shout echoed down from somewhere above.

Her reverie broken, Mirika twisted away. 'I'm coming. I just…'

There it was, lying beside the slab. Skidding across the rubble, Mirika snatched up the reliquary, only for it to break apart in her hands. She couldn't explain it. One moment, it was as solid as… Well, as solid as a rock beneath her hands. Then the onyx shell was broken fragments slipping through her fingers, and a golden orb, no larger than an eyeball, sat cradled in her palm.

'Oh, spit.'

Mirika stood motionless for a long moment, the orb's warmth seeping into her skin. Then she stuffed the orb into her haversack, and flung herself at the rope.

CHAPTER FIVE

The snow returned as night fell, this time as gentle showers more suited to fairytale than the dour reality of the frozen city. Mirika watched it from her hidey-hole within the collapsed house, an alchemist's fire burning at her back.

Yelen lay snoring away beside it. She'd not so much fallen asleep as passed out, exhausted by the pell-mell run across the valley, the tomb wisps dancing along air currents in their wake. The narrow escape in the barrow had spurred them on to unsuspected vigour, neither one wanting to chance that the wight would follow them into the open daylight. Azra had sworn that it wouldn't – that the sunlight burned them like fire. Then again, Mirika clove to the truth of Azra's stories far less readily than she had a day ago. But fear-lent endurance carried a body only so far – Yelen had been dead on her feet by the time they'd reached the relative safety of the streets. They'd chosen a suitable shelter, set a fire in the doorway to discourage wild animals, and called it a night.

Wolf-voices howled on the night air. Mirika glanced at the fire. It blazed merrily, the bright tongues more than enough to keep the pack at bay. They'd find easier prey elsewhere. There was no shortage of unprepared fools in Frostgrave. And she'd nearly been one, hadn't she? But for Yelen…

Mirika stared out through a jagged crack that served her as a window. The barrows of the Lower Reach shone in the intermittent moonlight, their wisps dancing and bobbing as they had in the day. She saw other shapes, too. Dark and shapeless at that distance, they flowed across the rises like oil across water, creeping tendrils of the greenish light writhing like snakes around them. Mirika had chosen their campsite specifically so she'd see any pursuit. So far, nothing had even stirred in their direction. Nothing had even approached the iron-fenced perimeter, much less entered the streets. Still, she was determined not to touch the timeflow until well away from the Lower Reach. The memory of the wight's caress had only faded so far. Not that it mattered. The moon broke through often enough to give warning. She'd keep watch the whole night if necessary…

Not that Mirika felt tired. As ever after a close call, her mind and body were abuzz. She could scarcely credit the distance they'd travelled that day, nor the exertions she'd made. She felt as though she could have walked the rest of the way to Rekamark, Yelen slung over her shoulders. It didn't matter. She'd sleep tomorrow, in her bed at the *Guttered Candle*. The anticipation of the almost-clean sheets and the warmth of the hearthfire did much to banish the horrors of the day.

Hoisting up her haversack, Mirika drew forth the golden orb. She still harboured a certain anxiety at the destruction of its onyx case, but those worries had faded with the daylight. By its very nature, a reliquary was a container, not necessarily a thing of value in itself. It seemed only logical that Master Torik had sought this very orb.

She turned it over and over in her hands, the metal warm against her bare skin. She saw nothing engraved on its surface, and her prying fingers found no join, no seam. It was featureless. Perfect. That alone made the orb valuable – that it was fashioned of gold made it doubly so. But there had to be more to it than that. Master Torik had little eye for art, and appreciated only items of a practical nature. And he'd all but said that the reliquary was vital to curing Yelen. How had he put it? *The last piece of the puzzle.* Ergo, the orb had some practical use.

But it was beautiful, all the same. Mirika held the orb tight, staring at it as if examination alone would yield up its secrets. She longed to bathe it in the light of times past, to see what secrets the timeflow concealed. But for the memory of the barrow, and the wights cavorting less than a mile to the south, she'd have done so. Instead, she clutched it tight and listened to Yelen's soft snores until the feeble rays of dawn crested the eastern hills.

* * *

'Pick up the pace, sleepy-head! The day's a-wasting!'

'I'm coming! Don't be so blasted cheerful about it.'

Yelen sighed, for the fifth time that afternoon wondering where Mirika found her energy. She herself had slept ten hours, give or take. Still the grey clouds of slumber clouded her mind. Still her limbs felt heavy as lead. Nonetheless, she did as instructed, all the while planning vengeful rebuttal once the sleepless night caught up with her older sister. Gratitude only went so far, after all.

At least there'd been no nightmares – presumably thanks to her deliberate abstinence from chanin tea. But maybe not. Maybe Azzanar was simply lying low. Maybe the part of her subconscious that worried over the demon's growing confidence had been as tired as the rest of her. Maybe anything. That, Yelen reflected, was the problem when you were losing your grip on your mind – all analysis became suspect.

And what of Azzanar? She'd been almost... helpful. And demanded no cost – the first thing Yelen had done once she'd clambered to the surface had been to check the tattoo. It hadn't changed. Perhaps the demon realised her days were numbered, and sought to win by slyness what she was about to lose by force? The thought provoked a savage smile. If that were the case, she was in for bitter disappointment.

Little by little, the lifeless cobbled streets fell away beneath Yelen's feet. The dark waters of the Nereta River appeared on the horizon, the fluttering banners and bright murals of Rekamark close behind, a splash of riotous colour amongst the cold drabness of the ruined city. Each blazon marked out territory, be it belonging to a delver-gang, a trader's post, a dispossessed noble's home-in-exile, or one of the other settlers who called Frostgrave their home. A hundred paths led to the frozen city – most terminated there – and there was a story behind every one. Not that Yelen cared.

Twice in the next hour, their path crossed that of outbound travellers. The first was an elderly enchanter, bent almost double beneath the weight of his pack and the tool-belt strung across his shoulder. A pair of colossal timber constructs stomped behind him, their barrel-chested frames festooned ropes that in turn supported sacks of all shapes and sizes. The enchanter nodded politely, but gave the sisters a wide berth, cleaving close to the opposite side of the street before vanishing into an alleyway.

Yelen shook her head in amusement. Caution was good, but either one of the old man's towering escorts could have flattened both sisters into paste. Perhaps he hadn't wanted the bother of rinsing the blood off their fists afterwards. The constructs *had* been beautiful pieces, delicate, swirling patterns tracing across their featureless faces. Probably they were as close to family as the old man had any longer.

The second group was a different matter. Numbering a dozen or so in all, they marched up the rubble-strewn cobbles with the faultless step of soldiers on parade. Their shields bore blazons of spread-winged eagles, and their armour gleamed. At the very rear strode a heavyset woman in a sigilist's layered robes and white mantilla. The paymaster, no doubt.

'Toy soldiers, out for an afternoon's stroll,' muttered Mirika.

Yelen stifled a giggle. 'Or fresh off the boat.' There *was* something childlike, almost innocent, in the earnestness on the approaching faces. Newcomers to Frostgrave, for a certainty. She wondered what they'd thought of Rekamark.

The sigilist halted abruptly. 'Can I help you?'

Mirika opened her mouth to reply. She closed it again as Yelen dug an elbow into her ribs, not trusting her reply.

'Where are you headed?' Yelen asked.

The woman frowned – judging by the lines on her face, it was something she did a great deal of – then clearly decided the information would do no harm. 'The Lower Reach.'

Azzanar laughed softly, breaking what had been a long and welcome silence. '*You'll not see them again. What a shame.*'

Yelen sighed. She didn't like the woman's attitude, but to say nothing made her as bad as the voice in her head. 'Watch your step. The barrows aren't as quiet as they seem.'

The sigilist looked the sisters up and down, perhaps weighing the value of Yelen's advice against her ragged appearance. Then she sniffed, leaving Yelen in no doubt as to the conclusion reached. 'We've nothing to fear.'

That parting shot delivered, the sigilist lengthened her stride to rejoin her column.

'*You can't help some folk, poppet.*'

Gods help her, but Yelen agreed.

Mirika shook her head in silent mirth. 'You know who that was, don't you?'

'Should I?' asked Yelen.

'That, little sister, was Mariast Levonne.'

'What? *The* Mariast Levonne?'

'The Green Widow herself. No trap untriggered, no ambush unembraced. She's a treasure, is our Mariast. I wonder if those soldier boys know how many expeditions she's led to their doom?'

Yelen shrugged. The credulousness of others was hardly her problem. 'No supply of idiots around here.'

'True. Lives a charmed life, that one.'

'Must be her winning personality.' Yelen held her deadpan expression a heartbeat longer, then collapsed into a fit of giggles. 'Come on. I want a drink, a bath and a fireside. I hear them calling.'

* * *

Rekamark's gate, like the rest of the settlement, was an ungainly affair, braced at either end by ageless stone, and held together with rusted nails and rotting rope. The wooden leaves didn't look as if they had been built, but had instead crawled into the gap between the two buildings and died. Mirika knew Yelen viewed it as a parallel to humanity's tenuous foothold within Frostgrave. She preferred to treat it as a symbol of the ingenuity and determination that made life at all possible.

A thin, dark-haired figure detached itself from the shadows between the gate's leaves as they approached. He ambled over, the confidence of his stride matched by that on his craggy, moustachioed face. 'If it isn't the Semova sisters. Profitable saunter, was it?'

Mirika knew that face well. Even if she hadn't, the spider-brand on his cheek spoke volumes. 'That's our business, Kardish.'

He offered a disinterested shrug. 'This side of the gate, sure. If you want through, it's another matter.'

Yelen exchanged a glance with Mirika and rolled her eyes. 'Oh, come on. Flintine's trying this again?'

'*Mister* Flintine expects those who benefit from his protection to show their appreciation.'

'And did Mariast's bunch of hopefuls show their appreciation?' asked Mirika.

Kardish sniffed. 'There's no charge for outbounds.'

He didn't fancy his odds at extorting from a small army, more like, Mirika decided. Maybe Flintine really was trying to tithe returning expeditions. Theoretically, the old man's gang *did* contribute the most swords when a fractious giant or a troll pack took it upon themselves to have a crack at Rekamark's ramshackle wall. Not that it really mattered. Rekamark may have looked like a town – if viewed charitably – but it was really just a huddle for survival. No one owed anyone else nothing. More likely, Kardish was throwing his master's name around in search of easy profit. In theory, it'd be a lucrative business. For every delver who resisted, there'd be another who palmed over a cut in the hope of avoiding a brawl.

'What do you think?' she asked Yelen.

'Doesn't matter what she thinks,' interrupted Kardish. 'It's how things are.'

Yelen ignored him. 'I think we've nothing to pay.'

That was true. Orb aside, they'd nothing to show for their foray beyond the Broken Strand. Unless Kardish was prepared to accept payment in stale supplies, which seemed doubtful.

'Like my sister told you,' said Mirika, 'we can't pay.'

His eyes narrowed. 'Then you won't mind opening up your packs for me to take a look, will you?'

He stepped closer, hand going to the hilt of his sword. Two hulking figures emerged from the shadows behind the gates, clad in patchwork leathers akin to those worn by Kardish. Mirika recognized both faces. Two of Flintine's musclemen, too stupid to stumble about Frostgrave proper, and instead tasked with 'collecting' debts inside Rekamark. Not that their presence proved Flintine's approval of Kardish's actions – they could equally well have been promised a cut of his takings. Not that it would have mattered, Mirika decided, setting her hand on her own sword. They weren't getting the orb.

Kardish checked his advance, allowing the bruisers to reach his side. 'Let's not do anything foolish. I'm sure I can think of some way you can pay your debt…'

Thin fingers closed around Mirika's arm. Yelen turned her back on Kardish and fixed Mirika with a steady stare.

'Maybe we should head back out. We've still a few days' supplies – enough for a delve on the edge of the Grey District. That'll meet the fee.'

'No.' Mirika hissed the word, annoyed that Yelen could even consider backing down. 'We let him do this once, we'll never cross that threshold for free.'

Irritation flickered across Yelen's face. 'I'm tired and cold. You're tired and cold. You really want to make a fight of this? There could be a dozen more of them behind the wall.'

'I'm not giving them anything.'

Yelen's brow tightened. 'You see? This is precisely what I meant. You don't listen to me.'

'Did you forget about the Gilded Rose? We go back out there, and there's a good chance we'll bump into them. I'd rather tussle with Kardish than cross that knight of Cavril's.'

Yelen stared unflinchingly back. She didn't understand. Or she didn't care.

Mirika's patience, already strained by Kardish's ultimatum, snapped. 'Then again, I guess it won't be your problem for much longer, will it? Not with you leaving.'

Yelen's lip twitched, her gaze turning cold as the snows. 'Do what you want.'

She stepped aside, leaving Mirika with the not entirely pleasant sensation of having won an argument by unfair means.

Mirika shook the feeling away, kindling her growing anger with the guilty warmth in her stomach. If Kardish wanted a fight, she'd give him one he'd not forget. 'Get out of our way.'

Kardish snapped his fingers, and the two heavies started forward.

Mirika smiled. After the horrors of the barrow, she needed this. She reached into the timeflow. Her tempo glinted like gold beneath her fingers.

* * *

Yelen didn't really see her sister move. Then again, she seldom did when Mirika cut loose.

The heavy to Kardish's left crumpled, mewling in pain. He struck the roadway, hands clasped across his groin, expression adrift on a sea of private pain. Mirika stared triumphantly down at him. Then she darted away, her sword scraping free of its scabbard and meeting the second thug's blade with a dull chime.

'*That looks entertaining,*' said Azzanar. '*Are you sure you wouldn't like a go, poppet? You only have to say the word. It'll be fun.*'

'I'll pass, thanks.' Yelen ground out her reply through gritted teeth. She couldn't believe what her sister was doing. She didn't doubt Mirika would win the skirmish. It was more the aftermath that concerned her. Kardish wasn't the type to forget humiliation. They'd be looking over their shoulders the whole time they were in Rekamark.

Mirika struck her opponent's blade aside and rammed her boot up between his legs. By luck or judgement he twisted aside, the kick going wild. His meaty fist grabbed at Mirika's flailing braids. It closed on thin air. Kardish, always alert to the risks of personal intervention, backed towards the gate.

'*She's very impressive.*'

'I'm sure she'd agree with you.' Belatedly, Yelen remembered that Azzanar was the enemy. 'Shut up.'

'Pardon me, I'm sure.'

The demon laughed all the way back to the recesses of Yelen's mind.

Mirika ducked under a lazy sword swipe, and rammed her heel into the heavy's instep. He howled with pain and reeled away, then slumped as the pommel of Mirika's sword cracked into his head. Yelen winced in sympathy. Though not fatal, it was a vicious blow by her sister's standards.

Kardish thrust two fingers into his mouth and a shrill whistle rang out. Six more heavies loomed in the gateway, an assortment of cudgels and blades held ready.

Yelen started forward, worry mingling with her anger. 'Mirika!'

She grasped the meaning at once, turning towards the gateway. 'I guess this was old man Flintine's idea, after all.'

Yelen hurried to Mirika's side. 'Let this go. We'll come back.'

'No! I'm just starting to enjoy it.'

She grabbed her sister's arm. 'You can't take all of them.'

Mirika's eyes blazed. 'Watch me.'

Yelen flinched, taken aback by the wildness in her sister's eyes. For a heartbeat, Mirika looked like a stranger, the shadows falling across her face all wrong. Then the moment passed, the unfamiliar giving way to the all-too recognizable smirk of a Mirika certain in her course.

'Perhaps she needs help?'

'I've heard enough out of you, too,' snapped Yelen. A horrible thought struck. 'Are you doing this to her?'

Mirika's expression tightened. 'What?'

Azzanar laughed. *'Oh, poppet. That's simply too priceless for words.'*

Mirika pulled free. Distracted by the voice in her head,

Yelen didn't notice until her sister pounced on Kardish. Seizing him by the throat, she slammed him against the gate. Timber scraped on timber, the impact drawing the binding ropes taut.

'Unhand me!' Kardish's choked demand barely reached Yelen's ears.

Mirika leaned closer, her grin one of pure revelry. 'Are you sure? There's a toll.'

'Get her off me!' His second shout was aimed at the heavies marshalling in the gateway.

As one, they started forward.

'Stay back! I mean it!' shouted Mirika.

The heavies ignored her.

Yelen ran towards the gate. As she ran, Mirika's first victim rose up on his hands and knees and grabbed at her ankle. She staggered, righted herself, and stamped down on the fellow's other hand. He bellowed with pain, and pressure on her ankle vanished.

'*I don't rate your odds, poppet. Let me help. After all, I'll be gone soon, won't I. What harm can it do?*

The heavies closed in on Mirika. What harm indeed? thought Yelen. It didn't matter that her sister had provoked this fight. She had to help. 'Alright, but I'm warning…'

Kardish screamed.

It began as a low wail but swiftly grew in pitch and volume. Her acceptance of Azzanar's offer interrupted by the outburst, Yelen stared at him. Nothing had changed. He still stood with his back to the gate, Mirika's hand locked about his throat. But as Yelen watched, a change crept over Kardish. His black hair turned grey, then white. His flesh sagged, the skin stretching oddly across his face and hands as years rippled faster over him than all others nearby.

'Stay back!' shouted Mirika. 'Stay back! Or I'll keep going until he's dust!'

Confounded, the heavies checked their advance.

Yelen felt sick. She'd always known Mirika could do such a thing if she wanted – it was no different to what Azzanar had helped her do in Szarnos' tomb, not really – but she'd never witnessed it before. It felt wrong. Obscene. 'Mirika! What have you done?'

Her sister rounded on her. 'We're going inside. They won't stop us. Not now.'

As predicted, the heavies parted. Yelen wasn't sure if that was because they were afraid for their boss's life, or their own. She couldn't blame them.

Mirika shifted her grip on Kardish and half-shoved, half-carried him into the gap. The now-old man took tottering, uneven steps, upright only by dint of the hand on his collar. The thought of him resisting, or even reaching for his sword, was laughable.

'Yelen!'

'I'm here.' Yelen followed her sister through the gate, expecting a heavy hand to fall on her at any moment. It never did, and soon they were through into Rekamark proper.

A thin crowd had gathered beyond the gate, drawn by the commotion. They clustered around the ice-crusted fountain, but made no move to interfere. You didn't, not in Rekamark. Yelen glanced back over her shoulder. The heavies hadn't followed. 'We're clear,' she muttered. 'Set him back to normal.'

They reached the frozen fountain. Still Mirika didn't reply. Yelen thumped her none too gently in the ribs. 'Now. Do it!'

At last, Mirika turned. Her eyes, so lately full of excitement and anger, were wide and haunted. 'I'm trying.' Her voice shook. 'It's not working.'

She set Kardish down beside the fountain. He slumped against the rim, eyes staring unblinking across towards the gate. His skin was pale, almost papery in texture. A cold fist tightened around Yelen's stomach.

'He's dead.' Mirika's face was nearly as pale as Kardish's. Her voice was little more than a whisper. 'What have I done?'

Yelen swallowed to ease the sudden pressure in her throat. Her anger scattered like smoke on the wind. It didn't matter what Mirika had done, or why. Not now. She glanced back towards the gate. The nearest of Kardish's heavies bore the creeping frown of a man stumbling towards action. She tugged at her sister's arm. 'Come on. Before this gets worse.'

Mirika didn't respond, but stared numbly down at Kardish. At her victim. 'I can fix this. I can. I *will*.' She took the corpse's hand in hers and closed her eyes.

Yelen squatted at her side. 'Rika. He's gone. You're not a corpse-twitcher. And if we don't get going, his friends will send us to join him.'

Mirika nodded mutely and rose to her feet. With a sigh of relief that did nothing to ease the tension in her gut, Yelen took her sister's hand and led her away into the crowd.

They'd just reached the alleyway when the first scream rang out.

* * *

Mirika walked in a haze, her footsteps guided through Rekamark's tumbledown alleys and reclaimed streets by Yelen's insistent tugs. External sights and sounds blurred together with the red rush in her head, and the frantic pounding of her heart. How could she have done it? She didn't kill. That had been her rule from the first, and now… And now…

But hadn't Kardish deserved it? He'd been ready to injure, perhaps even kill. And not just her, but Yelen too. How many beatings lay at Kardish's feet? How many deaths? What did it matter?

Of course it mattered. What had she been thinking? Mirika couldn't remember. There was only the rush as she'd manipulated Kardish's tempo; the texture of the rushing timeflow deeper, richer than it had ever been. A symphony of harmonies, where before there had only been a thin, thready melody dancing from moment to moment. She'd heard more. Distant, tantalizing notes whose memory faded the more she grasped for them. They'd cut off as Kardish began screaming.

Mirika's breathing shallowed, but her pulse kept racing. Not with guilt, but excitement. Fulfilment. She had the sense of standing on a precipice, staring out across a golden future. Yes, Kardish's death had been a mistake, but she'd learn from it.

'Mirika?'

Yelen's urgent enquiry dragged Mirika from her introspections. The world snapped into focus, the last elusive notes vanishing from her senses. The sheer, austere embankment wall stretched away below. Ahead, the turgid ice flows of the Nereta River eddied about the timber skeletons of the abandoned wrecks choking its northern waters. Poor Yelen. As worried about her as ever. Didn't she see that it was alright?

Mirika met the watery blue stare head on. 'I'm fine. You don't have to worry.'

'I don't have to worry?!' Yelen flung out a hand. The extended finger trembled. 'You killed him.'

The spark of guilt returned. Mirika smothered it. Strange how that became easier the more you did it. 'People die around here all the time.' Not only that, she didn't say, but they often died under unusual circumstances. It was expected, with so many wizards having made their homes in Rekamark, and with dozens more constantly passing through.

Yelen's cheeks flushed. 'It's not normally my sister who kills them!'

She didn't understand, Mirika realised. She wouldn't. Not until she calmed down. Then they could talk about it properly. Once there was time to explain. 'Were we followed?'

'What do you think? You know what this place is like. They're probably fighting over the contents of his pockets as we speak.'

It was an unkind assessment, Mirika thought, but not cruelly so. The line between delver and scavenger was a fine one. Not all employers were as generous with their coin as Master Torik or Cavril Magnis.

'Please tell me you've got the orb,' she said.

'Me?' Yelen looked away, incredulous. 'Get your head together! I couldn't take it even if I wanted to, you're clutching it so tightly!'

For the first time, Mirika realised she had her hands clutched across her chest, the smooth, hard shape of the orb pressing against her breastbone and wrists. Slowly, reluctantly, she eased her grip, and let the haversack dangle by its straps. 'I forgot.'

Yelen shook her head. 'Flintine won't, not once he hears. What are we going to do?'

Mirika winced, but Yelen was right. 'I'll sort it.'

'How? How will you sort it?'

It was a good question, and one to which Mirika didn't yet have the answer. 'Don't worry about it. I said I'll sort it.' She drew in a breath of the salty, riverside air. The last skeins of confusion parted. 'The important thing is to get home and let Torik work his cure. And then…' She paused, reluctance at the coming lie softened by necessity. 'Then we'll talk about how we get back to Karamasz.'

Yelen's expression softened. 'Okay. Have it your way. But we're not done talking about this.'

Mirika nodded. 'I know,' she said softly. 'I know.'

CHAPTER SIX

'How do I look?'

Yelen sank back against the wall and considered her response. Truthfully, Mirika didn't look like Mirika any longer. The red silks of the time walker's robes were just a touch too ostentatious, and clearly designed for warmer climes – not revealing as such, but figure-hugging in a way that cold weather gear could never really achieve. Then again, there was no need for furs, not with the fire crackling in the hearth of Mirika's bedchamber. Well, save for the bearskin rug beneath Mirika's naked feet.

'You look... Impressive.'

Mirika grimaced. 'Then why do you say it like that?'

'Like what?'

'Like you're trying to swallow something unpleasant.'

'Perhaps I don't see why you have to play up to him like this.'

Mirika peered into the mirror – unlike the one in Yelen's own room, this one was whole, and bounded by an ornate wooden frame – and fiddled with the golden clasp that kept her braids in their top-knot. 'It doesn't do any harm. And the happier Master Torik is, the better this will go. Besides, *I* think it looks splendid.'

Yelen sighed, as much at herself as at her sister's showiness. She knew she was hiding in their bickering. It was familiar, comfortable. Not like the conversation that forever loomed on its periphery. The one in which they discussed the man Mirika had murdered.

She stared out of the window and across the Nereta River. A pale afternoon was shaping up to be a foul evening, with crowded skies promising heavy snows.

'*I don't see why you're so upset, poppet,*' said Azzanar. '*It wasn't like he didn't have it coming. And it was accomplished with such flair.*'

'You'll forgive me if I don't find your approval comforting,' murmured Yelen.

A honeyed chuckle dripped across her thoughts. '*I can't help it if you're jealous.*'

'Jealous?' But that was part of the problem, wasn't it? If she set aside Kardish's death – and Yelen was just practical enough to accept it wasn't any great tragedy in the grand scheme – part of the emotional tumult beneath *was* driven by envy. Mirika's talent soared to new heights, while Yelen was on the cusp of giving up the only thing that made her special. She couldn't even time walk without her sister. She'd be normal. Ordinary. No better than any of the other hirelings that crowded Rekamark's tangled squalor, or died in droves amongst Frostgrave's untamed districts. The truth was, without Mirika, Yelen Semova wasn't anything special. She hated that, she realised. Almost as much as she hated the demon bonded to her soul.

Yelen bunched her fists. No. She couldn't think that way. It was exactly what Azzanar wanted. How did the saying go? Better a queen of the damned than a servant of the chaste? Something like that. It was a fool's consolation.

Azzanar's promises were fleeting, and the price was an eternity as an empty voice in her own body. She'd be glad to be rid of the demon.

But why then was she starting to feel Azzanar was more a kindred spirit than her own sister? At least the demon was always honest. Increasingly, Yelen had the impression that Mirika was anything but. Had she meant what she said about going back to Karamasz? Yelen wanted to believe, so much so that she didn't dare press, in case the offer vanished like morning mist beneath sunshine. If it was true, it was true. If it wasn't, then that would only lead to an argument, and she wasn't sure she could face that. After all, she hadn't exactly been forthcoming herself, had she? Otherwise she'd have told her sister just how often Azzanar tiptoed through her waking thoughts…

'Jealous?' Mirika turned from the mirror, brow knotting.

Yelen shook her head. 'It doesn't matter, just make sure you rein in the dramatics for Torik's guests.'

And guests there were. She'd peeked in through the arras before creeping up the back stairs. Torik had been in full flow, his rambling diatribe punctuated with the gesticulations of his right hand, and the crystal decanter bobbing dangerously back and forth in his left as he refilled his guests' goblets. An elementalist and his apprentice, judging by their singed robes and lurid facial tattoos. From their stoic expressions, they were every bit as bored as Torik was in his element. But few turned down an invitation to the *Guttered Candle*. There was always a nugget of wisdom buried in the spoil heap of Endri Torik's gruff digressions.

'You're not coming down?' Mirika plucked the orb from its resting place on the battered dresser and rolled it lightly from hand to hand. 'He'll be too pleased to finally get his hands on this to say anything else.'

Yelen stared down at her wrist. At the sliver of pale skin amongst the black. 'No. It's not worth the risk. We've no idea how long this cure of his might take. I can't afford to upset him until afterwards.' *And then I might just set this whole place ablaze,* she didn't say. 'I'll get some sleep, only… Mind if I stay in your room? It's not as draughty as mine.'

Mirika smiled. 'I suppose not. At least until I get back.'

* * *

The soft murmur of unfamiliar voices cut off as Mirika pushed the arras aside.

Master Torik beckoned her forward. 'Ah, my dear. Join us.'

She obeyed, crossing the tapestry-hung hall. As ever, the banquet table was set for a score of guests, even though Master Torik was alone save for two others. Reaching the table's head, she offered him a shallow bow – more of a nod, really. 'Master. I hope I'm not interrupting?'

'Of course not.' The power of Master Torik's voice always surprised Mirika. By all appearances, the man was more billowing robe than flesh and bone, his hunched posture suggesting he'd snap if a gust of wind caught him unawares. But the voice had the solidity of the roots of the mountains. 'Kasrin and Molok were on the point of leaving anyway, though I'm glad to have the chance to introduce you. Gentlemen, this is my apprentice, Mirika Semova. My apprentice, and my heir. She is my voice. Please, always treat her with the respect owed to me.'

Mirika stifled a scowl at the latter title. Not that she

wasn't flattered, but Master Torik clearly saw a longer association than she did herself. Especially now she knew the truth about how he treated Yelen.

The taller of the two elementalists – the most senior, if the firebrand tattoos and the better cut of his robes were anything to go by – inclined his head ever so slightly. His bushy eyebrows and thicket of a beard couldn't begin to hide his disappointed scowl. He certainly didn't look like a man who'd been on the point of leaving. 'Miss Semova. A pleasure.'

She returned the gesture, noting that the apprentice said nothing. Possibly he was forbidden to say anything at all. Some wizards took a dim view of their pupils speaking out of turn.

The creases on Master Torik's face shifted into a satisfied smile – or to the closest he ever came to such largesse. 'Let me show you out.'

After a heartbeat's reluctance, both visitors rose – the apprentice with a sidelong glance at his unfinished goblet of brandy. No wonder. When Master Torik had purchased the *Guttered Candle*, he'd inherited the finest cellar in Rekamark, for whatever that was worth.

Skeletal hands tight around the head of his walking stick, Master Torik eased himself upright, free hand clutching at the table for support.

Mirika started forward. 'Stay, master. I'll do it.'

Master Torik shook his head, his sparse white hairs brushing at his collar in time with the jerky movement. 'Nonsense. You've had a long journey, and on a difficult road, I'll wager.' He gave a small dry chuckle. 'Sit. Eat. Let these old bones make themselves useful while they may.'

Mirika took a reluctant seat as her master shuffled his

way towards the tavern's entrance hall, guests in tow. There was still enough untouched meat and bread on the table to leave half a dozen souls with stuffed bellies, but she found the horror – and the excitement – of the afternoon had left her with no stomach for it. The servants would have their fill when they arrived in the morning. Instead, she plucked an empty goblet from the table, and decanted a generous measure of the brandy. The sharp, sour flavour rushed over her tongue, the warmth of it welcome even before the roaring banquet hall fire.

By and by, Master Torik returned, his gait as shuffled and awkward as ever. Mirika made to stand, but subsided at his insistent wave.

'Sit. Sit. I meant it.' He sank back into his chair, letting the walking stick fall to rest alongside. 'Kasrin's such a bore, but one must observe the formalities. Used to be a student of mine, not so very long ago.'

'He was your apprentice?'

'Nothing so formal.' The wrinkles shifted into an unreadable pattern. 'A shared interest, that was all. Long before I came to Felstad. How such a stolid fellow came to bind his fate to the wildness of flame, I'll never understand. Perhaps he bores it into submission, eh?'

The words dissolved into laughter, and the laughter into a frenzy of coughs.

Mirika leaned forward, concerned. Whatever the old man had done to her sister, he'd shown her nothing but kindness. Besides, Yelen still needed him. 'Master?'

He waved her off, and dabbed his mouth with a handkerchief. 'It's nothing. I feel the chill more than I used to, that's all.' He leaned closer, his rheumy eyes gleaming, and his words taking on fresh urgency. 'Do you have it?'

Mirika withdrew the orb and set it on the table, the golden skin appearing almost molten in the firelight.

Master Torik extended a hand towards the orb. He checked the motion, his hand still an inch or two away, and pressed his fingers to his lips. 'Oh, my dear.' He laughed softly. 'I knew you'd not fail me.'

'I regret that the reliquary broke,' Mirika said, the brief memory of the barrow enough to provoke a shiver even in the swelter of the banquet hall. 'We had a few problems along the way.'

A touch of winter crept into Master Torik's tone. 'Your sister's influence, no doubt.'

'It was no one's fault,' she replied. 'The Gilded Rose…'

'Magnis? Hmphh. Must he keep dogging my steps?' Rising anger collapsed into a paroxysm of coughing. 'No matter. It's here now. As is your sister, I assume?'

'She is.' That was the closest Master Torik ever came to asking after Yelen's health, Mirika realised. How had she not noticed before? 'But… There was a complication at the gate.'

Master Torik's gaze didn't leave the orb. He stared at it as if transfixed, as if he sought to imprint its every detail on his mind. 'Yes. Flintine's people have been making trouble for a few days now. I presume you handled it?'

Mirika winced, but there was no going back now. 'Kardish died. I… killed him. I didn't mean to. I lost control.'

He broke away from the orb, pale eyes meeting hers. 'No, you didn't. You took control. Of your talent. As I've taught you to.' A thin, wheezy chuckle escaped his cracked lips. 'I always knew I'd chosen wisely.'

Mirika frowned, not at his assertion, but because the

expected reprimand had failed to arrive. 'But I've put you in danger. When Flintine finds out what happened…'

Master Torik waved the words away. 'Flintine will understand. It's the game he plays. I'll sprinkle crowns into his thuggish palms, and he'll quieten. A small enough price to pay for this.'

His gaze returned to the orb, the accompanying expression almost hungry.

'And you'll use it to cure my sister?' Mirika leaned forward, searching his face for any trace of a lie. 'Her tattoo's all but black. The demon almost has her.'

He snorted. 'Inevitable. Her will is weak, her soul prone to temptation. She doesn't have the strength to resist, and it's wearing her away, piece by piece.'

With a supreme effort, Mirika kept her disgust hidden. How had she never seen this side of Master Torik before? She swore to herself that it didn't matter. Once he'd kept his side of the bargain, he'd never see either of them again. Whatever it took. 'But it can save her?'

'Oh, it'll change everything.' He nodded gently to himself. 'Bring it through to the sanctum, and we'll get started.'

* * *

Suppressing a pang of reluctance, Mirika set the orb in the waters of the marble font. She wasn't sure where Master Torik had found that particular piece, just as she was ignorant as to the origins of the angel-winged lectern, and most of the items on the sanctum's shelves. They were the fruits of a long and productive life, collected over a span beyond the reach of most mortals. Only time walkers like her master could hope to live for so long, thinning his tempo, stretching it out for decades, even centuries. Master Torik had often hinted that she could do the same, but the idea had never truly appealed. *Why outlive your loved ones?* she'd asked. He'd laughed, and told her she'd change her mind once the first grey hairs showed.

'I'll fetch Yelen,' she said, heading for the stairs.

Master Torik shook his head. 'Let her sleep. You and I have work to do.'

He tottered past the chest-high grotesque, sat ingloriously askew across the cellar's rear corner – Boriz, Yelen had named it, though Mirika wasn't sure why – and began gathering items from the nearest shelf. A stoppered vial. A chunk of tiger-striped gemstone.

'What do you need from me?' Mirika asked.

'Hmmm? Keep your hand on the orb. Let me know at once if it starts to grow hot.'

His words triggered a stray memory. It had once before, hadn't it? Back at the Broken Strand, when she'd dropped the reliquary. There was still so much she didn't know. 'What is this thing? I travelled a long way to get it, and I still don't know.'

Master Torik knelt down, the walking stick trembling as it took his full weight. 'It's a reservoir, of sorts. A wellspring of power. Szarnos mastered the secrets of life as fully as he conquered Felstad in days of old. He thought if he trapped enough of his magic, his priests could weave him a new life from the threads. At least, that's what the legend says.' He plucked a piece of chalk from behind his ear, and started scratching a series of flowing runes across the floorboards. 'Too bad for him that his priests all died when the new king came to power. Felstad's rulers elevated paranoia to an art form.'

He fell silent, and returned his attention to his scrawlings. The floor was already covered in similar shapes and sigils, Mirika noted. The work of hours, if not days. Master Torik had been preparing for this for some time. 'And the power within will allow you to banish the demon?'

'It can do more than that. Like I said, it'll change everything.'

No wonder Cavril had wanted it so badly, thought Mirika. Perhaps she should reconsider staying on as Torik's apprentice...

One last, fussy scribble, and Master Torik staggered to his feet and braced both hands against the lectern. 'That should do it. It'll soon be over.'

The chalk sigils blazed a piercing blue. Mirika gasped for breath as a suffocating wave of... *something* crashed over her. The breath wouldn't come. The compacted dirt of the cellar fell away, yet remained impossibly firm beneath her feet at the same time. She couldn't speak. She couldn't move. Even her thoughts, ordinarily so swift, flowed like treacle.

Through dimming eyes, she saw Master Torik regarding her, his eyes alight with interest, not concern. 'Don't fight it, my dear. Talented as you are, this is beyond you.'

What had he done? What had she let him do? Mirika reached for the timeflow, but it edged further beyond her grasp with each attempt. The orb blazed beneath her hand, the heat of it the only sensation she could any longer feel. The confines of the cellar seemed so distant, the angles of reality shifting under the strain of Torik's spell.

Mirika's thoughts faded beneath a black and choking cloud. She struggled, but the cloud fed on her resistance, replacing her perceptions with its own. She felt thoughts pressing against hers, cold and hard. Torik's. They were Torik's. Fragments of memory fell away, subsumed into the dark mass, replaced by vistas she'd never seen, sensations she'd never felt.

In a single, horrifying moment of clarity, she knew what he intended. What Torik had meant when he'd spoken of her as his heir. *Always treat her with the respect owed to me. I have chosen well.* The words took on new meaning. She could have wept. Perhaps she did, but could no longer feel the tears.

No! She'd wouldn't allow it! She reached again for the timeflow. Again it deserted her. There had to be a way. Torik wouldn't win. He couldn't! And Yelen. It had all been a lie. He'd never had any intention of helping her. None.

Desperate anger became the spark to ingenuity. The orb. A wellspring, he'd said. A reservoir of power, waiting to be used. Torik wasn't the only one who could tap into it.

Mirika focused on the warmth beneath her hand and bent her will upon it, as she'd been taught. The black cloud came on, swallowing every scintilla of her being. Karamasz became only a name. Yelen a fading face, and a sense of regret. She screamed for help, though she no longer understood her own words, and forgot the sound of them before the echoes faded. A heartbeat on, and the woman knew only the warmth beneath her hand – that, and a fading determination.

And then, in the moment before all that was left of Mirika Semova blinked into nothing, the orb blazed brighter. A cold thunderclap broke across her thoughts, and a third presence joined the battle.

CHAPTER SEVEN

Yelen staggered, lost in the blizzard. Bracing her feet against the wind, she cupped a hand across her brow and searched for a light, a patch of shadow – anything that could have been her sister. She saw nothing. Just white swirling upon white. She couldn't even remember where she'd seen Mirika last.

'Mirika!' She howled the words, matching the wind fury for fury. 'Mirika!'

'*She's not there.*' A dark figure drew up at Yelen's side, her body little more than a patch of shadow lit by gleaming crimson eyes. '*And you need to wake up.*'

Yelen shoved the figure aside, and stumbled on a pace. 'I need to find my sister.'

'*She's not here,*' the figure snapped. Her hair writhed like serpents. '*This is a dream. Wake up, poppet! Before you get us both killed!*'

Shadowy hands closed around Yelen's wrists. Claws pierced her skin. She gasped in pain, but there was no blood, only molten ice. She stared numbly at the wounds, shivering uncontrollably. 'You're hurting me!'

'*I haven't started yet!*'

Yelen yelped as a dark hand struck her across the cheek. Her head snapped back. The snows spun.

* * *

Yelen awoke. Her vision swam. The sour stench of sulphur crowded the back of her throat. But more than anything she felt cold. Heavy and cold.

She jerked upright to a chorus of creaking and cracking. Chill wet lumps slithered from her arms and back. She shrieked and rolled off Mirika's bed, shoulder cracking painfully against the floor.

At last, her vision cleared. The hearth was dark, the ashes covered with a fine drifting of snow. The dresser and most of the bed were encased in ice. And the wall – the wall with the window that gazed out across the Nereta – was gone. There was only a jagged hole in the timbers, and the raging snowstorm beyond.

Yelen gazed around, dumbstruck. She barely heard the whip-crack of the shattering beam, or the roof issue its last, creaking wail. She stared vacantly up as the mass of wood and ice plunged towards her, knowing that she'd never get clear in time, even if her frozen, throbbing legs could be coaxed to motion.

The Clock of Ages' dolorous chime split the air. The plunging beam slowed to a crawl. A familiar energy roared through Yelen's limbs, burning away the cold, the indecision.

She scrambled aside in the same moment the timeflow reasserted itself. The beam crashed down, most of the roof riding hard upon its heels. The bed shattered to matchsticks beneath the impact. Then it vanished through the floor as the mass crashed onwards, taking half the room and Mirika's beloved bearskin rug with it.

Yelen retched, the taste of sulphur suddenly too much to bear.

'*Don't be ungrateful, poppet. That one was free. Move, before you need another.*'

Yelen ripped back her sleeve. The clock was indeed unchanged, still showing half an hour to Thirteen. She had the sense she'd missed something important in Azzanar's words, but her disoriented mind couldn't begin to guess at its nature.

'*Move, poppet, move! Before the rest comes down!*'

Yelen stared dumbstruck at the hole in the floor. The hole that had taken her boots and most of her travelling clothes. Pausing only to grab her travelling coat from the hook by the door, she flung herself towards the stairs. As she did so, a grinding crash spoke to a fate narrowly avoided.

* * *

Yelen staggered down stairs clogged with debris and drifted snow. Already, her fingers had fallen numb – without boots, gloves or layers of mufflers and furs, the travelling coat alone was of little protection against the merciless cold of a Frostgrave night. But there was no going back. It was forwards or nothing.

Wind gusted up the ruined stairwell. She clutched at the banister for support. What the hells was going on? The *Guttered Candle* had been no fortress, but it had been sturdy enough. Had Flintine taken Kardish's death so badly he'd hired a wizard to assault Torik's home, regardless of the consequences of such an act? Where was Torik? More importantly, where was Mirika? Finding no comfort in her questions, Yelen stumbled on.

Snow swirled across the banquet hall, the flakes driven by a biting wind that rushed in from where the west wall had once stood. The floor and tables – at least, those Yelen could see through the storm – were thick with drifted snow. Here and there, a lantern cast its oily amber glow, but for the most part the room lay in the grasp of darkness. One shadow seemed stronger than the others; taller, more fully formed.

'Mirika?'

The wind howled, snatching Yelen's words into the wild night. She stepped forward. Her foot skidded on a patch of ice, slipping from the bottom stair. She grabbed for the banister, staying upright through good fortune as much as any other factor.

A cold hand closed around her ankle.

Yelen glanced down, ramming a fist into her mouth to suppress a shriek. Torik lay at her feet, his face a mask of blood, and the lower half of his body hidden beneath splintered timber and a broken blanket of snow. His eyes stared vacantly up at her, unfocused, unseeing.

Gripping the banister tight, Yelen tried to tear her foot away. Tried, and failed. His grip was like steel. She threw a hurried glance across the room. The shadow had gone, swallowed up by the darkness leading to the entrance hall. Had it been Mirika? Or whoever – whatever – was responsible? And if it wasn't Mirika, then where was she?

Lent strength by desperation, she strained against Torik's grip a second time, and this time tore free. His lips moved, but the storm swallowed the thready words.

Free at last, Yelen stepped away. But something held her back. She hated Torik, as she was sure he despised her, but if he was still alive...

With a last reluctant glance across the snow-laden banquet hall, Yelen crouched beside the old man's body.

His chest shuddered as it rose and fell. Blood bubbled on his lips. No. Not dead. But neither was he long for this world.

'What happened?' she asked.

'Do not follow her.' Torik's whisper was barely audible. 'I have been a fool. And I have paid.' His agitated eyes darted back and forth.

'Where is she?' Yelen demanded. 'What have you done with my sister?'

'She was to be mine, body and soul. Young eyes to see out new decades. Strong limbs to replace these aged bones…'

Torik's words grew muted in Yelen's thoughts. Bile crowded her throat. The words were different, but the sentiment was one she'd heard over and over in her thoughts and dreams. She grabbed at the hem of her coat so tight that her hands hurt. She didn't trust what she'd have done with them otherwise.

'You never had any intention of helping me, did you? You were studying me, learning how the possession works.' Just saying the words made her want to vomit. 'How to…' She swallowed, unable to finish the thought. 'She trusted you! And you…'

The cold of the storm was nothing now, a dim memory scoured away by the blistering heat of anger. Not for herself. She'd never trusted Torik. But Mirika?

'*Kill him, poppet. You'll feel better.*'

Yelen placed a hand against Torik's neck. She felt the cold, papery texture of his withered skin. She could. It'd be so easy. And well-earned. 'Where is she? Tell me, old man!'

'Szarnos has her now.' Torik broke off, his body convulsing in a great, wracking cough. 'All the while, I thought she was mine, but his claim was the stronger.'

So the shadow had been Mirika? She'd done all this. And Szarnos? Gods. The orb.

'*Kill him, and let's go. I didn't wake you up just so we could freeze to death.*'

Yelen ignored the demon's encouraging whispers. 'Where is she?' she said again. 'Where's my sister?'

He gave a gurgling laugh. 'Gone. She's Szarnos now. Or soon will be. You are joined in damnation.'

Yelen stared at him, anger and fresh horror mingling hot and cold in her veins. Azzanar was right. She *would* feel better for killing him. She tightened her grip around his throat. Felt a surge of satisfaction at the sudden panic in the old man's restless eyes. But no. She'd lectured Mirika about Kardish's death. Killing was no more the answer now, than then. In any case, Torik was already half gone from exposure. He'd go the rest of the way before the hour was out.

She wouldn't kill him, but she didn't have to help him either.

'The frozen hells are calling you, vulture. I hope Belsanos' demons tear you to shreds.'

Rising, Yelen made her way towards the entrance hall. She didn't look back.

* * *

Yelen had thought she couldn't get any colder. Frostgrave proved her wrong within moments of crossing the *Guttered Candle*'s ruined threshold. But still she staggered on, following the line of fresh footprints along the embankment's crest, arms clasped tight across her chest as the insidious cold burrowed ever deeper into her numb flesh.

'This is a fool's errand, poppet.'

'Then I'm a fool!' Yelen spat the reply through chattering teeth.

'You heard him. She's gone.'

'And Torik has never lied to me, has he?'

Azzanar snorted. *'You're going to get us both killed.'*

'I. Don't. Care. I'm not giving up on Mirika. I saw she wasn't herself after she killed Kardish. I should have pushed, but I didn't. I knew Torik couldn't be trusted, but I didn't push. Don't you see? This is my fault. I'd rather die than give up on her now.'

And that was the problem, wasn't it? She'd always given up. Not just during their return expedition from the Tomb of Szarnos, but their whole lives together. Much as Yelen had chafed at the idea that her big sister always knew best, she'd always backed down. Never challenged. Never really fought her corner. She'd yearned for responsibility over her own life, but she'd never sought to claim it. If she had, maybe things would have played out differently. Now it was too late.

No. Never too late. Not while she had breath left in her body.

Yelen stumbled on along the embankment, her numbed mind trying to make sense of Mirika's destination. The bulk of Rekamark lay to their backs. There was nothing this way apart from the unbroken river. No bridges, just jagged rocks, beached hulks and empty sky.

Her bare foot brushed against stone. Her numbed ankle buckled and she fell face-first in the snow. She swore, loudly and foully as the cold exacerbated the pain.

'*Poppet, please.*' For the first time Yelen could recall, Azzanar genuinely sounded concerned. Not for her, of course. At least, not directly. '*You're so cold it's prickling at my skin.*'

Yelen clawed at a rusted railing, hauling hand over hand until she was on her feet. She'd let the demon push her around, too. Well, no more. 'I'm not stopping. Get used to it, and help me.'

Hunger pierced the sheen of concern. '*Are you asking for my assistance?*'

She rubbed her palms together, each feeling like a cold lump of meat to the other. 'No. I'm giving you a choice. You can either help me, or die with me.'

Azzanar's tone darkened. '*I won't be threatened.*'

'Really,' replied Yelen, taking another unsteady pace through the snow. 'Then why did you wake me up? Why help me survive the tavern's collapse?' She felt oddly giddy. Despite everything, she wanted to laugh. 'All this time, and I never realised. You're as trapped with me as I am with you.'

Azzanar hissed softly, but said nothing.

'So what's it to be?' asked Yelen. 'Live together, or die in the snow?'

The cold abated, not much, but enough that she felt the familiar rush of contact with the timeflow. The swirling snows slowed, the once hectic dance of flakes now the laziness of autumn leaves upon the breeze. Yelen drew back her sleeve. The clock hadn't changed. She loosed a shuddering, triumphant laugh, and tried to forget the mottled reds and blues of her skin. 'Thank you.'

'*It's a reprieve, nothing more,*' said Azzanar archly. '*The cold's still killing you. It's just doing so more slowly. You're still running out of time.*'

Yelen stilled a reply behind chattering teeth. The demon was right. She had to hurry.

She plunged on through the snows, always following the trail of footprints. Mirika's stride – at least, Yelen hoped it was Mirika's, for she didn't know what she'd do otherwise – didn't waver, but continued straight as a die along the embankment. The paces were evenly spaced, as if she was out for an afternoon stroll in the balmiest of weathers. Yelen knew her own were ragged, uneven, just as she knew the fact that her feet no longer hurt was nothing to celebrate.

Moments bled into minutes, the passage metered by each leaden footstep, but made uncertain by her contact with the timeflow. It was the longest she'd ever spent submerged in the ticking of the Clock – her past excursions had been brief, necessarily so once the truth about Azzanar had emerged. The world took on an unfamiliar beauty, the ruddy sheen of its altered state a match for the pounding behind her eyes.

At last, Yelen glimpsed the sight she'd longed and dreaded to see. Mirika stood at the Nereta's edge, the time walker's robe a bloody slash against the snow. Bare feet on the edge of the embankment's rampart, she stared out across the waters, face hidden by coils of unbraided hair whipping back and forth in the wind.

'Mirika!' Yelen screamed the word, her voice raw from worry and from the cold. 'It's me!'

Her sister didn't turn, didn't give any sign of having heard. But even the sight of her gave Yelen fresh strength. Setting her shoulders against the wind, she forged on.

'I saw Torik! He told me what he tried to do! Let me help!'

No response.

'I know you can hear me!'

At last, Mirika turned. Her eyes were black as the abyss, her expression taut, like she sought to remember something long since forgotten. Golden light pulsed beneath her pale skin, its brilliance rising and falling with the fury of the storm. In her hands, clasped tight to her chest, was the orb.

'Be gone.'

Yelen's heart caught in her throat. The voice was her sister's, and yet not. Something else resonated between the words, like fingers scratched across a chalkboard, or a terrified, dying screech. Some distortion caused by the clash of their disparate timeflows? The cold, writhing sensation in Yelen's guts told her otherwise.

'No! I've come this far. I'm not going back without you.' She extended a shaking hand. 'Please. Don't leave me!'

Mirika's expression shifted. No longer remote and confused, but tinged with heartbreak. 'Yelen?' Her voice was her own again, free of influence. 'I'm already gone.'

Without another word, she stepped off the edge of the embankment.

'No!'

Yelen threw herself forward, hands clutching for a hand, an arm – a fistful of robe. They closed on nothing but air.

She fell to her hands and knees on the embankment's edge, already knowing her sister was lost to the Nereta's inky waters, lapping at the ice-sheeted stones, twenty feet below. Except there were no waters, just sheeted ice, its angular tendrils creeping across the river. At their head already a dozen paces away, Mirika marched across the frozen crests, arrow-straight for the distant bank.

'Mirika!'

The snows swirled again, and she was gone.

'No!' Yelen tried to scramble upright. She slipped sideways into the snow, her knee cracking against stone.

'*She's gone, poppet.*'

Yelen shook her head so violently her neck creaked. 'No. I can still follow.' Gaining her footing, she peered over the edge, gauging the distance.

'*Don't be ridiculous. You'll break both legs jumping down. And that's if you don't plunge straight through the ice.*'

'I don't care! Don't you get it? She's my sister.'

Far below, the river ice darkened, dissolving once again into the Nereta that had given it birth. At once, the storm lost its potency, the howling wind dropping almost to nothing. The clouds parted, and the long-banished moonlight flowed across the virgin snows.

'*It's done, poppet. Let her go.*'

* * *

The temperature had risen with the storm's departure, but Yelen barely felt it. She had no eyes for her surroundings, nor the prickling pain as feeling returned to her extremities. There was only the leaden ache in her chest. With every step, it threatened to drag her down. She wanted to let it, but kept walking anyway – one sullen, sluggish step after the other, trudging steadily into the heart of Rekamark.

There'd been no point returning to the *Guttered Candle*. What the freak storm hadn't levelled, the snow had buried – Yelen had seen that much from a distance. Endri Torik lay sealed beneath the ruins of his home like a latter-day king in a barrow, a treacherous corpse surrounded by the treasures he'd possessed in life. There was no shelter to be had there, nor warmth, and even lost in her fug of grief and hopelessness, Yelen would need both if she wasn't to join the old man in the frozen hells. So instead she let her feet guide her on for what seemed an eternity, what few wits she had remaining locked in a vicious cycle of grief.

The tick of the Clock of Ages slipped from her mind as she walked the empty alleys, the world losing its ruddy hue as her tempo snapped by into sync. Azzanar either no longer had the strength to sustain their place within the timeflow, or no longer cared to do so. Yelen didn't ask. The longer the demon stayed quiet, the better she liked it.

Yelen longed for sleep. Every aching muscle begged her to sit for a moment, regather her flagging strength, but she didn't dare. She knew that if she closed her eyes, even for a moment, she'd never open them again.

But where to find help? There was no shortage of doors upon which to knock – at least, now she'd left the riverfront behind – but the knack lay in knocking on the right one. Choose poorly, and Yelen knew she'd be floating in the Nereta's waters come morning, throat slit ear to ear.

Her thoughts coalesced like molten treacle, urged on by the percussive crunch of feet in the snow. Azra had a squat somewhere over on the north side. He'd help her, assuming he were sober – which he probably wasn't. Who did that leave? Selsa the apothecary? His shop was considered neutral territory by most of Rekamark's squabbling gangs. Yelen nodded to herself. Yes. Selsa. She'd have to pay, but he'd accept a debt of service – his apprentices kept signing on with delver-gangs, too eager for adventure.

'What have we here?'

Yelen's heart sank as she turned to face the speaker. He sat on the rubble beneath a lopsided archway, itself the sole survivor of a long ago collapse. She didn't know the face, but she did recognize the angular spider-brand on his cheek. Another of Flintine's gang. Ordinarily, that would be bad enough. Today? After what had happened to Kardish…?

'I want no trouble.' Yelen almost didn't recognize her own voice, it was so raw and cracked.

Scratching his bald pate, the man rose to his feet. 'You hear that, Tan? She doesn't want trouble.'

A burly woman emerged from a shadowed corner across the street. 'Should've thoughta that before dusting Mister Flintine's favourite lieutenant this afternoon, shouldn't she?'

'Loved him like a son, so I hear.' The man paused. 'Or at least enough to offer a thousand crowns for whoever brings him one of the killers in consolation. Guess we're lucky to have found you first.'

Yelen knew she should be scared, but she'd no emotion left to spare for a couple of street-stalkers. She'd a good idea what Flintine had in store – a slit throat was the least of it – but could she really say anything to change her fate? 'I didn't kill him.'

The man slid two curved swords from their shoulder-sheaths, and spun them lazily about his wrists. 'Then you can tell Mister Flintine. He likes a good story, doesn't he, Tan?'

The woman rolled her eyes. 'On occasion. Stop playing with her, Garth. It's been a long, cold night.' She shifted her gaze to Yelen and unlooped a small, vicious cudgel from her belt. 'You *are* coming quietly, aren't you?'

Yelen sighed. She could scream her lungs out. Someone would hear, but no one would come. You were on your own in Rekamark after dark. What did it matter anyway? What did any of it matter anymore? Better a queen of the damned than a servant of the chaste. 'Help me,' she said simply.

Garth halted a pace away, beetle-brow knotting in confusion. 'What did you say?'

'I said, "Help." As in, "You win, I'm asking for your help."'

'You what?'

Tan squinted as she drew nearer. 'She's touched, that's what she is.'

Yelen gritted her teeth. 'It's very simple. I need your help. Now are you going to give it, or not?'

'*Oh, I'm sorry. Were you talking to me?*'

At last, thought Yelen. 'Of course I'm talking to you.'

'Mister Flintine's not going to have much fun with this one.' Tan shook her head. 'Reckon she's had one knock too many.'

Azzanar snorted. '*Sorry. Not in the mood. Maybe you'll remember that next time you threaten me.*'

Yelen couldn't believe what she was hearing. 'They're going to kill me! Us!'

'*Not yet they're not. The beating comes first, but I won't feel a thing. Consider this a lesson in manners.*'

Something inside Yelen snapped. She didn't care anymore. Let them do their worst. Let Azzanar think she'd won. What did it matter? Mirika was gone. 'Fine. Get it over with.'

'Thanks,' said Garth, sarcasm dripping from the word.

'Step away, Garth! She's coming with us!'

The newcomer's voice came from back along Yelen's

stumbling path. She recognized the sharp, waylander's edge to the woman's syllables, but her cold-addled brain couldn't place why. It wasn't until the woman drew close enough for the moonlight to reveal the shock of blonde hair and the worn eyepatch that realization dawned.

'Back off Serene!' Tan stepped to block her path. 'We saw her first.'

'That's nice. She's still coming with us.'

In response, Tan closed a meaty hand around Yelen's upper arm. 'Us? Way I remember it, you lost an eye the last time you went two against one in a fight.'

Serene laughed – a thin, dry sound wholly lacking in humour. She crossed her hands behind her back, the movement setting the tails of her greatcoat dancing. 'Yeah, but Danno and Rosk lost more than that, didn't they? Who would you rather be? Me, or them?'

Yelen watched dully as the two women squared off. Now the Gilded Rose wanted her too? She decided she'd rather take her chances with Magnis than Flintine. Not that it was her choice. Not while she was in Tan's vice-like grip.

Garth stepped past her, and tapped Serene in the chest with a sword point. 'Last chance, Serene.'

The one-eyed woman nodded. 'I was thinking the same thing.' She raised her voice. 'Kas?'

The whistle and thud came as one – a fraction before Garth's bellow of pain and the soft thud of his sword striking the ground. He spun away, the black shaft of an arrow protruding from his shoulder. Yelen winced as Tan tightened her grip, but glimpsed the archer, all the same. He sat perched in an otherwise-empty first floor window above and behind Serene, another arrow already nocked to his bow.

Serene shrugged, hands still clasped behind her back. 'Thanks, Kas,' she called. 'Put the next one in his eye, would you?'

'Left or right?' Kas' languid drawl echoed up the street. Southern as the blazing sun, it was hopelessly out of place in the frozen night.

The archer who'd been with Magnis' gang in the tomb?

Serene leaned in close to Tan. So close, that Yelen was treated to a lungful of her greatcoat's musty stench. 'What do you reckon, Tan? Left…' She ducked a little to the side, ostensibly giving her partner a clearer shot. '… or right?' Serene ducked to the other side. 'Or maybe we'll just call this a friendly misunderstanding and go our separate ways?'

'Misunderstanding?' Garth staggered upright, face mottled with pain and fury. 'I'll show you a misunderstanding.'

An arrow struck the ground a foot or so immediately to his front, sending a small spray of snow into the air.

'Sorry!' called Kas. 'Slipped. Next one goes in his eye.'

Tan, evidently quicker on the uptake than her partner, let go of Yelen's arm and intercepted Garth while a crippled arm was the worst of his woes.

'Leave it, Garth. They can have her. Not like we don't know where she'll be, is it?'

Tan spat at Serene's feet, retrieved Garth's fallen sword and looped an arm beneath his shoulders. Yelen watched them shuffle away through the snow, fighting a fresh onset of weariness.

'Thanks.'

Serene grinned. 'Don't thank me yet, love. Cavril wants a word, and you've a lot of explaining to do.'

CHAPTER EIGHT

'Mirika!'

Yelen stat bolt upright, bedsheets spilling away. Wakefulness came slowly. The memory of cold clung to her bones, accompanied by the dull, muffled pain of ill-treated joints. The half-remembered nightmare faded, her pulse dwindling alongside.

The soft lantern-light and the crackle of the smoky fire drove out the last traces of cold, but raised new questions. This wasn't her room. It wasn't even the *Guttered Candle*. The stone walls hung with tapestries, the flagstones were lost beneath piled furs. The wooden door sat square within its frame, something those in the *Guttered Candle* had never managed. The chamber possessed a luxuriousness that Torik had never embraced, much less permitted Yelen to partake of. A faint aroma hung on the air, sour and herbal. The cause of her grogginess? Had she been drugged? Was that why her memories ended with Serene's hand on her arm?

Memory separated from the cocoon of dream. Yelen bunched the bedclothes beneath her fists. It was all true. Mirika. Torik. The *Guttered Candle*. Flintine's thugs. She felt sick. How many times since leaving Karamasz had she wondered how her life could get any worse? Now she knew.

What time was it? There were no windows, no trace of the sky outside. An hour could have passed, or a day. Did it matter? Mirika was gone. Yes, Yelen told herself firmly. It mattered. The Gilded Rose – for presumably it was they who had her – didn't know she was awake. Assuming they stayed ignorant, she might yet slip away. But to where? Her life, such it as it had been, was gone. Return to Karamasz, perhaps? Rekamark – indeed, Frostgrave had a whole – had offered her little before. It promised nothing now. But what of Mirika?

Yelen recalled the dead look in her sister's eyes as she'd stepped off the embankment. Lost. Hopeless. Could Mirika be helped? Even saved? Yelen doubted it, and hated herself for doing so. But the situation was too similar to her own to hold out much hope. If Torik had spoken true, the long-dead Szarnos now wore Mirika's body much as Azzanar sought to occupy Yelen's own flesh. Was there any coming back from that? Yelen didn't know – she'd bent all of her thoughts to ensuring that her own transformation never came about, and never once thought to enquire if it could be reversed. And even if it could, what hope did she have of finding Mirika? The frozen city was vast, below ground as well as above. She could search a lifetime, and still not find her. And that was assuming she didn't end up a feast for wolves, trolls or others of Frostgrave's hungry denizens. Were their situations reversed, Yelen wouldn't have wanted Mirika to take that risk.

Remorse crowded the back of Yelen's throat. She choked back a sob. It helped nothing to think that way. Not while she was the 'guest' of the Gilded Rose. One step at a time. Get out. Get clear. Then decide what to do.

Given strength by renewed purpose, Yelen swung her feet out of the bed. Belatedly, she realised that the nightgown wasn't hers any more than was the room. She stared down at her feet. They were pinkish and tender, though that wasn't any great surprise after her barefoot trek through the storm. Indeed, she'd been fortunate not to have lost extremities – but there they were, all ten toes a match for her ten fingers.

The lack of clothes, though, that presented a problem. Assuming she could get outside, a young woman in a nightgown tended to attract entirely the wrong manner of attention. And that was if Yelen had any intention of roaming Rekamark without boots and coat, which she didn't. That left precisely one option, though she hated to take it.

'Are you there?' she asked softly.

There was no reply. Not even a breathy chuckle.

'Come on, I know you're listening.'

Still nothing. Yelen shook her head in disgust. All this time, she'd longed for a little privacy and now, when she needed Azzanar's help, the demon was nowhere to be found.

Perhaps she was free of the creature? No. She couldn't be that fortunate. Besides, there was still the slight taste of sulphur at the back of her mouth. Azzanar was still there. And if she wasn't talking, it probably meant she was sulking, if demons did such things.

Yelen took a deep breath. 'I'm sorry.'

'*Well, that was gracious.*' Sarcasm dripped from the demon's every word.

'You're a demon. I don't think you get to quibble about grace, or lack thereof. You should be glad I'm prepared to talk to you at all.'

'*Oh I am, poppet. I can't wait for you to bark some more orders at me. Shut up! Help! Fetch! Beg! It fulfils me in ways*

I can't even begin to describe.' Azzanar paused, her sense coiling and shifting as she embraced her theme. *'It's like the good old days, before the war. Before the fall. Know your place. Keep to your instructions. I didn't choose any of this, you know. I can't help what I am.'* Her tone, ordinarily so strident, grew pitiful. *'I have feelings too…'*

Yelen winced. 'I'm… Wait. No. I refuse to feel sorry for you. You're not the victim here. I am.'

'Oh well,' Azzanar's sense performed the mental equivalent of a shrug. *'It was worth a try, don't you think?'*

She sounded disgustingly pleased with herself. From morose to malice in an eye blink. Not that it changed anything, much as Yelen wished it were otherwise.

'I need…'

The door opened, admitting Serene, a heavy bundle tight in her hands. The greatcoat was gone, granting full view of the tattered open-necked shirt and threadbare grey trews. Her appearance, unkempt as ever, was a poor match for the room's opulence, but she moved with that familiar confidence, giving the impression that her every action, her every gesture, had been planned out in advance. Yelen envied her that. Especially now.

'Don't you knock?' Yelen asked.

'Not me, love.' The eyebrow above Serene's good eye twitched. 'Gutter scum, me. No finer feelings to mention. Not that you've room to speak, carrying on in your nightclothes.'

Yelen glanced down at her gown. Though filthy from the night's wanderings, it covered her rather more completely than Serene's garb covered her. Likely the other woman was simply the sort who loved to get in the last word. There was a lot of that going around. 'Well, if someone hadn't taken my coat, and I still owned any other clothes, I'd be wearing them, wouldn't I?'

Serene drifted closer, still with that same, easy confidence. 'No doubt you would.' She set the bundle down on the end of the bed. 'You'll find everything you need there. Boots might be a bit large, but you'll manage.'

Yelen frowned, surprised. On the one hand, now they knew she was awake, her chances of escaping the Gilded Rose were greatly reduced. On the other, there was little to gain from antagonizing Serene. 'Thank you. And… for saving me last night.'

Serene's shoulders twitched in an infinitesimal shrug. 'Just don't get any ideas about wandering off. You've some explaining to do, and Cavril wants to hear every word. If I have to bring you back, I won't be so gentle next time.'

Yelen's frown deepened into a scowl, all thoughts of treading carefully abandoned at the other woman's sneering tone. 'So you'll skip drugging me and go straight to striking me senseless next time?'

'Drugging you?'

'I can still smell it.'

Serene sniffed ostentatiously. 'That? That's the balm Marcan mixed to stop your fingers and toes blackening and dropping off. No laughing matter, stumbling around in the snows with bare feet.'

'Then why can't I remember anything?'

'I don't know, love. Maybe because you passed out halfway back, and I carried you the rest of the way? Feeling proper glad about that right now, I can tell you.'

Yelen felt her cheeks warm with embarrassment, but couldn't bring herself to apologize. 'I guess I'll get dressed.'

'You do that.' Serene stared stonily at her for a moment

longer, then left the room, setting the door firmly to behind her.

Ignoring the creaks and groans of abused muscles, Yelen heaved upright and examined the pile of clothing. Boots, gloves, shirt, a fur-lined jerkin and trews. Her own coat, the rents and tears earned during the recent expedition's excitement stitched closed. 'Well?'

'*Well what?*'

'Do you believe her?'

Azzanar laughed. '*So suddenly my opinion matters? Are you sure she didn't knock you on the head?*'

'That's the question, isn't it?' murmured Yelen.

Why *did* she want Azzanar's opinion? Did she really want it at all? Like it or not, the demon was the only ally she had right now. Well, not ally, exactly. But they had the unarguable common ground of survival. Mostly, Yelen suspected she simply wanted a familiar voice to talk to. She supposed she was fortunate that way. Lots of folk had a destructive influence, goading them to foolishness. At least she knew hers was real, and not a splinter of her own psyche.

'Still,' she went on, 'Magnis would hardly go to the trouble of providing clothes if he were wanting to kill me.' Not that the Gilded Rose *did* kill, at least as far as common tattle went. But with things the way they were, Yelen wasn't ready to make assumptions. At least, not optimistic ones.

'*That's the thing about clothes, though, isn't it?*'

'What is?'

'*Easy to take off the dead. They're a good gift with which to earn your trust, in that they cost nothing, if reclaimed.*'

'They cured my frostbite.'

'*So they say.*'

'So I *shouldn't* trust them?'

'*I'd say that you shouldn't trust anyone. It didn't do your sister much good, did it?*'

Mirika. Overcome with grief, Yelen sank against the bed. 'Is there any chance that she's alive?'

Azzanar shifted, flowing back and forth across her mind as she considered. '*Her body, yes. Though I can't speak for her mind. You can't help her.*'

'But you would say that, wouldn't you?' After all, if there was hope for Mirika shaking off Szarnos' influence, where did that leave Azzanar?

'*Yes, I suppose I would. So I suppose we're back to "don't trust anyone". Including me.*'

Based on the accompanying chuckle, Azzanar saw nothing appalling in that state of affairs. Not so Yelen. Again, she fell back on her own advice. One step at a time. That much hadn't changed. It could do no harm to speak with Magnis, but it wouldn't hurt to have a backup plan.

She took a deep breath. 'I may need your help.'

'*Anything for you, poppet. You know that. Provided you ask nicely.*'

* * *

After dressing, Yelen left the bedchamber to find Serene waiting outside.

'Took you long enough.'

Yelen offered a smile she didn't really feel. 'Wanted to look my best for my captor, didn't I?'

Serene shook her head and started off down the corridor. 'This way.'

Yelen followed her escort past a series of closed doors

and out into a vast, vaulted chamber – the transept of a temple, unless she missed her mark. High, arched windows confirmed the assessment, though if they'd once contained any stained glass, it was now long since gone. More tapestries covered the openings, with timber planking visible behind. A fire-pit burned in the centre of the nave. Most of the smoke was drawn up through a hole in the roof by the howling wind beyond, but enough escaped to carry the warm, heavy scents of woodsmoke and cooked meat to Yelen's nostrils. A cluster of battered armchairs was arranged around the flames. As Yelen approached, a familiar figure rose from one, his gilded robes glinting in the firelight.

'Yelen. So you're awake.' For once, Cavril Magnis' easy charm was in abeyance. His eyes were watchful, cool. 'I trust the clothes are a suitable fit? We're not exactly spoilt for choice, hereabouts.'

'They're fine,' Yelen replied, drawing closer. In point of fact, everything was a touch on the large side, but she was hardly in a position to choose. 'Thank you.'

Magnis waved her words aside. 'It's nothing, truly. What do you think of my humble home?'

'Very impressive.'

And it was, in a 'faded glory' sort of way. Yelen had occasionally visited the strongholds of other delver-gangs – normally to trade, occasionally to act as lookout while her sister 'liberated' an item or two from their stashes. Most were broken-down ruins, choked with rubble and with walls braced against collapse – their statuary and relics long since traded away for food or fresh hirelings. By contrast, the Gilded Rose's base seemed largely intact. Even the altar remained whole, its gold leaf and sapphire gemstones still in situ. It seemed that Cavril Magnis, much like the late, unlamented Endri Torik, liked to live in some comfort.

Yelen wondered what else they might have in common.

'You worship Solastra?' she asked.

Magnis' brow furrowed. 'What? Oh, the altar. I've a nodding respect, nothing more. I find that life is simpler if the gods don't notice you, so why desecrate holy ground and invite their attention? Won't you please sit? We have much to discuss.'

Azzanar stirred. '*You're being watched.*'

Yelen threw a slow glance around the room as she approached the fire-pit. The demon was right – she was indeed being watched. Marcan and Darrick sat at a table halfway between the fire-pit and the impressive, double-leaved doors at the nave's far end. Ostensibly, they were playing cards, but they had entirely too few eyes on the game, and too many on Yelen for her to feel comfortable. Kas sat up in the rafters, his legs dangling out over the nave, and a stone jug held loosely in his hand. Only Kain was absent, and Yelen was grateful for that. From what Mirika had told her, the knight was the most dangerous of the lot. If things went poorly, better Kain was elsewhere.

Reaching the fire-pit, Yelen lowered herself into one of the chairs. 'Is this where you tell me why I'm here?'

Magnis shook his head. 'Later.' He gestured to a small table set at the side of Yelen's chair. Bread. Fire-blackened meat. Even a pair of withered apples – Yelen couldn't remember the last time she'd seen anything approaching fresh fruit. 'Eat something first. You must be starving.'

The words set Yelen's stomach rumbling in sympathy. She reached out for a hunk of bread.

'*How do you know it isn't poisoned?*' asked Azzanar.

Yelen checked her hand an inch from the plate. Why would it be? If Magnis had wanted her dead or stupefied, he could easily have had Serene see to it while she slept. Caution was one thing. Paranoia was something else. Besides, she *was* starving.

'It's quite safe,' said Magnis. Apparently her worries had not gone unremarked. He plucked a charred leg from the plate and took a hefty bite, talking all the while. 'A touch overcooked, but better that than the other way around.' He swallowed, and offered the rest of the leg to Yelen. 'I seem to still be standing.'

Reaching a decision, Yelen snared the bread from the plate. 'I don't mean to be impolite. I'm not at my best.'

'Quite understandable,' he replied, stripping another mouthful of flesh from the bones. 'And I imagine that your charming passenger's not making life any easier for you.'

'*What did he just call me?*'

Yelen froze, the bread not yet at her lips. 'You know about that?'

'After your performance at the tomb, how could I not? You were *not* subtle.' The blond moustache twisted, framed by a quizzical expression. 'Whatever possessed you to make such a bargain?'

She flinched. For a heartbeat, she was back in the darkened tent, hands covered in blood and the pentagram blazing around her. 'That's my business.'

Yelen wolfed down the bread, as much to excuse her from talking as to address her ravenous hunger. What did Magnis want?

'Very well,' said Magnis. 'A curiosity only. Let's talk about my business. Where is the Orb of Szarnos?'

'*So that's the reason for his kindness,*' purred Azzanar.

'*Watch your step, poppet.*'

'Why do you think I know?'

Magnis shrugged. 'Frankly, I don't. But with the *Guttered Candle* levelled and dear old Endri levelled with it, I have few approaches to explore. I'm asking nicely, am I not?' He leaned closer. 'My associates retrieved you from an unfortunate situation, did they not? I think politeness demands that you answer.'

'*Don't tell him. If it matters that much, we can use it for leverage – a guarantee of safety.*'

Yelen held her tongue and reached for a piece of meat.

Magnis sat back in his chair, fingers drumming at the armrest. 'I understand your reluctance, but I assure you I don't care that you killed Endri.'

Yelen looked sharply up. 'I didn't kill him.' The accusation hurt more than she could have imagined. But was that because she'd left him to die, or because she'd lacked the courage to kill her tormentor – the man who'd doomed her sister?

'*Careful, poppet. He's goading you.*'

'Honestly, it's of no account,' said Magnis. 'He was an infuriating swine at the best of times, and he had fewer good times than any man I've ever met.'

'*Say nothing. Silence is your…*'

'Mirika did it,' Yelen snapped. 'Except it wasn't Mirika.'

'*Or just start blurting things out,*' hissed Azzanar, sarcastically. '*After all, what harm can* that *do?*'

'Mirika did it,' Magnis repeated flatly. 'And then she stole the orb?'

Yelen glared at him, but there was nothing to be gained by silence any longer. 'The orb took *her*. Torik tried using it to steal her body. It went wrong and something else's in there now. My sister's gone. She stepped out onto the frozen

Nereta and strode away into the night.'

The words spilled out like water from a breached dam, the one chasing the next. By the time they petered out into silence, Yelen felt her eyes dampen with long-denied tears. She drew in a long, rasping breath and stared into the fire.

'I don't know where the orb is,' she said at last. 'I wish I did, because then I'd know where to find Mirika.'

'*Oh, bravo. I hope you never get a taste for playing cards.*'

Magnis gazed at her for a long time, the muscles in his jaw tensing and relaxing but his eyes never wavering. Abruptly, he looked up and over Yelen's shoulder. 'Well?'

'Matches what I saw,' said Serene. 'The older one was proper out of it, then stepped off into the river, orb in her grasp.'

Yelen broke away from contemplation of the fire and stared accusingly at Magnis. 'Why ask, if you already knew?'

He met her gaze, the aloofness melting from his eye to be replaced with a soft empathy that made Yelen's heart ache. 'We all come to Felstad seeking gold, but honesty's a far rarer prize. I had to be sure you'd be truthful with me. I'm sorry about your sister.'

The conversation's course, so different to the one she'd expected, threw Yelen off balance. Might Magnis even help her, if it came to it? If so, a little flattery couldn't hurt. 'For what it's worth, she respected you. She was seriously considering your offer.'

His eyes brightened, accompanied by a smile that was just the wrong side of arrogance. 'Of course she was. I'm Cavril Magnis. No one can resist me.'

Yelen bowed her head – mostly to hide the slow smile creeping over her face.

'*I can't believe you're falling for this,*' hissed Azzanar. '*He's stringing this out. He's waiting for something.'*

Yelen understood the demon's suspicions. Tattle had it that Magnis' skills at misdirection went deeper than the illusions he crafted. Those traders who didn't despise him for his ability to haggle a price down far past their holdout point admired him for generous terms, unexpectedly offered. Not that the latter were any better off than the former, of course. It was simply that the deficit lay elsewhere, their attention misdirected by the famous Cavril Magnis charm. An easy smile and a concerned nature carried a body a long way, even in Frostgrave.

She believed most of what she'd heard, but now she was here, face to face with the man himself…? The stories were a candle set beside the heart of the sun. He'd have been a sensation in Karamasz, twisting the guilds to his personal profit, or skipping from bedchamber to bedchamber leaving undying infatuation and broken hearts in his wake. But perhaps, just perhaps, Magnis' effortless charm was not so effortless as it appeared. Mirika had many times dipped into the timeflow without appearing to do so, nudging her reflexes and perceptions simply by moving at different pace. Yelen had even done it herself, on those occasions where she'd embraced Azzanar's power. Perhaps Magnis was the same, his charm a careful trick to perception achieved through sorcerous means?

Yelen sat back and met Magnis' gaze. 'I'll resist you just fine.'

The confident smile collapsed like foundations worn away by the sea, replaced by an expression so crestfallen, so woeful, that Yelen almost retracted her challenge. Almost. She wasn't sure what held her back, only that she had the distinct impression that it was all an act, played out to an audience of one. And so it proved. An instant later, the smile was back – this time with a hint of devilry about the corners. 'I reckon you will, at that.'

'*Stop playing games, poppet. We agreed how this would go. Act before he can.*'

Yelen glanced around. Darrick and Marcan were still engrossed in their card game – or at least as engrossed as they'd been before. Kas didn't seem to be paying her any attention at all. He lay stretched, full length, along the beam, seemingly as secure as a child in a bunk, despite the fact that the beam was at least a score of feet higher off the ground than any child's bed. Serene remained in post, a little behind Yelen and to the side, her face as unreadable as ever.

The demon *could* be right, Yelen allowed. It could be a trap. But to what purpose? They already had her. They already knew what she knew.

'So why am I here?' she asked. 'You don't expect me to believe you had me picked up off the streets out of kindness.'

'Maybe you remind me of my sister. I haven't seen *her* in years, so why not help you?'

'You expect me to believe that?'

Magnis levelled an accusing finger. 'You know, you're entirely too cynical for your age. Mind you, so was Elien, last I saw her. The similarity is uncanny.'

That was rich. He was what, five years her elder? Ten at the outside. 'A life in the Karamasz guttermarch and this awful place brings certain attitudes to the fore.'

'That's true, that's true. As it happens, there *is* something else you can do for me. But first, there's a little unfinished business that needs attending to.' Standing, Magnis raised his voice. 'Darrick, would you be so good as to show our other guests in?'

Darrick pushed back his chair, the feet scraping on the flagstoned floor as he rose.

Yelen turned her attention back to Magnis. 'What other guests?'

He spread his hands. 'Alas, you've attracted a modicum of attention this last day or so – especially with that altercation at the gate. That's no good for anyone. I can't have Rekamark in uproar.'

At the far end of the room, one of the massive doors creaked open, propelled by Darrick's prodigious strength. A man entered. Nondescript by the standards of Rekamark's denizens, Yelen wouldn't have paid him a second glance, save for the fact that he bore Flintine's spider-brand.

'*He's selling you out! I warned you, poppet.*'

'You did,' Yelen murmured. The irony of the last few minutes didn't escape her. She'd told Magnis she'd resist him, but she hadn't, had she? He'd woven his honeyed net, and now she was trapped within it. 'We'll do this your way.'

'*At last, she sees sense.*'

Magnis reached out as Yelen rose, but she ignored him. Sulphur choked the back of her mouth. Her left wrist prickled with sudden heat. She didn't need to look to know that the clock had advanced, that another sliver of her soul had been lost. Then the thunderous pulse of the Clock of Ages swept across her, and her tempo broke free of reality's grip.

Serene was the nearest, no more than an arm's length away, but under the circumstances an arm's length was an impossible distance. Yelen, her personal tempo now twice that of the other woman's, ducked aside from the comically slow lunge. Yelen gave Serene a gentle shove as she glided past, just enough to send her off balance. Then she ran for the doors.

'I didn't see another way out, did you?'

'*I only see what you see,*' sniffed Azzanar. '*I just pay more attention. But no, it's that or the chimney.*'

Yelen spared an upward glance. In theory, she *could* push her tempo enough to run up the wall and reach the rafters, but she didn't fancy taking the risk. Besides, she didn't want to use Azzanar's power more than strictly necessary. She didn't trust the demon to give her fair warning before she reached the limits of what she'd bartered for.

Nonetheless, the upward glance wasn't wasted. Without it, Yelen would never have seen Kas plunging towards her, arms outstretched.

It was a well-judged leap, or would have been against any other opponent. Had Yelen simply been running twice her normal speed, her momentum would have prevented her from turning aside. It would have delivered her into Kas' grasp. But Yelen *wasn't* running twice as fast – the world was simply moving twice as fast around her. She threw herself aside. Kas plummeted past in slow motion and thudded into the floor.

Two down, one to go, including Flintine's man.

Darrick and Marcan were next, their images refracting into a dozen duplicates as Yelen closed. It was the same trick Magnis had used in the tomb – if you didn't know which was real, how could you be sure to evade your opponent? At least neither had drawn a weapon. Flintine was obviously offering more for her alive, for whatever consolation that was.

Yelen drew up short. She wasn't worried about Marcan – the swarthy fellow's arms were every bit as stocky as his legs – but Darrick's reach was another matter.

'*Brave heart, poppet. Like I showed you.*'

Taking a deep breath, Yelen increased her tempo yet further, doubling and redoubling it, then redoubling it again. She knew she couldn't hold herself at that speed for long, not without burning through the power Azzanar had bartered her. Would it be enough?

The mirror-images flickered like a candle in the wind. Not much, barely even a heartbeat, even with each moment drawn out to breaking point. It was enough. Darrick and Marcan – or rather, their originals – remained as solid as they ever had, one at either end of the peculiar crowd.

Yelen's tempo snapped back as she released her grip. Already moving, she charged through the line of doppelgängers without slowing, shards of light bursting around her as the images disintegrated.

She doubted Flintine's henchman even saw her coming. Mirika Semova was a time witch, everyone knew that. Her sister? Her sister was ordinary. Yelen was past him before his sword had even cleared its scabbard, and through the door before his warning shout – made turgid by their disparity of tempos – had fully sounded.

'*See, poppet? Easy.*'

Yelen forgot her hatred of the demon, just as she always did when revelling in the tide of the timeflow, and joined in with Azzanar's honeyed laughter.

The world suffered a grating, dizzying lurch. A metallic taste joined the bitter sulphur. Yelen's hips and shoulders slammed into the antechamber's flagstones, the impact shaking loose her grip on the timeflow.

'Magnis said you'd try to run,' said Kain, cracking the knuckles of one gauntleted hand with the other. 'Now give it up before I stop going easy on you.'

Shaking her head to clear the spots of colour from behind her eyes, Yelen clambered to her feet. The door behind Kain was ajar, the drifted snows of the temple approach bright in the afternoon sun. All she had to do was reach the door, and she was free.

'You got lucky, that's all.'

Ignoring the red buzz in the back of her head, Yelen reached into the timeflow and darted past Kain.

Suddenly, impossibly, a gauntleted fist was in her path, driving hard into her stomach.

Yelen struck the flagstones a second time, gasping for breath, her grip on the timeflow broken. 'How are you doing this? You're not fast enough to match me.'

Kain cocked her head. 'I don't have to be. I've seen your eyes. That's all I need to know where you're going. Now pack it in before I really hurt you.'

Yelen rose, wincing as the dull ache in her ribs added its complaints to the one at the side of her head.

'*Don't give up, poppet. Nearly there.*'

Yelen stared longingly at the doorway. 'I won't.'

So Kain thought she was predictable? Fine. She'd teach her otherwise.

Reaching into the timeflow a third time, Yelen feinted to Kain's right and flung herself to the knight's left, aiming kick at the back of her knee for good measure.

The boot never connected. Kain's hand, however, took Yelen across the throat, bearing her backwards and slamming her against the wall fit to rattle her teeth.

'Now, you going to behave, or do I have to squeeze?'

Yelen clawed at the gauntleted fingers, but Kain's grip was solid as stone.

'*You'll have to kill her.*' Excitement buzzed through Azzanar's silent voice. '*She can't stop you if her bones are dust.*'

No. She couldn't kill her. Could she?

'Stop struggling,' growled Kain. 'I really *don't* want to hurt you.'

'What's the difference?' Yelen gasped. 'You're going to hand me over to Flintine.'

Kain drew back. 'Who told you that? That creature looming over your shoulder?'

Azzanar went suddenly still, a prey animal caught in a predator's sight.

'Wait,' said Yelen. 'You can see her?'

'I see the shadow of her, dripping poison into your ear.' Kain snorted. 'Magnis isn't handing you over to Flintine. Could've done that while you slept, if he'd wanted. The next part happens easily enough, whether you're awake or I give you a little tap to quiet you. So what's it to be?'

Yelen tensed. She wasn't yet done. She could still reach into the timeflow – not to kill Kain, but maybe age her enough to slow her down.

'Consider this,' breathed Kain. 'Who really gains if you run off into Rekamark? You? Or your poisonous shadow?'

The words brought Yelen up short. Who indeed? Alone, she had no one to rely on but herself and Azzanar. Which was just how the demon would want it. Was that what lay behind the warnings of poison, of betrayal?

'*Don't listen to her!*'

Ironically, Azzanar's words tipped the balance – or rather, the desperate note of triumph denied. Feeling like a fool, Yelen let her body go limp.

* * *

'Mister Flintine will not be happy with these terms.'

Magnis sighed. 'Stop hedging, Lasro. Of course he'll be happy. It's practically the definition of something for nothing. Ten per cent of our next haul to drop the contract on Yelen. It's a good deal. Won't have to pay out that thousand crowns, for a start.'

Lasro stared down into the fire, the very image of a man wrestling with a weighty decision. But he was lost, Yelen saw as much from the sly glint in his eye. Ten percent of a Gilded Rose haul was a good cut, by anyone's standards. Lasro might have been one of Flintine's top lieutenants, but Magnis had been running rings around his like for years.

Yelen shifted from foot to foot, but subsided when Kain gave her neck a warning squeeze. It almost didn't matter. She couldn't escape now if she wanted to; even if Kas and Serene – both nursing fresh bruises – hadn't bolted the door. She wasn't used to manipulating the timeflow, and the fatigue of it had hit her like an avalanche. At least Azzanar was quiet, if not entirely absent. Yelen could practically feel the demon staring at Kain through her eyes.

Lasro stirred, set his jaw and gazed at Magnis. 'Mister Flintine wants Kardish's killer.'

Magnis spread his hands. 'She's well past his reach. Yelen's innocent.'

'Then why offer the tithe?'

That was a very good question, thought Yelen. Magnis might not want for coin, but there was a difference between that and spreading it around with abandon. She couldn't see how she was worth it.

'Because I understand that this isn't just about Kardish,' said Magnis. 'I understand that Mister Flintine has a reputation to protect. I'm offering the tithe to compensate him for any… distress the situation has caused.'

Lasro nodded. 'Very well. But the tithe will be fifteen per cent, not ten.'

'Twelve.'

'Agreed.'

Lasro rose from his chair. 'And it comes through me. You can send word from the gate.'

Which meant that Flintine would receive ten per cent, thought Yelen, while Lasro would pocket the difference without his master knowing.

Magnis got to his feet and offered a polite bow. 'Delightful. Darrick will show you out. Darrick?'

Lasro started off towards the door, the big man at his side. They made for a curious pair, with Darrick taking only two steps to three of Lasro's. Yelen stood in silence until Lasro had passed into the antechamber. 'So, what now?'

Magnis glanced at her with disinterest. 'I think you can let her go now, Kain. There'll be no more tricks, will there?' There was more amusement than rebuke in his tone.

The pressure on Yelen's neck vanished.

'Why didn't you tell me?' she said, massaging the base of her skull. She tried not to think on the portion of her soul she'd lost, seemingly to no avail and – worse – for no good reason.

'You hardly gave me a chance, now did you?' said Magnis mildly. 'Perhaps now we can talk about what you're going to do to pay me back.'

Yelen sighed. There it was. For all the pretence of altruism, there was a price for the Gilded Rose's intercession. She wasn't surprised. 'And I have no say in this, I suppose.'

'If you want one, but it's very simple.' Magnis grinned. 'I want that orb. You want your sister back. You're the key to both.' He shrugged. 'So, are you in?'

Yelen stared at him, mouth agape and eyes wide. She knew she looked ridiculous, but she didn't care. 'Mirika's... What? She's still alive?'

He nodded. 'I think so. I hope so. At least for now. But time's short, so we have to move quickly. Are you interested?' He gestured towards the door. 'Otherwise, you know the way out. We'll manage without you.'

It was all Yelen could do not to burst out laughing. Mirika was alive! How could she not accept Magnis' offer? 'Damn right I'm in. What do you need?'

It was only after she'd spoken that Yelen realised she'd made a poor job of resisting Cavril Magnis' charm.

CHAPTER NINE

The banners of Rekamark were a distant blaze of colour on a grey skyline. Yelen shook her head in wonder. Home for less than a day, and now she was on the move again, heading back into the cursed districts of Frostgrave. She felt no great sense of loss. The *Guttered Candle* hadn't been her home, not really. Her home was with Mirika.

She turned her attention to Cavril Magnis, trudging through the snows a few paces to her side. Of the company, he was the only one not laden down with haversack and bundles of kindling. The perks of being in charge.

'You really think we can save her?'

'I truly hope so. That orb really needed flesh and blood it could dominate. With that not forthcoming, the possession isn't complete.' He arched an eyebrow. 'Unless your sister always longed to give up her body for a desiccated old spirit? I've heard tell that a liche and his host can share their existence, if the proper deal is struck. Though to be honest, all of those stories end badly.'

Yelen halted, hunching and straightening her shoulders to set her haversack in a new position. 'Why?'

'Why do you think? Living forever's the ultimate selfishness. I can't imagine it inclines one to share.' He shrugged. 'Still, I've occasionally wondered if I'd have what it takes to twist a mouldy old spirit to my will. Maybe Mirika's seized that opportunity?'

She shuddered. 'Not so I know.'

He nodded. 'Then it'll be up to you to get through to her. From what you've said, Mirika was fighting Szarnos' influence. You'll give her the reason to fight harder.' He pressed a spread palm to his chest and offered a knowing smile. 'While I, Cavril Magnis, will contribute a few choice charms to weaken the orb's hold, and attempt a little persuasion of my own.'

Yelen shook her head at the wizard's self-aggrandizing manner and concentrated on following the trail of footprints. The Gilded Rose were strung out in a long line, their formation more suitable for a pleasure hike than a delving expedition. Then again, with Rekamark still in sight and the Lower Reach yet some way ahead, dangers were few and far between until night fell. And she had the impression that not all of Magnis' hirelings cared greatly for each other.

No, that wasn't true. Darrick and Marcan seemed to get on well enough – judging by their shared, bombastic refrains of rimelander folk songs, anyway. They were belting one out now, the lyrics echoing back along the streets towards Yelen. Something about a tavern maid of questionable judgement and a bet, if the snatches she caught were anything to go by. Tasteful, by rimelander standards, but Yelen felt sure it wouldn't last.

A dozen paces ahead of the duelling vocalists, Kas stalked lightly through the snows, bow slung across his shoulders and a thoughtful expression on his face. Occasionally, he'd judder to a halt, cock his head, and head off in a new direction. He never once glanced back, seemingly confident that the rest of the company would follow without question.

Serene marched as far behind the rest of the company as Kas strode ahead, the nonchalant expression cracking into something approaching distaste only when the notes of the raucous duet became particularly strident. And Kain? She brought up the very rear with a glower a few degrees colder than the chill northern wind.

Up ahead, Kas straightened, beckoned to his left, and set off along a new street. Magnis half-turned, repeating the gesture for Serene and Kain, and quickened his pace.

'You're sure he knows where he's going?' asked Yelen.

'It hardly matters. If Szarnos really is in control – and I don't think either of us is prepared to question *that* – he'll be heading back to his tomb, or at least to the Temple of Draconostra. He'll feel safe there – safe enough to set about, erm… consolidating his situation. You've heard the stories. Not a fellow for improvisation, old Szarnos. He'll have some goal in mind.'

Yelen grimaced. Magnis had tried, but there was no way to describe her sister's plight that didn't make her skin crawl. And, truth be told, their course so far had more or less retraced hers and Mirika's steps of the previous day. But there was no guarantee that would last. 'And if you're wrong?'

'I've learned not to question Kas' instincts,' said Magnis. 'He has a talent for tracking. How do you think we followed you to the Tomb of Szarnos in the first place?'

'I assumed we were after the same thing. Like at Markriese. I didn't think there was a mystery to it.'

He laughed softly. 'Goodness no. I'd narrowed down

the location, but that was all. Old Torik kept his secrets close, even from his apprentice.'

Yelen frowned. There had been something in the way he'd spoken… 'You were Torik's apprentice?'

'For a time, and for my sins. Don't look so surprised, I think the old fool taught half the wizards in Rekamark at one time or another. Liked to play the patriarch, did Torik.' Without breaking stride, Magnis performed a flowery bow. 'Dispensing wisdom from on high. Or rather, dispensing what looked like wisdom. There's no fool like an old fool.'

Realization dawned. 'You were using him, weren't you? To get leads on stuff worth delving.'

Magnis had the grace to shift uncomfortably. 'Less than you might think. Torik talked a lot, but it was mostly guesswork. Either that, or he kept most of the good stuff close to his chest.'

Yelen smiled. 'What's the matter, upset that the old man might have outwitted you?'

He sniffed. 'I'll have you know, I'm above such things, Miss Semova. Though I must confess, things became a lot easier when you and your sister came on the scene. I knew it was only a matter of time before he sent you after the orb. Under the circumstances, I'm doubly sorry you got there first.'

Yelen recalled her last glimpse of Mirika, pale skin shot through with golden light, eyes dark as pitch. 'Me too,' she said softly. They walked in silence for a time, the sound of their footsteps drowned out by another boisterous refrain from up ahead. 'This orb… What is it? Really, I mean.'

'Ah,' said Magnis. 'That was the cause of many an argument before I departed Torik's tutelage. He always maintained that it was a sort of thaumic lodestone – a power source capable of fulfilling truly outrageous magic.'

'Like possessing my sister...' Yelen tailed off, sickened at the very thought.

Magnis didn't seem to notice. 'For one, though I doubt that would have taken more than a fraction of its potential. The overture to a symphony to come, if you will. I'm sure Torik had great plans for the balance of the orb's power, once he'd acquired a body young enough to carry them out.'

'But you didn't agree?'

'It didn't make *sense*.' Magnis' tone took on fresh urgency. 'Why would Szarnos just leave a vast reservoir of thaumic power behind for others to use? The legends are clear that he was a meticulous planner, with a recourse for every eventuality. And what eventuality is more certain than death? No. I always suspected the orb was a phylactery, containing not just a portion of Szarnos' power, but his soul.' He shrugged. 'Dangerous things, unless you've a strong enough will to conquer the spirit inside. Liches will make do with old bones if they have to, but they'd much rather have a warm body, or better yet, a willing pupil. There's no shortage of cautionary tales, if you know where to look.'

'Then why do you want it so badly?' asked Yelen. 'Surely it's of no use to you, now you know the truth.'

Magnis laughed. 'Oh, it's still valuable enough, to the right person. But I wouldn't say it's useless. Forewarned is forearmed, and I'm sure a fragment of Szarnos' personality is far less ferocious than the whole. You, of all people, should know the possibilities. You proved that back at my humble abode.'

Yelen rubbed at her left wrist, knowing even then that the itch was all in her mind. 'I don't control her. I made a bargain. A foolish one, as it turned out.'

'Then perhaps the trick is not to fight, but to ensure every bargain goes your way?'

She shook her head. For all his confident talk, Magnis had no idea what it meant to be shackled to a creature like Azzanar. No one did, except maybe Mirika, if there was any longer anything of her left. Yelen shook the horrific thought away as soon as it formed. Mirika could still be saved. She *had* to believe it.

'*You should take your handsome new friend's advice,*' said Azzanar. '*You'll have a lot more fun if you just embrace your destiny.*'

Yelen slowed, allowing Magnis to go on ahead. A quick glance confirmed that Serene was still half a dozen paces back and out of earshot.

'I'm never letting you out again,' she hissed, too low for her voice to carry. 'You tricked me.'

'*Tricked you, poppet?*' The demon's voice thickened with anger. '*I only did what you asked.*'

'You let me believe that the Gilded Rose meant me harm! Pick. Pick. Pick. Until I believed it. Until I was desperate enough to call on you!'

'*Hah! If you want to see who tricked you, you need only look in a mirror. Your problem isn't with me, poppet, it's with everyone. You always think you know better. Better than me. Better than Cavril Magnis. And better than your sister.*'

'Shut up! It's not like that. You and I? We're done. I'll go to the grave before I give you anything else.'

Azzanar laughed. '*But you've said that before, poppet. Remember? Sooner or later, you always let me out. And it's not like dear Master Torik can "cure" you any longer. Not after you left him to die in the snow.*'

'Shut up!'

Yelen didn't realize she'd screamed the words until they echoed back. Magnis halted and stared back at her. Foolishness and anger fought for control, swirling like fire. She didn't even know she was trembling until a wiry arm settled around her shoulders.

'Seconded!' shouted Serene. 'Stow that awful racket, will you Darrick?'

'But it's folkloric.'

'It's obscene, is what it is. Put a sock in it.'

The big man's face creased with irritation. 'Or else?'

Serene's free hand drifted to her belt, and a dagger's pommel. 'You really have to ask? Remember how Marcan's having trouble counting to ten of late?'

Darrick laughed uneasily. 'Cavril wouldn't let you.'

Magnis shrugged. 'Oh no, Cavril's not getting involved. He's just out for a nice afternoon walk.'

Darrick packed it in. Nudging Marcan in the ribs, he ambled away down the street. Magnis shook his head in weary amusement, and followed.

'Ah,' said Serene. 'Peace and quiet. At last.'

'Thank you.' Yelen had the feeling the other woman knew she'd not been protesting at the singing, but couldn't bring herself to ask.

Serene let go of her shoulders, and picked up her pace. 'You're not the only one with voices, love. Just remember – they've only as much power as you give them.'

Yelen watched her go. She was right. Azzanar couldn't do anything. Not if she didn't let her. Not if she stayed strong. 'Like I said,' she whispered. 'We're done. Stay out of my thoughts.'

The demon chuckled. '*Oh, I will. But think on this, my dear, darling child. I'm close to the surface now. So close that I can feel the wind on my face. That changes things.'* Her tone hardened. *'You'll beg for my help before we're done.'*

All at once, the skies seemed greyer and darker than before. Yelen swallowed away the taste of sulphur, and followed Serene down the street.

* * *

The chorus of wolf howls raced along Yelen's spine, setting her nerves on end. She glanced back and forth, eyes searching the ruins to either side. She already knew she wouldn't see them. You didn't. Not until the pack was ready to strike. Humans weren't the only beasts made treacherous by a life in the ruins of Frostgrave.

Kain waved an arm above her head, finger tracing a circle in the air. 'Close up! They take you, and you're on your own. I'm not coming after you.'

Magnis smiled his easy smile. 'You'll come after me.'

'That's different. You're paying.'

'Charmer,' muttered Darrick. He waved at Yelen and raised his voice. 'Come on, girl. Might not be much eating on you, but still enough for temptation.'

Yelen nodded acknowledgement and picked up her pace. She arrived at Magnis' side at the same time as Kas. The tracker had his bow unslung, and an arrow nocked.

'I don't like this,' he said. 'Something has them riled.'

The howl came again.

Serene cocked her head. 'Sounds like hunger to me. Same as normal.'

Marcan muttered something unintelligible under his breath. 'Kas is right. They're afraid. Heard 'em this way up in the Grey District a couple years back. Lost most of my company when they gathered their courage.'

Serene laughed quietly. 'You always say that. Once – just once – I'd like to go a whole expedition without hearing one of your stories.'

Marcan ran a gloved hand through his beard. 'Ain't just the supernatural that's worth respect hereabouts. If all these graves *do* open one day, I'll wager every crown I have that them rotting bones will come a poor second to tooth and claw.'

'That's what? Ten crowns in all?' Serene shook her head. 'An easy stake given you drink ten times that in a night.'

'Suit yourself,' he rumbled. 'But when…'

'Enough!' Magnis' tone was unusually severe. Either the wolf-voices had him worried too, or he was just sick of hearing his hirelings quarrel. 'There's no point taking chances. Kas, are we safe to press on, or should we hole up for a few hours?'

Yelen didn't much like the sound of that. Dusk was still hours away, but she knew from experience that the wolves would only get louder and bolder as night approached. If they stopped now, they'd not start again until dawn. Precious hours in which Mirika might be lost for good.

If she wasn't already.

'I'm going on.' She was surprised at how steady her voice sounded, given that her innards were twisted tight by fear.

Marcan snorted. 'That's a bad idea.'

Yelen met his gaze. 'I'm still going on. She's my sister.'

'No loss there. You're easy on the eye, but that's all. Not like you're earning your passage.' A bushy eyebrow twitched. ''less you start being a bit friendlier, I wouldn't mind that.'

'Shut it, Marcan,' said Serene. 'Credit the girl with better taste, yeah?' She turned to Yelen. 'Be sensible, love.

You know how it works. You go out there alone, you're a dead woman walking. Frostgrave doesn't care that you're young and pretty. It'll kill you just the same.'

'You can't stop me.' They didn't need to know that Azzanar had forsworn offering all aid.

'*I* can.' Kain offered a rare, glacial smile. 'At least, if I'm asked to. What's it to be, Cavril?'

Magnis steepled his fingers and pressed them to his lips, tilting his head ever so slightly this way and that in silent contemplation. 'What do you think, Kas?'

The tracker shrugged. 'They're still off to the west. Leastways, so far as I can tell. We stay close, we can keep moving, but if they cut round ahead of us we'll need fire, and plenty of it.'

'Then we keep going. But we stay together, and we stay quiet.' He offered a wry smile. 'I want a better place in the history books than "eaten by wolves".'

Darrick shrugged. 'You get eaten by wolves, there'll be no place in the history books. You'll just be a grisly footnote in one of Marcan's stories.'

Magnis shot him a patient look. 'I rather think that's my point.'

Yelen felt a burden lift from her heart. It was tiny, compared to what remained, but she welcomed it. One step at a time. It was as true now as it had been in Rekamark.

'But there'll be no more talk about going on alone,' Magnis went on, his gaze coming to rest on Yelen. 'We're in this together. That's how it works.'

Yelen had no doubt that the words were for her, and her alone. The elation of the moment before crumbled beneath a profound feeling of foolishness. She really *didn't* want to press on alone, and there was no guarantee Magnis needed her enough to suffer a challenge to his authority, even indirect as it had been. She nodded her mute acceptance.

Magnis' lip twitched. Not a smile, not quite. 'Yelen, perhaps you'll take a turn up front with Kas? He's getting old. I'm sure a pair of young eyes would be welcome.'

She glanced at the tracker's lugubrious expression, neither welcoming nor rejecting. 'Sure. Why not?'

* * *

Yelen passed the next hour in Kas' company, trying to ignore the intermittent howls. It had been months since she'd heard Frostgrave's wolves so active. On that occasion she and Mirika had sought refuge in a crumbling watchtower and hunched close to their fire. In the end, the wolves had grown silent when the snows returned, having the good sense to seek the shelter of their lairs. This time, however, the darkening skies remained clear, and the ululating howls continued to ring out.

Kas spoke little, breaking his silence only to call out obstructions on the rubble-strewn hillside that led down to the Lower Reach. Though the tracker kept an arrow nocked the whole time, his posture remained as relaxed as ever, and that in turn helped Yelen's nerves to settle, at least a little.

Azzanar's parting shot still hung heavy on her mind. *I'm close to the surface now. That changes things.* What did it change? Was it just more of the demon's double-talk – another attempt at manipulation? What if it wasn't? There'd been an edge in Azzanar's voice Yelen hadn't heard before, as if the demon had finally abandoned playing at friendliness, and was now prepared to do whatever she could to seize control.

Yelen bit her lip. There had to be something she could do. She glanced up the hill, to where the rest of the Gilded Rose made their descent. Maybe not her. Maybe someone else.

For all Magnis' talk of Kas 'getting old', there was certainly nothing wrong with his eyes. Even in the failing light, he caught sight of the sunken footprints before Yelen. Then again, she doubted he had more than forty winters behind him. Perhaps fewer. Folk aged fast in the frozen city, assuming they were permitted to age at all. Beckoning her over, he crouched beside the tracks, the foot of his bow braced against the snow-covered ground.

'Small feet. Uneven paces. Your sister's been this way. Knew we'd find some eventually.'

Yelen peered at the tracks. 'You're sure?' She didn't doubt his conclusion, not exactly, but she didn't see why he was so certain the footprints belonged to Mirika.

Kas scratched his bristly head. 'Barefoot? Only two ladies I know of crazy enough for that, and you're standing right beside me.'

He had a point.

'What about these others?' asked Yelen. There were at least half a dozen other sets of footprints leading away down the hillside, all heading in roughly the same direction as Mirika's trail.

He shook his head. 'They're too old. See where the edges have melted? They're heavier, too. An even step. Precise. Someone's company of soldiers, perhaps.'

Yelen thought back to the approach to Rekamark the previous day. It felt like a lifetime ago. 'We passed Mariast on the way in. She was heading to the Lower Reach.'

'The Green Widow?' Kas purred with laughter. 'So they're all dead by now.'

'Probably.' Yelen stared at Mirika's footprints, distant doubts coalescing. 'You said these are the first tracks you've found.'

'That's right.'

'So how have you been following her?'

Kas stood upright. 'There's a scent on the air – one the wind can't shift. It's dry. Stale. Like death.' He stared away down the hillside. 'Those wolves? They're not hungry. They're afraid of your sister. So am I.'

Without another word, he stalked away down the hillside. Yelen suppressed a shudder, and followed.

∗ ∗ ∗

Magnis brought the company to a halt as dusk came on. Marcan set a fire and packs were broached for a meal of chanin tea, salt beef and dry bread. Yelen ate her share of the latter, but drank only water. She still remembered the dream from the last time she'd imbibed chanin. Maybe that *had* been all Azzanar's doing, but she wasn't prepared to take the risk.

Most of the company crowded into the tumbledown ruin that served as their encampment. Darrick sat in the lee of the empty doorway, his thick fingers dancing along the stem of a wooden flute. The low, mournful melody hung upon the air like smoke from the fire. Yet somehow it reminded Yelen of happier times, distant though they were.

Kas, his bow finally set aside, sat propped up in the corner. Serene sat beside him, greatcoat bundled at her back, shoulder buried up against Kas' ribs, and her head resting on his shoulder. The sheer matter-of-factness of it all made Yelen smile. She'd caught no hint of affection earlier in the day, but she supposed that neither was much given to letting their feelings show. Even now, their position could perhaps have been taken as nothing more than a desire for shared warmth. But Yelen marked how a little of the tension had faded from around Kas' dark eyes, and how entwined fingers clasped tight against Serene's thigh.

Magnis sat alone in the opposite corner, eyes closed in sleep or contemplation. Marcan remained by the fire, so close that Yelen was sure his beard would catch light. He tended his self-appointed charge with an occasional prod of a crooked stick, sending sparks dancing around the blackened cauldron.

Only Kain remained outside. She stood some way distant, her back to the doorway, the blade of her sword resting against her shoulder.

'Isn't she coming in?' asked Yelen.

Marcan glanced disinterestedly up from the fire. 'I doubt it,' he rumbled. 'Thinks she's better than us, doesn't she?'

'She thinks she's better than *you*,' Kas corrected wryly. 'It's not the same thing.'

Marcan shot him a sour look. 'Har har. And maybe she is. But she's still here, isn't she? You only get three kinds in this godforsaken place. Outcasts, exiles and thieves. I wonder which she is.'

'Why don't you ask her?' asked Serene.

'Why don't *you*?'

'You forgot me.' Magnis spoke without opening his eyes, a wounded note in his voice. 'What am I?'

'That's easy,' said Serene. 'You're all three.'

'Harsh words. Very harsh.' Magnis' grin belied his injured tone. 'Though I'm not sure one can be an outcast *and* an exile. They're the same thing, surely?'

Darrick lowered his flute, the last note faded beneath the crackle of the fire. 'Exile has a certain ring of authority to it, while being outcast *could* simply be fleeing a baying mob. Or even self-inflicted.' He spoke precisely and crisply, a tutor enlightening particularly dim students. It stood in stark contrast to his brutish, mangled features. 'So while an exile *is* an outcast, an outcast isn't always an exile.'

'So you *are* all three,' said Serene.

'It would appear so,' Magnis agreed, his eyes still closed. 'And all the more magnificent for it.'

The corner of Kas' mouth twitched. 'Perhaps we should add "braggart" to the list. What do you say, Marcan?'

The bearded man snorted. 'Not sure. I don't make the rules.'

'Have you forgotten that this "braggart" keeps coin in your pockets?' said Magnis. 'Keeps you fed and sheltered? I think I'm due a little more respect.'

Darrick cocked his head. 'Surely only a braggart would make such a claim?'

'Oh dear. Beset on all sides by calumny. It's a wonder I go on.'

Yelen thought Magnis looked awfully cheerful for a man so beset. Then again, she was surprised at the easy camaraderie of her travelling companions. She and Mirika had crossed paths with the Gilded Rose so many times in the past months, and each encounter had only reinforced her impression of grim, ruthless mercenaries, chasing gold crowns – just like pretty much every other delver gang in Frostgrave.

But Mirika had been right. The Gilded Rose *were* different, and it stemmed from Cavril Magnis himself. She tried to imagine Torik enduring the mockery of his underlings as Magnis had, and abandoned the attempt. Hells, she couldn't picture herself doing it, were she in his position. In another, such self-deprecation might have come across as stagey, or manipulative, but Magnis didn't seem to care that he was the butt of the joke, so long as someone was laughing.

No wonder Mirika had wanted to join them. The Gilded Rose, oddly assorted though they might have been, were a family of sorts. All save one.

Coming to a decision, Yelen beckoned to Marcan. 'Pass me some more of that meat, would you?'

He grunted, and tossed her an oilcloth-wrapped bundle. 'For a skinny thing, you can't half put it away.'

'It's not for me.' Careful not to touch the cauldron itself, Yelen ladled a helping of tea into a battered tin mug. For the first time, she noticed that Marcan's right hand had only three fingers and a thumb. The little finger was missing, the stump tied off by a worn bandage. 'Your hand. How did that happen?'

Marcan held up his hand, examining the missing digit as if for the first time. 'This? It's a reminder that I'm not to gut pretty young time witches just because they beat us to a prize. Only last I saw, she's walking around, and I'm short a finger.'

He glared at Serene, who stared back unrepentantly. 'You were warned.'

Pieces clicked into place. Serene's quip about Marcan only being able to count to ten. The distant memory of Magnis instructing her to 'give him a reason not to forget'. It seemed that Magnis' family enforced its rules.

With that realization, the fire lost a little of its warmth. Yelen gathered up mug and food, and retreated outside.

***

'I heard you talking about me.' Kain spoke without turning.

Yelen jumped, and wondered why she'd done so. She wasn't trying to sneak up on the older woman, after all. No. She knew why. Kain scared her. Not just for her manner, but because of what she could do. What she could see. Perhaps fear wasn't the right word, but *respect*. Then again, that implied some form of equality, and there was none. 'I brought you some food.'

'Did you?' Again, Kain spoke without inflection. No gratitude, no dismissal.

Yelen laid her burden down on the crest of a shattered wall and drew her coat tighter. After the warmth of the fire, the evening air cut even more sharply than before. Still Kain didn't move. She remained as motionless as the wall-side statue that served as her partner in vigil. It too bore knightly armour. It too affected an unhealthy stillness. Had Kain been covered by a light dusting of snow, the two would have been all but indistinguishable.

'If you wanted to go inside, I could keep watch for a time.'

In fact, that was the last thing that Yelen sought. She wanted to get out of the wind, back to the seeming safety of the ruin – wanted it all the more with each fresh howl that split the greying skies. But the offer had to be made.

At last, Kain turned. 'What do you want?'

Yelen hugged herself tight, rubbing at her upper arms to drive away the cold. 'I told you. I thought you'd like some food.'

The knight inclined her head and fixed Yelen with a stare. 'What do you *really* want?'

So much for the subtle approach. 'Back in Rekamark, you said you saw a shadow on my shoulder, dripping poison into my ear.'

'Yes.'

'Is… Is she still there?'

'Oh yes. She's part of you. A second shadow cast by darkness, rather than light.'

'I didn't ask for this. It was a conjurer, back in Karamasz. He said he could help me be more like my sister. Help me ride the timeflow.' Yelen knew she was babbling. She hadn't meant to speak of this at all. Hells, she hadn't told anyone else this story. Even Mirika didn't know it all. But there was something about Kain's stare. It didn't invite honesty. It demanded it. 'I never asked for *this*.'

'Are you sure of that?'

Kain's expression didn't flicker, but Yelen knew she'd seen through the lie all the same. Truth was, she'd been so enamoured of becoming more like Mirika, she'd never stopped to consider the implications.

'I was so jealous. Mirika could do so much, and all I could do was time walk – and even then it only worked with both of us together.' And now she couldn't even do that, Yelen realised with a start. The one piece of chronomancy that had been hers, not Azzanar's, and without Mirika it was lost to her.

Kain issued a thoughtful grunt. 'So that's how you escaped at the Tomb of Szarnos. I confess, I've seen it done before, though seldom better. Many would kill for such a gift.' She paused, accusation rumbling beneath the words that followed. 'Most would be satisfied with such a gift.'

Yelen shook her head in misery. She'd told herself the same thing many times since that fateful day, but to hear it from another... 'She speaks to me. Calls me "poppet".'

'How nice.'

'It's not.' Yelen's breaths shuddered in her throat. With an effort, she brought them under control. 'You know what a poppet is? It's a straw doll that you throw into a Midsun bonfire to implore Solastra to heal a loved one. It's a sacrifice. The poppet dies in flame so another might live. That's what I am to her!'

'Why tell me?' asked Kain.

'I thought… Well, I thought you might be able to help me. You can see her. No one else can. I thought you might know a way. I'll do anything.'

'Why not return to the conjurer? He brought forth the beast. Surely he can banish it?'

'Because he's dead.' Yelen closed her eyes, remembering the blood. The panic. 'I think I killed him.'

'I see.'

Tears of shame stung Yelen's cheeks, their bite all the more bitter in the cold wind. 'Can you help me?'

Kain offered a slow nod. 'There is a way.'

Yelen caught her breath. 'You can? How?'

'I can cut out your heart.'

Yelen stared at her, hope dispersing as soon as it had arrived. 'Pardon me?'

The corner of Kain's mouth twitched. 'You said you'd do anything. The road to damnation is a sheer slope. The downward path is easy, but the return journey is harder. Do you still want my help?'

All at once, Kain seemed taller and broader than before, the sword monstrous in her hands.

'I…' Yelen staggered away backwards, heels dragging against the cobbles. 'No… No!'

She stammered the words, wary of saying anything that might provoke Kain to precipitate action. When she was halfway back to the broken door, she turned on her heel and fled the rest of the way, chased on by Kain's parting words.

'Thank you for the food.'

CHAPTER TEN

'This is a bad idea,' muttered Darrick.

Yelen followed the big man's gaze through twilight's gathering darkness. Beyond the twisted iron railings, the Lower Reach was alive with wisp-light, the captive spirits dancing their mad gavotte of flickering colour above the barrows. But though she agreed with Darrick, she said nothing. Mirika's trail led straight through the Lower Reach.

Marcan snorted. 'You're soft. Isn't nothing to this place but tricksy lights and empty cowls. Nothing for the likes of us to worry about.'

Darrick rounded on him, finger wagging. 'It never ceases to amaze me…'

'Enough.'

Magnis didn't shout, but the two immediately ceased their quarrel all the same. Another reminder, had Yelen needed one, that for all the Gilded Rose's easy badinage, there was only one leader. Once his decision was made, he brooked no argument.

'It's what? Ten hours, dusk 'till dawn?' said Magnis. He raised his voice. 'How long to go around, Kas?'

'Fifteen hours. At least fifteen hours.'

Magnis paced up and down the line, meeting the eyes of each companion in turn. 'The sands of time are slipping away, and the weather's good. We can't afford to lose ten hours, let alone fifteen. Six hours for sleep?' He shrugged. 'We'll have to. After all, we all of us need rest. But that means we press on while we can. Even in the dark. Even through the Lower Reach.'

Darrick stirred. 'We camp in the Lower Reach, we'll lose a lot more than fifteen hours.'

'He's not wrong,' said Kain. 'It's one thing to keep moving. Staying put like a tethered goat is something else.'

Magnis shook his head woefully. 'Have you so little faith? I've a plan. I *always* have a plan. Serene?'

The woman mutely shrugged off her pack, opened it and tossed a bundle to Magnis.

He caught it easily, and held it up. 'Blackroot, silver dust and blessed incense. Corpsefire, that's what they call it in the south. Its light burns undead if they get too close. We've enough of these to ring a small camp, and they'll burn for a good twelve hours. All the time in the world.'

Yelen had never heard of corpsefire, and had no idea whether Magnis' claims were true. Yet he'd spoken with such surety that it was all but impossible *not* to believe him. How much of that was his magic at work? Or did she have it backwards? Did Magnis even command that much sorcery, beyond a few simple parlour tricks? Was he, in fact, much more than an enterprising huckster in fine robes?

Magnis handed the bundle of corpsefire back to Serene. As he did so, he offered Yelen a sly wink, as if the whole thing were a joke, and they were the only two to share in it. She didn't know how she felt about that.

'I still don't like it,' rumbled Darrick.

Magnis spread his hand. 'Fine. You don't like it. Feel free to head back. We're already down twelve per cent on this expedition, so I'm all for saving a few crowns where we can.' As if on cue, the wolf-howls picked up again. 'Of course, *they'll* have our scent by now. Not a journey I'd care to make alone.'

Without another word, Darrick turned his back and lumbered away towards the gateway.

Magnis rubbed his hands together. 'Glad we've sorted that out. Kain? Would you be so good as to bring up the rear?'

* * *

Yelen spent the early part of the journey in the middle of the company, Serene to her front and Magnis at her side. All semblance of a leisurely hike had long since fled, the strung-out line of before now reduced to a compacted, huddled blob, hurrying through the fading light. There was no singing, and very little speech – the consensus that no unnecessary sound be uttered every bit as unspoken as it was immediate.

Through it all, Yelen kept an eye on Kain as often as she could. The knight's threat had faded, and she'd halfway convinced herself the threat to cut out her heart had been a bleak joke. Even so, Yelen felt better when she had eyes on Kain than when she did not. Even Azzanar's furious threats had lost their sting – as much because the demon remained silent as to any other factor. Distant perils lost their potency in the light of the barrow-wisps, and their constant reminder of sleepless malice nearby. On her last near-disastrous trip through the Lower Reach, Yelen hadn't seen anything in the barrow save for light and shadow, and was hopeful to keep it that way.

The trail of Mirika's footprints ran arrow-straight through the snowy hummocks, varying course only to keep to the valley between the summits. Other sets – those left by what Yelen presumed were Mariast's band of toy soldiers – wove back and forth, vanishing into the distance only to rejoin the trail hundreds of yards later.

'Searching for something, looks like,' said Kas.

They weren't the only ones. Yelen had the impression of shapes moving beyond the tenuous light of the lanterns. Not men – or not living ones, at least. But she never saw them save for out of the corner of her eye. Maybe they weren't there at all, but figments of a sleep-addled mind?

'Their sleep has been disturbed.'

Her mind elsewhere, Yelen fair jumped out of her skin at Kain's sudden words. She held her tongue for a moment, willing her galloping pulse to subside. 'You think Mariast cracked a tomb?'

'Why else come here? This is no place for the living.' Kain's utterance had the finality of tombstones slamming home. 'They'll keep their distance until nightfall.'

Magnis shook his head. 'Mariast's never been careful. She's looking for anything that can turn a profit, and to hells with the consequences. She's not the most complex example of humankind.'

Serene snorted. 'Not like you.'

He arched an eyebrow. 'I have hidden depths, I'll have you know.'

'They must be *very* well hidden.'

* * *

As night drew close, Magnis called a halt. Producing one of the corpsefire mixtures from his haversack, he tipped a little into each of two dented metal bowls. He closed his eyes and ran an open palm across one, then the other. As his hand passed, each mixture came alight with white flame.

'Here.' He passed one to Yelen, and another to Darrick. 'I don't think our hosts will be brave enough to bother a group of our size for a while yet, but this should keep them polite.'

Yelen took the proffered bowl and cupped it in her hands. The flame had a heady scent. It was rich, sweet and held a lingering note of tree sap – a fragrance so far in Yelen's past it took a moment before she recalled what it was. 'It smells of springtime.'

Magnis grinned. 'I suppose it does. No wonder the undead hate it so.'

Marcan's brow creased. 'What're you talking about?'

'Spring is the death of winter,' said Darrick, his reverent eyes fixed on the flame. 'And nothing embodies winter like a wight.'

Most of the earlier tension had gone from his voice, Yelen noted. The reality of the corpsefire was clearly more reassuring to him than the mere idea of it. She glanced around. Was it her imagination, or were the barrow-wisps giving them wider berth than before? The shadows beyond most certainly were. Try as she might, Yelen couldn't glimpse a single one. She hugged the bowl closer, only then noticing that the fire gave out no heat, as other fires did.

They set off again, Kas' lantern bobbing along to light their path, the company's mood more relaxed than before. Yelen had the sense that although Darrick had been the only one to voice his concerns, all of her companions were grateful for the safety offered by the soft, white light. All of them apart from Kain, of course. For all the concern on the knight's face, she could have been walking in sunlit fields, without so much as a single care to weigh her down.

Little by little, Serene drifted back from her place at Kas' side, and fell into step with Yelen. 'How are the voices?'

Yelen watched her closely, unsure of how much to say. 'Better. Quiet.'

Serene laughed softly. 'I heard you arguing with yourself before. Seemed familiar.' She tapped her temple. 'Mine aren't real, of course. Which comes as good and bad. Means I can ignore them easier than you, but it also means I can't get rid of them. Yours is, though, isn't it? Real, I mean?'

Yelen nodded tightly. 'Too real. How did you know?'

'I may not be as well-read as Darrick, but I've picked up a few things, here and there.'

The two walked in companionable silence for a time, and Yelen found her thoughts turning to Serene. Though she'd not realised it before, she suspected the other woman wasn't a great deal older than herself. It was the missing eye that had worked the deception – that, and Serene's seemingly boundless confidence.

'What brought you here, Serene? To Frostgrave?'

She shook her head. 'You first. Fair's fair.'

Yelen winced at the memory. 'It was this or the pyre. When I and my "voice" first came together, I went a little crazy. Drew too much notice. We needed to go somewhere Karamasz's lawkeepers wouldn't follow, so we came here. You?'

Serene kicked at a hunk of ice. It skittered away from her foot and rolled to a halt at the foot of the nearest hummock. 'Lost the taste for my old trade. You know how it is. You learn a set of skills, take the stiff's money, try to make them happy. Then you realize that no matter how good you are, you're only

ever one dissatisfied client away from lying dead in the gutter.'
She sighed. 'So I gave up cutting throats and took ship up the
Nereta.'

Yelen frowned at an explanation that had ended in a very
different place to the one she'd expected. 'And your voices –
they came with you?'

'Tried drinking them away, but it turns out I had a
conscience. Who knew?' She ran a hand across her eyepatch.
'Lost this in a brawl. Would've lost the other, if not for Kas.
Now we look after each other.'

'And Magnis?'

'He pays well, but he's a smooth-tongued rogue.'

'You don't trust him?'

'Love, I don't trust anyone, 'cept for Kas.'

A few paces ahead, Kas came to an abrupt halt. Yelen
started guiltily, thinking he'd overheard their conversation.
Serene, apparently, had no such worries.

'What is it?'

Kas raised his lantern. 'See for yourself.'

At first, Yelen couldn't see what he meant. The warm amber
glow of the lamp shone down on the ever-present snow,
churned at her feet and then drifted up towards the flank of the
barrow. Snow, and a lump of ice.

A lump of ice that had once been a man.

He knelt on a rising knee, his back to the barrow, arms
crossed in front of his face as if to ward off a blow. His eyes,
wide with terror, glittered like gemstones in the lantern-light
– his whole body did. Icicles hung from his arms, and from the
pauldrons of his armour. They were bent backwards, as if they'd
somehow formed in the teeth of a ferocious wind. Yelen knew
the livery, if not the face. One of Mariast's toy soldiers.

'There's another one over here,' rumbled Marcan.

Yelen tore her gaze to the other side of Mirika's trail.

This one stood nearly upright, frozen stiff in the act of a two-handed sword swing.

'Not a pretty business.' Marcan lowered his lantern and gave the figure an experiential prod with the tip of his sword. The soldier swayed, then toppled like a falling tree. He struck the ground, and shattered into a dozen pieces.

Kain stepped forward and laid a heavy hand on Marcan's shoulder. 'Show some respect!'

'What's the harm? He was already dead, wasn't he?'

'And so will you be, one day.'

He smiled wolfishly. 'Won't matter none to me, will it? I'll be long gone.'

Magnis stepped between them. 'That'll do. Kas, what do you think?'

The tracker shrugged. 'Seems obvious to me. Mariast's expedition was attacked. These two died, and the rest fled.' He peered downed at the mass of churned snow, and tilted the lantern away along the barrow's flank. 'That way, I reckon.'

Darrick stared into the kneeling corpse's eyes. His hands danced across his heart, making the sign of the sun. 'I said this was a mistake.'

'Really?' asked Serene. 'I don't think I heard, you were so quiet.'

'This isn't funny, Serene.'

'No, it's not. And it's also not the work of a wight, neither. Not any wight I've ever heard of anyway.'

The big man swallowed, and nodded. 'You're right. So what happened?'

'That's obvious, don't you think?'

'Mirika.' Yelen stuttered the word, not wanting to give it voice, but wanting to hear another say it even less. 'My sister did this.' She took a deep breath. One way or another, there was worse to come, but she had to be sure. 'We need to find the others.'

***

It didn't take long to reach the rest of Mariast's expedition. Their footprints, previously so measured, so ordered, now left only a mass of disturbed snow in their wake. Kas led the company sure-footedly around the lower slopes of two barrows, and up the gentle rise of a third. As before, the barrow-wisps scattered before the corpsefire, but Yelen barely noticed, too afraid of what they might find.

'Stay together,' hissed Magnis. 'One of you strays too far from the corpsefire, you'll feel an icy hand on your shoulder.'

Weapons out, the Gilded Rose reached the crest and moved through the jumble of monoliths and barrow-stones. Yelen clutched her dagger tight, more for comfort than out of any expectation it would do her any good if it came to a fight. It didn't help. Not even a bit.

'I have them.'

Kas took a long step over the low stones of a ghost-fence, and onto the summit proper, wisps dancing frantically away from his approach. Yelen shrugged off Serene's restraining hand and followed. She had to know.

The skirmish below had been as nothing to whatever battle had occurred on the barrow-top. Here, boots had churned the snow so badly that the bare, permafrosted soil glinted in the lantern light. There were ice-locked bodies everywhere, a ghastly tableau of terrified and contorted faces, each one caught in the act of defiance, or of flight. Yelen knew they'd never thaw. More statues to join those already atop the buried tomb.

'I've found her!' Darrick's tremulous shout echoed between the monoliths.

Yelen reached his side a fraction after Magnis.

'For the love of…' The master of the Gilded Rose took a deep breath before pressing on, a little of his customary confidence back in his voice. 'Keep your voice *down*, Darrick. We're risking too much simply by being up here.'

Yelen didn't have to wonder what he meant. The darkness had taken on a brooding, almost angry, quality. Bad enough that the living transgressed on the territory of the dead at all, but to defame the summit of a barrow with their presence…?

Magnis shook his head. 'Well, that's another legend brought to a squalid end.'

Mariast's frozen remains lay in the snow on heels and haunches, one hand raised up in defence, or perhaps in the act of some last, desperate conjuration.

'Aye,' said Marcan. 'She'll find plenty of familiar faces waiting for her in the frozen hells.' He shot a glance at Kain. 'I hope that's not too disrespectful?'

Kain glowered at him, but said nothing.

Serene snorted. 'No one'll miss the Green Widow. She's killed more new blood than the giants of the Grey District.'

'I will,' said Kas. 'She still owes me money.'

'More fool you for thinking she'd pay.' Serene's tone was light enough, but her eyes didn't leave Mariast's glittering face. 'Your sister did this?'

Yelen choked back a reply, and settled for a nod. She didn't know, not for sure, but between the storm that had levelled the *Guttered Candle* and the way the Nereta's waters had frozen beneath Mirika's feet…

'Kas?' said Magnis. 'We have any outbound tracks?'

The tracker extended a lazy hand. 'One set, leading away

down the slope over yonder. Even spacing, bare feet.'

'Then she's still alive.' Magnis leaned in close to Yelen, and lowered his voice. 'I know this looks bad, but there's no blood, and no sign of the orb. Maybe Mariast tried to take it? I wouldn't put it past her to have a crack at robbing a lone wanderer.'

Yelen didn't answer. Kardish had been bad enough, but this? A dozen dead in all. She couldn't believe her sister was capable of such a thing. But maybe that was the point? Kardish had died of old age, his tempo stretched to breaking point. There was no sign a similar magic had been used on Mariast's band. Mirika *hadn't* done this. It had merely been her hand that had wielded Szarnos' magic. Magnis was right. There was still hope.

She looked up to say so, but Magnis had drifted away to Kain's side.

'This isn't what I signed up for.' The knight spoke softly, her words barely carrying to Yelen's ears.

'I know,' he replied, just as quietly. 'But we've come too far to turn back when it's within our grasp. I've already waited long enough.'

Yelen twisted away, partly to disguise the fact that she'd heard at all, mostly to conceal her disgust at Magnis' true priorities. He didn't care about Mirika. This was all just a means to an end.

She stared again at Mariast's ice-locked corpse. 'I'm still coming for you, sister,' she whispered. 'Alone, if I have to.'

***

Magnis finally called a halt nearly two hours later. By Yelen's estimate, they were halfway across the Lower Reach – an impressive achievement owing as much to the surprisingly clement weather as to the decision to press on. She tried not to think about it. Things were bad enough without tempting a snowstorm.

As campsite, Kas chose the shoulder of a collapsed barrow, partway between two ghost-fences. Some calamity in years past had caused a landslide, burying the entrance of that particular tomb. No one wanted to risk callers, corpsefires or no.

Magnis placed a ring of a dozen bowls in all, each two or three paces from the next. That created a protected space large enough to house the whole company, as well as a single, conventional fire, lest the cold claim lives even as the wights were held at bay. Twelve brilliant white flames to mark a ring of safety against an uncaring night.

Barrow-wisps bobbed and wove beyond the fiery perimeter like flies at a window. Yelen peered out into the darkness, trying to catch a glimpse of their masters, but saw nothing. It didn't mean they weren't there, of course. She felt sure they were close by.

'Delightful.' Magnis rubbed his hands together, a man well-pleased with his efforts. Not that he ever seemed less than impressed with himself. 'Six hours to go. Three two-man watches means four hours sleep apiece, and very glad of it we'll be.'

He fished in the pocket of his robes and tossed a small hourglass at Marcan. The swarthy man fumbled the catch, cursed floridly and stooped to pick it up from the snow.

'You and Kain take the first,' said Magnis. 'Tas and Darrick have the middle, and I'll take the last with Serene.'

'What about me?' said Yelen.

'Get some sleep. You had a difficult night, and tomorrow's a long day. You'll need it.'

She pursed her lips. 'I'll stand my turn like everyone else. I don't want special treatment, and I don't need coddling.'

Marcan snorted, then gasped as Serene drove an elbow into his belly.

Kain lowered herself onto the remnants of an ancient boundary wall. 'Never turn down a good night's sleep when it's offered. The road stretches on. Your turn will come.'

'She's right,' said Magnis. 'Let this lot have a broken night's sleep. That's part of what I pay them for.'

Yelen considered, and nodded. The more she thought on it, the less she wanted to give up what little rest lay ahead. Especially as she expected Azzanar to be waiting in ambush, as she had many times of late. 'What about you? Who's paying you?' The question, spurred on by her recently overheard conversation, came out more arch than she intended.

Magnis seemed not to notice. 'Why, providence of course. I aim to leave behind a legend that will awe generations to come, and I'd rather be remembered as a dashing, generous fellow who shared his companions' burdens. You wouldn't deny me that, would you?'

She forced a wry smile. 'I suppose not.'

'Good, because it's your turn tomorrow. I'm not that generous.'

CHAPTER ELEVEN

Despite Yelen's fear that Azzanar was lurking, waiting to manipulate her dreams, her slumbers passed without the demon's honeyed voice. More than that, there were no dreams, no nightmares – just the blackness of oblivion, lit from within by the white light of corpsefires, and of smouldering kindling.

She awoke twice, stirred from sleep by some sound, or a forgotten fragment of memory, striving to become a dream. Each time, Yelen stared into the light of the nearest corpsefire, drinking in that strange, impossible spring-scent until she dozed calmly off to sleep.

Then she awoke once more. This time, into darkness.

The corpsefires were out. And the darkness was alive with movement. Watchful. Patient.

Yelen licked dry lips, not daring even to breathe lest it draw attention. Her heart thudded against her ribcage, the sound so loud she couldn't fathom how it hadn't yet given her away. How could the fires be out? Twelve hours, Magnis had said. Why had no one raised the alarm?

Slowly, a hair's breadth at a time, Yelen craned her head. At every moment, she expected the darkness to surge towards her, for the wisps above to enfold her in their sickly green light. How had it come to this? Had the Gilded Rose abandoned her? Was she dreaming? No. It couldn't be a dream. The ground was cold beneath her, and the hurried thump-thump of her heart too painful for mere imagination.

At last, a familiar figure crept into view.

'Darrick?' The whisper crossed Yelen's lips before she could stop it.

The big man sat atop the boundary wall, back set against the collapsed barrow. His uneven face – normally so ruddy and full of colour – was a pallid and mottled blue. His mouth lay open in a silent, distended scream. His eyes stared blankly into the darkness. To all appearances, Darrick looked as though he'd died screaming in terror. But how had she not heard him?

With a breathy hiss, a section of darkness detached itself from the black of night, and surged towards her.

Yelen instinctively rolled away through the embers of the campfire, too terrified even to scream. She felt a flare of sharp, savage heat as embers burst around her. Then white light enveloped her. She'd been wrong. Not all of the corpsefires were out, only those to her front.

The billowing darkness screeched as its impetus carried it into the light. Yelen had a brief glimpse of skeletal claws and pale green eyes. Then it was gone, coiling back into the safety of the dark, steam trailing behind it.

Yelen rolled to a sitting position, taking in the state of the campsite for the first time. Yes, six of the corpsefires still burned, offering a semicircular haven to one side of the fire. She wasn't sure what worried her more – the four piles of bundled blankets that should have had bodies in them, or the two that were occupied, but deathly still.

Eyes darting back and forth across the roiling darkness, Yelen crossed to the two occupied bundles – both in what she clung to as the 'safe' side of the campsite. She turned the first over, and found herself staring back into Magnis' taut, wide-eyed face.

He, at least, wasn't dead – or not yet. His lips worked feverishly, his eyes twitching like a man locked in a waking dream. She'd seen that expression before, on Mirika's face after she'd escaped from the barrow, but this was a thousand times worse.

Something in the darkness hissed, regathering its courage.

Yelen waved a hand in front of Magnis' face. 'Cavril? Cavril, wake up! Please wake up!'

He offered no response. No indication he'd even heard.

Abandoning her attempts to rouse Magnis, Yelen scrambled through the snow to Kain's side. The knight was every bit as senseless as her employer, her expression of dread all the more disturbing for how out of place it looked on a face normally so stoic.

Mirika had spoken of a wight crawling around inside her head. Talking to her. Embracing her. She'd made light of it at the time, but that's what Mirika always did. Had the horrors of the barrows, unable to reach their prey still in the light, turned to more insidious methods? If so, why hadn't she been affected? The answer was obvious. Yelen had one thing that the others lacked: Azzanar. She couldn't imagine the demon consenting to some mere undead vestige claiming a soul she considered rightfully hers.

Azzanar. She'd sworn not to seek the demon's help. But this was different, wasn't it? This was about more than her. At least two other lives hung in the balance. Maybe as many as five, if her missing companions weren't already dead. No one would blame her.

Yelen choked back a sob. One companion dead. Two beyond her reach. Three... gone. But where? What was she to do? What could she do? There had to be something.

'Think, Yelen, think.'

She could stay in the half circle. She'd be safe there. Or would she? What if those corpsefires went out too? And what then? Mirika. Azzanar. The Gilded Rose. Was she to spend her whole life being saved by others?

No.

Yelen wasn't sure what corner of her soul sparked that defiance, but she clung to it as if it were the most precious of gemstones – as if it were the sole cord that bound her to her absent sister. She didn't have Mirika's abilities, she might have been alone, but she wasn't helpless.

Yelen peered into the dark, to where the other bowls had rested – *had* being the operative word. Some had been upended, emptied into the snow. Others were full of snow themselves, their fires doused from within. It wasn't accidental. Someone had done it on purpose, but who? One of the missing trio. That made sense. Marcan, Kas or Serene. But why? Yelen shook the thought away. It didn't matter. Not now. The important thing was that *if* the other fires had been sabotaged, the others *should* keep burning.

The darkness surged. Yelen's heart leapt into her throat. She flinched away, tripping on Kain's prone body and nearly upending another of the corpsefire bowls. Once again, the wight spiraled away as the light of the corpsefires touched it. But it had come closer this time. So close, its chill backwash rose goosebumps across her exposed flesh.

Yelen was moving before she even realised she'd decided to act. She dived forward, out beyond the protective corpse-light, fingers scrabbling for one of the extinguished bowls. It tipped, dangerously close to spilling its contents into the snow. Then her hooked fingers caught against the rim, and it was hers. Another moment – another panicked scrabble at arm's length – and she had a second bowl.

Out in the darkness, the wight finally realised Yelen had left the sanctuary of the light. Darkness writhing about it, the spirit issued a low, hissing screech and surged to claim her.

Yelen was already shuffling backwards. As the wight closed, her heel caught on a haversack. She toppled backwards, clutching the purloined bowls tight to her chest so as not to spill their precious contents.

The fall saved her life. The wight's claws met empty air above her head. Then it shrieked and withdrew, driven back by the light.

Breath fluttering, Yelen scrambled to her knees and set the bowls down beside the fire. So far, so good. She tried not to think about the other wights she'd glimpsed as she'd fallen, or how close the first wight's pale claws had come to seizing her as she'd fallen, and turned her attention to the bowls.

The contents were sodden, drowned by thawing snow. Sodden, but not useless.

Yelen glanced at the fire. It had gone untended too long, the dull red embers covered in a thick layer of ash. But that was okay. She could work with that.

Seizing the haversack that had so lately saved her life, she ransacked its contents until she found the very thing she sought. Numb fingers scrambling at the pouch strings, she tipped the contents into the fire.

The result was everything she could have wanted. The alchemist's powder caught light at once, the dying fire bursting into brilliant, furious life. Yelen thrust fresh kindling in the flames. The blaze stabilized, the warmth of it every bit as much a relief as the hope it offered.

Perhaps sensing circumstances shifting against it, the wight hissed its voiceless challenge and swept towards her.

Yelen didn't retreat from the pale claws. 'The hells with you!'

Wedging her toes beneath the nearer of her two salvaged bowls, she kicked the contents into the flames.

The corpsefire mixture crackled as the fire took it. A great hiss of steam joined the leaping flames. Then the air was full of the scent of springtime, and a white light ten times as brilliant as those on the periphery.

The wight had no chance to evade, and no time to retreat. The rippling darkness of its robes burned in the light like parchment in flame; its pallid, misshapen bones melted like snow in sunlight. With one last, thin wail, it was gone – its spirit at last cast into the frozen hells it had evaded for so long.

'I hope that hurt!'

The panic of recent moments subsided in the rush of victory. Yelen's breaths still came hard and fast, but elation now drove them as much as desperation. More. The creatures could be fought. They could be beaten.

Yelen glanced at the fire, still blazing white. She suspected the corpsefire mixture wouldn't last as long as it would have in the small bowl, but it offered a reprieve, and she was grateful for it.

The darkness billowed and hissed, but no wight sought to challenge the light that had claimed its brother.

Knees skimming through the snow, Yelen knelt beside Magnis. His face was calmer, his breathing steadier. Whatever enchanted dream had claimed him was receding, driven back by the light and scent of the vast corpsefire burning a few paces away. Kain too seemed better. The expression of terror gone from her features.

A scream split the air.

A piercing, drawn out wail, it was identifiable neither as a man's nor a woman's, a cry of terror or of pain. It lingered, then faded, leaving an aftermath almost as wearing on the nerves as its sudden onset.

Yelen flicked her eyes across the empty bedding. Marcan. Kas. Serene. She didn't much care about Marcan, still hadn't forgiven him for gutting Mirika like a hog. But Kas and Serene had been friendly – certainly more welcoming than she'd have been under similar circumstances.

But what could she do? Her dagger was a pitiful weapon against such foes. Kain's sword lay scabbarded beside its sleeping mistress, but Yelen had no idea if she could heft the thing, let alone defend herself with it.

Again, the temptation arose to plead with Azzanar, to beg for her help. Again Yelen crushed it down. She'd already proved she didn't need the demon's help. She could do so again. Her eyes fell across the second bowl she'd rescued from the darkness, and the spark of an idea formed.

Yelen all but ran to the bundle of kindling. She selected three of the longest, straightest branches and bound them together with strips torn from Darrick's bedding, wrapping the cloth thicker and tighter at the far end. She scooped the snow from the rescued corpsefire bowl and drained away the slushy, icy water. She lost some of the mixture along the way, but it didn't matter – or so she hoped.

Oil from one of the lanterns joined the mixture, creating a slimy, foul-smelling mulch that she scooped onto the makeshift torch's padded end. The porous cloth drank in the mixture. Wiping her hand on the remains of Darrick's blankets, Yelen whispered a prayer to whatever god or goddess might be listening, and thrust the end of the torch into the campfire. Searing white flames burst into life at its head.

Yelen pressed a hand to her mouth to still the involuntary peal of delighted laughter. Now she had a weapon.

No longer afraid of the circling wights, she retrieved another of the silent, snow-choked bowls from the perimeter and tossed the mixture onto the fire. The white light leapt to new heights, a promise that it would keep Magnis and Kain safe from the wights' clutches a while longer yet.

Taking a deep breath, Yelen plunged into the darkness.

* * *

It wasn't hard to follow her missing companions' trail. Wights didn't leave footprints, and four sets led away from the camp. Yelen wondered about that, until she found a fourth set tracking back towards the fire. She'd already accepted that one of her companions had betrayed the others, and this felt like proof.

Abandoning the returning trail, she pressed on after those that remained. On she trudged, the bravado of her pursuit fading as the warmth of the fire grew more distant. Twice, wights barrelled out of the darkness. Twice, a sweep of the torch sent them back. But she'd come too far to turn back now. Squaring her shoulders, Yelen pressed on, trying not to think about how the torch's light already seemed dimmed, how the barrow-wisps began crowding closer.

The tracks divided beyond the low stones of a ghost-fence, two pairs veering off around the side of the barrow, one continuing ahead with ragged, uneven steps. Not really knowing why she made the decision, Yelen hurried after the lone trail, her urgency fed by the dying torchlight, and a horrible premonition of what she'd find.

Kas sat propped against the plinth of a spread-winged statue, one hand slack in the snow, the other pressed against a ragged wound in his side. The snow around him was dark with blood, and his skin rubbery and pale. But he still lived, if barely, his chest rising and falling in fitful bursts. His sword, the blade unblooded, lay half-hidden in a nearby snow drift.

The last of Yelen's newfound bravado faded at the sight. She couldn't do anything for him. She doubted anyone could. But a wight wasn't to blame for this. They didn't need blades to kill, and they wouldn't have left him alive. No. This was something else. Kas' assailant had wanted a slow death.

'Kas?' Yelen crouched beside him. 'Who did this to you?'

Awareness flickered into his eyes, violent action hard on its heels. Giving voice to a wordless moan, he flailed at Yelen with his free hand. But there was no strength behind the blind, desperate blows, and his eyes stared blindly past her.

Yelen seized the flailing hand in hers and held it close. 'Kas. It's me. It's Yelen. I'm not going to hurt you.' His struggles faded as the words sunk in. 'Please. Tell me who did this.'

'Led me from the camp.' His croaked words were little more than a whisper, and Yelen had to strain to hear them. 'Cut me open. How…?' His voice faded.

Yelen leaned closer. 'How what? Kas? Kas!'

He gave a last, shuddering breath and lay still, his hand slipping from Yelen's.

Yelen wasn't sure how long she knelt at Kas' side, her thoughts a whirl of loss and anger. Someone *had* betrayed them, Kas had all but said as much. All the signs pointed to Darrick – after all, whatever happened, had happened on their watch. Had he disposed of Kas and then… And then what? The memory of the returning footprints surfaced. Staggered back to the camp to die? Why? Darrick had been terrified of the very idea of entering the Lower Reach. Had he offered up his companions to the wights, hoping the trade would leave him untouched? If that had been his plan, it had failed badly. Though Yelen had never seen a wight's victim before, the mottled blue skin was a common enough feature of delvers' tales. A wight's embrace. She and Mirika had even joked about it, not far from where she now stood.

And if not Darrick, what were the alternatives? Serene? Yelen didn't think so. She'd seen too much genuine affection between her and Kas. She couldn't imagine Serene wanting him harm. No. Marcan was more likely. She'd believe almost anything of the squat, brutish fellow. And if the two were together, it hardly boded well for Serene, did it?

Certainty hardened as the facts fell into place. Marcan had killed Kas. He'd taken Serene, and doused the fires so that the wights would finish what he'd begun.

The torch crackled. Yelen stared at it in growing alarm. Its light was fading. She'd lost too much of the corpsefire mixture to the snows. The breathy hisses of the wights grew louder, the darkness taking shape as their courage returned with the dying of the light.

Grabbing Kas' abandoned sword, Yelen retraced her tracks through the snow. She'd not find Serene before the torch failed, but maybe she'd make it back to the camp. No. She *would* find her, and they'd *both* make it back to the camp. And if Marcan had harmed Serene like he had Mirika, she'd make damn sure he'd pay.

Yelen retraced her outbound footsteps, wights hissing at her heels. The return journey seemed longer, sufficiently so that she began to wonder if she'd somehow gone astray. But no, at last she came to the divergence, hers and Kas' outbound tracks meeting the two sets that vanished around the side of the barrow.

Yelen pressed on through thinning snows. Permafrosted soil underfoot gave way to stone slabs. The low stone walls of the barrow approach, once scarcely waist-high, now reached high above her head, held in place by crumbling buttresses. Grotesques peered down from the ridges, their horned faces seemingly delighted with her approach. And there, dead ahead, where the footprints thinned to nothing on bare stone, the looming barrow-gate, its ancient timbers clasped with rune-set iron.

The night went oddly quiet. Yelen turned around, staring back through the darkness. The wights had gone as if they'd never been. Instinct warned her not to take heart from the sudden development. Azzanar had said that the wights of the Lower Reach were territorial. Yelen suspected she'd crossed into the domain forbidden to her pursuers. The servants of another king, perhaps?

Or maybe, she thought, her skin prickling at the idea

of it, this was the territory of something so terrible it put fear into the cold hearts of the lesser wights.

Swallowing hard, Yelen pressed on before the implications convinced her to turn back.

As Yelen grew closer to the gate, she saw that she'd been mistaken, tricked by the melding of darkness and shadows. Of the two great, iron-bound doors, only one was still closed. The other had collapsed, its rusted iron hasps no longer able to support the desiccated timbers. The remnants of the broken door lay at a drunken angle across the threshold, dust thick around it.

The torch crackled in Yelen's hand. Though the flame still burned, it increasingly did so with the familiar smoky orange of lamp oil, and not the comforting white blaze of corpsefire.

'This is a really, really bad idea.'

But even so, she clambered over the collapsed door and into the barrow.

The space beyond was scarcely wider than the gateway, the walls dressed with lumpen, uneven black stone. Gold glinted from alcoves as she hurried along the passageway, the metal's gleam barely diminished by the thick layer of dust. A delver's fortune, just sitting there, waiting to be claimed, but Yelen ignored it and pressed on.

Further in, the passageway met another running crosswise, offering three possible routes deeper into the barrow. Fortunately, footsteps showed through the dust as plainly as in the snows above. Two pairs. Still two pairs. Reluctantly, Yelen began to doubt her theory about Marcan's betrayal. Why would he kill Kas, and then lead Serene into the barrow? Yelen could almost have believed that it had merely been a freak gust of wind that had broken the ring of corpsefire. Were it not for Kas, lying lifeless in the snow, that was.

The footsteps took the leftmost passage. Yelen followed, eyes and ears straining for any sign of a threat. They found nothing, but that did nothing to set her mind at ease. There was something about the air in the barrow – something pressing on her thoughts. Cold. Malevolent. Say what she liked about Azzanar – and she had – but at least there was always a warmth to the demon's presence.

Yelen passed through chamber after chamber. The crude stone gave way to polished obsidian, traced with gold. With each step, the pressure in her mind grew steadily worse. It drove her on as much as it goaded her to flee, repellent and alluring at the same time. Her progress slowed as she began imagining shapes gathering in the darkness. Yelen's eyes told her there was nothing there; her ears agreed. But her mind would not be convinced.

Thus when a shadow *did* move, she almost ran it through without thinking.

Marcan held up his hands, shrinking back into his hidey-hole between two sarcophagi. 'Easy, girl. It's me.' His voice wavered a tone or two above its normally rich baritone.

'Where's Serene? How did you get here?'

Bloodshot eyes stared into hers. 'I was dreaming, wasn't I? Except I wasn't. Woke up with that… that thing looming over me, eyes boring into me. I ran for it, but this place is like a bloody maze, and pitch dark. I've been wandering for hours.'

More like minutes, Yelen judged. 'I heard you screaming.'

He shifted uncomfortably, a flush of colour in his cheeks going some way to restoring his formally healthy complexion. 'Not proud of that, but you didn't see it. We get out of this, I'm heading back north. I'll take rangifers and white apes over what's down here.' His features contorted in sudden alarm. 'You *do* know the way out?'

'Where's Serene?'

Marcan shook his head. 'She's gone by now. No sense dying too.'

Yelen pursed her lips. 'Where is she?'

He grabbed for the torch. 'Give me that!'

Yelen stepped away, and brandished her borrowed sword. 'I'm not leaving her.'

'Don't be stupid,' he growled. 'Don't make me take that off you.'

She knew it would ordinarily have been a threat worth heeding – Marcan was far stronger than she. But he was unarmed, his sword presumably back at camp, and his every swaying motion betrayed a body on the brink of collapse. Maybe he'd win, but it'd cost him. 'You can help me find Serene, and we all walk out of here, or you can take your chances in the dark. What'll it be?'

'I told you, she's dead.'

'Then she won't be hard to find, will she?'

The beard bristled, and Marcan nodded. 'Have it your way.'

Yelen released a breath she hadn't realised she'd been holding. 'Lead on.'

It transpired that Marcan's claim of the barrow being a labyrinth was less than accurate. Even with his meandering attempt at escape muddying the once-clear trail of footprints, they had no trouble retracing his steps through the vaulted chambers. Yelen suspected that between the oppressive presence and the pitch-blackness of the barrow, he'd simply panicked. Not that she said as much. She didn't know how long the threat of the sword would keep him honest. Even a small provocation might spur him to chance a fight for the torch. Fortunately, Marcan had either recovered his courage, or was too broken inside to consider breaking their agreement.

Marcan drew up a handful of paces from a partially collapsed arch. 'We're here,' he whispered.

Yelen had known as much before he'd spoken. It was as much the pounding pressure in her head as the wisps of green mist curling around the base of the arch. A deep, resonant hiss echoed along the passageway, the voice those of the wights outside, but richer, more sonorous.

Regathering her courage, Yelen pressed her back against the passage wall, and crept towards the arch. She knew the light from the torch would surely give her away long before whatever lurked within caught sight of *her*, but instinct was instinct. With the insidious pressure mounting inside her thoughts, she welcomed anything that helped her feel concealed, unnoticed.

Slowly, carefully, she peered around the edge of the archway.

The chamber beyond was easily twice the size of any she'd seen so far inside the barrow. The walls were lined with alcoves. Each held a stone sarcophagus, some fractured with age, some still whole. And at the far end, beneath the marble gaze of a horned statue, Serene lay motionless on a stone bier, a golden torc at her throat and gemstones in her hair. Whether she was alive or dead, Yelen couldn't tell. At her side stood a shadow wreathed in green mist – the same mist that hid the flagstoned floor from view. As the hissing chant grew in pitch, a stone dagger glinted in the shadow's pale hand. Barrow-wisps swirled above, their patterns shifting with each breathy refrain of the shadow's chant.

The sight of it made Yelen want to turn and run, to flee for the entrance and the illusory safety outside. The pressure in her mind urged her to lay down torch and sword, to take her place upon the bier beside Serene, and await the knife's kiss. Choking down both impulses, she glanced at Marcan. He had his eyes pinched closed, his lips working furiously. He felt it too.

'I'll drive it back,' Yelen breathed, scarcely crediting the evidence of her own ears. 'You grab Serene, and then we run for it.'

He stared at her, face tight. 'You're mad.'

'Probably.' She forced a smile. 'But do you want to die screaming, or laughing?'

Marcan shook his head and sighed. 'You are mad. Go. I'm right behind you.'

Yelen took a deep breath, her nerve wavering now the prospect of action was before her. Then she stepped around the archway, and into the chamber.

She moved softly, quietly, but still each footstep sounded as loud as the crack of a broken twig in a silent forest. But the wight didn't turn, its shapeless, shadowy back remained towards her, all of its attention focused on Serene's motionless figure.

The creature's hiss grew louder, more insistent as Yelen approached, the sound finally breaking up into the rolling syllables of some forgotten tongue. Yelen's arms grew heavy, her thoughts sluggish. Fear replaced by yearning. Was not each step bringing her closer to the one calling for her? To her rightful place upon the bier?

Yelen scrunched her eyes closed. It didn't help. The compulsion remained. Sleep. Submit. Join the slumbers of eternity. She wanted to clap her hands over her ears, silence the sonorous, breathy voice. But how was she to do that with torch in one hand and sword in the other? So she did the only thing she could. Throwing subtlety to the winds, she screamed a wordless challenge, and charged.

The wight spun around at once, its creeping chant building into a hiss of rage. Green eyes flared, and the creature twisted in on itself like a waterspout, or a snake suddenly surprised.

Yelen screamed louder, more to drown her fears than for any effect it might have on her foe. Blood thundered through her ears, driven by a racing pulse. But this was a good thunder, the sort that filled her heart and lungs with courage, with strength.

She thrust the torch forward. The wight screeched and retreated along the length of the bier, scraps of darkness and mist trailing behind. Yelen's confidence soared. She could do this!

Another lunge. Again the wight retreated. Yelen didn't know how long the spirit would remain at bay, but she was determined to enjoy every moment.

'Marcan!'

Yelen risked a glance behind. Marcan edged forward, eyes on the wight.

'Hurry up! I don't know how long I can hold it.'

The wight lunged.

Her attention on Marcan, Yelen barely saw the spirit move. She responded instinctively, lashing out not with the torch, but with the sword. Steel bit into the swirl of robes. The wight screeched and flinched away, the blow meant for Yelen's heart instead raking her shoulder. She cried out – not with the pain of it, but the sudden icy cold. The wight hissed in triumph, and surged forward again.

This time, Yelen was ready. Ignoring the creeping numbness in her shoulder, she thrust the torch into the mass of shadow and mist. The strike was slowed by deadened muscles. But it was fast enough. The wight, unable to check its momentum, fell onto the lit torch.

Its robes caught light, the brilliant white flame spreading across the desiccated cloth as swiftly as they would across sun-bleached scrubland. A terrible keening wail echoed around the chamber. The wight flailed madly, Yelen forgotten as the cleansing flame took hold. With a last tumultuous howl, it fled for a side passage, and vanished into the gloom.

The scream faded with distance. Then it rose in pitch and volume, joined by other loathsome voices.

Her sense of triumph curdling to renewed fear, Yelen glanced back at the bier. 'Marcan…?'

He ripped the torc from Serene's neck and tossed it into a corner. 'Yeah, I have her.' With a grunt, he heaved the woman onto his shoulder, spilling the gems from her hair. Without a backward glance, he loped for the archway.

Yelen glanced at the floor – at the discarded torc and scattered jewels. A king's ransom, enough to buy passage back to Karamasz, and to find a comfortable life. She wanted none of it – she wanted nothing from the barrow but her life.

The distant voices grew louder, nearer. With one last glance in the direction the wight had taken, Yelen fled after Marcan.

* * *

Yelen had expected Marcan's burden to slow him, but he carried Serene as if she weighed nothing at all. This was perhaps a testament to the man's physique, but Yelen suspected fear played the greater part. He waited impatiently at each junction, eyes darting at every shadow as the wail of the awakening barrow rose to fresh heights.

With each step, the numbness in Yelen's shoulder intensified, but she hung onto both torch and sword for grim life, knowing that to abandon either was to invite disaster. Each backward glance betrayed shadows gathering in passageways lately abandoned – the barrow's inhabitants had no intention of letting the upstart living go unpunished, but Yelen had taught them to respect the flame.

The torch flickered.

Yelen stared at it in alarm. It'd last until they reached the camp. It had to.

Another turn, and they were in the entrance chamber. A breathless scramble after that, and they were outside.

The chill morning air washed across Yelen's face, driving away the lingering effects of the barrow-chant. Somehow, it was warmer outside than in the barrow's depths. Or was that hope she felt? Exultation soured as she tried to raise the torch higher. Her arm, frozen at the wight's touch, responded sluggishly. She swayed, suddenly dizzy – the exertions of the night at last catching up with her.

'Follow the footsteps,' she said. 'They'll lead you back.'

Marcan regarded her appraisingly. 'Lead *us* back, you mean.' Without waiting for a reply, he slipped an arm around Yelen's waist and lent his strength to hers. 'Can't leave you behind, not now.'

Yelen opened her mouth to protest. Then she closed it again as a fresh wave of tiredness swept over her, and she realised she'd be glad to have the support.

On they staggered, Marcan seemingly tireless and unhindered by the burden of one unconscious woman, and one rapidly becoming so. Yelen tried to remember how many paces it was to the camp, but the memory eluded her – in the dark, everything looked the same, and terror had driven many details from her mind.

She still heard the wights behind, and surely there were others waiting ahead. Would the ghost-fences keep the group from the barrow from pursuing into rival territory? There was no way to know. There was only the trail of broken snow, and the frail promise of sanctuary at the far end.

'They're still following,' rumbled Marcan. 'Not sure we'll make it.'

'We'll make it,' said Yelen, shrugging free of his supporting arm. She glanced behind, saw the darkness moving. They were closer than she'd thought, and gaining all the time. 'We're nearly there. Just keep going. I'll hold them back.'

Marcan bristled. 'No. Give me the sword. I'll do it.'

'No. Serene can't walk, and I can't carry her.'

He looked sharply away. 'Have it your way.' He paused. 'Listen…'

Yelen shoved him. 'Just go, will you? Otherwise it's not going to matter who stays.'

He gave a sharp nod, and trudged off along the trail, Serene lolling on his shoulder, and barrow-wisps spiralling above his head.

Yelen set her back to the wall and held the torch as high aloft as her numbed shoulder would allow. A minute's head start, then she'd follow.

The torch sputtered and died.

Darkness rushed in, sparks of green wisp-light the only source of illumination. Low, breathy hisses washed over her like laughter. Abandoning the spent torch, Yelen took her borrowed sword in both hands, and waited for the crippling fear to return.

To her surprise, it didn't. There was only a dull, angry rumble deep in her guts. Maybe this was how it was for everyone in their last moments, she thought numbly. One last burst of defiance before the end.

'I'm sorry, Mirika,' she whispered.

The darkness surged. Green eyes shone.

Yelen threw herself aside and landed heavily in the snows. A cold, dry backwash swept over her. The wight hissed with frustration and swirled back around, pale fingers glinting in the wisp-light.

The sword felt cold and heavy in Yelen's hands as she swung. The desperate blow bit deep into the wight's faceless cowl. Its angry screech became a keening wail, and the robes collapsed empty at Yelen's feet.

She didn't see the second wight's approach. She only felt the cold, sharp pain as its claws raked her upper arm.

Yelen lurched away from her new assailant, icy numbness spreading across her shoulder. She sliced at the wight. The fresh leadenness of her sword arm made the blow clumsy. The spirit swooped away, leaving only a few scraps of severed cloth in the snows.

Green eyes blazed all around.

'Come on!' Yelen shouted. 'Scared of me, are you?'

A wight darted towards her. She swung the sword, and the spirit jerked away.

Yelen spun around, never turning her back on a wight

for more than a moment, using the threat of her borrowed blade to keep them at a distance. But with each revolution, they grew bolder, withdrew with greater reluctance. They knew she was tiring. They knew it could only end one way.

She could see their humpbacked silhouettes now, the darkness within the darkness betrayed by the dancing light of the barrow-wisps. Would they leave her dead in the snow like Darrick, Yelen wondered, or drag her back to their tombs, and make her as they were? She gave a thin, mirthless laugh. Azzanar wouldn't like being shackled to a spirit any more than she would a corpse. There was solace in that, but it was thin and bitter as ash.

The wights closed in a final time. Yelen marshalled the last embers of her strength, and gripped the sword tightly.

'Enough! She is mine.'

The shout rumbled like a landslide, ice and rock grinding together in a promise of icy death. It reverberated in the pit of Yelen's stomach, stripping away what remained of her confidence with each mournful syllable.

The wights shrank away before Yelen's disbelieving eyes, their fear of the new-come voice seemingly every bit as abiding as her own.

A new shape gathered in the darkness, its outline picked out by the flickering barrow-wisps. It was tall and cadaverous, the scarlet robes hanging awkwardly from an angular, fleshless body. Green light blazed from hollow eye sockets, casting peculiar shadows across the skull's empty, skeletal rictus. Yelen had seen it before, at repose. The body of Szarnos the Great urged to new and ghastly life.

Yelen stared in horror as the apparition approached. It was one thing to hear legends of ancient sorcerers come back from the dead, but quite another to see one with her own eyes. She wondered distantly how this could be. What use had Szarnos for Mirika if he'd reclaimed his own body?

'Abase yourselves, worthless creatures!'

Szarnos spread his arms wide. The wights cowered like the mortal vassals they'd once been. Yelen sank to her knees, not wishing to draw the undead sorcerer's attention more than she already had. Not that the words 'she is mine' occasioned much comfort so far as that went.

A hand tugged at Yelen's arm. 'Not you, girl.'

Startled, Yelen turned and found herself staring into Kain's expressionless face. The knight was still pale, and had dark, brooding shadows under her eyes, but she was no undead apparition.

'Snap out of it.' Kain reinforced her point with a vicious tug on Yelen's arm. 'He can't keep them fooled forever.'

Yelen glanced at the wights. Not one of them paid her any heed. Realization dawned. 'Magnis?' she whispered. 'That's Magnis?'

'Good thing this lot's brains are all rotted away, or they'd know it too. Now come *on.*'

Yelen allowed Kain to lead her away, but kept her eyes on the huddled wights. Was it her imagination, or were some of them looking restless? Magnis' illusion was convincing to her living eyes, but how long would it trick the senses of the undead?

'I have returned!' boomed Magnis. 'And claim these lands as I did before! Return to your tombs, and await my command!'

Not one of the wights moved.

Yelen and Kain drew parallel with the worm-eaten image of Szarnos. As they did, the first wight rose from its abasement. A bony claw extended from beneath a tattered sleeve, and a sibilant challenge hissed across the darkness.

'Told you,' muttered Kain. 'Move!'

For his part, Magnis clearly hadn't given up. 'You defy me? Have you forgotten the power I wield?' The Szarnos-image struck a bombastic pose, arms spread as if to encircle the world.

'What is he doing?' hissed Yelen. 'I've seen drunken mummers more convincing.'

'That's Magnis,' said Kain. 'His illusions are flawless until he opens his mouth.'

More wights rebelled, joining the first in hissed accusation. They flowed across the snow, their numbers growing. Ahead, Yelen glimpsed the most beautiful sight she'd ever seen – a soft, white glow lighting the shoulder of the barrow mound. The camp. They were nearly back. Almost safe.

The air filled with a venomous hiss as the wights surged forward. The Szarnos-image shattered like breaking glass, and Magnis fled towards Yelen and Kain. 'Go! Go!'

He thundered past Yelen in a spray of snow. Kain gave Yelen a shove. 'You heard him.'

'What about you?'

Kain shrugged her bastard sword from its shoulder sheath. 'What about me?'

Yelen nodded, not wanting to force a reprise of her own earlier argument with Marcan. Then she set off after Magnis, leaving Kain to her work.

She glanced back over her shoulder as she ran, fearful of what she'd see.

Kain held her sword at high guard, the blade levelled at head height. A wight howled out of the darkness. The sword flashed, so fast that Yelen barely saw it move. The wight collapsed with a sound like ripping cloth. Then Kain took a long step back, the sword back at guard.

Yelen looked again several times over the course of her retreat. Each time the scene was the same: a yowling shape severed by a blur of steel, Kain's armoured form making an unhurried retreat across the snows. For all the concern the knight displayed, she could have been sparring, and with unskilled children, at that. Once again, Yelen wondered where Magnis had found her.

At last, Yelen reached the fire, the light as welcome as the alien warmth. Serene sat shuddering beside the flames, Magnis at her side. Marcan reclaimed his sword, and moved to the light's edge to watch Kain at work, his open-mouthed amazement obvious even through his beard.

Serene stared up at Yelen as she approached, her eye red-rimmed and her face pale. 'Kas?'

Yelen hesitated, but what was there to say? 'I'm sorry.' She felt Darrick's cold dead gaze on her as she spoke the words. The certainty that he'd caused all this returned, harder than ever. Nothing else made sense. 'It was Darrick. He lured Kas from the camp, and left him for the wights in the hope they'd leave him alone. Kicked over the corpsefires, too. All for nothing. The wights had refused his sacrifice, and killed him instead.'

Marcan spat.

Magnis stared blankly at the blue-tinged body. 'I should have sent him back.'

'Should've cut his throat, you mean.' Serene spoke the words through taut lips.

'Maybe. He's paid now.'

'Doesn't help Kas, does it?' She twisted away, her words choked off.

Kain stepped into the circle, her sword once more in its sheath. 'They've gone. Even the dead know when they're on a hiding to nothing.'

'They'll be back,' said Magnis. 'They won't let our trespass stand, and I don't fancy trying that trick again. It takes a rare talent and a deal of effort to root an illusion in an undead mind, even if I do say so myself. I'm not sure it'd work again.' He peered thoughtfully at Yelen.

'I didn't have any choice,' said Yelen, unsure why she felt so defensive. 'I couldn't leave them!'

'Damn right she couldn't,' muttered Marcan. 'Hells, Cavril, I know you think we're all expendable, but there are limits!'

Serene said nothing. Her eye was closed and her interlaced knuckles were white as snow.

'You did the right thing, girl.' For once, Kain's voice held a note of approval even... of warmth. 'And you've more than earned your passage, hasn't she, Cavril?'

'What?' Magnis tore his gaze from Darrick's corpse. 'Yes. Twice over. Gather whatever's useful from their packs, and we'll head out. Everyone carries a corpsefire bowl. I want to be gone from this place.'

* * *

When dawn arrived, it found the denuded company of the Gilded Rose on the crest overlooking the Lower Reach. They'd walked without rest or food through the early hours.

Magnis and Kain had taken lead and rearguard respectively. Neither seemed any the worse for their wight-sent dreams, and possessed both strength and alertness that Yelen knew was wholly lacking from herself. Marcan and

Serene trudged at her side, each lost in private worlds, one of humiliation, and one of grief. Yelen had tried to give Serene Kas' sword, only to be refused.

'Keep it,' she'd said. 'You've earned it, love. And gods know you might yet need it.'

Only when the barrow hills were lost beneath the ridge, and the sun burning bright in the sky above, did Magnis call a halt.

'An hour, no more,' he said, as Marcan coaxed life into a fire. 'Some food will do us all good, but I don't want to get caught up here if another storm comes in.'

Yelen nodded absently, but a greater worry remained with her. It had grown like a canker in her thoughts, fed by cold and sorrow. 'What's the point?' she demanded. 'We've lost the trail, haven't we? How will we find it without Kas?'

Serene flinched at the name. Not much, but enough to make Yelen feel guilty.

Magnis spread his hands. 'Everything we've seen suggests your sister's retracing her steps. We'll keep on, and hope that holds true.'

'And if it doesn't?'

'One problem at a time, girl,' said Kain. 'No point planning for a tomorrow that won't come. Unless you've a better idea?'

Yelen bit back a retort. Truth was, she hadn't even a *worse* idea. She told herself that she should be glad that the Gilded Rose were prepared to press on after the disaster in the Lower Reach. She was tired. She knew she was tired. Weariness made everything seem hopeless. Mirika was alright. She had to be. 'I'm going to take a walk.'

Marcan glanced up from the smouldering kindling. 'Don't go too far. Wolves don't come up here, but there's always something looking for a warm meal.'

'I'll come with you.' Serene half-rose, but subsided as Yelen waved her down.

'I just need to clear my head. I won't wander, I promise.'

Magnis exchanged a look with Kain. The knight nodded, almost imperceptibly.

'Very well,' said Magnis. 'You've earned that much.'

Yelen set her back to the group and retraced her steps through the trees until she made out the dancing barrow-wisps far below. She wasn't sure what had driven her to look back one last time. Perhaps it was the fact that she'd left more than Darrick and Kas behind. Part of *her* was still there. The part of her that had always needed someone else to get her out of trouble. What if that was what she'd needed all along – not to run from Mirika's shadow, but to cast her own? In either event, it dismissed Azzanar's claims of a future in which she begged for the demon's aid. That alone was progress.

Yelen cast a glance back the way she'd came, but saw nothing but the trees. None of the company had followed her. 'I've beaten you,' she whispered. 'I don't need you. I can look after myself.'

'*Oh really?*' said Azzanar. '*Is that what you think just happened?*'

Yelen grimaced. She hadn't thought the demon had been listening, but perhaps this was for the best – an opportunity to put her in her place. 'Yes. I'm learning to stand for myself. You and I came together because I wanted to be like Mirika. But I don't have to be like Mirika. I can be myself.'

The demon chuckled, wending sinuously around her thoughts. '*Oh, the lesson's not over yet.*'

The certainty in the silent voice sent a shiver down Yelen's spine. 'What do you mean?'

'*I confess, I'm surprised you handled that without pleading for help. That's normally what you do, after all. When I set this little game in motion, I thought it would force your hand, but it doesn't matter. Like I told you before, I'm close to the surface now. Things are different. Especially when you're asleep.*'

The cold shiver settled in Yelen's gut like a lump of ice. Kas' last, garbled words took on a different meaning. *Led me from the camp.* And he'd fought her at first. She'd thought that the panicked action of a dying man, but it wasn't, was it? Led me from the camp.

You led me from the camp.

Slowly, as if in a dream, Yelen set a hand to her dagger and tugged if from her sheath. It came slowly, reluctantly, and a glance at the blade revealed why. It was crusted with blood.

Yelen stuffed a fist into her mouth to stifle a gasp. 'No! No. I didn't.'

She fell to her knees, scrubbing desperately at the blade with handfuls of snow, as if erasing the blood would likewise remove the guilt. Fragments of memory flooded in. Taking Kas by the hand. Blood warm on her fingers. The weight of the rock as she struck Darrick's senses away. All distant, like a horrible dream, but too real to deny.

'It wasn't me!'

'*Oh, but it was, poppet,*' laughed Azzanar. '*At least as far as the others will be concerned. And believe me, I'm just getting started.*'

CHAPTER TWELVE

The storm returned less than an hour after the company set off again, confirming to Yelen that the brooding city hated her, and everyone she associated with. This time, the storm was more wind than snow – a development that came as both good and bad. Good, because it meant the company could see well enough to proceed. Bad, because the combination of violent gusts and unsteady ground made the going even more treacherous than before.

As in their escape from the Lower Reach, Magnis took the lead and Kain the rear, with Yelen and the others plodding on in the centre. No one spoke. Or if they did, the wind snatched the words away before they reached Yelen's ears. That was fine with her. She didn't want to talk to anyone. She didn't even want to think. More than at any point since she'd fallen in with the Gilded Rose, Yelen felt alone in a crowd.

Unfortunately, there was no hiding from her own thoughts in the strange isolation of the storm. They buffeted her just as surely as the winds, and their daggers of guilt were every bit as sharp as the gale's teeth.

She'd killed Kas, and Darrick. Yelen tried telling herself that it hadn't been her will that had struck the blows, only her hands, but it didn't help. Azzanar had no power without her, no means of interacting with the outside world. If she hadn't been present, the two would still be alive.

It didn't take much to know *why* Azzanar had acted as she had. In one fell swoop, she'd taken revenge for the slights Yelen had heaped upon her, and placed her host in a situation that required her help were it to be survived. That the latter half of the gamble had failed was the only bright point, and it was a slender comfort. If Azzanar could seize control of her body at will, then what good did it do to keep resisting her? No, Yelen decided. The demon couldn't control her at will, otherwise she'd have already done it. She needed her host weak to do so, and no one was at a lower ebb than asleep.

Then and there, Yelen realised that if she were to have any chance of staying in control, she'd not be able to sleep. It was impossible. She could perhaps manage for a day, maybe even two, but the next time she closed her eyes it would be Azzanar who opened them, not her.

Hours passed, punctuated by the howl of the wind and the spray of ice across Yelen's face. As the imposing bulk of Blackstena crematorium appeared in the distance, another unpleasant thought occurred. Azzanar had suppressed her memories of the previous night. Who was to say that there weren't more memories – worse memories – waiting to be uncovered. Yelen found it all too easy to imagine exactly what Azzanar had said with her voice in order to lure Kas from the safety of the camp, and she was certain the demon's imagination was a deep, dark ocean whose deeps she'd never plumb.

But what else could she do? Confess to the Gilded Rose that she'd murdered two of their friends? That she'd sabotaged the circle of corpsefires, leaving them at the mercy of the wights? Magnis might listen to the truth. Kain? Not likely, not following the offer to cut out her heart. Marcan? No chance. And Serene…

Time and again, Yelen ran the conversations through her head, always imagining the worst of all possible outcomes. But then, what positives were there to consider? The course, such as it was, seemed certain. If she could only stay awake until they found Mirika… It would change nothing for her, of course, but at least she'd have done all she could for her sister.

If it wasn't already too late…

* * *

Blackstena crematorium was much as Yelen had last seen it, though the room in which she and Mirika had taken shelter was foul with troll dung. Marcan declared it too fresh to take chances, so he and Kain made a full circuit of the ground floor while Magnis and Serene set up a temporary camp in a relatively clean side chamber. Yelen still couldn't bring herself to speak to them, and stared moodily out across the furnace room. Part of her hoped that the others wouldn't return – two less people with whom she'd be forced to share her guilt.

Behind her, the fire crackled into life.

'Ah, that's better. Cavril Magnis triumphs again.'

'Yes, Cavril,' Serene tried to sound scathing, but Yelen could tell her heart wasn't in it. 'Truly, you have mastered a trick known to any child over the age of four.'

'You didn't see me last night. I was magnificent. Yelen will tell you.'

215

Dully, Yelen realised a response was required. 'Yes, I suppose you were.'

Magnis shook his head. 'Suppose? A true master is never appreciated in his own lifetime.' He stumbled to his feet, brushed himself down and set a billy can on its tripod above the flames. 'If you'll excuse me, I'll leave you ladies to hold the fort, while I see how our errant companions are faring. The mood Marcan was in, I imagine he'll be searching every nook and cranny.'

So saying, Magnis crossed into the furnace room and vanished into the maze of passages. Yelen watched him go, only belatedly realizing that the very last thing she wanted was to be left alone with Serene.

'I never thanked you, did I?'

Yelen turned from the doorway. Serene sat facing away, poking the fire with a stick. She had her sleeping blankets wrapped around her like a cocoon. For the first time since Yelen had known her, she looked strangely fragile.

'You don't have to,' said Yelen, the words tasting like lies. 'I just did what needed to be done.'

'That's not what Marcan said,' Serene replied, her voice flat and lifeless. 'He told me he'd have left me, but you gave him no choice.'

Yelen couldn't think when they'd had the chance to speak of it between the walk and the wind, but nodded anyway. 'Fear's hard to control. Not sure any of us were ourselves last night.'

Serene poked at the fire. 'Don't be so sure, love. I've seen a lot of men and women at their lowest moments, just before the end. That's the moment in which you find out who you truly are, or that's what they say. Boiled down to the essence. Marcan didn't like what he saw. What about you?'

'I did, at first,' Yelen admitted. 'But I keep thinking about the others, how they died.'

Serene's shoulders slumped, just a fraction. 'Kas wouldn't want you carrying guilt for him.' She spat into the fire. 'As for Darrick, I hope he's getting his penance in the frozen hells.'

'I hope he's getting what he deserves,' said Yelen carefully. Despite her earlier resolution, she was gripped by an overwhelming desire to confess to Serene, and to hells with the consequences. But there was such a thing as too much honesty. 'I can't tell you how sorry I am about Kas.'

'He used to tell me he wasn't much of a catch,' said Serene. 'And he was right. But he was mine. That's what mattered.' She gave the fire a vicious stab with the stick. 'You know what I wish? That the wights hadn't got to Darrick.'

She didn't have to explain why. But for all the implied violence in Serene's words, her tone was more sorrowful than defiant. At a loss for anything to say, Yelen did the only thing she could – she sat down beside the other woman and held her close.

For a time, the only sound was the crackle and sputter of the flames, and the gentle burble of the water in the billy can as the heat took hold. It was hypnotic, soothing, and with the warmth of the fire and after a night in which she'd had far less sleep than she'd originally supposed, Yelen found herself drifting, nodding...

A blood-curdling roar echoed along the furnace hall, jolting Yelen from her near-slumber. She leapt to her feet, hand going to Kas' sword. 'What was that?'

'Sounded like a troll.' Serene was already at the door, daggers in hand. 'Stay here.'

She hurried off down the furnace hall, the tails of her greatcoat flapping behind. With one last glance at the fire, Yelen hurried on behind.

Magnis was waiting for them at the foot of the broken-down stairs leading to the upper levels. 'Nothing to see, ladies. There *was* a troll left in the building. Kain and Marcan are seeing to its eviction.'

Another roar rang out, followed by a dull, meaty *thwack*.

Serene moved toward the stairs. 'I'm going to help.'

Magnis set a hand on her shoulder. 'I think Marcan's working out a little... anxiousness.' Serene offered him a baleful stare, and he snatched his hand away. 'However...'

Serene ran up the stairs without a backward glance. Magnis shook his head. 'You wouldn't know it, but I used to command respect, once upon a time.'

Yelen glanced at the stairs. 'She's not herself.'

'Understandable. But who is, around here?' He sank against the wall. 'The Magnis luck strikes again, no doubt. Perhaps I shouldn't have come here?'

'Here?'

'To Felstad. I had some notion of raising enough funds to hire an army, but I suspect I underestimated the difficulty of such a course.'

Yelen frowned, her own difficulties forgotten. 'But you're already wealthy.'

'Oh, I am, am I?'

'Everyone says so. Azra, for one.'

Magnis snorted. 'So it must be true.' He shrugged. 'I'm not poor, certainly, but armies are expensive, and so are their rations.'

Yelen opened her mouth to speak. The troll roared again, this time more with pain than with rage, or so she thought – so she *hoped*. A peal of deep laughter rang out after. Marcan, at least, was enjoying himself.

'Shouldn't we help?' Yelen asked, as soon as she had any chance of being heard.

Magnis shook his head. 'Kain will step in if they get into any difficulty. Fifty like her and I wouldn't need an army.'

'Why do you need one at all?'

'It's a long story, but it boils down to a very messy war over inheritance.' Magnis' lips twisted ruefully. 'Suffice to say, a distant cousin argued with my great-grandfather's choices, and resolved to take by force that to which he was unentitled. My parents are dead. My sister's gods alone knows where. I doubt she's dead – Rufrick never could resist a pretty face.' His voice tightened. 'The rest of my branch of the family are either hanging from gallows or grovelling at Rufrick's feet. I don't wish to sound dramatic, but I'll see him dead if it's the last thing I do. If he's harmed Elien, that death may take some time coming.'

Magnis smiled, as if the matter were of no mind, but Yelen wasn't fooled. Beneath his carefree, almost flippant exterior, Cavril Magnis was wound very tightly indeed.

'That's horrible,' she said. 'I'm sorry.'

'Life is never what we'd make of it,' said Magnis. 'That's why I want the orb. I've three buyers fighting over it. The price won't buy me the swords I need, but it'll be a huge step forward.' Another bellow split the air. 'Oh dear, that one sounded like it hurt. And now you know the terrible tale of Cavril Magnis. I'd be grateful if you didn't tell the others. Kain aside, they think I'm only in this for the thrills. I'd hate to disillusion them.'

Yelen reflected that it wasn't all that long ago she'd believed exactly the same. 'Why tell her? For that matter, why tell me?'

He smoothed down his moustache. 'You think someone like Kain would hang around a delver gang without a deeper cause lingering in the background? She's looking for a purpose, not a score.' He shrugged. 'As for you? Well, I suppose it suddenly occurred to me that we're both in this because of our sisters. Family. At once a curse, and a blessing.'

Yelen allowed herself a small smile – the first such smile since leaving the Lower Reach. 'You're not wrong. I was on the brink of leaving Frostgrave, I wanted a life outside of Mirika's shadow. Now I just want her back.'

A meaty *thud* echoed down the stairs, closely followed by a sharp clatter of falling rubble. Magnis peered up the staircase, shrugged and turned his attention back to Yelen.

'Are you going to tell me the rest?'

Yelen started guiltily. 'I don't know what you're talking about.'

'You've not been right since last night. Hells, you look worse than I feel, and I was lost in dreams of skeletal fingers peeling my flesh away, strip by strip.'

Did he know? For the first time, Yelen considered that Azzanar's deeds might not have gone unwitnessed. Sure, Kain and Magnis had been lost to the wight-sent dreams when she'd 'woken' herself, but before…?

The need to confess – to tell someone, anyone – was overwhelming. Yelen didn't trust it. There was no sharing of this burden. Magnis might not have been so close to the dead as Serene was to Kas, but they'd still been his companions, allies – possibly even his friends. There was no telling how he might react, and Yelen still needed the Gilded Rose's help – assuming Magnis didn't have her killed outright.

'It's nothing,' she said. 'Last night's hitting me hard, that's all.'

Magnis nodded. 'I'm not surprised. Running headlong into a barrow? That's either brave or foolish.'

'And impersonating an undead sorcerer isn't?'

'Well, perhaps a little. But the hierarchy of the departed is rigid as iron. Some say it's part of the magic that binds them. Others, that it's simply survival – the lesser fearing the strong.' He shrugged. 'Either way, to have a liche like Szarnos the Great loose within the barrow was akin to dropping a pike into a millpond. I thought it'd buy some time, and it did.'

Yelen nodded. The sounds of trollish eviction still sounded from above, but they came ever more infrequently – presumably one party or other was getting tired.

'The water must have boiled by now,' she said. 'I'll check.'

'I'll come with you,' said Magnis easily.

He shadowed Yelen along the furnace hall, never that close, never that distant. He *did* know. He had to. It couldn't be concern. He'd shown no such consideration for the others – hadn't even evinced remorse at the previous night's deaths. He had to be playing her along, giving her the chance to betray herself, but why? Why wait?

As Yelen reached the welcome warmth of the fire, another thought occurred to her. What if Magnis didn't know? What if she dozed off and Azzanar took control once more? How many more would die unwarned?

The billy can burbled happily, the water indeed coming to the boil. Yelen ignored it and took a seat on an alcove's lip.

Lately, every choice had seemed like no choice at all. Was that what Azzanar had meant when she'd claimed Yelen would beg her to take over? Easier to let go than to keep stumbling on? No. Not yet. Not while Mirika still needed her.

'I need you to promise me something.' She threw up her hands in exasperation and stared down at the fire. 'I don't know you well enough to know whether a promise will bind you, but I need it, all the same.'

Magnis regarded her silently for a time, his customary insouciance in abeyance. In fact, his expression was one of utter seriousness, as solemn as a priest absolving sin. Folding his arms, he sat down beside the fire. 'Let's hear it.'

Yelen hesitated, but there was no going back. 'That you'll help Mirika, no matter what.'

He frowned. 'Of course. We already agreed as much.'

She searched her memory, but found nothing stronger than implication. At best, there'd been a pledge that the Gilded Rose would help *her* help Mirika. It wasn't enough. 'I need to hear you say the words. Please.'

Magnis pursed his lips, but nodded. 'Very well. I swear, on what little remains of the Magnis family name, to do all I can to help your sister. Good enough?'

Yelen considered. The phrasing was slightly different, but she supposed it was close enough. Set against the larger doubt that any promise could be worth anything, such quibbling seemed trivial. It was still far from a guarantee, but what guarantees were there to be had in Frostgrave? 'Thank you.'

'What's this about?'

'Last night. Darrick didn't kill Kas.' The words tumbled out, each practically trampling the one that came before. 'Azzanar did.'

Magnis went still, his expression unreadable. 'Azzanar. This demon of yours?' His voice hardened. 'How was it done?'

'I don't know,' said Yelen, miserably. 'She kept me from remembering until we were out of the Lower Reach, and I still see only flashes, even now.'

Magnis glanced at the doorway. He still hadn't called for help, though Yelen found little solace in that. Confession hadn't lightened the burden, as she'd hoped. If anything, it pressed down upon her heavier than before.

'She took over when I slept. She made me do those things.'

'You should have told me.'

'I didn't know she could! It's never happened before. You have to believe me.'

Magnis closed his eyes. 'Can you think of any reason I shouldn't have you killed for this?'

'No.' The reply came easier than Yelen had expected. But then that was the thing about the inevitable, wasn't it? 'Not so long as you keep your promise about Mirika. Give me that, and I won't fight. None of the rest matters, not anymore.'

'What are you doing? You can't do this! I won't let you.'

Azzanar coiled angrily around Yelen's thoughts, thrashing madly as she tested her cage. Each struggle ended in failure. Whatever power she had while Yelen slept, she had none in the waking world. At last, Yelen's burden eased, or perhaps it was more that her will to shoulder it increased, strengthened by the satisfaction that Azzanar would perish alongside her. The demon had gambled, and she had lost.

Magnis ran a hand down his face, tugging at the ends of his moustache. For the first time, he looked weary – a man beset by worries greater than his years.

'Well then,' he said at last. 'It's just as well one of us has more imagination, isn't it?'

Yelen stared at him, suspicion crowding her thoughts. Azzanar ceased her thrashing.

'What do you mean?'

Magnis rubbed his hands together in front of the fire. 'You didn't kill Kas and Darrick. It may have been Yelen Semova's hands that did the deed, but the malice wasn't hers.' He shook his head. 'No. You saved us all last night, and don't you think I've forgotten it.'

'You don't understand! I put you all in danger.'

'But not knowingly,' said Magnis. 'And even if you had an inkling that this Azzanar of yours could have done what she did, I'd find it hard to blame you. I've lost more companions in Felstad than I care to remember. Sometimes I knew the risks greater than they, but I pressed on anyway. Because Elien needs me, and because Rufrick must pay for what he's done. I've no right to judge you.'

Yelen hardly believed her ears. 'Then what do we do?'

'Nothing in the grand scheme has changed. I want the orb, you want your sister back. We press on. Even with a couple of hours sleep – gods know I need them – a brisk pace will bring us to Szarnos' tomb before nightfall. Can you stay awake until then?'

'I think so.'

'Good.' He grinned. 'I'll keep my promise if I have to, but I'd rather you were there to see it done. I've a legend to build, after all. A sackful of crowns might procure an army, but reputation keeps it loyal. Well, mostly.'

'But what if I'm wrong,' said Yelen quietly. 'What if Azzanar breaks through again?'

The grin faded. 'Forewarned is forearmed. I'll be

watching, and I'll make sure Kain is too. Say nothing to the others – especially not to Serene. She doesn't have my… ah, pragmatic nature.'

Yelen read the implications all too clearly. 'I understand.'

Magnis shrugged. 'Who knows, if the orb contains the power I think it does, maybe it can be used to break Azzanar's hold.'

'That's what Torik claimed.'

'A lie is always more palatable if wrapped inside a truth.' Magnis snorted. 'In any case, I'm not Torik.'

'And if Mirika's not at the tomb?' Yelen already knew the answer. If Mirika hadn't in fact returned to Szarnos' tomb, the trail was cold as death, and there was no hope for any of them.

'Then we deal with that if it happens.'

'One step at a time.' Yelen reflected that her life was increasingly a series of single, disconnected steps.

'Precisely. And at this moment, that first step involves a nice, strong brew of chanin tea to keep your eyes open and infernal interlopers behind those eyes, where they belong.'

'Where who belongs?' Kain stood in the doorway, arms folded and suspicion gleaming in her eyes.

Yelen started guiltily and opened her mouth to speak.

'Us, of course,' said Magnis, offering Yelen a half-wink. 'How goes the troll hunt?'

'Over and done with,' said Kain. 'I left Serene slicing off its claws. Reckons Old Selsa will pay handsomely for them. Something about a cure for baldness – I didn't ask for details. Marcan's still checking the upper floor. He'll not find anything.'

'Anyone hurt?'

'Only in their pride.' She cracked a rare smile. 'Marcan,

in particular, seems almost back to normal. For him.'

Magnis shook his head. 'Well, we can't have everything.'

* * *

After discussion with the rest of the Gilded Rose, Magnis eventually settled on calling a three-hour rest – enough to take the edge off the previous night's lack of sleep, but not so much that they'd lose too much of the day.

Marcan, in particular, seemed greatly enthused by his victory over the squatting troll – and this despite a new collection of bruises – and confidently claimed they could press on through the Broken Strand by night, if need be. It didn't take any great perception to see that he was glad to be back on comfortable – if dangerous – ground, presented with perils he understood.

That said, neither he nor Serene were pleased to be excluded from watch duty. Magnis ruthlessly crushed their objections, citing their experiences of the midnight hours and claiming that he, Kain and Yelen had suffered less. Kain had raised an eyebrow at that, the gesture so brief that Yelen was sure that she'd been the only one to see it. She was just as equally sure that Kain had meant it that way.

So it was that Yelen found herself sharing the first watch with Magnis, and the second with Kain.

The first passed painlessly enough, even though Yelen spent much of it pacing back and forth along the furnace hall to stave off sleep. Bravado aside, she found that she was desperately tired, and didn't trust herself to remain by the fire without nodding off.

It seemed Magnis felt the same way. Though he didn't say anything over the course of their watch, Yelen felt his eyes on her with every passing moment.

Once again she wondered at Magnis' true nature. Beneath the erudite, carefree exterior, he was a driven man – moreover, he was kinder than she'd ever have expected. Twice now he'd set aside the danger of having her close, and offered only help and understanding. Yelen told herself that it was because he needed her to get through to Mirika, but she didn't come close to convincing herself. The Cavril Magnis charm at work, probably, but she found that she didn't mind. She needed all the hope she could get.

Eventually, the sands of the hourglass passed away, and Kain took Magnis' place. Unlike her paymaster, the knight made no pretence of standing watch over anything other than Yelen.

As the winds rose outside, Kain matched Yelen pace for pace, never so close as to be threatening, but never far enough away that Yelen could no longer feel her unrelenting gaze between her shoulder blades.

Finally, Yelen could take no more. On the next circuit of the furnace room, she ground to a halt, boots crunching through the floor's detritus, and spun to face Kain. 'So he's told you?'

'He has.'

As ever, the knight's expression gave no clue as to her thoughts. That only made her answer more infuriating.

'And?'

'And my offer remains open, should you choose to take it.'

'That offer being to cut out my heart?'

'Indeed. It will likely come to that before long, whatever happens.' Kain shrugged. 'I won't judge if you lack the strength to see this through to the end.'

Yelen's half-formed response dissipated as the meaning of Kain's words sank in. No recrimination for Kas and Darrick's deaths. No horror that Magnis seemed content to allow her continued presence in the Gilded Rose. Just an insinuation that she was too weak to continue. That she'd buckle under the strain. In its way, the challenge was no different to that set by Azzanar herself. *You won't be able to see this through. You'll beg me to end this.*

'And you think I should keep fighting?' she asked.

'That's not for me to say.'

'That's not an answer.'

'Of course it is. It's merely not one that you want to hear.' Kain stepped closer. 'It doesn't matter what I think. It doesn't matter what Magnis thinks. It doesn't even matter what that hellspawn in your soul thinks. All that matters is what you choose, and that you have the strength to see it through.'

Yelen laughed softly, bitterly. 'I'm Yelen Semova. I don't get to make choices.'

'Really?' Kain took another step, her dark eyes burning into Yelen's. 'Seems to me you made plenty of choices last night.'

So Magnis hadn't told her everything. 'That wasn't me.'

'Who? The girl who saved our lives? Who ran headlong into the depths of a barrow for people she barely knows? You made those choices. Plenty would have done otherwise.'

Yelen shifted uncomfortably. 'I was lucky.'

'You were. But to have luck, you must first place yourself in a situation where you need it. That takes strength. Perhaps you have more of both than you realize.'

'Easy for you to say.' Yelen swept out her hand to encompass the room. 'All of this? This isn't who I am. It isn't what I want. You don't understand. Why would you? You're a warrior. I'm just a gutter rat, running from one poor choice to the next.'

Kain cocked her head, a quizzical frown on her lips. 'And if you could choose the way the next few hours go, what would that be?'

She didn't even have to think. 'I want Mirika back.'

'Then make that happen.'

Yelen laughed softly. 'As easy as that?'

'Of course not. But the first lesson a warrior learns is that you don't always get to pick your battles. The second thing is that any battle – *any* battle – can be won through sacrifice.' She arched an eyebrow. 'What are you prepared to sacrifice?'

'Whatever I have to.'

Even as she spoke the words, Yelen felt a new determination. It burned like the heat from a fire, but was kindled within, not without.

Kain peered into her eyes, and nodded. 'I suppose we'll see.'

For the first time since she'd awoken, the knight turned her back on Yelen and strode off. Yelen frowned, confused. Had Kain truly been waiting all that time just to deliver that message? Or had she simply been watching to see how close Azzanar truly was to the surface – Yelen wasn't sure how Kain was able to see the demon, but didn't doubt for a moment that she could.

'You know what Magnis told me about you?'

Kain turned unhurriedly, her expression once again unreadable. 'I'm sure you'll tell me.'

'That you're looking for a cause.'

She shook her head, soft laughter spilling from her lips.

'I've had a lifetime of causes, and of unjust and ignoble battles dressed up as righteousness and duty. Now I want nothing more than crowns in my purse, and I find I'm the happier for it.'

Yelen stifled a frown. Somehow, she'd expected more from Kain. The older woman carried herself with such deliberate confidence, it seemed wrong for her to have such simple – even mercenary – goals. 'So I owe you, do I, for the advice?'

Kain shook her head. 'Consider it payment in kind for last night. And wisdom from one lost soul to another. May it serve you well.'

Without a backward glance, she left the furnace hall and returned to the campfire. Yelen watched her go, uncertain where she now stood with Kain. But one thing was undeniable. She *did* feel better. Perhaps her battles could be won, after all.

CHAPTER THIRTEEN

Even the Wailing Reach seemed subdued that afternoon, its wind-blown voice screaming only fitfully through the trees. All in all, it lent Yelen the impression that she and the frosty expanse had more in common than she could have guessed.

Certainly, she didn't know how she felt about the members of the Gilded Rose who, like her, plodded wordlessly on into the teeth of the wind. Two knew the truth, and two knew only the lie. Two believed they owed her their life, while two knew her hands bore the blame. The only advantage to the situation was that if Azzanar did take over, there'd be no shortage of hands eager to see the demon finally pay.

And Azzanar was growing stronger, there was no doubt about that. The taste of sulphur was back, and thicker than ever. Several times, Yelen had glimpses of places she'd never seen, overlaid across the snowscape like waking dreams. Chambers of black stone and raging flame; mountains like rotten teeth against a blood-red sky. The visions cleared as quickly as they formed, chased away by frantic shakes of the head, but the smell that came with them, all decadence and charred flesh, lingered long in Yelen's nostrils. And through it all, Azzanar's silent laughter echoed through her mind.

Distracted by one such vision, Yelen missed her footing. It was a simple enough mistake, easily made even without distraction. Instead of solid stone, her boot found only shifting ice. A splintering *crack* and she fell, feet slipping away into the iced-over chasm.

Fingers scrabbled through the snow, but found no purchase. Feet kicked at empty air. A desperate glance below revealed only bleak rock, twenty or thirty feet below. Not enough to be fatal, just to break bones, for all the comfort that gave.

Yelen's hips slid into the chasm. Fingers closed around a trailing root. Her shoulder jolted, the shock travelling up her arm and yanking her grip free. Her struggles grew more desperate, but that only hastened her slide.

Yelen jerked to a halt, the seams of her coat digging into her armpits. Then she was moving again. Upwards. Knees and boots scraped over the chasm's edge and the pressure on her collar vanished, leaving her sat unceremoniously in the snow.

'Watch your step next time,' rumbled Marcan. 'I'm not climbing down after you.'

Yelen nodded, sucking down short shallow breaths as her racing heart slowed. 'Thank you.'

He shrugged, the motion almost invisible beneath his mountain of furs, and reached down to help her up. 'Shame to come all this way and no further.'

'It would.'

Yelen took the proffered hand in hers, and let Marcan hoist her upright. Then, without another word, she pressed on after the others. Serene was barely a dark shape in the swirling snows, Kain and Magnis entirely lost from sight. Had she been at the back of the company, rather than

Marcan, Yelen realised, they might not have known she was missing until it was too late.

It seemed Marcan was of similar mind. From that moment on, Yelen sensed he was never more than a pace or two away, hovering like an overprotective guard dog. Was it concern that drove him? The need to repay a debt? She wasn't sure. But Yelen felt better for it, all the same. Between the visions, and the growing weariness from too much travel and too little sleep, she was glad to have someone looking out for her – even if it was the brute who'd almost killed her sister.

* * *

Eventually, the wind-blown pines gave way to the shattered buildings of the Broken Strand. Not that Yelen realised it at first. The storm followed them from the ridgeline, not abating as it should, but growing in ferocity. It howled through the close-knit streets, the gusts transforming flurries of snow into razor-edged torrents of ice.

Three streets in, Yelen found herself bent almost double against the wind, as if the burdens of her soul now weighed down her body also. The others fared no better. Marcan in particular was so caked with snow that he looked less like a man than one of the yeti whose furs he sported.

Nor did the visions help. For every fifty paces Yelen took into the biting chill, she took two in the sweltering heat of the fire-wreathed land, a hot wind of ashes scalding her frost-numbed face. There was no preparing for the shock of it, and the aftermath always left her sick from the rush of sulphur, but still she staggered on.

Perhaps an hour into the Broken Stand, Magnis beckoned the company into the dubious shelter of a sunken watchtower. There, out of the wind's incessant howl, he unpeeled the scarves from across his face, revealing an unusually downcast expression.

'We're paying for an easy passage of the upper reach.' He breathed onto his hands and massaged his cheeks. 'I've never seen it so bad down here.'

'Fine time for that famous Magnis luck to desert us,' murmured Serene. 'We can't keep on into this.'

Marcan shook his shoulders to clear the snow, his furs making the motion appear not unlike that of a dog shaking itself dry. 'She's right. We can just about handle the storm, but it'll be dark soon, and you know what that means.'

Yelen knew what it meant. With the dark, the trolls would emerge from their lairs. But she knew Marcan's implications went further. He wanted to abandon the pursuit, or at least delay it until better weather or daylight.

A sick feeling gathering in her stomach, she crossed to the nearest window. An accident of fate had seen its pane of glass survive the watchtower's collapse – albeit riven by a massive crack that marred it top to bottom. Before the events of the Lower Reach, it had been a simple gamble – if one conducted in the face of unknowable odds – offsetting each delay against losing Mirika's trail, and the hope that the orb had not completely consumed her. Not now. The stakes had changed. It wasn't any longer a question of how long Mirika could resist, but how long Yelen herself could stay awake in order to keep Azzanar at bay.

Magnis sank back against the wall. 'Kain? What do you think?'

'Hard to say,' she replied. 'Most trolls aren't so stupid they'll venture out into this mess. But it only takes one and a run of bad luck. Depends whether you think we're owed some good.'

Yelen turned back to the window. That was three against pressing on, even if Kain's reluctance had been couched in careful terms. That was it, wasn't it? She gripped the stone sill, Azzanar's silent laughter dripping across her thoughts. The taste of sulphur returned. The storm beyond the glass became a flurry of ashen fragments against an angry sky.

'No,' Yelen muttered. 'I'm not giving up. I'm not.'

'*Not in your mind, perhaps. But your body tells a different story,*' Azzanar purred. '*I'll make a deal with you. Let me out now, and I'll spare your friends. I won't – we won't – lay a finger upon them.*'

Yelen gripped the sill tighter. 'I thought you told me I'd beg.'

'*Perhaps I'm feeling generous. A gift, offered out of fond memories from those days in which we were friends.*'

'We were *never* friends,' Yelen hissed.

'*Oh we were, poppet. And now I'm all you have. Don't let pride trick you. This is over. Be sensible. Take the bargain.*'

The room spun. Yelen slumped against the sill. Should she take the offer? It was only a matter of time, and she *did* have Magnis' promise to save Mirika. That, combined with Azzanar's bargain to leave the Gilded Rose be… Maybe it was time to stop fighting.

A hand fell on her shoulder. 'Yelen?' Kain's voice sounded echoed, distant. 'You alright, girl? There's a decision to be made.'

The vision of fire cracked like the windowpane, splinters of frozen streets and storm-tossed skies showing through the cracks. Why was Azzanar making this offer, if her victory was so certain? For all the demon's protestations, they'd only ever been reluctant allies at best. Yelen could think of only one reason – it was a distraction.

Yelen stared through the window, focusing her gaze on the central chink of the 'real' landscape. The cracks in the inferno-racked vision grew wider, its shards splintering and fading. The snowstorm rushed in, drenching the world in a blanket of gusting white. Or almost so. As the winds gusted again, the curtains of snow parted, revealing a small, dark figure in the distance, hunched against the elements.

A dark figure, and a gleam of gold.

Heart leaping, Yelen spun around and stared up at Kain. 'I'm going on.'

Serene grimaced. 'Have sense, love. We'll be lucky to survive the night.'

'But Mirika's out there!' Yelen pointed at the glass. 'I just saw her.'

Magnis exchanged a look with Marcan, the doubt on his face plain even through his beard. 'Kain?'

The knight shrugged. 'I saw nothing. Not saying she didn't.'

Yelen stared back through the window. She saw only snow and the dark silhouettes of eroded stone. Had she imagined it? Was she now so desperate that she'd summoned a hallucination of her own to vie with Azzanar's? Certainly she was tired enough.

A stray memory clicked. What had Kain said? About lacking the strength to see things through? Did she have the choice to do what had to be done? Yelen took a deep breath, searching for the confidence that had led her into the barrow long hours before. To her surprise, it came at her call. 'I'm not asking you to come with me, but I'm going on.'

Marcan shook his head. 'You're mad.'

'She is.' Magnis laughed under his breath. 'I'm starting to think she fits in around here better than she imagines.'

'That's not funny, Cavril. You shouldn't encourage her.'

'Why not?' He pushed away from the wall. 'I'm going with her.'

'You're what?'

'Think about it.' Magnis drew up to his full height and squared his shoulders, the effect spoiled somewhat by his snow-cast and bedraggled appearance. 'We all saw the remains of the *Guttered Candle* and what happened to the Green Widow. And now this storm, just as we're catching up with her? Does anyone think it's a coincidence?'

Serene offered a lopsided frown. 'When you put it like that…'

'You're not considering this?' interrupted Marcan.

'It makes sense. What if Mirika's covering her tracks? Using the storm to stop pursuit? If we hole up every time the weather turns sour, we'll never catch up.'

'Using the storm?' Marcan rumbled. 'She's a time witch, not an elementalist.'

'*Mirika's* a time witch,' said Magnis. 'Who knows what Szarnos is capable of? And it's Szarnos we're following, not Mirika.' He offered an apologetic shrug to Yelen.

Kain started for the door. 'Then we should keep moving.'

Marcan shook his head. 'Not you too.'

'Just as long as he's still paying.' She stared at Magnis. 'You *are* still paying?'

His chapped lips formed a grin. 'Naturally.'

'Then I'm going. The sooner we catch our stray lamb, the sooner I can get back to the warmth of civilization.'

Magnis nodded. 'Serene?'

'What the hells. I'll come.' She arched her back, joints snapping back into position with soft but audible clicks. 'Yelen followed me. I'll follow her.'

Yelen's cheeks warmed, part pride, part guilt. 'Thanks.'

'Thank me by having a better sense of direction than I did, love.'

Magnis turned his attention to Marcan, a squat, sullen shape in the corner. 'Leaves you, Marcan. What's it to be?'

He scowled. 'Better five together in a storm than one alone in the night, I guess. Besides, you run into a troll, you'll be glad to have me around.'

* * *

Despite Marcan's fears, no trolls came with dusk. Unfortunately, neither did the storm abate. But Yelen no longer felt the icy spray in her face, nor the knotted, dull tension from shoulders braced against the winds. Fierce as the storm was, it couldn't hide the footprints. Staggered and uneven, they began less than two hundred paces from the sunken watchtower and ran along the snow-clogged cobbles, already half-filled by the unforgiving snows.

'How far ahead is she?' yelled Marcan, his basso rumble scarcely audible above the howl of the storm.

'No idea,' Serene replied. 'Maybe Kas could have…'

She scowled, leaving the thought unfinished.

Yelen didn't care. The footprints were the first proof she'd not imagined Mirika's presence in the snows. After all, who else would be out here alone, in this weather? No one was that crazy. Mirika was alive! There was still hope, and Yelen sensed she wasn't the only one who felt it. There was an energy to the company now, a vigour that lent pace to their journey. No one complained, not even when the drifted snow grew waist deep – not even Marcan. After the near-disaster of the barrows, every member of the Gilded Rose wanted something, *anything* to go their way.

But as time wore on, Yelen came to love and hate the footprints equally. Loved, because they showed that Mirika was still alive, hated because they proved she was still ahead, still beyond reach. But Yelen preferred the latter over the former. More than anything, she dreaded rounding a corner and finding Mirika lifeless in the snows.

They found plenty of other bodies, or remnants thereof. It seemed that not all the Broken Strand's trolls had sought to ride out to storm – or at least had been sufficiently wracked with hunger to risk its icy teeth. As dusk slid into night, Yelen's count reached an even dozen of the brutes, frozen solid as Mariast's luckless toy soldiers, encased in glittering ice already half-hidden by the snows.

Yelen peered at the brutish faces in the lantern light, and tried not to think about the consequences for herself and the Gilded Rose. Magnis seemed to think she could reach Mirika, even through Szarnos' control. What if she couldn't? She'd certainly failed two nights ago on the banks of the Nereta. With an effort, she pushed the thought to the back of her mind. One step at a time. She'd not even laid eyes on Mirika since that brief glimpse back at the watchtower. There was no sense borrowing trouble from the future.

Half-blind, and wearier by the moment, Yelen led the Gilded Rose through the streets, eyes straining for a glimpse – *anything* – of Mirika. The infernoscapes came and went, but they'd lost their power now Yelen knew them to be mere trickery, another tool of Azzanar's to batter her resolve. How close she'd come to giving up! Kain had been right. There was always another choice, another path.

The street opened out, the storm lessening in ferocity now it was no longer funnelled by crumbling buildings. A new shape loomed in the lantern light, dirty grey against a black and storm-cast sky. The Temple of Draconostra. They'd made it.

'Well I'll be…' Marcan pointed at a slender figure, dark against the snows.

'You already are.' Serene shook her head in wonder.

'Mirika!' Yelen shouted. 'Wait!'

The wind swallowed the words, but the figure turned all the same. Dark, empty eyes stared out from a face shot through with golden light, unbraided hair dancing like snakes in the wind. Had Yelen stumbled across her by chance, she'd not have recognized her sister. As it was, the apparition she'd become made her soul ache.

'Mirika!'

The figure hunched away along the temple approach, the wings of the storm closing to hide her from sight.

'Mirika!' Yelen started forward down the hill.

'Look out!'

Marcan's cry of warning and the deep-throated bellow came as one. A mass of furs slammed into Yelen's shoulder. The air above her head parted before a massive bunched fist, and then she plunged into a snow drift, lantern falling from her hand.

Marcan shouted again – this time equal parts pain and a *whooph* of expelled air. Propelled by the troll's brutish strength, he flew back across the street. He rebounded off a column, and fell unmoving into the snows.

With a roar of victory, the troll knuckled towards Yelen, the twisted bough of its club scraping along the cobbles behind. She scrambled to her feet, already knowing she couldn't escape the beast. Too slow, her numbed hands grasped at the hilt of Kas' sword.

The blade was only halfway clear of the scabbard when the troll reached for her with a prehensile hand.

'Die!'

Suddenly Serene was there, daggers flashing at the troll's wrist. Blood sprayed across the snows. The troll jerked back its hand, roaring in pain.

Serene wasn't done. Turning a pirouette as graceful as any dancer, she lunged at the beast's belly, the two gleaming dagger-points slicing into furless flesh.

The troll reeled, roaring madly in its brutish tongue. Then, moving with a speed at odds with its bulk, it swung the club in a massive arcing blow.

Serene twisted aside. It wasn't enough – the bough struck her shoulder a glancing blow. She spiralled away and fell awkwardly to one knee. Her daggers, ripped from her grip, were still lodged in the beast's belly.

Yelen forgotten, the troll lurched towards Serene. But Yelen hadn't forgotten the troll. More importantly, she hadn't forgotten the lesson in courage she'd learned amongst the barrows of the Lower Reach.

'Get away from her!'

Yelen knew her blow was clumsy even as she swung – even before it skidded on the thick, greasy pelt of the troll's arm. But harming the creature wasn't the point. All she wanted was to distract the beast's attention from Serene. And in that, she succeeded beyond her wildest nightmares.

The troll rounded on Yelen, the foul wind of its

confused bellow thick in her face, and its hot spittle splashing her skin.

It swung blindly, the bough aimed by instinct, rather than sight. Yelen went backward before it, the gnarled timber passing inches from her nose, then darted inside the troll's reach before it could reverse the swing.

This time, her blow possessed all the force she could have wished for it. The steel cut down through greasy fur, down through the leathery hide. Blood gushed. The troll flailed, but Yelen had learned from Serene's mistake and had already dived beyond its grasp.

As her elbows and knees jarred against cobbles, the troll's club-arm drooped, the weapon dropping from its fingers. For a moment, it stared dumbly at its hand, troglodyte brow furrowing in confusion, then rounded on Yelen.

She scrambled back on hands and heels, at last regaining her footing. The clawed hand reached out for her. The troll flinched away as Yelen struck, then lunged. Its fingers wrapped around the sword, the blade slicing deep as it ripped the weapon from her grasp.

'No!'

The troll flung the sword away and advanced, a loathsome chuckle on its lips. Yelen darted aside. This time, she was too slow. A leathery hand closed around her throat, and dragged her towards the drooling maw.

'Let me go!'

Yelen hammered and clawed at the troll's hand, but its flesh was like wood.

'Kain! Kain! Where the hells are you?'

But of the knight, or of Magnis, there was no sign through the raging snows.

She needed a weapon.

Yelen's gaze dropped to the troll's belly and Serene's daggers. Abandoning her attempts to break the beast's grip, she reached for the nearest hilt. Her fingertips brushed the polished steel, but no more.

The troll drew her closer, the acrid stink of its breath washing over her face. Yellowed fangs parted.

Again Yelen reached for the dagger. Again, her fingers found no purchase.

'Hands off, you stinking brute!'

Marcan's bellow sounded a heartbeat before the dull, wet thud of his sword thrust took the troll in the back. The creature roared in pain, the arm holding Yelen dipping.

At last, her fingers closed around the dagger's hilt. With a wordless scream of triumph, Yelen ripped the blade free of its fleshy prison, reversed her grip, and rammed it, two-handed, into the troll's bloodshot eye.

The creature bellowed one last time, went limp and toppled backwards like a felled tree.

Yelen fell with it, smothered by a face full of the beast's stinking pelt. Coughing at the smell of it, but her blood racing, she rolled clear and lurched to her feet.

Marcan wiped his blade clean in the snows, the motion made oddly stiff by a limp he'd not possessed minutes before. 'Smoothly done. If I didn't know better, I might think you were getting a taste for this.'

Yelen shook her head. 'Not me.' But her blood was racing with more than fear, she knew that. Part of her had enjoyed the fight. Well, the *winning* of the fight, anyway.

Something sour dripped off her top lip and into her mouth. Suppressing a shudder, she grabbed a handful of clean snow and wiped her face clean. The sharp, scratchy needles of ice against her skin were a price gladly paid.

'I don't know,' Serene ambled over, one hand massaging her abused shoulder. 'A couple of dozen wights one night, now a troll. Cavril had better be careful. Might be that you'll steal his legend out from under him.' Crouching beside the dead troll, she reclaimed her daggers and set about cleaning them meticulously in the snows.

'Where is Cavril, anyway?' asked Yelen, reclaiming her sword. 'Or Kain, for that matter?'

'We're here.'

Yelen turned to see Kain and Magnis approaching down the hillside. The former held a troll's severed head by a hank of discoloured pelt and the faded gold and blue heraldry of her armour was caked in blood spatter. The latter, like Marcan, had picked up a fresh limp from somewhere.

'*Your* troll had a hunting partner shadowing us,' Kain went on. She let the head fall into the snows and prodded the corpse with a toe before turning her gaze on Yelen. 'You do most of this? Fancy that.'

Her piece said, Kain strode off downhill towards the temple.

Yelen glanced at Magnis, who was making considerably heavier weather of walking. 'Are you hurt?'

'Mostly my pride.' He grimaced, the expression quickly turning into a wince. 'A troll tried using my ribs as a punching bag. In my haste to retreat, I slipped on some ice. Would've been a most ignoble end if Kain hadn't been around.'

'Here, lean on me.' Yelen slipped an arm around his waist. 'Can't have the great Cavril Magnis falling over a second time, can we?'

His eyes narrowed, but he sank against her shoulder all the same. 'You're disgustingly cheerful for someone who nearly had their face chewed off. Is that troll spittle in your hair?'

Yelen ignored him. 'She's here, Cavril. Minutes ahead of us, that's all.'

* * *

Yelen couldn't escape the sense of repeating history as she crept through the tunnels. She'd made the same journey less than a week ago, fretting about the preparations to open the vault, and the possibility of the Gilded Rose following hard on their heels. At the time, Mirika had cautioned her not to worry, just as she always did. And she'd been right, in a way. The Gilded Rose were never the danger – it had been Torik all along. They'd both been betrayed long before they'd even set foot in the tomb.

Once again, Marcan had the lead and Kain the rear. Magnis had declared he was fit to continue under his own power once they'd escaped the storm, and now hobbled a pace or two to Yelen's front, just as Serene did a pace or two behind. Yelen found it strange to think that a week ago they'd been her rivals, if not her enemies. So much had changed.

Yelen couldn't help but think what might have been had she and Mirika fallen in with the Gilded Rose, and not Endri Torik's schemes of immortality. She shook the thought away. It was useless to speculate. If Magnis could help her, then all to the good. If not, she'd carry herself off into the snows before she let sleep take her. Kain had been right about that as well. Victory could always be won if you were prepared to sacrifice for it, and Yelen would gladly lay down her life to stop Azzanar from harming Mirika… or her friends.

Even now, she could feel the demon gloating – the warm, honeyed chuckle that spoke to a pleasure deferred, but not denied. The flashes of the burning world came more frequently now, keeping pace with Yelen's growing tiredness. Each time, she girded what strength she had left and drove the visions away.

A little longer. That's all she needed.

At last, they arrived in the tomb proper – the room in which Mirika had nearly died.

'Is she here?' hissed Serene.

'She's here.' Kain pointed up to the head of the zigzag stairway. Soft golden light glimmered away between the colossal statues. 'I'd be happier if I knew why.'

'Just be glad we've found her at all.' Magnis turned to Yelen. 'Are you ready for this?'

She hesitated. The course of the coming minutes would make the horrors of recent days worthwhile, or douse them deeper in tragedy. But what choice was there? 'What do you need me to do?'

'I'll distract her. You talk to her. Get her attention. If there's any part of Mirika left behind those eyes, she'll listen to you.'

'And if that doesn't work?' growled Marcan.

Magnis hesitated. 'It'll work.'

Marcan and Kain shared a bleak look behind Magnis' back. Their paymaster didn't see it, but Yelen did. 'I have to do this. No one else needs to come.'

'We're here, aren't we?' said Marcan. 'Shame to trudge all this way and not see how it ends.'

Serene nodded, but said nothing.

'Thank you,' said Yelen, the words feeling empty and useless on her tongue. Then she pushed past Marcan and began the long, slow climb up the stairs.

* * *

Harsh syllables danced on the air as Yelen ascended, the voice Mirika's and yet not. As on that fateful night by the Nereta, a dry, dead screech underlaid every unfamiliar word, a sound so hateful it set Yelen's nerves dancing anew. Though the words were strange, their sense was all too similar to those of the wights of the Lower Reach. But it didn't matter. The sound of Mirika's voice redoubled Yelen's courage. She wasn't lost. Not yet. She could still be reached.

'*You need to give this up, poppet.*'

'And you need to shut up,' muttered Yelen. 'I don't care what you think.'

Azzanar laughed softly. '*Your sister's gone by now. That withered old soul has waited centuries. He'll have smothered her without a second thought. All you can do is destroy him in return, and I doubt you've the strength for that.*'

'A few days ago, I might have agreed with you. Things are different now.'

'*They are indeed. Truly, poppet, I'm impressed, and it's made me reconsider. You've enough life for us to share. I'll take the nights, and you the days, how does that sound? All you need do is walk away.*'

It was all Yelen could do not to laugh out loud. 'You think I'll fall for that? If I walk away, I'll be yours night *and* day.'

Azzanar snorted. '*Even if that were true, you go up and you'll die.*'

'Maybe. Maybe not. But at least I'll know I did everything I could to help Mirika.'

'A delightful sentiment, I'm sure. They could carve it on your headstone. Except you're not going to get one, are you?'

Yelen detected an edge of fear beneath the demon's sarcasm. She drank it in, revelled in it. She didn't think for a moment that Azzanar's offer was genuine, but the demon was worried about what was to come – that she and Yelen would both perish at Szarnos' hands... at Mirika's hands.

'So be it.'

Azzanar hissed and retreated from Yelen's thoughts. It felt good to deny her – if only one last time.

A hand fell on Yelen's shoulder as she approached the final landing.

'Let me go first,' whispered Magnis. 'I'll distract her, you remind her of who she is.'

Yelen nodded tautly, a knot forming in her stomach. With a last flash of a smile, Cavril Magnis sprang up the final handful of steps.

CHAPTER FOURTEEN

'Mirika!'

Yelen heard a tremor in Magnis' voice. Not much, maybe not even one she'd have noticed a few days ago, but it was definitely there. Had the master of the Gilded Rose reached the limits of his bravado? She eased her way up the last couple of stairs and peered cautiously over the top step.

The chanting ceased. 'Who are you to address me so?'

Mirika's voice was almost unrecognizable, subsumed by the slithering, whispering presence from the orb. Her hair hung lank and white with frost, her time walker's robe was stained and tattered, and what little of her flesh Yelen could make out was mottled blue and shot through with golden light. Yelen swallowed away a dry throat. Could Mirika really come back from this

Magnis took a long step away before answering, drawing Mirika's attention further from the stairs. When he spoke, he did so in puzzled tones. 'I'm Cavril Magnis of the Gilded Rose. You must remember – we know each other well.'

Yelen frowned at that. Magnis and Mirika barely knew one another. They were rivals, nothing more. Or were they? Was Magnis exaggerating their relationship to break through Szarnos' hold, or had her jibes about flirtation hit closer to the mark than she'd believed? It'd certainly explain why Magnis had set so much at stake. Maybe the orb wasn't his real concern.

The orb pulsed. Mirika clasped it tighter to her chest. 'You are a speck, nothing more.'

Magnis frowned, and took another long step away from the stairs, hands clasped behind his back. Sparks of light danced on his fingertips, weaving tapestries of burning filament and dancing ash. Yelen recalled his claim of weaving charms to loosen the orb's grip. Were these those charms? Whatever he had in mind, it was clear he didn't want Mirika seeing them.

'That hurts, Mirika.'

She laughed, the sound of it like cracking ice. 'Mirika is gone.'

'I don't believe that.' Magnis' image blurred into two duplicates as he circled around the ledge, each walking in perfect step with the original. 'The Mirika I knew was strong enough to fight. Still is, or I'd be dead already.'

Mirika shifted to keep him in view, her back fully turning to the stairs, and to Yelen. 'Maybe she has yielded, content to be part of my designs.'

Magnis and his doppelgängers wove about one another, like a street huckster's cards in a game of Find the Lady. Yelen soon lost track of which was the original, and which were the illusions.

'And what could a withered old soul like you offer such a vibrant young woman?' asked Magnis. He jerked a thumb back at the open vault – the vault Yelen had opened on her last visit – and the jumble of bones within. 'To be honest, I'm not sure you're her type.'

Mirika raised a hand. Bluish-white light flared across the ledge, mist dancing in its wake. A doppelgänger shattered into fragments of fading light.

Yelen started forward. Her head hadn't even cleared the uppermost step when a heavy hand fell on her shoulder. Glancing back, she found herself face to face with Kain. The knight gave a short, sharp shake of the head and Yelen subsided.

Magnis clicked his fingers, and another image burst into being. 'You'll have to do better than that. I'm not some chancer little poor old Mariast. I'm Cavril Magnis. I aim to be remembered.'

Another freezing blast shattered a doppelgänger. Magnis shook his head and clicked another into being.

'And I'm still waiting to hear why you think Mirika would have anything to do with you. At least most demons offer great beauty and long life. Look what you've done to the poor woman. I've seen better-looking creatures moaning and scraping at the inside of barrows.'

Mirika screeched and destroyed another of the mirror-images. Magnis clicked another into being, but this time Yelen marked the pinched look on his face. Kain's grip on her shoulder tightened.

'You are tiring,' crowed Mirika. 'How many more can you manage, I wonder?'

Another flare of frozen light. Another doppelgänger shattered.

Magnis gritted his teeth. He clicked his fingers, and this time two images sprang into being. 'Try me. Thing is, I think you're tiring too. I recognized a few snatches of that lovely dirge you were singing. A resurrection chant.' He nodded back at Szarnos' long-dead bones. 'Surely you're not trying to get that body moving around again? Hate to say, but I think it's had its day.'

The orb pulsed. Mirika lowered her hand. 'You're clever.'

The four images of Magnis shrugged as one. 'It's not for me to say.'

'Then let me make you an offer, Cavril Magnis who would be remembered.' Mirika held out the orb. 'Take the orb. Join with me, and I will release this woman. I will cherish your friends, eradicate your enemies. Your name will echo across the ages… And the wrongs upon your bloodline shall be undone.'

Magnis went still as stone. 'How do know about that?'

'I am Szarnos the Great. Little escapes me. Not your innermost desires. And not your companions, cowering on the stairs.'

Mirika spun around. Yelen found herself staring into her once-sister's cold black eyes. The temperature of the air plunged. Ice crawled across the steps, flowing into the cracks in the stone, forcing them wider.

Magnis started forward. 'No! Wait!'

Mirika rounded on him, the orb again clasped to her chest.

Kain's restraining hand became an open-palmed shove into Yelen's shoulder blades. 'Move!'

Yelen flung herself up the last few steps, boots slipping on the fresh coating of ice. The stairway lurched and groaned under her feet, rubble spilling away as the spreading ice tore the stone apart.

As Yelen reached the top, the stairway collapsed entirely. She flung herself forward, fingers clawing at the flagstones of the landing. The impact drove all breath from her body, her knee cracked painfully against stone. But she held on for dear life, feet kicking at emptiness as she hauled herself up.

Below, the upper part of the stairway slid into darkness. As it did so, something heavy landed behind her, gloved fingers latching onto the landing's edge. Marcan. A quick glance behind revealed Kain and Serene perched precariously on the broken remains of the stairway, some yards away.

Mirika advanced on Magnis. Her hand swept out, and the illusions disintegrated beneath a barrage of frozen light. Magnis cried out and flinched away.

Yelen hauled herself onto the ledge and reached down for Marcan.

He shook his head. 'I can see to myself. Help Cavril.'

Yelen spun around to see Mirika bearing down on Magnis.

'So what is it to be?' asked Mirika. 'Remembrance and revenge, or a life and death forgotten by all?'

'I know you're in there, Mirika,' said Magnis, backing away. 'Now would be a good time to prove me right.'

The orb pulsed. White light gathered around Mirika's outstretched hand.

'Mirika! No!' Yelen half-ran, half-stumbled across the ledge, positioning herself between Magnis and her sister. 'You can fight this. I know you can! Being stubborn's got you into trouble for as long as I've known you. Let it do some good for a change.'

Mirika stood still as a statue, the white light dancing around her hand. 'Your words mean nothing.'

Yelen drew herself up. Had Mariast felt anything at the end? Would she? 'Then why do you care if Cavril accepts your bargain, or not? Why try to animate your old body? She's fighting you, isn't she?' Yelen cast her mind back. What had Magnis told her about the orb? 'Mirika, listen to me. He needs a willing host. I can't imagine anyone more unwilling. You can beat him, I know you can!'

'Worthless,' hissed Mirika. But the glow around her hand faded a fraction – or at least Yelen *thought* it did.

'Then why am I still alive?' demanded Yelen. She stepped closer, scarcely believing her audacity. From the corner of her eye, she saw Marcan haul himself heavily onto the ledge. 'I'm no use to you as a host – there's already at least one mind too many rattling around my soul. So kill me, if you can. But I don't think she'll let you.'

The orb pulsed. Mirika stared down at it, her features slackening. 'Yelen?' A little of Szarnos' influence had faded from her voice. 'I... I can't fight him much longer. You have to go.'

'No. I want my sister back. I'm not abandoning you.' She took a deep breath. 'You'll have to kill me, because I'm not leaving.'

Magnis stepped to Yelen's side. 'Just put down the orb.' He spoke smoothly, the serenity of his tone a contrast to the weariness on his face. 'You'll be able to think clearly again. You'll be yourself. You'll be free.'

Mirika glanced from Yelen to Magnis and back to Yelen again. 'I... I don't... I can't...' Her eyes widened, and her lips drew back across her teeth in a rictus of silent pain.

'Mirika!' Yelen started forward, reaching for the orb.

A squat, fur-clad figure beat her to it.

'Give me the bloody thing!' Marcan's hands closed around the orb.

Mirika screamed. A cold wind tore across the cavern. Stone buckled and rumbled beneath Yelen's feet.

'Look out!'

Magnis shoved Yelen, sending her sprawling. As she struck the ground, a stalactite shattered into fragments on the spot she'd been standing.

The wind picked up its pace, howling around the stone walls. An impossible storm of snow and ice coalesced around the centre of the ledge. At its heart, Mirika and Marcan stood locked in silent battle, each seeking to wrest the orb away from the other.

Yelen staggered across the trembling ledge, icy shards slicing at her face and plunging stalactites shattering around her. The winds grew stronger with every step; the creak of tortured stone echoing louder.

'Yelen, wait!'

She ignored Magnis' cry and set her shoulder to the rising wind. Mirika was a handful of paces away, no more. 'I can reach her!'

The rumble of stone reached a new pitch, the dull crescendo pierced by a chorus of sharp *cracks*. The ground beneath Yelen's feet heaved and fell away. This time, she fell with it. Mirika and Marcan slipped from sight, lost in a tumult of grinding, plunging shadows, and then the darkness swallowed Yelen whole.

* * *

'*I hope you're enjoying your defiance.*'

Yelen opened her eyes into blackness. Her thoughts gummed together like honeycomb, but the dull pain and damp warmth at the back of her head told her everything she needed. She'd been unconscious. Had Azzanar…?

She sat upright, and jerked to a halt as her head struck stone. Dizziness rushed in. Everything hurt.

Yelen sat up again, more carefully this time. A figure crouched beside her. Slender. Dark-haired. So familiar in another context that it took Yelen a moment to recognize her own face. Or rather, her own face when her body was hers no longer.

'*Don't worry, I've done nothing.*' Azzanar stretched a lazy hand around the darkness. Her eyes glinted red. '*After all, where is there to go?*'

Yelen took a deep breath and stared up into the grinning face. Fragments of memory stirred. Mirika. Magnis. Marcan. 'You're not real. I'm imagining you.'

'*Well, yes and no.*' Red eyes gleamed in a face at once more beautiful and malevolent than Yelen knew her own would ever be. A black tongue flickered over thin lips. '*You've had quite a knock. It creates… opportunity.*'

Bile choked the back of Yelen's throat. 'What have you done?'

Azzanar laughed. '*Nothing. Not yet.*' She ran her fingers across Yelen's cheek. They were warm. Too warm. As if a fire lay kindled inside. '*That moment I promised you? It's coming.*'

'I'm not begging you. I'm never begging you.' Yelen spat the words.

'*Yes, poppet. Just as you say, poppet.*' Azzanar picked at her nails. '*I suppose I'll leave you to it, then. Let me know when you decide to be reasonable.*'

The demon turned sideways, and was gone.

Yelen took another breath to steady herself and peered into the darkness. Her eyes adjusted to the lichen-lit gloom. The roof was a mess of jumbled stone, the walls no better. Her haversack lay a short distance away. Memories of the collapsing cavern dredged up from the depths. How far had she fallen? Where were the others?

Her eyes settled on a hunk of cold and lifeless ice away towards the wall. At first, Yelen wondered why. Then, she realised it wasn't ice at all, but frozen flesh – a bearded head shattered from a body buried by the cave-in.

Marcan.

Yelen twisted away, her stomach tensing. 'You fool. What did you do?' She hated herself for the words, but could find no others. She'd been getting through to Mirika. If Marcan hadn't grabbed the orb…

And if Marcan was dead, where was Mirika?

'Yelen? Yelen is that you?'

Magnis' hoarse words came from somewhere behind Yelen. Moving slowly, gingerly, she rolled onto her front and peered into the darkness. Mirika would have to wait.

'It's me. Keep talking. I'll find you.'

'No hurry. I'm not…' Magnis broke off in a fit of coughs. 'I'm not going anywhere.'

Yelen set off on hands and knees. It transpired that the space behind her was more open than that which had lain ahead. One of the tomb's colossal statues had fallen in such a way that its broad shoulders tilted a jagged slab of rock away from the rubble-strewn ground. There, lying on a spoil heap level with the statue's chest and one arm pinned beneath a boulder, was Cavril Magnis. His face was pinched and smeared with blood, but his eyes were alert as ever.

Yelen scrambled over and sank back onto her haunches. 'Can you move?'

Magnis jerked his head at his pinioned arm. 'I'm afraid the cavern has a stony grip on me.'

'Marcan's dead.'

He nodded wearily. 'Lot of that going around.' He raised his free hand from his side. Blood gleamed in the lichen-light. 'It would seem I landed badly.'

Yelen stared bleakly down at Magnis' chest. The left-hand side of his robes glimmered black and sticky in the pale light.

'So much for the legend of Cavril Magnis,' he muttered softly. 'So much for all of it. I let you down. I'm sorry.'

She stared at him wordlessly for a long moment. How could he say that? 'You didn't. And we're getting out of here.'

He laughed, the sound quickly giving way to a gurgling cough. 'I must be delirious. I'm sure I just heard you say…'

'I said we're getting out of here,' she repeated, more certain this time.

Yelen leaned forward, set her palms against the boulder pinning Magnis' arm, and braced her boots against the ground. She gave it an experimental shove. It rocked slightly, dust spilling away from the sides.

'You'll bring it all down on us,' muttered Magnis.

'I don't think so.' Yelen shifted her hands, seeking a better grip. 'There's no other weight on it. You've been lucky.'

'Not the first word that comes to mind.'

'Be quiet, and keep pressure on that wound.'

'Yes, mother.'

Satisfied that her grip was as good as it would get, Yelen threw her weight behind the boulder. It shifted inch by inch, then tipped away, crashing into the caved-in wall.

Dust cascaded from the ceiling. Yelen held her breath, releasing it only when it became apparent the rumble wasn't about to collapse in on them.

'Can you move it?'

Magnis winced and shook his head. 'Something's grating.'

Yelen glanced from his arm to his chest, weighing up her choices. 'It'll have to wait. The chest wound comes first.'

Scrambling back across the rubble, she retrieved her haversack and encountered her first fragment of good fortune – her lantern had survived the fall intact enough to take a light. Not that light offered much encouragement – a clear view of Magnis' injuries only confirmed their severity. His left forearm was a mass of mottled bruises, and the torn cloth of his robe revealed a gash that ran the length of his ribcage, often as deep as the bone.

Ignoring his feeble protests, Yelen cut open and peeled away the blood-soaked robes and bound the livid gash as best she could – which in truth was not very well at all. Magnis uttered no cry throughout, though his breaths hissed and flickered through his teeth.

At last, Yelen tied the final knot in place, and sank back on her heels. 'It's not pretty, but it'll hold for now.' Her voice trembled as she spoke the lie. At best, the binding was a stopgap. Even if it stopped the blood flow, infection was a certainty. 'Let's take a look at your arm.'

'Wait.' Magnis held her back with his good hand. 'I need you to promise me something.' His voice was stronger now, some inner fire bubbling to the surface. 'I've no right to ask, but I have to. If I… Promise me you'll help Elien.' His hand fell away. 'I'm her brother, she has no one else… Always loved roses…'

His strength spent, Magnis sank back and his eyes closed.

'Magnis? Cavril?'

Yelen leaned forward, heart in her throat. Magnis' chest rose and fell, the breaths shallow but rhythmic. She sighed with relief, in a way glad that he'd passed out. How could she promise to help Elien Magnis? She was on borrowed time every bit as much as Magnis. Just as death reached out for him, Azzanar reached out for her. And yet...

Moved by an instinct she couldn't quite identify, Yelen leaned forward and kissed Magnis on the forehead. 'If I can, I will.'

As Magnis slept, Yelen turned her attention to his mangled arm, splinting it as best she could with branches from the haversack's kindling bundle. Like her other effort, it was a long way short of perfect, but it would have to do.

That done, Yelen turned her attention to the makeshift cavern that doubled as both shelter and prison. Lantern in hand, she scoured every inch of rock, looking for some chink of light that would betray a possible escape. She didn't dwell on the new problems that would arise if she found one – namely, the shifting of tonnes upon tonnes of rock. Similarly, she tried not to let her thoughts linger on darker prospects. There was no proof, none at all, that she and Magnis weren't the only survivors of the collapse. Serene, Kain and Mirika could all be dead, and Yelen found no consolation in the thought that if Mirika was dead, then Szarnos was entombed once more.

At last, Yelen found what she was looking for. Behind the half-buried statue that had saved Magnis' life, a gentle draught set the lantern flickering. And where there was an air current, there was maybe a way out. Moments later, she had it – a crack between two fallen stones. It was too small to shine the lantern through – too small to admit even the tips of her fingers – but it was better than nothing.

Unfortunately, every stone Yelen tested remained fixed solidly in place, wedged tight by the pressure of those above. There was no danger of a secondary collapse because there was no chance of her shifting even a single rock. At least, not by herself. The thought of it revolted her, but what else could she do? If she did nothing, Magnis would die for certain. She'd die for certain.

Pressing up against the crack, Yelen shouted as loud as she could. 'Kain! Serene! Can you hear me?'

The only reply was her own voice echoing back on her. No. That wasn't true. There *was* something else coming from the other side. A distant but familiar voice, chanting unfamiliar words. Mirika – or rather Szarnos. Not that there was any point expecting help from that quarter.

'Kain!'

The shout echoed again without response. There was only a muffled sound, easily taken for the backwash of the echoes.

Yelen sank back against the uneven wall. So that was it. No choices left. She closed her eyes. When she opened them again, Azzanar sat opposite, red eyes gleaming in the lantern light, the cold stone darkening her translucent mockery of Yelen's form.

'You're not real.'

'*I'm real enough, poppet. I thought it might be nice to talk face to face.*'

'How considerate.'

'*I believe you've something you want to ask me.*'

'Want to? No.' Yelen glanced back at Magnis. 'But I don't have any choice.'

The demon smiled. '*So you say.*'

'Can you – can we – do anything for him? Mirika altered her tempo to heal her wrist.'

Azzanar arched an eyebrow. '*It's possible. But if there's an infection, you won't want to see what that does when dipped into the timeflow.*'

Yelen pulled back her glove and stared at the clock tattoo. Just a sliver of bare skin left, then darkness. Not enough, in other words. 'If I do this, you need to promise to go far away. You're to leave my friends alone.' It felt odd to use the word about the survivors of the Gilded Rose, but Yelen could conjure no other to do the job. 'You're to leave Mirika alone, assuming they manage to save her.'

'*Is there really anything I can say that you'll believe, poppet?*'

'Not really. I suppose I'll have to trust you.'

Azzanar leaned closer and set her hands on Yelen's. Strange, to feel the touch of something that wasn't really there. '*And you can, poppet. I love you. Who knows you better than I?*'

Mirika. Yelen didn't say the name aloud – likely the demon was thinking it anyway. 'And you'll heal Cavril's wounds, and free him from this cave-in?'

'*I can't make any promises about the first, poppet. Some wounds, time doesn't heal. As to the rest, a bargain is a bargain.*' Red eyes met Yelen's; earnest and unwavering.

Yelen met the gaze, as if she could divine the demon's motives with a stare. Azzanar was always at her friendliest when she stood to gain something, and Yelen now offered her everything she'd ever desired – she'd every reason to be accommodating. Yet doubt remained. Not for the first time, Yelen wished she'd inherited more of an awareness of the Clock of Ages, that she could do more than the shared time walk with her sister. But then if she could, she'd not be where she was, would she?

'Alright,' Yelen breathed. 'In exchange for healing Cavril, and freeing him from here…'

She shuddered, remembering the dream – caught behind a mirror while Azzanar took her place. But there was no other way. Not unless she wanted Magnis to die.

Azzanar's hand brushed her cheek. '*Say the words, poppet.*'

'And you'll take us far away from Frostgrave, and never harm my friends.'

The demon leaned closer still. Her face, almost touching Yelen's, wore a smile of anticipation. '*Say the words.*'

'I…' Yelen's mouth went dry. 'I…'

'Yelen!' Kain's shout echoed clearly around the confined space. 'Where are you, girl? Answer me?'

'Kain?' Yelen pulled away from Azzanar, and pressed her face to the crack in the rubble. She glimpsed the knight standing on the lower slope, battered and bruised, but hale. 'Kain? Where have you been?'

'Where have *I* been? I've been calling for you, but you didn't answer. You taken a knock to the head?'

'Yes. No.' Yelen glanced back at Azzanar, the truth of the matter rushing in. The demon had manipulated her perceptions again, feeding her sense of hopelessness and abandonment, but the spell had broken – seemingly not a moment too soon. 'I was confused, but I'm seeing things clearly now.'

Azzanar hissed, black tongue flicking across her teeth, and vanished.

Yelen turned her attention back to Kain. 'Cavril's in here with me. He's hurt. Can you get us out?'

'Patience, girl. I'm thinking.' Kain vanished from sight. The sound of rock scraping on rock rang out. 'I think so. It's not too badly packed from this side. No guarantees, though.'

Yelen glanced back at Magnis. 'Just do your best. It's better than our other options.'

At the back of Yelen's mind, Azzanar growled.

In the event, Kain's best was very good indeed. Though Yelen's heart skipped a beat every time she heard a boulder skip and scrape away down the slope, fearful that the makeshift ceiling would fall in upon her, no such collapse occurred. With a yawning groan, a rock beneath the crack toppled away, occasioning a spill of rubble down the slope. Part of Yelen's footing slipped away with it, and she scrambled back to stable ground. The resulting gap was large enough to accommodate Kain's head and shoulders – easily broad enough for Yelen to crawl through.

Kain stared impatiently up at Yelen. 'You coming out, or you just getting comfortable?'

'It's Cavril. He can't squeeze through here, not in his state.'

Kain nodded and patted the boulder to her left. 'This one's our best bet. Put your shoulder to it, and we'll see if it'll shift.'

Yelen did as instructed, trying not to think about the tonnes of rock still above their heads – tonnes of rock looking for the merest excuse to plunge down. 'Ready.'

'On three. One. Two… Three.'

Yelen straightened her legs and threw her full weight at the rock. Nothing happened. Then, with a creaking, cracking screech, it rumbled away in a torrent of dust. Overbalanced, her footing lost on the loosened scree, Yelen nearly went with it – would have done, had Kain not shot out a gauntleted hand to grab her.

'Hold on. It's a long way down.'

And it was. A lantern set a little to Yelen's right showed the rubble pile sloping off for at least the height of a three-storey building. Steadying herself, she peered up. A long way down it might have been, but it was a longer way up. The lantern light hinted at jagged stone, but revealed nothing of the darkness above.

'How far did we fall?'

'No idea,' said Kain. 'Too far. Serene's looking for a way out.'

That news awoke a spark of joy. 'She's alive?'

'She is. No idea what happened to Marcan, though.'

Yelen shook her head. 'He's dead. Mirika killed him… And Magnis? I've done what I can, but it doesn't look good.'

Kain nodded. 'Let me see. Don't wander off.'

The knight passed through the gap in the rocks. Yelen perched on the rubble and hugged herself. She'd been so close to giving up. Azzanar had nearly taken her. No. She'd nearly handed herself over. And for what?

She sat in silence for a time, the distant echoes of Mirika's chant blurring with muttering from inside the cave-in. Seven had set out, now only three remained – four, if she counted Magnis, which Yelen wasn't sure she should. She wasn't even sure she should count herself. After all, it was only a matter of time, wasn't it?

'I heard you talking.'

Yelen started guiltily. Magnis stood in the entrance to the cave-in, his good arm across Kain's shoulders. His face was pale, save for the grey circles beneath his eyes. A haversack hung from the knight's free hand.

'Talking?' asked Yelen.

'About me. To your… other half, I presume?'

Yelen nodded, not sure what to say.

'Don't give yourself away, Yelen, not for me.' He laughed softly, and winced. 'It only hurts when I laugh. And when I breathe.' He offered a wan smile. 'But Kain tells me you did a good job with me. So thank you. I'm sure I'll be back to my obnoxious self in no time.'

Yelen glanced at Kain. The knight shook her head.

'You need to rest,' said Yelen.

Magnis twitched his head. 'Don't fuss so. Plenty of time for… for that later. I made a promise, and I aim to keep it. Just see that you keep yours.'

Yelen nodded. So he'd heard that too. 'I understand.'

Kain frowned. 'The girl's right. You need rest, and medicine.'

'I need a great many things,' said Magnis, 'and I'm not going to find them here, or anywhere between here and Rekamark, am I?' He paused, but Kain said nothing so he pressed back on. 'No. Onwards it is, assuming you're prepared to carry me a little further?'

The knight hesitated. 'As far as you need.'

'Good. Now where has Serene gotten to?'

* * *

As it transpired, Serene hadn't gotten far at all. She emerged from a side passage as they reached the bottom of the slope, her appearance even more dishevelled than was usual. Her greatcoat was scuffed and torn in several places, and her blonde hair was filthy with rock dust and matted blood. Her face was wan in the lantern-light, almost haunted. Nonetheless, she moved as lightly as ever, climbing the rubble pile as sure-footedly as a mountain goat. Her stricken expression deepening when she caught sight of Magnis.

'Marcan?' she asked.

Yelen shook her head.

Serene shrugged. 'No loss.'

It struck Yelen as a heartless comment, but she suspected that a Serene bereft of Kas was a very different woman to the one she'd come to know.

'Have you found a way out?' asked Kain.

'Not exactly,' Serene replied. 'But I did find Mirika. Amongst other things.'

Yelen frowned, put on guard by her tone. 'What's that supposed to mean?'

'You'd better see for yourself.'

CHAPTER FIFTEEN

The diminished company of the Gilded Rose travelled in silence, Serene leading and Yelen bringing up the rear. Magnis hobbled along between, the bulk of his weight resting on Kain's tireless shoulders, and his broken arm bound tight across his chest by a makeshift sling. Though he plainly sought to stifle the sounds, every few steps brought forth a quiet hiss of pain. Yelen tried to ignore them, just as she tried not to think on the harsh syllables of Mirika's chant ringing louder and louder in her ears. Not that there was much solace to be found in their surroundings.

The deeper tunnels were different to the rough craftsmanship of those above. Dressed stone fronted the bare rock, lining funerary alcoves in which skeletal dead lay locked in ice, frozen in contemplative repose. Yelen quickly lost track of how many such interments they passed, but the number ranked beyond hundreds.

That number climbed steeply again as Serene led the way into a vaulted chamber and across a stone bridge. Lantern light danced across the ice-crusted cylindrical walls, but couldn't begin to broach the darkness beneath the bridge's span. And alcoved within those walls, like books set upon a library's shelves, lay yet more frozen dead, swathed in funerary garb, skeletal arms folded across their empty ribs and bony fingers gripped tight around the hilts of rusted swords.

'I never dreamed this was here,' whispered Magnis. 'I'd heard stories, but…'

Yelen eyed the nearest skeleton. Its timeless grin seemed to leer at her through the ice, a promise of her own mortality yet to see fulfilment. 'What do you mean?'

He shook his head wearily, and motioned for the company to keep moving.

Serene led them on, the tunnels heading ever deeper below ground, the echoing chant growing ever louder, more oppressive. Then, just as Yelen was on the brink of calling for a break, the passageway opened out once more. Responding to Serene's frantic gesture, Yelen pressed herself against the passage wall, and peered through the archway.

The buried temple, for such it must have been, was far grander than anything Yelen had yet seen within Frostgrave. The nave and the peaked roof called back to the Gilded Rose's base of operations, but everything here was on a far grander scale. The robed statues interspersed between yet more of the stacked funerary alcoves, their upraised arms forming the supports of the roof. The gilded warrior-figures lining the frozen-over pool running the length of the nave. The high windows, lit from within by pale green light. All spoke to spectacle designed to cow onlookers, to strip away certainties and replace them with those uttered from the steps of the cracked, black dais and its golden altar. All of it locked beneath inches of Frostgrave's ageless ice.

Mirika stood before that altar, arms outspread, the orb clutched in one hand. Green wisp-light played about her fingers, dancing about the tattered-winged statue overlooking the altar and spiralling across the stone pews choked with ice-encrusted dead. Some wore tattered robes, others were clad in rusted and distorted scraps of armour. All sat in silence beneath the rows of mildewed banners.

The chant reached fever-pitch, then died away in a choked snarl of frustration.

'It's not working.' Her whisper echoed along the nave, Szarnos' dry, bitter tones stronger than ever. 'How are you fighting me? It shouldn't be possible.'

Mirika's clenched fist slammed down on the altar, and the chant began anew, louder this time.

'I told you she was stronger than you thought,' muttered Magnis. He eased himself off Kain's shoulders. 'I need to talk to her. Help her throw off Szarnos' influence.'

'And how well did that work before?' asked Serene acidly.

'This time Marcan's not going to come charging in to spoil everything, is he?' Magnis sank against the wall and glanced at Yelen. 'You want your sister back, don't you? This is the only way.'

Yelen stared at him in silence. The worst of it was, Magnis was right. They were both on borrowed time now. Azzanar wasn't going to give up tricking her. It was only a matter of time before she won. And as for Magnis… The stain was across his robes, proof that her attempts to bind his wounds had only delayed the inevitable. Chances were neither of them were making it back to Rekamark. Mirika was all that mattered now.

She nodded tautly. 'Alright. What do you want to do?'

'To talk. Just talk.' Magnis nodded towards Mirika.

'Szarnos isn't having it all his own way. That means Mirika's still in there. If I go up there alone – no illusions, no weapons – she won't feel threatened. Szarnos won't be able to harness her fear.' He looked back at Yelen. 'You, of all people, should know how powerful a tool that can be.'

Yelen had to give him that. The only times she and Azzanar had ever seen eye to eye – the only times they'd cooperated with one another – was when they'd been in danger. What if Mirika *had* been holding Szarnos back during their last confrontation? And then Marcan – a man who'd tried to kill her in almost that very spot – had interfered. How would Azzanar have twisted that? How had Szarnos?

'I don't like this, Cavril,' hissed Serene.

He laughed softly. 'I don't much know that I like it either, but options are few and time fleeting. At least this way I'm the only one at risk.'

'Not alone,' said Kain. 'You'll never walk that far, even if Szarnos doesn't freeze you solid.'

'I'll manage. I'll have to. If this looks at all like a confrontation, it won't work.' The corner of Magnis' mouth twitched. 'And you, Borodna, promise a fight like no one I've ever known.'

'I still don't like this,' said Kain, flatly.

'I'm not asking you to like it. I'm *telling* you to do as instructed. That's why I pay you.'

She stepped away, eyes narrowing. 'So that's the way of it?'

'It is.'

Mirika's chant broke off in a stream of guttural curses. An iron candelabra clattered across the flagstones, propelled by a frustrated sweep of her hand.

Yelen came to a decision. 'Let him go.'

Serene's good eye widened. 'You can't be serious.'

Yelen flung a finger towards the altar. 'Look at her… him. Distracted, off-balance. There'll never be a better time. We can't fight Szarnos – we all saw what happened to Mariast when she tried. Maybe Cavril's right.'

'And if he's not?' asked Kain.

Yelen glanced at Magnis. He straightened slightly, and met her gaze unblinkingly.

'Then it's his choice,' she said.

Kain nodded. 'Go.'

Cavril eased gingerly away from the wall and took Yelen's hand in his. 'I'll bring your sister back to you. I promise.' With a last squeeze of her fingers, he passed through the archway and began the long walk up the nave.

Yelen watched him go, stomach aflutter. She couldn't shake an ominous feeling. Magnis was surely walking to his death, and yet he seemed so confident of success.

'*I can't believe you listened to him.*' Azzanar slumped against the archway and shook her head. '*A mind of mirrors, that one.*'

'You're one to talk,' muttered Yelen. 'He's dying…' She paused, strangely ashamed to have said the word aloud. 'Mother always told me to trust the word of a dying man.'

Azzanar laughed. '*In my experience, the drowning will say anything, clutch at any straw that might reverse their circumstances.*' She shook her head and traced a fingertip through the air. It left a trail of fire that sparked and faded. '*But if your mother told you otherwise, I'm sure that's fine.*'

Yelen watched Magnis' staggered, lurching steps along the aisle. Mirika still faced the altar, the chant and angry curses now so overlaid as to no longer be distinguishable.

The ominous feeling grew. She told herself Azzanar was wrong, was sowing discord just as she always did, but still…

Warned by an itching in her shoulder blades, Yelen glanced over her shoulder and found Kain staring unblinkingly at her.

'What does she say?'

Yelen frowned, and Kain jerked her head towards the archway – towards Azzanar. The demon straightened like a child caught in an act of misrule, and vanished.

Serene frowned. 'What does who say?'

'That we shouldn't trust him,' said Yelen. She'd thought Kain's claims of being able to see Azzanar were figurative. Apparently not. 'But she would say that.'

Kain's lip twisted into a half-frown. 'Perhaps. I'd say we're about to find out.'

Yelen turned her attention back to the nave. Magnis drew to a halt. Setting his good hand on the end of a pew, he propped himself up.

'Szarnos! I'm here to parley.'

Mirika spun around, harsh syllables of the chant dying on her lips. 'And what do you have to offer that I cannot simply take?'

Magnis didn't reply for a long moment. He leaned against the pew, chest rising and falling as he recovered his failing breath. 'At this moment, almost anything, I'd say. She's still fighting, isn't she?'

The familiar blue-white light formed around Mirika's hands. 'She will yield in the end.'

'Don't be so sure. She's a time witch, and stubborn with it.' Magnis coughed, and wiped his mouth with the cuff of his sleeve. 'How's she doing it? Meddling with her tempo just enough to dislocate your incantations?'

The glow around Mirika's hands intensified. 'I will not be mocked.'

Magnis didn't seem to notice. 'Go ahead. Kill me. It won't do you any good. But I've an offer that will.'

Azzanar appeared on the edge of the archway, this time out of Kain's sightline. '*And I thought he was going to talk to Mirika. I suppose he must have changed his mind.*'

Yelen swallowed back a rebuke, but she couldn't shake the feeling of unease. 'He'll bring Mirika back. He promised.'

'*Poppet, mortals make and break promises all the time. It's practically a sport. Why would he be any different?*'

A hand fell on Yelen's shoulder, the suddenness of it all but making her jump out of her skin. 'Something's not right,' muttered Kain. 'I'm going out there.'

'He said to stay here.'

'I know what he said.'

'No.' Yelen stared at her hand, suddenly planted in the middle of the knight's chest. She wasn't sure how it had got there – wasn't sure how she'd had the audacity to bar Kain's path, but she had. She squared her shoulders. 'He'll keep his word.'

Kain remained silent just long enough for Yelen to contemplate just how easily the knight could break her in half if she so chose. 'I hope you know what you're doing.'

Yelen glanced at Serene, whose eye flickered back and forth, and whose knuckles whitened on a dagger's hilt. 'So do I.'

In the temple proper, Mirika hunched forward a step. 'I'm losing patience.' Szarnos' harsh tones rippled through the words. 'Make your offer, if you indeed have one to make.'

Magnis straightened. 'The woman's no use to you as a host. Set her free.'

Mirika clutched the orb tighter to her chest. 'No! I have waited centuries. She will yet embrace me. My legacy will continue.'

'Maybe. Maybe not. But what if she didn't need to?' Magnis made a jerking half-bow. 'I accept the offer you made before. I will take her place.'

Azzanar chuckled. '*So the drowning man has found his straw.*'

Mirika knelt and extended her hands, the orb clasped between them. The icy glow faded from about her fingers. 'Agreed. Take the phylactery. Let me guide you. Wield my legacy as your own.'

'No!' shouted Yelen. She ran through the archway, boots skidding on the icy flagstones. 'You can't do this, Cavril!'

Mirika hissed. Magnis rounded on Yelen. 'I can. I must.' He spoke quickly, pleadingly. 'It's the only way. You want Mirika back, don't you?'

'And what about Elien?' she demanded, skidding to a halt. 'What happens to her?'

'But that's just it,' he said, eyes gleaming. 'I can do more for my sister with Szarnos' might behind me than I ever could with mere coin. There's an army here. You've seen a portion of it, but I felt it as soon as we arrived. It's writhing, waiting to be reborn. Your sister's holding it back, but I'll embrace it, give it purpose. Think of it! I could break Flintine's hold on Rekamark forever, and that would just be the start.'

Yelen stared at him, slack-jawed. The image of Cavril Magnis she'd built up in her head – the roguish but honest man she'd believed him to be – shattered into pieces. Just one more illusion. 'This was your plan all along, wasn't it? You never had any intention of selling the orb!'

Magnis gave a lopsided shrug, and winced. He pressed his good hand to his side, and spread his bloody fingers. 'We are what circumstances make us.'

Mirika stood unmoving before the altar, orb still held at arm's length. To all appearances, she'd heard nothing. Apparently Szarnos saw no reason to involve himself in the argument. More likely, Yelen decided, he wanted to do nothing that might jeopardize his willing host.

Yelen stepped closer. 'I won't let you go through with this.'

'*We* won't let you,' said Kain, taking up position on Yelen's left. 'This isn't the answer.'

'You've gone mad, Cavril,' said Serene, circling around to Yelen's right. 'This isn't what Kas and I signed on for.'

Magnis sighed. 'You're not seeing this as you should.'

'I see a man who seeks control of an army of the dead,' said Yelen. 'When has that *ever* worked out for anyone? Give me one example. Just one.'

'It doesn't have to be like that. I'll be in control, not Szarnos. A partnership of flesh and spirit.'

'You told me that such deals always ended badly, remember?' shouted Yelen.

'And none of them were struck by me,' snapped Magnis. 'I know what I'm doing.'

Metal slithered on metal as Kain drew her sword. 'Listen to yourself. Can you even hear what you sound like?'

Magnis' expression slackened with disappointment. 'You're threatening me?' His eyes darted back and forth, from Kain to Serene and back to Yelen. 'I know what I'm doing. More to the point, it's my choice!'

Yelen stripped off her glove, baring the clock-tattoo. 'I used to think that! Look at me now!'

'And you think we're the same?'

She looked away, disgusted. 'I thought we might be. Not anymore.'

'I'd hoped it wouldn't come to this, but I can't allow you to stop me.'

Yelen took another step. 'You're in no position to stop anyone. You can barely stand.'

He ignored her, shifting his attention to Yelen's right. 'Serene. About Kas. I assume you know it wasn't *really* Darrick who killed him?'

A cold fist closed around Yelen's stomach. 'Cavril…'

Serene glanced from one to the other. 'What are you talking about?'

'Someone whispered sweet nothings in his ear, lured him from camp,' said Magnis. 'Then she cut him open, and left him for dead in the snow, didn't you Yelen?'

'It wasn't like that!' Yelen pleaded. 'It was…'

Serene's scream, more a wild animal's than a woman's, drowned out the rest of Yelen's words. She covered the distance between them in an eye blink. Her hands closed around Yelen's robes, flinging her back against the high-sided pew.

'I trusted you!'

'It wasn't me!'

Serene's forearm slammed across Yelen's throat. A dagger-point gleamed. 'He was mine! He was all I had, and you took him from me!'

Azzanar settled in the pew behind Yelen and chuckled softly to herself. '*Would you like some help?*

Suddenly, the pressure on Yelen's neck vanished. Serene pinwheeled backwards, propelled by a gauntleted hand tight around her collar.

Yelen slumped, rubbing at her throat.

'Go!' Kain twisted the dagger from Serene's hand and shoved her to the floor. 'Stop him.'

Magnis had set off along the aisle once again, drawing ever closer to the proffered orb.

Yelen pushed off from the pew and ran in pursuit. The cold air raked her lungs as she closed the distance.

Magnis' lead shortened, but his head start was too great. Two paces, maybe three, and he'd reach Mirika's side. Yelen's legs pumped in one last effort, covering the remaining ground.

As she closed, Magnis' image splintered into two, both reaching for the orb.

Yelen had only a split-second to decide. She threw herself forward, hands clutching at the left-most Magnis' waist.

They met the edges of his robes, and passed straight through.

With nothing to cling to, Yelen overbalanced and fell. She struck the icy flagstones just as the illusion burst into glittering fragments, the impact jarring all breath from her body.

Magnis' fingers closed around the orb.

Golden light suffused the air, so blinding in its intensity that Yelen threw up a hand to shade her eyes. Through slitted fingers, she saw two dark shapes fluttering amongst the brilliance, one standing tall, the other kneeling. A deep, thready booming sound filled the air, its rasping passage like the breath of some vast, slumbering creature rousing to wakefulness. A thousand skittering voices pressed in on

Yelen's thoughts, their words mingling and overlapping like echoes of wind through the Broken Strand. Then they faded, swallowed up by the dolorous, rumbling notes, and the light glimmered down into nothing.

A hand found Yelen's and dragged her upright.

'See? There is nothing to fear.'

Yelen reluctantly allowed a cupped hand to tilt her chin, bringing her gaze into line with its owner's. Cavril Magnis still *looked* like Cavril Magnis. The golden light still ran beneath his skin as it had beneath Mirika's, but it no longer resembled invasive tendrils, but a wash of brilliance lighting it from within. Only the eyes were wholly different. Cold and black, they peered out onto the world like moonless skies, unreadable and unknowable. A golden hemisphere glinted in the centre of his breast, the ring of charred cloth revealing where the other half of the orb had buried into flesh and bone. Yelen recalled all the times her sister had held the orb close, as if seeking to enfold it in her flesh, and felt sick.

'The deal is struck, and I am an apprentice once again.' Szarnos' rasping tones bubbled beneath Magnis' words, but they were much softer than they had ever been when Mirika had spoken. 'I will learn all he can teach me.'

Yelen pulled away, uncomfortable beneath the inky stare, and sank to her knees beside Mirika. Her sister lay face down where she'd collapsed, unmoving. 'Mirika?'

'She'll recover,' intoned Magnis, laying a hand on Yelen's shoulder. 'There'll be little lasting harm.'

'I'll see for myself, thanks.'

Yelen shrugged the hand away and gently eased Mirika's tangled hair aside. Her face was pale, with deep red circles beneath fluttering eyelids, but she was breathing.

Yelen sighed with relief, and stroked her sister's cheek. Even in so sorry a state, Mirika looked better than she had in days – she should have been riddled with frostbite and gods alone knew what else. Maybe Szarnos had kept his word. Szarnos, or Magnis, or whoever was truly in control.

'So what happens now?' asked Kain. She had a sullen-looking Serene pressed face-first against one of the pews, arm twisted high behind her back.

'Let go of me!' snarled Serene.

Kain jerked the arm higher. 'Stop struggling, or I'll break your arm. Don't test me.' She turned her attention back to Magnis. 'I asked you a question.'

He shook his head at the disrespectful tone. 'Now, you leave. Return to Rekamark.'

'And you're not coming, I take it?'

'Everything I need lies within these catacombs. Szarnos' magic will sustain me, just as it heals me now, and will guide me in the days to come.' His eyes bored into hers. 'Think of the wonders I'll see. Perhaps I *will* become a legend after all.'

That cinched it, thought Yelen. It had to be Magnis in control, or mostly so. But for how long? 'He's using you.'

'And I'm using him. Symbiosis.' He crouched beside her. 'I was dying, Yelen. No legend. No hope. Now you have your sister back. I promised, and promises are important.' He pinched his eyes shut and shuddered with unrecognizable emotion. 'It will take some time yet before Szarnos and I are fully aligned and my wounds are healed. But when that is done, I'll be untouchable.'

'You can't control him,' said Yelen bitterly. 'He'll twist everything you seek to achieve.'

Magnis scowled. 'You're not listening.'

'Why would I bother? I don't know who you are anymore.'

'Then go. I've kept my promise.'

For a moment, disappointment glinted in Magnis' dark eyes, then he rose to his feet, arms outspread. Pale light rippled out from his hands, enfolding the ice-locked dead seated in the frontmost pews. Jagged cracks spread across the glittering surface as the mouldered bones within stirred to unlife.

'Remarkable,' whispered Magnis, the strains of Szarnos' voice growing in pitch beneath his own. 'Such power, so readily. And this is but a taste. No more illusions. No lies of light and sound. Just the deepest and most final of all truths.' The golden light beneath his skin deepened, spreading like spiderwebs along his veins. When he spoke again, all trace of the suave, cultured tones had gone. There was only Szarnos' guttural rumble. 'Go. While I still permit it.'

A chunk of ice dislodged from the nearest skeleton and shattered into a hundred pieces. A bony arm flexed and grasped at the stone armrest. Magnis rounded on Yelen, dark eyes gleaming and bereft of recognition. 'Go!'

'Yelen?' called Kain. 'There's nothing more to say.'

Yelen stared at Magnis, himself lost in rapt wonder at the awakening congregation. Then she gazed down at the sister she'd feared gone for good. She wanted to cry for joy and sorrow in equal measure.

'Do you need help?' asked Kain.

'No,' Yelen replied, gathering Mirika up in her arms. 'I have her.'

* * *

At last the black, suffocating clouds parted. Mirika didn't trust it at first, expected the oppressive voice to return to her thoughts. When it didn't, new sensations flooded in – feelings that she'd forgotten existed. Hunger. Pain. And cold. Cold above all.

Mirika sat upright, gathering the bundle of blankets and too-large clothes tight about her. She sucked in a deep breath, hating and relishing the icy spikes that prickled at her lungs. Muffled sounds resolved into familiar forms. The crackle of flame. The grinding of boots on stone. And voices. One voice in particular.

'Yelen?'

Mirika opened her eyes and immediately regretted it. Dark and light blurs fought for dizzying primacy. She raised a trembling hand, shielding her eyes. A dark blur grew closer, its presence shrouding the light.

'Mirika?' Warm arms enfolded her in an embrace almost bruising in its enthusiasm. 'You're awake? How are you feeling?'

'Like death.'

'That's not funny. How much do you remember?'

Mirika wanted to lie, for herself as much as for Yelen, but what was the point? She'd still know, just as her sister would still worry. 'All of it. I remember all of it.' Nausea flooded in with recollection. 'Mariast. Her toy soldiers. Marcan.' Her gorge tightened. 'I think I'm going to be sick.'

'Just breathe deeply. It'll pass.'

Mirika almost managed a smile at that. 'You don't know that.'

The embrace tightened. 'You might be surprised,' whispered Yelen, her breath warm on Mirika's ear. Then she withdrew.

Moments trickled past. Flickering shadows resolved into shapes. The leaping flames of a fire. A rubble-strewn slope reaching up into the darkness. Yelen, her eyes bright with elation as she knelt tending the flames. The Gilded Rose's knight... What was her name? Kain? Standing watch close by.

'Where am I?'

'Somewhere beneath the Tomb of Szarnos,' Yelen replied, stirring at the billy can. 'It's your fault. You brought us here.'

'I remember,' Mirika said softly. She remembered Marcan looming out of the darkness. The moment of panic. The smothering sensation as Szarnos took control. 'Where's the other woman?'

Yelen's expression soured. 'Serene? Looking for a route to the top.'

'Alone? That's dangerous.'

Kain snorted.

'Not as dangerous as keeping her down here,' said Yelen. 'She thinks I seduced and murdered her lover.'

Mirika tried to envision her little sister doing either, and quickly abandoned the attempt. 'And did you?'

'Not exactly.' Yelen held up her wrist, showing a clock face that was all but black. 'She comes out when I'm sleeping, wears me like a second skin.' Her lips twisted into a rueful smile. 'Told you I knew what I was talking about.'

The implications crowded in. It was too easy to guess why the clock had wound on. 'Yelen...'

She shook her head. 'I don't want to talk about it. You're back. That's all that matters.'

'You shouldn't have come for me.'

Yelen held out a steaming mug. 'Would you have come for me?'

Mirika frowned. 'Of course. You're my little sister.'

'And that cuts both ways,' Yelen replied, in a tone that brooked no argument. 'Now stop being ungrateful, and drink your tea.'

Mirika fell silent and cradled the cup in both hands, savouring the warmth as it seeped back into her bones. 'You're different.'

'I told you, Azzanar's closer to the surface. It's bound to show.'

'I don't mean that. You're calmer. More confident.' She forced a smile. 'You're not arguing with me.'

'Don't be fooled. If I start screaming, I'm not sure I'll stop.' Yelen glanced in Kain's direction. Then, apparently satisfied the other woman wasn't listening, she leaned closer. 'I told you once that I wasn't sure who I was without you. I've a better idea now.' A faraway look came into her eyes. 'Shame it's too late to be of use.'

The warmth of the mug did nothing to dispel the chill provoked by those words. 'What do you mean?' Yelen looked away. 'Yelen, tell me.'

'Azzanar nearly killed us all in the Lower Reach, all to get me to give up the last of myself,' she spoke quietly, her eyes downcast. 'She'll do it again, first chance she gets. I can't stay awake forever.' She took a deep breath and gazed defiantly into Mirika's eyes. 'As soon as we're out of here, I'm going to go for a walk. Any direction, doesn't matter, so long as it's away from you. Serene will do the rest. Azzanar won't win. I won't let her.'

Mirika gripped the mug until her knuckles whitened. 'Yelen, no.'

'There's no other way. We've known for years it might come to this.'

'You're talking about killing yourself!'

'If the alternative's Azzanar killing anyone else, then I can live with that.' She smiled a watery smile. 'If you'll pardon the expression.'

Mirika bit down an angry response she knew would only make matters worse. In a way, it didn't surprise her. Come what may, Yelen always seemed to have a plan – even if they were never so ghastly as this. 'And what do your new friends think of that?' she hissed.

'We've discussed it. Why do you think Serene hasn't slit my throat already?'

Anger and despair crashed across Mirika, seething like the waters of a mill race. 'No. I won't let you.'

'You can barely hold that mug. I see your hands shaking.'

'You might be surprised.' Mirika embraced her rising anger, let its warmth bring her new strength. 'There's another way. There's always another way.'

'Or maybe I made a terrible mistake, and it's time to pay the price. Azzanar's my fault. My burden. Too many have suffered already.'

Mirika leaned forward and grabbed her sister's hands. 'No. We can still beat this. You can't throw a rock in Rekamark without hitting a wizard, and we'll go further afield if we have to.'

'You're not listening. I'll not make it back to Rekamark. It's my decision, and it's made.'

'What does Cavril think?'

Yelen's mouth parted, a peculiar look in her eye. 'What did you say?'

Mirika paused, the expression on her sister's face scratching at a hazy memory. 'Cavril. What does he think?'

Yelen sprang to her feet and pointed away into the darkness. 'Cavril's back down there. He offered himself to Szarnos to set you free, and he was too bloody happy about it if you ask me!'

'No. That's not right. It can't be.'

'I thought you said you remembered everything?'

'I do. I did.' Mirika shook her head in a vain attempt to clear it. 'No. Nothing after I brought down the vault. I thought you'd ripped the orb from me or destroyed it, or something. Not this. Why didn't you tell me?'

'I just did!'

Kain, pretence at privacy abandoned, stalked around the fire. 'What is it, girl? What do you know?'

Mirika closed her eyes. 'Szarnos isn't the only one. There's a dozen more just like him, and he wants to wake them up.'

* * *

'It would seem I'm no longer your most pressing issue, poppet. How sad.'

Yelen stared at Mirika, thoughts skipping as she strove to grasp the enormity of what her sister had said. Szarnos was bad enough. A second? A third?

'You're sure?' she asked.

Mirika nodded, eyes scrunched closed. 'It was the only thing he wanted. Over and over, the same black thoughts pressing down on me. I fought him, dipped in and out of the timeflow to render the incantations meaningless. But it came closer each time. Time doesn't mean much to the undead. It was like trying to drown a river.'

'Where are they?' asked Kain. 'The others?'

'There's a crypt beneath the altar. Twelve corpses. Twelve orbs. Szarnos was chosen to act as herald, to open the way for his brothers and sisters. His thoughts were thick with duty. They tasted like ash.' Mirika grimaced and looked away.

'The Hidden Court of Draconostra,' muttered Yelen. 'It's real. Gods, but we've made a sow's ear out of this, haven't we?'

'The Hidden Court?' said Kain. 'Magnis didn't say anything about that.'

'Maybe he didn't know,' said Yelen, casting her mind back. From the way his voice had changed, it had been starkly obvious Magnis' dreams of controlling the long-dead tyrant had been precisely that – fantasies burnt away beneath the liche's unyielding will. A willing host he'd offered, and such had he become. Not a partner, as he'd hoped, but a slave. His future was hers also. Unless there was another way.

'We can't let this happen. We have to go back.'

Kain shook her head. 'Not a chance. We're well out of that.' She spoke the words matter-of-factly, enunciating simple truth.

Yelen stared at her, disbelieving. 'You're not serious.'

She shrugged. 'Job's done. We get to leave with our lives, and we're damn lucky to do that.'

Mirika hauled herself upright, brushing a tangle of hair back from her face. 'I thought the Gilded Rose was better than that.'

'What Gilded Rose? Paymaster's gone. Half of us are dead. We're done.'

'Who's done?' Serene flitted out of the darkness like a ghost. Yelen flinched as the baleful one-eyed stare fell

FROSTGRAVE: SECOND CHANCES

across her. 'I've got us a way out. It's a steep climb, but manageable.'

Kain nodded. 'Good. Let's get moving. The sooner we're out of this place, the better.'

She turned away. Yelen grabbed her arm.

'Get your hand off me, girl.'

Yelen had thought gazes didn't come any more basilisk-like than Serene's. Kain's coal-eyed stare quickly proved her wrong. A week before, she'd have backed down. But a lot had happened since then.

'Don't you get it? This is our mess. Me and Mirika brought that orb out of the tomb, but you'd have done it if we hadn't. What happens next is on us.'

Kain's glare didn't waver, but help came from an unexpected quarter.

'She's got a point,' said Serene. 'I don't like it, but she's got a point.'

'You don't like it. *I* don't fight for causes,' said Kain flatly, addressing her words to Yelen. 'Or have you forgotten that, girl?'

Yelen met her stare head on. 'I remember you saying you'd had enough of causes dressed up in fake righteousness. I'm not proposing we fight a crusade against Frostgrave's buried hordes. Gods know we'd never manage it anyway. But look at the body count Szarnos has managed in a handful of days, without help. It's going to get much worse, and we can prevent it.'

Kain cast a hand back in the temple's direction. 'Did you see what I saw back there? We couldn't stop Szarnos when he was alone and your sister had him in check. Now he's raising an army, and Cavril is gone.' She clenched and unclenched her fists, and took a deep breath. 'Look, I'm not saying I don't feel responsible for this. I told Cavril it was a bad idea, and it was. But adding our corpses to the pile isn't going to change anything.'

'I'm still going.'

Kain sighed. 'Listen, girl. *Yelen*. It's easy to be an idealist when you're young and think you're invincible. Take it from someone who's lost too many friends. Some battles you can't win.'

'I thought all battles could be won, so long as you're prepared to sacrifice,' snapped Yelen, throwing Kain's own words back at her. 'Well I'm prepared to do whatever I can.'

And that was the key, wasn't it? she realised. Sacrifice had marked out the road to this point, and offered the only hope that the journey would go on.

Kain rounded on Mirika. 'Help me out here? She's your sister.'

Mirika snorted. 'You talk like I've ever won an argument with her. Besides, I happen to agree.'

Kain gave an exasperated growl. 'Don't you understand? I'm trying to stop you throwing your lives away. You can't beat Szarnos.'

Yelen choked back a frustrated retort. She had to be careful what she said. Some words, you couldn't take back, and some secrets were precious. 'I can. I know a way.'

Serene frowned. 'She's right.'

'What was that?' asked Kain.

'I said she's right.' She stepped closer, an energy in her voice that Yelen hadn't heard since Kas' death. 'Cavril tried to tell us, but we were so busy haranguing him that we didn't listen.'

'He told me he was dying,' breathed Yelen. 'That it would take time for Szarnos to heal his wounds, that afterwards he'd be untouchable. That means Szarnos is weak right now. He's vulnerable. Maybe for the last time.'

At last, Kain's mask of certainty cracked. 'The clever sod. That'd be just typical of him, wouldn't it? Every conversation a spiral stair.'

'I think he was trying to tell us without Szarnos knowing.' Yelen tapped the side of her head. 'Azzanar can't hear my thoughts, only my words. Perhaps it was the same for Cavril.'

Kain nodded heavily. 'You win. I'll come. But not for the cause, mark you. Because it's a friend's last duty.'

Yelen nodded. 'Understood. Serene?'

For a long moment, Serene stared appraisingly at Yelen. 'You promised me I'd have a chance to kill your demon. Can't do that if Szarnos kills you, can I?'

Yelen tried to ignore Mirika's stricken glance. 'Is that a yes?'

'It's a yes.'

'Mirika?'

'Do you even need to ask?' Her gaze settled none too lightly on Serene. 'I just hope you're right about this.'

'I am,' said Yelen.

And if Magnis' sacrifice wasn't enough, she resolved privately, another would serve every bit as well.

CHAPTER SIXTEEN

'*You're throwing your life away, poppet,*' hissed Azzanar.

Much to Yelen's relief, there was no sign of the demon – just her voice dripping across Yelen's thoughts. So too were the hallucinations of the infernoscape in abeyance. They had been since they'd rescued Mirika, now Yelen came to think about it. Likely Azzanar was husbanding her strength for something impressive. Yelen tried not to worry about it. She couldn't prevent the demon's machinations. She could only remain alert for them.

'*You're throwing* our *lives away.*'

Yelen pressed back against the wall at Kain's insistent wave. The chill of the ice seeped through her coat, setting her nerves atremble. The squeak-crack of pressured ice was all too similar to the sounds of the temple's thawing congregation.

'Then perhaps you want to help,' she muttered, too softly for the others to hear. 'No strings attached?'

'*I'll not be a party to this madness. You've lost your mind, poppet.*'

'Actually, I like to think of it as getting the most out of it before you steal it.'

Mirika tucked in close at her side. 'What is it?'

Yelen shook her head, not wanting to discuss the matter. Fortunately, Kain mistakenly thought herself the target of the question.

'Sentries on the bridge,' she said. 'Szarnos is stretching his muscles.'

Szarnos, noted Yelen, not *Magnis*. Kain's initial reluctance to believe had vanished. Or perhaps she found it easier to distance herself from her former paymaster. Much easier to think of their quarry as a monster to be destroyed, than a friend.

Yelen eased her head around the archway. Two skeletons stood in the middle of the stone bridge, tattered robes twitching in the burial chamber's strange convection currents. Pale lights burned in their eye sockets, and their hands clasped rusted blades. They swayed ever-so-slightly, each motion accompanied by a rattling creak.

'Easy,' murmured Kain. 'This'll be hard enough without them spotting you.'

Serene pushed to the front. 'Two? You're worried about two?'

'No,' replied Kain. 'I'm… Serene!'

Serene brushed off the knight's restraining hand and ran for the bridge.

The nearer of the skeletons looked sharply up and stalked forward, sword swinging. Serene ducked the blade, swivelling on the balls of her feet as she did so. A heavy boot lashed out, cracking into the skeleton's robed knee. The leg shattered, bones clattering away over the sides of the bridge. Overbalanced, the skeleton fell to its remaining knee. A second well-aimed kick sent its skull tumbling into the abyss, and then Serene had its rusty sword in her hands. She parried the surviving sentry's thrust, stepped inside the weapon's arc and rammed her shoulder into its chest. The skeleton vanished over the edge of the bridge, the green fire of its eyes plunging into darkness.

Serene pirouetted to face the archway, setting the purloined sword jauntily over her shoulder as she did so. 'And you were worried.'

Kain strode onto the bridge, and Yelen and Mirika on her heels. 'Not about them,' she growled. 'Szarnos' magic raised them. They're bound to him, and…'

'And he to them,' finished Mirika, a pinched expression on her face. 'He knows we're coming.'

'Don't be ridiculous,' said Serene. 'He'll be too busy digging out his brothers and sisters.'

A *crack* echoed up and down the burial chamber. Ice spilled away from an alcoved tomb to Yelen's right. A skeletal hand emerged, clawing at rock. A skull followed, eyes blazing beneath a rusted helm. More cracks sounded, followed by the scrabble of bone on icy rock. Green pinpricks burst into life all around the bridge.

'Apparently not.' Yelen shoved Mirika towards the far end of the bridge. 'Go! Go!'

A skeleton dropped onto the bridge ahead of Mirika, burial robes dancing.

'Look out!'

Even as Yelen shouted the warning, her sister blurred with accelerating tempo. The skeleton's lunge speared clean past Mirika's ribs. Serene's borrowed sword blurred, shivering the skeleton's spine. The creature dropped, no longer anything more than a bundle of ragged cloth and lifeless bone. Mirika dipped, fingers claiming the skeleton's battered sword. Then she was through the distant arch and into the dubious safety of the tunnel beyond.

Kain slid her sword free of its scabbard. 'You should be running.'

Yelen glanced upwards and immediately wished she hadn't. Skeletons swarmed from their burial alcoves, clambering downwards over the icy stone like spiders on a web. The air filled with the scrape and creak of timeworn bone. 'What about you?' she asked, unable to keep a tremor from her voice.

'I'll be right behind you.' Kain settled her sword into a two-handed grip and squared her shoulders. 'I need room to work.'

Yelen darted for the far end of the bridge. A bony hand snagged her ankle, sending her sprawling. Her knee jarred beneath her, but she clung to her sword for dear life.

Rolling onto her back, Yelen kicked at the hand scrabbling at her ankle. Bones ripped apart, and then she was free. Scrambling to her feet, she found herself face to face with another skeleton. Steel flashed, her instinctive parry clumsy. The skeleton's sword scraped along Yelen's blade. Twisting aside, she lashed out. The strike was artless as her parry, but no less effective for all that. Steel bit deep, severing the skeleton's arm a little above the wrist. Yelen's backswing split the creature's rusted chainmail, scattering the bones beneath. Then the way was clear, Serene and Mirika calling to her from beyond the archway.

'Come on!'

Yelen covered the remaining distance at a limping run, her knee burning with protest at every uneven step. Another hand clawed up at her from the flank of the bridge. She ground the fingers beneath her boot and pressed on. Only when she felt Mirika's hand on hers, dragging her into the tunnel, did she glance back.

And saw Kain, alone in the middle of the bridge, a half dozen undead crowding close about her, and more clambering to join them.

'We can't leave her!' Yelen pulled free of Mirika. 'We have to do something.'

Kain edged along the bridge, sword in a high, two-handed stance.

'And do what, exactly?' Serene buried her borrowed sword into a skeleton's skull, then kicked both sword and victim through the archway and into the abyss. A dagger glinted as she drew it from a sheath. 'Get in her way?'

The other woman's feral grin struck Yelen as inappropriate, almost cruel. But then Kain's sword flashed for the first time, and she understood.

The knight's first sweep cut the nearest skeleton in two, splintering yellowed skull through to grave-garbed pelvis in a single strike. Scarcely had the blade come to rest when it spiralled out in a whirling arc, parrying strikes to Kain's front and behind, before angling sharply down to cut the legs out from under a luckless skeleton. Slowly, unhurriedly, Kain stepped into the emptied space.

'I told you she was good,' said Mirika.

To Yelen's mind 'good' didn't even begin to cover it. Pace by pace, Kain made her way along the bridge's icy stones. Chimes of steel on steel and the crunch of metal on bone accompanied every step, the bastard sword dancing a grim ballet to the rhythm of Kain's tread. A skeleton collapsed with every strike, the animating magic dispersing as their bodies disintegrated. Others clattered forward.

A pair crawled hand over hand up the bridge's supports, cutting off Kain's path. Kain's thrust crumpled the chest of the first before its blow could land. Then she ripped the fearsome blade sideways through the ruined ribcage, beheading the second newcomer in the same brutal motion.

Yelen lost sight of Kain as three more skeletons dropped onto the precarious ledge before the archway. She ducked beneath a curved blade. Steel sparked on stone above her head as she thrust, her attacker collapsing as its spine shattered. Serene turned aside a second blade with a reversed dagger. Her lashing foot sent one skeleton tumbling into another, the momentum sweeping both into the darkness.

'Let go of me!' Yelen turned to see a half-risen skeleton clawing at Mirika's coat. 'I. Said. Let. Go!' Her sword hacked down with each terse shout. The light faded from the skeleton's eyes as its bones splintered. Mirika pulled away, breathing hard but her eyes wild. 'Hah!'

Yelen grinned, the precarious situation forgotten. The distant, dour woman she'd scarcely recognized had gone. This was the Mirika she remembered. Then the telltale crack and scrape of thawing dead grew to new heights, pinpricks of green light blinking to existence in the passageway ahead.

'Kain!'

The pommel of the knight's sword crunched down onto a veiled skull. Her last obstacle clear, Kain swept her weapon down into a low guard and stepped through the arch. 'Run!'

Mirika took off, Serene on her heels. With a last glance at Kain, Yelen followed.

* * *

Mirika ran pell-mell along the winding passage, aware of little save for the thunder of feet behind, and the green lights winking into existence in front of her. Her coat ripped beneath grasping fingers. Cold bone tore at her skin. Each time, she dipped just briefly enough into the timeflow to rip free, then thundered on.

Part of her wanted to laugh with the joy of the danger, but the rest of her feared what lay ahead. With every step, she felt the black force of Szarnos' will grow stronger – a melding of terror and nausea pricking at her thoughts. On a rational level, she knew that the orb could no longer claim her – Magnis had seen to that. But still, the thought – the possibility, however unlikely – of the liche crawling beneath her skin again…?

Bony arms closed around Mirika's neck, the momentum of her run half-dragging the skeleton out of its alcove. Stifling a yelp, she seized the creature's wrists and set its tempo skittering across the timeflow. Yellowed bone cracked, bursting into dust and then she was free. Lurching to a halt, Mirika aimed a kick at the lifeless skull, and sent it clattering away. A flush of satisfaction at the act of petty violence helped tamp down her unease, and she ran on.

Little by little, the funerary alcoves grew scarcer, and finally yielded to walls of dressed stone. Mirika jerked to a halt as hands – flesh and blood hands, this time – grabbed her arms.

'Hold up, will you?' said Serene, between rasping breaths. 'We don't want to plunge into that lot without the others.'

Mirika frowned and peered down the passageway, finally noting the green glow suffusing the next bend. 'That's the temple?'

Serene nodded, and glanced back the way they'd come. 'Next corner. You really don't remember any of it?'

Mirika shook her head. 'I'd like to forget the bits I can.'

'You and me both.'

'Even Kas?'

Serene grimaced. 'Especially Kas. What use are memories? Not that I'll have those for much longer, way this is going.'

Not knowing what to say, Mirika peered back the way they'd come. She tried to forget that Serene was only there because of Yelen's promise. Serene would kill Azzanar, and in that moment Yelen would be lost forever. If she wasn't already.

After what seemed an age, Yelen and Kain emerged from the darkness. Not at a run, as Serene and Mirika herself had, but one steady backward pace at a time. The women stood shoulder to shoulder in the confines, Yelen's sword thrusting and parrying with a confidence that seemed most unlike her sister. A lot really *had* changed.

Bone splintered. The last pair of green eyes plunged into darkness. At last, Yelen picked up her pace, jogging the last few steps to join Mirika and Serene.

'That's the last of them for now,' she gasped, plainly out of breath. 'But there are plenty more coming.'

'What I wouldn't give to have a firecaller along,' muttered Serene. 'Think of the flames roaring through that tunnel.'

'Wouldn't matter. He's waking the entire catacomb,' said Kain. Her tone remained steady as a rock. Where her companions all sported grazes and cuts from grasping hands and near misses, the knight remained unmarred. So far as Mirika could tell, not even a single skeleton had laid a bony claw upon her. 'No way out for us that way, not now. And the idea of fighting Szarnos with his army on my heels doesn't do much for me.'

Mirika felt the knight's dark eyes boring into hers. There was no escaping her meaning. 'You want me to collapse the passageway?'

'Can you?'

Mirika closed her eyes, and let herself drift on the timeflow. It responded readily – eager, almost, for her touch. 'I think so.'

'Wait a minute!' Serene pushed past Mirika and glared at Kain. 'You can't do that! What if there isn't another way out? We'll be trapped!'

'Should've thought of that before you rushed in, girl,' said Kain. 'We're already trapped. She does this, we'll at least have a chance.'

Serene lapsed into taut silence. The scraping and clattering of pursuing skeletons echoed along the tunnel.

Mirika glanced at the nearest arch, its stones already warped and buckled from centuries of erosion and settlement. It wouldn't take much. Drown it in the timeflow, stretch its tempo to breaking point... She'd have done it in a heartbeat even a week ago. Probably would have thought of it herself. Even with no immediate prospect of another exit. Now...? Now it wasn't her decision to make alone. 'Yelen?'

Her sister threw a look back down the tunnel and shrugged. 'Did any of us really think we'd be getting out of here anyway?' The tightness around her eyes undermined the levity of her tone. 'Do it.'

Mirika crossed to the archway and laid her hand on its twisted pillar. Her borrowed gloves, too large for her thin fingers, chafed at her skin. 'Everyone get clear. I can bring down the arch, but there's no way of telling where it'll stop.'

Serene retreated towards the distant glow. 'Mad. All of you. Mad.'

Mirika lost Yelen's response beneath the sudden rush of immersing herself in the timeflow. Light twisted from lantern-light orange, to crimson, to a deep and pulsing red. She took a deep breath, and plunged beneath the tick of passing seconds, reaching for the sonorous, unyielding tick of the Clock of Ages, the emptiness of the counter-beat. The tempo of the pillar – the whole archway – lurched to a new and terrifying pace. Thousands upon thousands of years ran away beneath her hand, all in the space of a heartbeat.

The mortar gave first, rotting away into thin, grey particulates. Then the stones themselves split asunder, the dust from their cores darker and coarser. Mirika gave the arch one last push and stepped away, colours snapping back to normality as she rose from the timeflow.

'That's done it! Move! Move!'

Yelen and Kain, already halfway to Serene, redoubled their pace. The archway's surviving stones crashed down, sending clouds of dust and ice spiralling along the passageway. The creak-crack of the advancing dead gave way to a deep, throaty roar as the rock succumbed to natural law. The roof split asunder, the newly opened cracks adding their own cascades of dust and rubble as the dolorous thunder rumbled along the passageway.

Mirika ran on, too wearied by her efforts to do more than skim the timeflow to speed her on. Chunks of stone crashed past, some no larger than a fist, others vast enough to crush her flat. All missed. By a hair's breadth, and never by more than the fraction of a second gained by her immersion in the timeflow, but they missed.

Mirika flung herself around the corner, a gale of dust driving her on. It gusted across the threshold of another, intact, archway, and flung her to the head of a stairway.

She had a brief glimpse of surroundings that were unfamiliar, and yet niggled at memory like old friends: a gleaming altar, rows of stone pews – the tattered-winged statue with a dragon's head. And the host of risen dead, their raiment a mix of priestly robes and warrior's chain, shambling up the stairs to greet her. Helpless in the rush of wind, Mirika skidded over the top step and plunged towards them.

'Not that way, girl.'

A strong hand closed around her upper arm, hauling her sideways over the stone banister and onto a tiered pew. Kain gave her a hard shove away from the stairs, and then dived after her.

As Mirika fell, the entrance archway snapped like a wishbone. The thunder of tortured stone redoubled, and the entire entranceway collapsed in a spill of boulders and shattered facing stones. The river of rubble crashed on, sweeping down the stairway, and snatching a vast portion of the rotting congregation into renewed oblivion.

A boulder crashed over Mirika's head, gouging a chunk from a pillar before crunching away into the darkness. Icicles plunged from the ceiling, and shattered all around. For long moments, the bedrock groaned and shifted, as if threatening to consume the temple as it had the entrance passageway. Then the deluge of dust and stone eased.

Serene's hand closed around Mirika's, dragging her

upright. 'If that's what happens when you shatter one arch, reckon you could've pulled the whole bloody catacomb down.'

Yelen shook her head ferociously, spilling dust from her hair. 'Wouldn't have worked. We need to be sure Szarnos is dead.'

'I could've lived with the risk.'

Kain eyed the surviving skeletons warily. 'Look alive. There's plenty of the welcoming party left.'

Mirika followed her gaze. The stairway was all but buried under a pile of broken stone, and much of the congregation buried with it. But at least two dozen skeletons still roamed the pews, the terrible creaking-clicking of their limbs oddly loud in the aftermath of the collapse.

'What about Szarnos?' asked Yelen.

'Haven't seen him,' said Kain, hefting her sword experimentally. 'Maybe he's under that lot.'

'No,' said Mirika, her thoughts assailed by flashes of compulsions not truly hers. 'He'll be in the crypt.' She pointed. 'Beneath the altar.'

'If he didn't know we were coming before, he will now,' said Kain philosophically.

Mirika coughed, and wiped at her streaming eyes. 'Unless he thinks we're under that lot. Gods know I nearly was.'

Her hand started shaking. Her knees buckled. Belatedly, she realised that a hurried meal didn't make up for days without food and drink – however much Szarnos' magic had kept her alive in that time.

Yelen caught her before she hit the dust-strewn flagstones. 'Take it easy, Rika. We'll manage it from here.'

She shook her head, annoyed at how tired she felt. 'I can fight.' But the sword felt impossibly heavy in her hand.

'I'm sure you can,' said Kain. 'But take it slow anyway, yes? Give the rest of us a chance to contribute. What do you think, Serene?'

'I think that if we get out of here alive, I'm killing you myself.'

Kain shrugged and sidestepped towards the nearest aisle. 'We get out of this alive, I might let you try. In the meantime, help me clear a path?'

Serene glanced at the skeletons swarming up the pews. 'No. But I'll let *you* help *me* clear a path.'

Kain cracked a smile. It was wolfish more than beneficent, malevolent more than amused, but it was the most beautiful thing Mirika had seen in years. 'Good enough.'

With a booming laugh, she ran towards the foe.

CHAPTER SEVENTEEN

Step by step, they approached the altar, broken bones scattering from their boots and empty eye sockets peering accusingly up from the ice-sheathed flagstones. Azzanar kept pace the whole way, her accusing stare unblinking as the sun. Up ahead, Kain vanished from sight, descending a narrow stair running behind the altar. Serene grabbed a skeleton by its neck and dashed its skull to splinters on the altar's black stone before following.

Yelen led Mirika through the green glow of the stained glass windows, eyes flicking left and right, watching for threats. Nothing came close. A pair of robed skeletons creak-clacked their way across from the temple's rear, a threat for later, not for now. The path was clear – or almost so. Serene's grunt and a crunch of bone suggested more trouble awaited in the crypt.

Her arm tight around Mirika's waist, Yelen descended the narrow altar-steps. Unblinking rime-crusted statues peered at her from alcoves in the stairway, six majestically robed figures to each side, their graven expressions hollow and yet burgeoning with malice. She suppressed a shudder. The Hidden Court, and they were walking into their lair. Sure, they were dead, but so was Szarnos. Death wasn't an obstacle if your plans were in place – it was an opportunity.

Yelen's certainty crumbled as she approached the dark opening beneath the altar. What business did she have in that place? Opposing something like the Hidden Court wasn't a job for a delver, it was a quest worthy of wizard – hells, an entire *college* of wizards.

'*They've awaited this moment for centuries,*' breathed Azzanar. '*Their return was foretold before Karamasz's first stone was laid. You really think you can interfere? You really think you'll survive?*'

'Look out!' shouted Mirika.

Yelen's world lurched as Mirika's weight, so lately a burden, became an urgent shove. The stairway took on a ruddy sheen, the descending edge of the ceremonial scythe slowing to a crawl. It arced down, parting the trailing tangles of Mirika's hair and slicing through the tails of her coat.

Yelen crashed face first into the wall. The halberd's blade sparked on a stone step. Mirika, balance lost, tumbled away down the stairs. The red light faded as the sisters' contact broke, time's natural flow reasserting itself.

The scythe, moving already, glanced off the statue to Yelen's left. She spun around, and found herself staring up into a skeleton's rigid grin. With a creak of bone, the creature raised the scythe high and swept it down.

Yelen threw herself forward. Her shoulder thumped into the skeleton's armoured chest. The creature slammed back into the wall with a crack of bone, its blow going wide. Dimly, Yelen realised that the last statue on the left had not been a statue at all, but a guardian waiting in ambush.

The world lurched again as the scythe's butt struck her head a glancing blow. A stair's uneven tread took Yelen in the ankles, tippling her back. Stars burst behind her eyes as the wicked crescent of the blade screamed down.

Yelen had no conscious memory of raising her sword in a parry. But raise it she did, one arm braced against the stairs, elbow locked; the other aloft in defiance. Steel clanged on steel, the sword-blade shuddering with the impact, the scythe blade juddering to a halt an inch from her brow.

'Get away from my sister!'

Yelen heard a splintering *crunch*. The skeleton staggered, the scales of its armour parting as a rusted sword-point pierced them from within.

The pressure on Yelen's sword slackened. She rolled aside. A second *crunch* sounded, and the skeleton collapsed in a heap of lifeless bone.

Mirika sank against a wall, sword dangling from her hand. 'That was too close.'

'"I don't think I'll be much use,"' mimicked Yelen, regaining her feet.

To her surprise, she didn't feel any fear, despite how close she'd come to death. Was it simply that she'd seen worse in the barrows of the Lower Reach, or because even her subconscious knew there was worse to come?

'Like you said, you've come a long way. *I'm* not letting *you* out of my sight.'

But despite the note of levity in Mirika's voice, she sounded bone-weary. With a nod, Yelen slid her arm beneath her sister's shoulders and they pressed on into the depths.

Aware how close she'd come to an ugly death, Yelen peered at every nook and cranny as they advanced. Azzanar remained silent, the demon presumably aware that her bleak prophecy had come within a hair's breadth of self-fulfilment.

They passed more of the guardian skeletons, their armoured forms lifeless and often limbless. A cluster lay at the point the stairs levelled out into a low-ceilinged vestibule. Ahead, there was only silence. Yelen preferred the clamour of battle. At least while there was noise, it meant the others were still alive. Silence offered only unknowns.

A handful of steps later, the musty air filled with the familiar guttural chant of Szarnos' incantations, and Yelen found herself wishing for silence to return.

A great iron gate loomed out of the darkness, its rusted leaves parting barely enough to allow passage. A bas-relief of a dragon spread tattered wings above, a corroded brass seal marked the floor below. Even through the thick coating of ice, Yelen made out thirteen jagged runes arranged around the circumference. Thirteen runes. The serpent-rune of Szarnos, and the twelve of the Hidden Court.

'You ready for this?' asked Mirika.

'Stupid question,' Yelen replied, tightening her grip on the sword. 'Let's just get it over with. But if there are other orbs down there, for gods' sake don't touch them.'

'Thanks for reminding me,' said Mirika drily.

Shadows shifted within the gate as they approached. Yelen jerked to a halt and raised her sword.

'Easy, easy,' said Serene. Blood gleamed at a gash in her greatcoat's shoulder. 'It's me. Kain sent me back for you. She thought you were in trouble.'

'You missed one,' said Yelen, more curtly than she'd intended.

'You're hurt?' asked Mirika, with rather more concern.

'I've survived worse.' Serene's tone told a different story. It wasn't apprehensive as such, but held a note of reserve Yelen hadn't heard before.

Apparently realizing she'd revealed more than she'd intended, Serene turned sharply away. 'Come, if you're coming. We're clear to the burial chamber. Going by the light show in there, we don't have much time.'

Another refrain of the guttural chant echoed over Yelen, its syllables like spiders on her skin. No. It wasn't the chant. A horrible realization gathered momentum, increasingly inevitable with each passing moment. 'Where did you say Kain was?'

'She's back there...' Serene's eye widened. 'Gods damn her!'

She hurtled back through the gate, the sisters on her heels.

* * *

Yelen heard confirmation of her fears long before she saw any proof. The pitch of Szarnos' chant dropped. The air hissed with the crisp fury of an icy wind. Kain's shout of rage and pain all but covered the dull, wet sound of steel tasting flesh.

Even with Mirika as a burden, Yelen all but sprinted over the threshold, Serene only a pace or two ahead. To Yelen's front, a low balustraded wall gave way to a stone hollow. Ornate stone plinths were arranged around the perimeter like the number on a clock face. Each bore a robed skeletal figure, hands steepled in silent repose, an obsidian cube clutched in bony fingers.

Kain and Szarnos stood on a dais at the hollow's heart, a golden statue of the tattered-winged dragon looming above them. Half the knight's face was red and blistered, the matching side of her armour glittered with frost.

The corona of white light around Szarnos' hands flared as Kain's sword hacked down. Ice thickening on her armour, the knight skidded across the uneven flagstones. She crashed against a plinth. The impact jarred the sword from her hand and rattled the reliquary in its dead owner's grasp. Slowly, majestically, the onyx cube tumbled. It struck the ground and broke apart, sending a golden orb rolling across the stones.

'Kain!'

The knight glanced up at Yelen's shout. 'Get out! He's too powerful!'

Szarnos bore down on Kain. Her hand closed on the grip of her sword. She rose, blade already sweeping out in a brutal arc.

'I said go!'

Szarnos' chant deepened into a throaty laugh. White light flared. The stream of magic caught Kain dead on, flinging her to the hollow's edge. Her sword struck flagstones, and shattered into a dozen pieces. A heartbeat later, Kain slammed into the wall. She collapsed unmoving, ice crackling and thickening about her armour.

Mirika stifled a gasp.

Serene growled and started towards the balustrade. Shrugging Mirika aside, Yelen grabbed Serene's collar. She dragged her down out of sight as Szarnos' black gaze tracked towards them.

'Let go of me!' Serene clawed and hammered at Yelen's hand.

'He'll kill you,' hissed Yelen. Had it been sacrifice or arrogance that had made Kain face Szarnos alone? Both, most likely. Not that she had any room to judge.

'So? We stop him here or no one stops him at all. Nothing's changed!'

Yelen nodded. She'd expected to feel fear, or apprehension. She didn't even feel remorse for Kain, alive or dead. Her spirit was at peace, calmer than it had been since leaving Karamasz. She wondered if this was how everyone felt in the moments before they died.

'You're right. Nothing's changed.' Yelen took a deep breath and glanced up at the balustrade. 'You cleared a path. It's my turn.'

Serene cocked her head, brow furrowing.

Mirika worked it out first. 'Yelen! No! This wasn't the plan.'

Yelen's resolve almost crumbled at the heartbreak in her sister's voice. Almost. She took her sister's hand, felt the familiar warmth that went deeper than friendship, deeper than blood. Deep as birthright. She clung to it, used it to ward away sudden nausea. 'This was always my plan. I'm sorry.'

'No!'

Then, before her doubts could coalesce – before Mirika could summon the strength to dive into the timeflow and stop her – Yelen vaulted the balustrade.

* * *

Szarnos turned as she landed, bluish-white light growing brighter about his hands. Black eyes gleamed. The chant died away.

'And what is this?' he hissed. 'You too seek my destruction?'

Yelen let the sword fall from her hand. 'Not me.'

She felt the liche's oily black stare burrowing into her thoughts, striving to unpick her secrets and intentions. He didn't even look like Magnis any longer, the skin pinched and white as bones reshaped into a form more pleasing to their new owner. Her eyes drifted to where Kain lay. For a fleeting moment, she thought she saw the knight's lips flutter in breath. Not that it mattered any longer.

'Then you've come to offer yourself?' A pale hand swept across the chamber. 'Give yourself to one of us. To the future.'

'You know what I want.' Yelen glanced up at the balustrade. In reversal of recent moments, Serene held back a stricken Mirika. 'My sister lives. My friends live. Give me that, and one more thing, and I'm yours. No resistance. No defiance. That's what you want, isn't it? Death is such a waste.'

'Most assuredly.' Szarnos stepped closer, lips cracking into a smile. 'And your last condition?'

'Tear this parasite apart, and send him back to the frozen hells.'

Szarnos hissed, anger rattling in his throat. An icy hand seized Yelen by the throat, hoisting her off her feet. 'What foolishness is this? What do you mean?'

Yelen met his gaze, unblinking. 'I wasn't talking to you.'

'*Oh poppet,*' gushed Azzanar. '*It'll be my delight.*'

* * *

Mirika watched in horror as the transformation overtook her sister.

Yelen's skin darkened to a deep, baleful crimson. Her fingers hooked into black claws. Fire flowed from her scalp, consuming her tightly braided hair to form a flickering, crackling mane. Her clothes smouldered in the sudden inrush of heat, hems charring at the edges as the demon unfolded from her soul. Her face remained unchanged, but the features took on a malice that Yelen had never displayed, not even in her darkest moods.

Until that moment, Mirika had never believed it would come to pass, that they'd always find a way to cheat fate. Not anymore. That realization hollowed out her soul, carving a void she knew she'd never fill. Yelen – no, *Azzanar* – writhed in Szarnos' grasp, staring directly up at Mirika with eyes like glittering rubies. There was no recognition in that gaze. None.

'What is this?' demanded Szarnos. 'What trickery?'

'No trickery,' sneered Azzanar, forked tongue flickering. 'Just precedence. She's mine. You can't have her.'

Claws raked Szarnos' wrist, spattering black blood across the flagstones. The liche hissed, and flung her aside. Green light, insubstantial as mist, spiralled up from the ragged flesh. It danced briefly on the air, then dissipated into nothing.

Azzanar landed with a cat's grace. She stood legs bowed, shoulders hunched and arms outspread, as if compensating for a tail she didn't possess – or at least didn't possess in that form. 'Foolish deadling. Playing at power. You don't understand true might.'

White light flared from Szarnos' outstretched hand, frosting the air behind. Azzanar sprang aside, bones scattering about her feet as she scrambled across a plinth. The corpse's reliquary shattered as it struck the floor, the golden orb rolling free before coming to rest at the foot of the dais.

'Defiler!'

Szarnos hurled another bolt of frozen light.

Again Azzanar darted clear. Ice spattered across the plinth, scattering the abused skeleton yet further.

'I'm demon,' she laughed. 'That's rather the point. A subverter of graven idols and desecrator of dusty tombs. You liches, always the same. Craving order. Where's the fun in that?' Azzanar crooked a curved claw at the golden statue. 'I'll bargain. Stop venerating that caricature of death. Worship me instead.' A dreamy look crept over her face. For a moment, but only a moment, she looked like Yelen again. 'It's millennia since anyone called me a goddess.'

Szarnos howled. He thrust his clenched fists forward. Mirika shuddered, her breath frosting in her lungs as the temperature plunged. Ice crept outwards from the liche's braced feet, and a storm of frozen shards scythed across the chamber.

This time, Azzanar stood her ground. With a throaty roar, she swept her hands behind her and leaned forward. A thick gout of soot-tinged flame burst from her gaping mouth. Steam hissed where fire battled ice for supremacy.

'I had no idea.'

With an effort, Mirika tore her gaze from the contest below. Serene was staring across the chamber, slack-jawed.

'Even when she admitted about Kas...' Serene breathed. 'I expected some infernal seductress... Not this. How the hells did she keep *that* contained?'

'I don't know.' Mirika spoke the words numbly. She felt like she was trapped in a dream. A nightmare. She wanted to leave, to do anything but bear witness to what Yelen had become. But she couldn't. It would have felt like betrayal. She stared at her hand, still warm from her sister's touch. The last such touch she'd ever feel. The sense of failure gnawed at her. 'I don't know.'

Azzanar's flames grew brighter, fiercer. The skin of her brow split, and black horns burst through, curling their way into existence.

Szarnos' knees buckled. The ice storm disintegrated in a shower of white light. The liche staggered away from the victorious flame, hands raised to shield his face.

'It is our time,' he spat. 'We will guide Felstad back to glory. The world will welcome our embrace. Immortal. Unchanging. Eternal.'

The flames billowed out. Azzanar hissed and sprang through the smoke, claws outstretched. Szarnos gestured, his hands trembling as he hauled them upwards. A wall of ice rose up to block the demon's pounce. Claws sent splinters flashing from the barricade, but it held.

'Can't hide behind that forever, deadling,' crowed Azzanar.

She lunged for the wall's nearest edge. Szarnos gestured again. Other walls sprang into being, weaving a jagged, uneven cocoon with the liche at its centre. Azzanar spat, and slashed desultorily at the wall. Her claws gouged deep, then she turned away in disgust.

'Stalemate?' whispered Serene.

The familiar chant grew into being. Quiet at first, muffled by the wall of ice, but it grew in depth and volume.

On the nearest plinth, a skeletal arm twitched.

'Not even close,' muttered Mirika. 'He can't beat her alone, so he's raising help.'

'I thought they wanted living hosts?'

'For that, they need to survive.'

'What do we do?'

Mirika closed her eyes and reached out for the timeflow. Fatigue set in at once – faster than it should have. Her tempo returned to normal with a sickening lurch. She staggered, sinking against the balcony for support. 'I don't know.'

Azzanar prowled the hollow, eyes flaring in frustration. 'You can't hide in there forever, deadling. I'd love to leave, truly I would, but a bargain's a bargain.' Something metallic skittered away from her foot. 'Oh, what's this?'

The demon ducked out of Mirika's sight. When Azzanar stood back up, her hands cradled a golden orb – the same one she'd earlier disturbed. She licked a fingertip, and ran it across the orb's skin. Steam rose wherever she traced, the orb's surface buckling and hissing as if subjected to tremendous heat.

'Yasimov of the Thirteen,' Azzanar breathed. 'Can you hear him screaming, Szarnos? Barely awake, and still the agony's tearing him apart.'

The chant from within the icy cocoon continued, deeper, louder.

'I suppose not.'

Azzanar clenched her fist and the orb liquefied, molten metal spattering across the floor. A terrible, shrieking wail howled through the chamber, like a rusty gear forced into movement, but a thousand times worse. Mirika clapped her hands over her ears to block out the noise. It didn't help. It rattled the roots of her teeth, set her spine aching in sympathy.

Azzanar shook her fingers clear. 'No empathy for Yasimov? Still, even immortals must feel jealousy. I'd know.' Her lips shifted into a sly smile. 'Let's try another.'

She crossed to the nearest plinth and plucked the reliquary from its corpse. Shaking the black stone once, she cracked it against the plinth like an egg. The reliquary shattered, the golden orb dropping into her clawed hand. 'How about Mirazka?'

Again the surface of the orb ran like water, the otherworldly scream raking across the chamber.

* * *

Yelen awoke in bed. Warm. Content. The familiar sights of her room recognizable even in the dark. The shelf and its thin collection of books. The wardrobe. The window that always whistled when the wind was in the east. The fire roaring in the hearth. The mirror.

The mirror...

Memory flooded back.

Yelen flung aside the bedclothes and ran to the mirror. The reflection in the glass wasn't hers, wasn't the room in the *Guttered Candle*, but how could it have been? The *Guttered Candle* was gone. Instead, she saw the gloom of the Hidden Court's burial chamber, and a cocoon of ice. As to her reflection, it was almost unrecognizable – a dozen stages further removed from the crimson-eyed doppelgänger who'd haunted her dreams and her waking thoughts.

Szarnos' harsh tones echoed around the bedroom-that-wasn't. Yelen saw a skeleton half-rise on its plinth. Azzanar plucked the reliquary from the cadaver's grasp. A rush of heat kindled in Yelen's bones, boiling up inside her like the deepest rage she'd ever felt, the fires of the hearth leaping in reply.

Both stone and orb disintegrated at Azzanar's touch. The scream rattled the glass in the mirror, the cracked panes in the window. The hearth crackled almost to nothing. The warmth bled from Yelen's limbs, leaving her giddy, breathless.

'What are you doing?' said Yelen. 'Stop toying with him before someone else gets hurt.'

'*Hush, poppet. I'm enjoying myself.*'

'The deal wasn't that you enjoy yourself.'

Azzanar plucked another reliquary from its unresisting host. '*And yet here we are. That's the life of a passenger, poppet. May as well get used to it.*'

Her tone was strident, assured, but Yelen wasn't fooled. They'd been together too long for that. 'You can't break through the ice, can you? You're trying to lure him out.'

'*Though it pains me to admit as much, you're right. I've never liked the cold.*'

Yelen frowned. Something didn't add up. 'Can't you shatter it? Melt it? You helped me destroy the stone of Szarnos' vault. It shouldn't take much to disrupt the tempo of ice – it practically yearns to melt.'

Azzanar laughed. '*A laudable suggestion, poppet, but impractical.*'

Yelen felt the words hang on the air, taunting her. 'That's rubbish. Everything you and I have ever done has been through control of the timeflow. How can you even say that.' Her knees buckled, and she grasped at the hearth for support. 'Unless…'

'*I've never so much as dipped a claw in the timeflow. I've stopped you from accessing it, that's all.*'

'No!' Yelen sank onto the bed. The timbers creaked. 'That's not true!'

'*I'm afraid so, poppet. It's hardly my fault you mistook a talent not yet bloomed for an absence of the same, now is it? I can't tell you how much work it's been keeping you from realizing once it finally sparked fully to life.*'

Yelen stared at her shaking hands. It wasn't true. It couldn't be. And yet she found she believed Azzanar. There was no slyness in the demon's mockery, no hint of a larger game at play. Just good old-fashioned gloating, of delight at a long-running joke at last reaching its punchline. She gritted her teeth and stared up at the grinning face in the mirror.

'So all this time, I've been trading pieces of myself for nothing?'

'*Precisely. I'd give you the slow hand-clap you so richly deserve, except I'm rather busy at the moment.*' Azzanar's lips twisted into a grin. '*Go back to bed, poppet. We'll have plenty of time to talk later.*'

Yelen buried her head in the pillow and screamed.

* * *

The scream of a dying phylactery faded away, replaced by Azzanar's crowing laughter.

'Still hiding, liche? That's eight of your fellows snuffed out. You can't win this race. Come out, and I'll leave the others be.' She plucked another reliquary from its resting place. 'Who knows, perhaps they'll be found in years to come. Plenty of delvers seeking their fortunes in this tawdry city of yours.'

The back of Yelen's abused travelling coat split. Two black-feathered wings spread wide. Azzanar threw her head back in rapture, fire danced across the tips of her horns. 'Ah, that's better. Like old times.'

Mirika tore her gaze away, unable to stomach the sight. Her eyes fell upon Kain's body, still frosted with ice.

A gauntleted hand twitched.

At first, Mirika didn't believe it, thought it the result of wishful thinking. Then the fist spasmed. 'She's still alive.'

'Not for long,' said Serene. 'Soon as she melts Szarnos, we'll find out if she bleeds.'

'Not Azzanar,' said Mirika, hoping the other woman meant the demon, and not Yelen. 'Kain.'

Serene shook her head. 'No chance.'

'I'm telling you, she moved.'

Serene scowled, then nodded. 'Keep an eye open. I'll take a closer look.'

Mirika glanced at Azzanar, still crowing at the unresponsive Szarnos. 'We'll both go.'

They kept low, careful not to disturb the scattered bones, and doubly careful to give a wide berth to the single remaining liche-corpse that lay in their path. Serene led the way. Mirika kept glancing back over her shoulder at what had once been her sister.

Another soul-wrenching scream echoed around the burial chamber. Liquid gold dribbled onto the ground.

'Three left, deadling,' mocked Azzanar. 'Don't you care? Won't you avenge them? Won't you offer yourself in their stead?'

The chant of resurrection guttered and died.

'I'll be damned.' Serene squatted at Kain's side. 'She's still breathing.'

Mirika scutched into the lee of the now-empty plinth and peered down. Kain might have been alive, but she was a mess. Her face was a mess of swollen and torn flesh, the entire left side of her body locked in ice. 'If I can get her free of this ice, can you carry her out of here?'

Serene scowled. 'I could, if I had any intention of leaving. I've a score to settle over there.'

'We'll argue about that part later.'

Mirika laid her hands on Kain's frozen pauldron, and reached into the timeflow. She didn't ease herself in as she had before, but dived deep, hoping her momentum would bring results before fatigue snapped her back into reality.

As before, tiredness set in at once. The Clock of Ages wanted her gone, but why? Had she truly overtaxed herself so badly in the temple above? Mirika shook her head. It didn't help to think that way. She'd work to do. She tied her tempo to the ice, flinging it into acceleration. Already melting beneath the heat of her hands and the fading warmth of Kain's flesh, it dwindled away as if beneath the summer sun.

Mirika held the tempo steady for one… two… three relative breaths. Then the Clock pushed back, hurling her clear.

'You alright?' asked Serene, her attention split between Mirika and the confrontation beyond the dais.

Mirika shook her head. 'My connection with the timeflow. It's not right, but I don't understand why.' She stared down at Kain. 'I hope it's enough.'

The ice cocoon exploded, flinging a thousand razor-sharp shards across the chamber, leaving a frozen mist in its wake. Azzanar's wings whipped around, shielding her face and body from the worst of it. Serene cried out as a shard tore a bloody furrow across her forehead. Mirika hunched deeper behind the tenuous cover of the plinth.

Szarnos charged through the frozen mist, fists encased in ice and the familiar white light crackling around his fingers. He screamed as he came; not the wailing death cry of the phylacteries' spirits, but the raw bellow of a being driven to madness out of loss and rage.

Azzanar's wings unfurled. Blood dripped from her face and from rents in her clothing. The tip of one horn ended in a ragged stump. Szarnos had hurt her, despite the desperate precautions.

'Now that's the spirit!'

Again she belched fire at the liche. Szarnos came on, robes alight, hair ablaze. An ice-encased fist clubbed Azzanar to one knee, the blow landing with more force than Cavril Magnis' spare frame should have ever possessed. As she could rose, his hands tore at her throat, the telltale spicules of frost creeping across her jawline and up her cheeks. Not to be outdone, Azzanar locked her hand around Szarnos' throat, the talons cutting deep. Blood sizzled as it hit burning flesh.

For a long moment, demon and liche stood locked together in their murderous embrace, neither moving, neither uttering a word. Then Szarnos sagged, his hands slipping free of Azzanar's throat as his burning corpse crashed to the ground.

'Winter doesn't last,' Azzanar sneered. She pressed a palm to her frost-clad cheek. Steam rose, the ice melting away at her touch. 'No one should know that better than a ruler of Frostgrave. Sooner or later, the fire always wins and the ice recedes.'

She opened her mouth wide, and fire flooded forth once more, reigniting the dying flames of Szarnos' body. The tortured flesh blackened and shrank as the bones twisted, a single charred arm seeming to reach up out of the flames before collapsing into ashen dust.

* * *

The heat of the flames receded, the hearth diminishing. Yelen leaned against the mantelpiece, breathless and dizzy.

'It's done, poppet. I keep my promises. You should be pleased.'

Yelen stared at the mirror. She didn't *feel* pleased. This wasn't a triumph. Too many had died, and died needlessly – many of them at Azzanar's hands. Cavril was the worst. Had anything at all of him been left when Szarnos had perished? Even enough to realize that his sacrifice had paid off? It almost didn't matter. It wasn't as though she could apologize for her final words to him.

She braced her hands on the mantelpiece, and stared deep into Azzanar's eyes with all the conviction she could muster. 'That's not all you promised me.'

Azzanar laughed. *'I've no quarrel with your friends. I'm having a* very *good day. But if they pick a fight…'*

'No,' snapped Yelen. 'I won't let you.'

'You don't have a choice. You've no power here anymore, poppet. That was the agreement.'

'That's not fair!'

Yelen knew the words sounded childish, just as slamming her fist against the mirror's glass was a petulant, powerless act. But an older, wiser thought gathered behind them. No, it wasn't fair. But then nor was it necessarily true, either. In their time together, Azzanar had claimed so much, but all of it had begun because Yelen had begged the demon to grant her access to the timeflow. And if that had been a lie, then what else?

She stared through the mirror. Mirika was too far away, and there was no suggestion she even realised what Yelen needed of her. That was the problem with having a voice in your head – it made conspiracy impossible. But there was still a chance.

Yelen looked again at the mirror, and noticed something she hadn't before. A slim crack, barely more than a hairline, ran from top to bottom. It wasn't just that she hadn't seen it before – she was damn sure it hadn't *been* there before.

She wasn't powerless. And she certainly wasn't alone.

* * *

Azzanar scattered Szarnos' ashes with a booted foot, and strode towards the nearest plinth. She cracked open the reliquary, and scattered the molten contents across the floor. The now-familiar death scream shrieked across the chamber.

'What a vile sound.' Mirika glanced down to see Kain's swollen eye flicker open. 'I have the memory of attempting something noble, and failing at it,' said Kain, her voice little more than a dying breath.

'Foolish, more like,' muttered Serene. 'Yelen took your place, in more ways than one.'

'Don't you believe it,' breathed Kain. 'That girl's smarter than you think.'

Another phylactery melted in Azzanar's grip. Mirika threw a disgusted look in the demon's direction. 'No. Not this time. My sister had a plan, but it was all about tricking us, not Azzanar. The demon's won.'

'Maybe,' said Kain. 'Have a little faith. She's…' She petered out, the rest lost beneath the soft rasp of breathing.

'You should go,' Serene told Mirika, 'before she remembers we're still here.'

Azzanar spun on her heel, the molten gold of the last phylactery spilling from her fingers. 'Oh, I've not forgotten. I promised to spare you, that's all.'

Serene put a hand to her dagger, and climbed to her feet.

Azzanar tapped the side of her head. 'She's shouting at me now, reminding me of the bargain. But if you raise a hand against me – if that dagger even comes close to touching my skin – then all bets are off, my poppets. For all of you.'

Mirika's blood ran cold. 'Yelen's still in there?'

'Of course. It's my turn now. That's how it works. We're going to have *such* fun. Maybe you'd like to join us?'

Azzanar's demonic countenance dissipated, like a river's reflection dispersed by a sudden pebble. The red-skinned monster vanished, and once again Yelen stood before Mirika, her clothing charred and torn, her eyes still blazing red. 'I've never had a sister,' said Azzanar. 'I wonder what it's like.'

The idea was so abhorrent Mirika couldn't begin to find the words to reply.

Serene circled around to Mirika's right. 'I still owe you for Kas, demon.'

'Please,' sneered Azzanar. 'As if you never killed anyone. You've washed the blood off your hands, but I can still smell it. Truth is, you loved cutting throats more than you ever loved him. Kas was holding you back.' She tapped a finger against her breastbone. 'I freed you.'

Serene tensed, ready to spring.

Mirika held out a warning hand. 'Don't do it, Serene. She's trying to provoke you.'

'Maybe I don't care.'

Mirika bit back an angry retort. She was going to die, didn't she see that? 'Yelen wouldn't want this.'

'Should've stuck around then, shouldn't she?'

Mirika glanced at Kain. No help there. The knight was still unconscious. Still dying, for all she knew. If only she'd been right. If only Yelen really had worked out how to beat Azzanar as well. But she hadn't. Her sister had accepted her fate, and had spent the last of her soul to see Szarnos defeated. Not that she had any right to judge, Mirika decided. They were all in this mess because of her, and now – if she was lucky – she might just have the strength to dip into the timeflow long enough to stop Azzanar's first pass burning Serene to a crisp. That, more than anything else, made matters worse. The connection to the Clock of Ages was still there, but it was muted. As if…

Oh gods, it really was that simple, wasn't it?

'Yelen,' muttered Mirika. 'You crafty…'

Serene sprang, dagger flashing.

***

Yelen recognized Serene's intent before she even left the ground. Recognized it, and was ready. The fires kindled, rising through her, begging for release.

She denied them.

The flames in the bedroom's hearth leapt to new heights, setting light to her nightclothes and searing her skin. Pain wracked Yelen's body, hot and cold all at once. She gripped the mantelpiece and screamed. But she held tight to the flames, kept them in her bones where they belonged.

'*What are you doing! Stop it! Stop it! At once!*'

Yelen raised her head as her hair caught light. Azzanar stared back, face twisted in fury.

'Me?' gasped Yelen. 'I'm doing nothing. I've no power here, remember?'

Then she laughed.

***

Mirika reached into the timeflow and flung herself at Serene. Her tempo responded sluggishly, but it was enough, speeding her into collision with Serene's shoulder just as the first flames spilled from Yelen's – from Azzanar's – lips. Both women went down in a tangle of arms and legs beside Kain. The fires flickered over their heads.

Mirika lost her grip on the timeflow in the same moment she hit the flagstones. It was less disorienting now she knew the reason – not that it'd help her survive the flames already tracking towards her.

Except they weren't.

Azzanar stood stock still, the last dribble of fire spiralling upwards from her lips with none to replace it. Her face was frozen in a look of fury. Her outflung hands trembled.

'I can't hold her for long,' Azzanar cried.

No. Not Azzanar, Mirika realised, scrambling to her feet. The voice was wrong.

Serene gathered herself. 'What's happening?'

Mirika's heart swelled with a sudden flush of glee. 'Yelen. She's fighting her.'

'Then I'll finish it.'

'No!'

Serene shoved Mirika aside and started forward, only to stagger immediately to a halt.

'Stay put, or I'll break your damn leg,' gasped Kain. Mirika glanced down. Kain had Serene's right boot held tight in both hands. 'She's your sister. You finish it.'

Azzanar's arms shook. The first tongues of flame trickled across her teeth. 'I'll send your ashes to the frozen hells for this!'

'I don't think so,' said Mirika. 'Turns out Yelen's smarter than both of us.' She flung her arms around Azzanar, drawing her into an embrace. 'Time to come home, little sister.'

Azzanar ranted and raged, her speech a litany of curses. Mirika closed her hand around her sister's, and let the pulse of the Clock of Ages sweep her up.

Everything vanished in a swirl of reds and blues, the dimensions and confines of the natural world falling asunder as the time walk took effect. Mirika closed her eyes and clung tight to Yelen's hand, afraid to hold on in case she'd guessed wrong, but more afraid to let go and risk losing her sister forever. She thought back to days before, when the time walk – their shared birthright – had saved her life. Now it would save Yelen's soul.

Or so she hoped.

The world settled. Up and down regained their meaning. Cold stone formed under Mirika's knees. Hesitantly, she opened her eyes. They stood on the burial chamber's upper level, in the very spot they'd witnessed Kain's fall – the last place they'd touched, giving their birthright purchase on inconstant time. The room itself was unchanged, strewn with bones, ashes and spatters of once-molten gold. Serene stood in the hollow, ankle still tight in Kain's grasp, expression torn between anger and disbelief. But Mirika had eyes only for the face before her.

'Yelen?'

Eyelids fluttered open. Blue eyes gazed back. Blue. Not red.

'It's me.' Yelen smiled. 'You saved me.'

'You saved me first.'

Ignoring Serene's confused look and Kain's rather more enigmatic one, Mirika flung her arms around her sister and wept for joy.

CHAPTER EIGHTEEN

The blizzard howled through the darkened streets of the Broken Strand, promising a night cold enough to see the trolls confined to their lairs. Cracked glass rattled in the fourth-storey window. Yelen shuddered, and drew her blankets tighter around her shoulders.

Across the street, the Temple of Draconostra lay as silent as when she'd first laid eyes on it. And yet it was different somehow. Forlorn, almost. As if its hour of purpose had come and gone, all for nothing. Szarnos the Great had returned to legend. The Hidden Court were banished to rumour and hearsay. And that wasn't all.

Yelen bared her wrist, and peered at the clock face tattoo, half-expecting it to have changed. It hadn't. The dial was no longer dark. There were only the numerals of the clock, dark against pale skin. For the first time in months, Yelen couldn't even feel the demon coiling in her thoughts. No visions. No whispers. No laughter. Azzanar had retreated. But for how long?

'Is she bothering you?'

Mirika stood in the doorway, firelight at her back and a concerned frown on her face. She'd hardly slept since Serene had finally found a clear passage back to the surface. None of them had. No one had wanted to pass a night in Szarnos' domain, whether he was languishing in the frozen hells or not. And so they'd staggered on through the rime-crusted chambers of slumbering dead, Yelen feeling like little more than a numbed corpse herself. Nothing in her life had felt sweeter than the first caress of the cold night air.

Yelen hastily covered her wrist. 'How's Kain?'

'Sleeping like the dead. I nudged her tempo enough to heal the worst of her injuries, but she won't let me do more. Says she doesn't want to wish her life away.'

'And Serene?'

'Keeping watch outside, and don't change the subject,' said Mirika. 'Is she bothering you?'

Yelen sighed, but decided she wasn't getting off the hook. 'No. I can't even hear her.'

Mirika drew closer and slipped an arm around her shoulders. 'Then why don't you sound happy? Perhaps you're free of her.'

'I'd feel happier if I understood why.'

'You stood up to her. Broke her hold. From what you told me, the bargain was all lies and incense anyway. Her strength came from making you believe you were weak.' Mirika shrugged. 'Does it need to be more than that?'

Was that it? Yelen wondered. Had her own belief in the consequence of thirteen o'clock been the only real power Azzanar had held over her? Hells, she'd all but pleaded for the demon to take over, at the end. She'd surrendered, given in. By her attitude, Yelen had made herself a slave. Without Azzanar's confession... Without the time walk pulling Yelen back to her earlier state, clutching tight to the secret the demon had unwittingly shared... The darkness of the tattooed clock face had once foretold inevitable damnation. Maybe like a page unwritten, the newly pale dial promised a life now Yelen's to shape.

'Then why can't I touch the timeflow?' said Yelen. And she'd tried. Gods, how she'd tried. In small ways at first, when Mirika's attention was elsewhere, then with increasing desperation. 'If Azzanar was all that was holding me back, I should be able to if she's gone.'

'Maybe it'll come in time.' Mirika offered a lopsided smile. 'If you'll pardon the expression. In the meantime, try to cheer up. You've earned a little happiness.'

Yelen scowled. 'Easy for you to say.'

'I don't know,' said Mirika. 'I reckon sharing my soul with Szarnos gives me a *little* more perspective than I had before.'

Yelen pulled away. 'So we're back to you-know-best, is that it?'

'No! Gods, no. Honestly, I don't know how you kept her captive all this time. Szarnos all but swallowed me. I wasn't strong enough. You were.'

Yelen shook her head. 'It's not the same thing.'

'Maybe not, but I'm proud of you, little sister, and I want you to be happy. Kain said something about rebuilding the Gilded Rose. She'd like us to be part of it. But if you want to go back to Karamasz, then so be it.'

'And what do you want?'

Mirika shrugged. 'I'm staying in Frostgrave – at least, if I can pay off my debt with Flintine. Kain told me about Cavril's bargain, but I doubt Flintine will settle for twelve per cent of nothing.'

She fell silent for a moment. Yelen knew her sister was recalling the moment of Kardish's death. They'd not spoken of it yet, but Yelen could well imagine the guilt Mirika felt. In its way, it wasn't so different to the burden she still carried over

Kas and Darrick.

'Anyway,' Mirika went on. 'I'm staying, and I'd rather you stayed with me. Whether you believe it or not, I'd be lost without you.'

Yelen looked away, cheeks warming with embarrassment. Outside, the wind rose to fresh heights. Her reflection in the window, as downcast in appearance as she was in mood, shook with the rattling panes of glass.

'I'm not sure I know where I want to be any longer,' Yelen said at last. 'Perhaps it doesn't matter where I am, as long as I'm *me*.' She took a deep breath, let the lingering aroma of fire-smoke fill her. 'I'll come back to Rekamark. Beyond that, I don't know. I've a promise to keep.'

'Cavril's sister?'

Yelen closed her eyes, recalling Magnis' earnest plea. In hindsight it was obvious that he'd known how events would unfold. 'Yes. I don't know how I'm to help Elien. Hells, I don't even know where to begin…'

Mirika flashed a grin. 'Actually,' she said, 'I've an idea or two about that. So does Serene, oddly enough. But we agreed not to tell you until you get some sleep. How long has it been now?'

Yelen opened. 'Too long. Alright, you win. Go on. I'll be through in a moment.'

Mirika lingered a moment longer, then slipped back through the doorway.

Yelen listened as her sister's footsteps faded. Mirika was right. Maybe she was owed a little happiness. Coming to a decision, she levelled a stare at her reflection in the glass. Blue eyes gazed back; serious, but with a hint of mischief. Or so Yelen hoped.

'Get some sleep, Yelen Semova. It's a long road ahead.'

She laughed, the stern expression in the glass collapsing into mirth.

Blue eyes flickered crimson then back to blue.

Yelen froze, heart pounding, uncertain of what she'd seen. She pressed fingers against the pane, examining her features once again. Blue eyes stared back. She sighed with relief.

'Just your imagination,' she muttered. 'Mirika's right. You need to sleep.'

'You do indeed, poppet,' breathed a familiar voice. *'Like you said, it's a long road ahead. You and I? We're not done.'*

SCENARIO

We hope you have enjoyed *Frostgrave: Second Chances* by Matthew Ward. This book is the first novel based on the popular tabletop wargame, *Frostgrave: Fantasy Wargames in the Frozen City* by Joseph A. McCullough. If you would like to learn more about the game, you can join the *Frostgrave: Fantasy Wargames in the Frozen City* Facebook group, or order the rule book from www.ospreygames.co.uk.

For readers who are already fans of the game, we present this exclusive two-player *Frostgrave* scenario, loosely based upon events in the novel.

* * *

CORPSEFIRE
By Joseph A. McCullough

The excursion into the Lower Reaches has proved more successful than anticipated, and several of the party are laden down with treasure. Night is falling, though. Better to make camp for the evening than to risk moving through the ruins at night. Thankfully, you brought several corpsefire lamps to protect you from the wraiths that roam this area. Unfortunately, it appears yours is not the only crew of explorers in the area tonight...

Set-Up

Before set-up, each player should roll a die. The player that rolls highest is the 'encamped player'. The other player is the 'raiding player'.

This scenario should be played on a 3x3' table. The table should be covered in ruins as per a standard game of *Frostgrave*. After the ruins have been set up, place six 'corpsefire' markers on the table so that they roughly form a 12" circle around the centre of the table. The encamped player should then place his entire warband inside this circle. Two of his figures (including either the wizard or apprentice, but not both) should be awake and standing up. The rest of the warband is asleep, and the figures should be placed on their sides. The encamped player should also place four treasure tokens anywhere he wants inside the circle, provided they are at least 1" from any of his figures.

The raiding player should then place all of his warband within 2" of a board edge of his choice. The raiding player should also place two treasure tokens anywhere on the board within 18" of the board edge opposite his starting edge.

Finally, the raiding player should place three wraiths (see *Frostgrave*, p.112) anywhere within 2" of the board edge opposite his starting edge.

Special Rules

Do not roll for initiative on the first turn. The encamped player automatically has the initiative.

All but two of the encamped player's figures begin the game asleep. These figures will not activate while asleep. To wake up a figure, the encamped player must make a move action and end that action in base contact with one of the sleeping figures. He may then wake up one figure as a free action. This figure stands up immediately, but cannot activate until the following turn. If an enemy figure moves into combat with a sleeping figure, or makes a shooting attack against a sleeping figure, that figure immediately stands up.

The three wraiths follow the standard rules for uncontrolled creatures with the following exception. If a wraith is ever called upon to make a random move, it will instead move directly towards the closest corpsefire marker. The wraiths cannot enter the circle made by the corpsefire markers until one of those markers is destroyed.

Any figure that is in base contact with a corpsefire marker, without an enemy figure within 1", may spend an action to destroy the corpsefire marker.

A figure within 1" of a corpsefire marker is treated as having a magic weapon while fighting against the wraiths.

Figures may exit any board edge in order to secure treasure.

Due to the darkness, the maximum line of sight in this scenario is 14".

Treasure and Experience

Treasure is gained as normal in this scenario. Experience is gained as normal with the following additions:

- +20 experience points for the encamped player if he has no sleeping figures on the table at the end of the game.
- +20 experience points for the raiding player if he destroys at least two of the corpsefire markers.
- +25 experience points for each wraith killed by a wizard or a member of his warband.